From Fall to Spring

INGRID LEKSAND

For my family

More juvenile offenders are due to be executed

There are 49 juvenile offenders, some as young as 15, on death row in Iran.

The Independent, January 2016

Prologue

'THE PAST IS A FOREIGN country; they do things differently there,' wrote L. P. Hartley. And how right he was. The past is a cruel Janus-faced monster, at one moment tearing you apart with a vengeance, and at the next propelling you into the stratosphere. It fills you with joy, flashing before you snapshots of warm, sweet sunny days before chucking you into an abyss of gloom and despair.

My past is no different, it seems. Since I retired from teaching English literature three years ago it has been haunting me – whether walking along quiet sandy beaches with my partner or rereading old classics or digging in my beloved garden – memories have been bubbling to the surface unbidden, inconvenient, unwelcome. André Brink, in his novel *An Instant in the Wind*, said 'The land which happened inside us no one can take away from us again, not even ourselves.' Mostly I want to forget it all, but it's not that easy: a newspaper article, a smell, a picture, a taste, is all it takes to awaken that dormant volcano. But lately, rather than fight them I decided to embrace them, to revisit my past, to remember how different it was.

I began following the blog of a young man from Tabriz in Iran. It's been my invisible thread to that once enchanting place. For him, the Islamic Revolution is history; he'd have learned about it in school or watched television documentaries and films. Recently he reported on the church attached to Anoushirvan Secondary School, which apparently is in desperate need of repair and renovation. His post on the school opened the floodgates on my memories. Now I can't stop them.

Close friends who know my story have been suggesting that I should write it down, but until now I never had the time or the inclination. Yet it seems that writing it down – writing it *out* – may be the only way to put the ghosts of the past to rest. And the more I dredge up from the well of my memories, the more I think there might, after all, be a story to be told.

I'm a better listener than a talker. I love listening to other people's stories. But when it comes to telling my own, I hang back. It's not because others won't want to hear it – I wouldn't be telling it for them – it's because I'm scared of unlocking the past and the guilt I feel for surviving.

So here I am, in my study with a fresh cup of coffee. The house falls into a sudden silence as soon as the door is closed. The noise of the dogs barking with excitement fades away as my partner takes them down to the beach for their first walk of the day. It's time to switch on the computer, open a fresh document and start writing.

But where should I start? With something shocking, to hold my readers' attention, or at the beginning, the way I experienced it, on a typical hot summer's day in Tehran.

Part 1

Shah unveils $68,000m five-year plan to boost Iran development

The Shah of Iran announced a $68,000m (£28,600m) revised fifth five-year plan, more than doubling the fund allocation and providing for an average annual growth rate of 25.9 per cent.

Under the revised plan, which ends in 1978, the country's per capita income is expected to rise from $556 to $1,521.

Mr. Abdolmajid Majidi, Minister of State for Economic Affairs, said that the most important objective of the planners was to increase the quality of life in Iran by offering a comprehensive social welfare programme, including free education, free health care, housing, social insurance and government subsidies to keep the price of basic consumer goods at fair levels.

The growth targets for agriculture and industry would make Iran one of the world's leading industrial countries.

The steel industry would be able to produce at least 10 million tonnes a year by the end of the plan period and expansion of the energy industry, including the setting up of nuclear generating stations, would raise electricity output to 23,000 megawatts.

The Times, August 1974

Chapter One

ON A HOT AND SUNNY August day I rushed home, hoping that the letter that was going to change my life and determine my future had arrived.

The streets were bustling; taxis and buses packed with commuters looked like stuffed jars of pickles. Impatient, hungry drivers were sounding their horns, polluting the air with noise that was worse than their vehicles' deadly fumes. It was just past two o'clock in the afternoon. Groups of children were playing together in the streets off the main road, enjoying their summer holidays. Those of them tired from playing all morning were slowly heading home, taking their time as if they were in no rush to get there. A mother leaning out of a window was calling her daughter in for lunch. The little girl, busy playing hopscotch with two boys in an alleyway, was concentrating on her steps and continued hopping from one square to the next, her colourful skirt floating in the air with every jump. The shopkeepers were pulling their shutters down and the city was getting ready for the afternoon *chort* – siesta – before the second half of the business day began again after lunch. The only peace and quiet seemed to be in the blue sky over Tehran, where not a trace of cloud could be seen.

Under my arm I held tight to a copy of *TIME* magazine while trying to read an article in *Kayhan International* that had attracted my attention. Tehran's daily English newspaper had an editorial with extracts from an article that had appeared two weeks earlier in *The Times*, the British daily, under the headline, 'Chancellor cuts VAT, aids ratepayers, eases dividend limits and accepts Iran loan.' After several attempts to read it, I had to admit defeat; it was too difficult to walk, concentrate on reading and not bump into passers-by.

When I got home the letter was behind the door. I had been waiting for it for over a month. My hands started to shake as soon as I saw the ministry's official envelope. My heart was pounding. This was my first job, the job I had dreamt of since I was a child. 'Whatever this letter contains will decide my future,' I said to myself. I ripped it open and, after a few seconds reading, a huge smile split my face.

At the end of June I had completed a course of long, hard training to become a secondary school teacher. Since I sat the last exam I had been thinking of nothing but my results. The thought of having my own class, my own students to teach, students whose futures I could shape, was absolutely thrilling. But I didn't just want to teach the syllabus that the Ministry of Education dictated. It was boring! I wanted my students to enjoy learning English. I wanted to introduce them to other topics in order to familiarise them with the outside world, and, in teaching them a foreign language, to open their minds and show them how the world perceived Iran. I truly believed I was capable of changing the world – or at least my world – by opening my students' minds.

'Dear Mr Azad,' the letter read. 'We are pleased to inform you that you have met all the requirements of the Ministry of Education's internal examination for the position of an English language teacher.'

I didn't even bother to read the rest; I didn't care – at least, not then. What I wanted was right there in the first paragraph. And of course I checked the salary they were offering: one thousand tomans a month – a small fortune!

I ran upstairs shouting. 'Mâdar, Mâdar, I've passed, I've passed.' Grandma came out of the kitchen, smiling and calm as usual.

'That's wonderful, my dear. Thank God. I knew you'd get it! Who better than you to teach our young adults. I'm very happy for you.' Her eyes filled with tears. 'If only your parents were here to see this. They would have been so proud of you. Teaching is the most honourable job. The future of every society rests on the shoulders of its teachers.'

Grandma used to be a teacher herself; she was one of the very first women teachers in one of the first schools for girls in Iran. She came forward and kissed me on both cheeks.

'Now, go and freshen up. Lunch will be ready in a few minutes,' she said.

While changing and getting ready for lunch, my mind raced through every dream I ever had of teaching. But hunger and the smell of Grandma's wonderful food hurried me to the table. She was an amazing cook; I've never had a dish taste better than hers anywhere else in the world.

I called my grandmother *Mâdar*, Persian for mother but also short for *mâdarbozorg*, grandmother. My mum I used to call *Mâmân*, like most Iranians. We always used to eat at the table in the kitchen. Our kitchen was quite spacious with a large window opening onto an enclosed patio. We didn't have freezers and I don't think dishwashers were available yet in 1974. All you could expect in an urban Iranian kitchen was a cooker, a sink, a fridge and a few kitchen cabinets. Our Hoover washing machine was the newest item in our home. We had a round table with four chairs, but the kitchen was large enough to fit a table for ten. I remember the white metal cabinets and the one with sliding glass doors where the plates and glasses were kept. They bore the scars of my childhood manoeuvres and accidents when I used to ride my tricycle in the house and bang into the furniture. I never liked our kitchen's neon light; it made it look like a carpenter's workshop.

Mâdar had already laid the table. She had made Fesenjân with Persian basmati rice. Fesenjân is an ancient dish made with boneless chickens, ground walnuts and pomegranate juice or purée. It is one of my favourites. During lunch Mâdar reminisced – again – about her first day as a teacher at her school. She had been thirty-two when she started her career at the all-girls school in Tehran, and was the youngest teacher in the school, teaching her favourite subjects, Persian literature and history.

'I will never forget my first day of teaching, Pedram,' she said as she served herself after filling my plate. 'No matter how I describe it, you'll never be able to feel my excitement on that day. I was entering a world that never existed before. Women teaching in schools? God, it was like a dream.' Her eyes were big with excitement as she recalled her life as a teacher. It was the biggest event in her life. 'This was a proper school – not like those classes that were held in some rich family's house exclusive to their children, or those religious classes held by the local mullah. This was a school open to everyone, free and compulsory. Reza Shah had abolished that dreadful black veil only nine months before and women could now be active members of the Iranian society. Women became free for the first time in centuries. We could do almost anything we wanted. We were in seventh heaven! For the first time I felt equal to your grandfather.'

Mâdar forgot about her food. Every time she recalled those days she went into a trance.

'I became his partner in life, not just a housewife,' she went on. 'We started educating other women who up until then were treated as creatures born to cook and look after the house and the children, or as fertile land for men to come and spread their seed on.'

This was not the first time she had told me about her life. She was so proud to be one of the first women teachers of our country that it made her feel almost noble. I could understand her sentiments perfectly. She was such a strong character and had so much determination, I could not imagine how she would have lived had Reza Shah the Great not introduced his reforms.

I noticed she was rubbing her knees under the table. 'Are they painful again?' I asked. She had been suffering with arthritis for a number of years, but she was still a very capable woman who hardly ever complained. She was always on the go, which made people forget she was in pain.

She shook her head and gave me a faint smile. 'Unfortunately, it's my most loyal companion. As much as I want it to go, it insists on keeping me company. You take things for granted nowadays,' she said. I knew she would change the subject. She never liked to complain or draw attention to her problems. 'In my day, every day was a challenge,' she added.

Roudabeh – Grandmother – was born in 1904; we didn't know the exact date because there was no national birth registry in those days. Her mother had been an illiterate housewife and her father, a civil servant with only a basic education. At sixteen she was married off to Jafar, a man ten years her senior and a colleague of her father's at the Ministry of Public Health. Her husband – my grandfather – was a doctor who had been trained by the Swiss medical delegation to Iran and worked at a military hospital known as Army Hospital 501. Working with Europeans had broadened my grandfather's mind. He had learned French, and that allowed him to read the works of many European – mainly French – writers, as well as Swiss and French newspapers. Due to his hard work and the various posts he held in the ministry, he was given the title of *Hakimod-Dowleh* – physician to the government – by Ahmad Shah, the last shah of the Qajar dynasty. His open-mindedness combined with Roudabeh's charisma and stamina made them the ideal couple for the modern family unit in early 1920's Iran.

At that time, what was left of the once mighty Persian empire was an empty, fragile shell on the brink of disintegration. Thanks to the Qajar Shahs, who had ruled for one hundred and twenty-nine years, thousands of square miles of Iranian soil had been lost through war to the British and the Russians. The country had no infrastructure, no communication, no education, no health and no transport system. The so-called central government was too weak to collect taxes in provinces where local chieftains were in power and ordinary people were at their mercy.

It was under such conditions that the newly-wed Roudabeh started her married life. Because of Grandad's job, they were frequently relocated to the provinces, having to live for years in remote places with no sanitation, where fresh running water and electricity were the stuff of fairy tales. Roudabeh miscarried her first child, something quite common in those days. Indeed, only her fourth pregnancy out of ten survived into adulthood. That was my mother. On Roudabeh's third pregnancy, she gave birth to a girl who they named Assal – meaning 'honey' in Persian. My mum remembered her. When they were living in Qazvin, a provincial town a hundred miles west of Tehran, Assal suddenly fell ill. My grandfather tried everything to save her. In the end they made the six-hour journey on horseback and by car to the Swiss hospital in Tehran. It turned out that Assal had tuberculosis. The Swiss doctors who worked with my grandfather were willing to send her to Switzerland for treatment. But she was too weak to make the long journey. They would have had to cross the Alborz Mountains to northern Iran, board a ship at Port Pahlavi for Baku in the Soviet Azerbaijan, and then take a train through Russia and Poland into Germany and, finally, Switzerland. In less than two weeks Assal had died. She was only ten. My grandmother never really recovered from this tragedy. She believed that if she'd stayed in Tehran, all her children would be alive today. I never asked her whether she blamed my grandfather for it or not.

Mâdar was twenty-one when my mum was born. Eleven years later, when the veil was abolished in 1936 and the women of Iran were given the chance to participate in everyday life, nothing could stop her. My mum was at school by that time, so Roudabeh could enter society without worrying about her daughter. She decided to pursue her lifelong dream of teaching and joined a team of teachers at Tehran's Namus High School, the first public school for girls in Iran.

Roudabeh had been an avid reader ever since she and her brother, Abdullah, attended Mullah Ali's classes. Her father was an open-minded man and, unlike many of his contemporaries, believed that both his children should be treated equally. So he had sent her with Abdullah to learn reading and writing by studying the Koran. Though girls were not allowed to be educated in public, Mullah Ali had agreed to make an exception for Roudabeh. He was in debt to my great-grandfather and his family who had taken care of him, educated him and sent him to Qom, Iran's holy city. If Roudabeh sat at the back of his class behind all the boys, kept herself completely covered, and promised not to ask any questions, Mullah Ali would teach her too.

Mâdar loved Persian literature. She knew by heart the poems of our world-famous poets, Hafiz, Omar Khayyam and Ferdowsi, as well as the contemporary ones like Forough. She was the one who introduced me to books and made me fall in love with them. One of my fondest memories from childhood is of sitting on cold winter evenings with my parents and Mâdar around the *korsi*. It was a specially built low wooden table under which was placed a brazier full of red-hot charcoal – later, a special electric heater. The table was then covered with a large thick blanket and usually topped by a decorative handmade tablecloth. We sat around it on futon-like mattresses, stretching our legs under the blanket and pulling it up to our waists. Our favourite game was poetic crambo, where one of us gave a line of verse, for which the others had to find another line of verse that began with the last letter of the previous line. Mâdar and I played in a team against my parents and, of course, we always won.

After we'd eaten lunch Mâdar left the kitchen to take her afternoon nap.

'Leave them,' she told me, pointing to the dishes on the table and in the sink. 'I know you can't wait to tell Parastou and Kamran your news.'

I smiled and said that I'd be seeing them that night. 'What are *your* plans for the evening?' I asked.

'I'm heading for the nightclubs!' she said, bursting into cheeky laughter. 'No, darling, *dâyi pireh* – the old uncle – is coming over tonight. I've invited my brother and his wife for dinner. I was there two weeks ago. Now it's my turn to have them round. Don't you worry about me. Go and have fun, but will you be having dinner at home with us or not?'

I asked her not to wait for me – I didn't know how long I'd be with Parastou and Kamran – and as she headed for her bedroom I lay down on the floor in the sitting room and stared at the ceiling. Guilt was pressing down on my chest. I took a peep at the ministry's letter. I had not told her the whole story and I wasn't sure how she was going to take it.

I turned round and grabbed the copy of *TIME* from the coffee table. A few months earlier, I had taken out a subscription to the magazine. It was my way of keeping in touch with events worldwide, as well as updating my English. The cover of the August 5th edition had the headline: 'The Vote to Impeach'. The Nixon saga had been all over the media and I was very interested in it. His resignation and the eventual transition to President Ford were hot topics of conversation everywhere in the world at the time. Nixon had been most helpful and understanding towards Iran and our needs. I just hoped that Mr Ford, the new president, would be as friendly as his predecessor. I'd had a conversation about it with Kamran a few days earlier, which had turned into an argument. Kami was not very keen on Americans.

Iran had always had a very close relationship with the US, particularly since the end of the Second World War, while the other two major powers, Britain and Russia, had always tried to invade us. The majority of people, especially those of the older generation, trusted the Americans more than the British or the Russians. American assistance after the end of the Second World War was welcomed by many in Iran. But others, mostly of the younger generation – Kami being one of them – thought of this assistance as 'interference' and believed that the US involvement in the 1953 coup d'état that toppled Dr Mosaddegh's government had tarnished the US's standing in the world as a supporter of democracy.

I told Kami that he had to look at the bigger picture: Dr Mosaddegh's nationalisation of Iran's oil industry took place at a time when Nasser, the Egyptian leader, had orchestrated a coup against Farouk, the Egyptian king, holding Egypt up as a model to other Arab nations and encouraging them to revolt and shift towards the Soviet Union. Kami could not see the connection between what happened in Iran and what happened in Egypt. He rejected my suggestion that the Iranian communists joined Mosaddegh under his banner of nationalism and were supported and encouraged by the Soviets. The communists hoped they could eventually take over the nationalist government, I argued, and ultimately topple the monarchy – just as had happened in Egypt. Such an eventuality would have had disastrous consequences, not only for the country but also for the region and the West as a whole. I wanted Kamran to see that it was Iran's national interests, coupled with America's fear of

Soviet expansionism in the Middle East, that convinced the US to assist us in bringing down Mosaddegh's government. I thought my perspective on the issue was obvious and it made me laugh, which just made Kami all the more angry with me.

I couldn't concentrate on the article in TIME – thoughts of beginning my new job in just over a month kept intruding – so I put the magazine aside. Though it seemed a long way away to the start of the academic year, I had plenty to do between now and then to make sure I was ready for my first day as a teacher. Textbooks in our schools were published by the Ministry of Education and teachers had a syllabus to follow. But I wanted my students to learn more than what was in the textbooks. I had it in mind to use articles from English newspapers. These would be a refreshing break from the otherwise rigid curriculum. I hoped my students would welcome the idea, and I began planning my classes in my head.

I had a pen pal in London. His name was Richard and we kept in touch regularly. Though we had never met, I felt as if we knew each other quite well. At the beginning of our correspondence, we each picked a famous monument or building in our own country and told each other about it. He wrote to me about Windsor Castle and I told him about Golestan Palace; he introduced me to Big Ben and I described Shahyad Tower; I matched his British Crown Jewels with our imperial collection; and when he related the mysterious history of Stonehenge, I told him about the ancient city of Persepolis.

I used to marvel at his descriptions of London. Having never visited another country, I wanted to impress him with my own ancient land and its customs, so I used to do a bit of research or visit places in order to keep my letters interesting. I was also very curious to know what the West thought of us. Richard would send me pieces about Iran that he had cut from British newspapers, and I showed them to my university friends. The articles were not always positive but they made us feel proud nonetheless. None of my friends had ever left Iran, so we were all rapt by Europe and its seemingly glittering lifestyle.

'Oh, here you are!' Mâdar broke my concentration. 'Weren't you going to see Parastou? It's well past five o'clock. The house was so quiet that I thought you'd already gone. I only had a little nap and I've been reading all this time, thinking no one was in.'

'Still plenty of time,' I replied. 'Do you fancy some tea?'

'What a silly question!' she replied. 'Would I miss my afternoon ritual?'

I went to the kitchen to prepare the samovar while Mâdar went out on the balcony. Once the tea had brewed I brought it out to her. The air was cool and pleasant in the shade of the huge plane tree that spread its branches over our building. We could hear the birds, a chorus of them, singing inside the leafy tree.

When we finished our tea, Mâdar took herself off to the kitchen to prepare dinner for her brother and her sister-in-law. She adored them. They were the only ones left in the family from her generation.

I took a quick shower and splashed some Old Spice on both cheeks. It stung a little. I looked at myself in the mirror, admiring my toned chest and flat stomach. I used to do fifteen minutes of stretches every day and swam as often as I could, but in recent weeks I had been a bit lazy.

When I was ready, I said goodbye to Mâdar and put the letter from the ministry in the back pocket of my jeans. My conscience was nagging me: *you should have told her the whole story.* But as soon as I walked out of the building a welcome breeze took the thought away with it.

Little boys and girls were out playing again in the alleyway, and their laughter and squeals filled the air with joy. Hoor Alley was a wide cul-de-sac off Amiriyeh Street. The neighbourhood was made up of middle-class families who had lived there for years. It was lined with two-storey houses; only the two buildings at the Amiriyeh Street end of the alley were apartments. Ours was above a branch of Bank Bazargani and the one on the opposite side was above a shop that was closed and empty most of the time.

Mossayyeb, the cucumber seller, had already put out his vegetables on the pavement in front of the closed shop. He was a man well into his forties, married with six children, who had sold his cucumbers from the same spot for as long as I could remember. The sun had dried and tanned his skin over the years and the wrinkles made him look much older than he really was. He was extremely courteous and always seemed happy, though every now and then he complained of a backache. 'These baby cucumbers are responsible for my backache!' he used to say. 'Thirty years of lifting them have aged me faster than I would have wished.'

When he saw me coming towards him he raised his hat and said hello.

'*Khânoum bozorg chetoran*? – How is the grand lady? – Tell her I have beautiful Isfahani cucumbers,' he continued before I could answer. 'All fresh. Smell them.' He approached me with a handful of baby cucumbers.

They smelled heavenly! I can still smell them now. I thanked him and said that I would get *khânoum bozorg* to pop down and buy some.

It was Thursday and traffic was building up in the streets as people started their short weekend. The week in Iran begins on Saturdays, as it does in most Islamic countries, so the weekends are on Thursdays and Fridays. Schools and some offices closed for a half-day on Thursdays and all day Friday. This proved to be economically damaging, especially at a time when our economy was growing. Our days off clashed with the regular working week in other countries, thus giving us only Mondays, Tuesdays and Wednesdays to do business with the rest of the planet. The government considered changing the weekend to bring it into line with the rest of the world, but the clerics objected, saying that such changes would drive the nation away from Islam and into the arms of the infidel Christians.

I walked down Amiriyeh Street to the junction where I had more chance of finding a taxi. Opposite Mihan Patisserie, one of the best known in the city in those days, I called a taxi and sat in the back with a young woman and her newborn baby. Two young chaps sat in the front next to the driver. In Iran, taxis pick up as many as four or five passengers going in the same direction. Inside the taxi, the red leather seats were covered with thick transparent plastic to protect them, and everywhere there were photographs and postcards of famous Hollywood actors, Iranian artists, religious shrines and mosques, a reflection of Iran's diverse and vibrant society in the

1970s. On the back of the driver's seat in front of me was a black-and-white picture of Gina Lollobrigida and Yul Brynner in a scene from *Solomon and Sheba*; on the back of the passenger seat were Bruce Lee and Norman Wisdom! Hanging from the front mirror were postcards from the Imam Reza shrine in Mashhad and a picture of Imam Ali, together with a small compass. Every time the driver braked, the front of the car lit up like a disco, with colourful lights flashing on and off. It didn't seem to bother the driver; I suppose he was used to it. Many taxi drivers decorated the interior of their taxis in this way. I never liked it. I thought it was tacky.

As we drove back up Amiriyeh Street, heading north towards Pahlavi Avenue, I saw Mossayyeb grimacing as he lifted a large sack of cucumbers onto his wooden cart, ready to go home. Driving in Tehran, a city of almost four and a half million inhabitants, was a nightmare. Hillman Hunters were everywhere. Originally British, but assembled in Iran under their Persian name, Paykan, these relatively affordable cars were the symbol of the middle-class Iranian family and the vehicle of choice, in distinctive orange and white, for taxi drivers.

On our way along Pahlavi Avenue we enjoyed the chirpings of thousands of sparrows hidden in the fifty-year-old plane trees that lined it while the taxi driver played the latest hit from Googoosh, the country's favourite pop star. The front windows of the taxi were down and the heat of the day had given way to mild humidity. The sun had started to set and dark clouds hid the crimson sky. You could smell the rain in the air; after such a hot day everyone would be glad of a downpour.

Large banners hung from the lamp posts bearing the slogan, 'Fewer Children, Better Life'. They were part of a nationwide campaign by the government to encourage families not to have more than two children. The taxi driver was talking about the campaign to one of the men sitting in the front.

'I'm really happy about this. Don't you think it's a wise thing?' He put his question to everyone in the taxi.

The young man sitting by his side was not so sure. 'Now they're trying to tell us how to live our life?' he complained. 'Give me a break! What is all this?' He sounded irritated, which I thought was a bit over the top – the smaller family size wasn't mandatory.

'Well, I wish they'd brought this in decades ago,' the driver insisted. 'Had I not had seven siblings we would have had a better life.'

No one said a word, so he continued: 'I'm at least grateful that families are finally being educated. It is so much easier for the parents, as well as the government, to provide better healthcare and education – a better life and brighter future for our children – when we only have one or two kids.'

The recent huge increases in oil revenues had given the government the opportunity to implement some of the best projects and the most advanced technologies on offer. It was as if the nation was taking a crash course in becoming modern, in catching up with the rest of the world.

After forty-five minutes of driving through heavy weekend traffic I finally reached the Parspours' place. Kamran lived nearby but we'd agreed to meet at Parastou's. They were students at Tehran University. Although I had graduated from the same university a few years previously, we still had many friends in common. The new academic year would be their final year. They were thinking of continuing their education by enrolling in masters' programmes. Kamran was eager to go abroad and continue his studies in England or the United States. But Parastou didn't like the idea of leaving her family; she was very fond of her younger brother, Ardavan, who was still at secondary school.

Parastou invited me in before we headed out to the cinema. Her parents had gone to see a ballet by Maurice Béjart at Roudaki Hall with friends. Kami was already there.

I was barely in the door when Parastou started. 'Spit it out!' she said, staring at me. 'I know that look. You have news.'

I smiled.

'Okay, what's happened?' asked Kami.

'Come on! I know you too well, Pedram.' Parastou wasn't going to give up. 'That smile on your face from the moment you walked in was like a flashing bulletin board.' She turned to Kami. 'Do you know something that I don't?'

She looked at me and then at him again. 'Am I missing something here?' she said, looking puzzled.

I burst out laughing. 'I passed!' I shouted. 'I got the job! I'm now a teacher.'

Kami, smiling, came forward and hugged me, congratulating me and slapping my back.

Then Parastou, as if she had just woken up, threw herself at me, hugging me, kissing me and screaming. 'Oh, my God! That's great news! I'm so happy for you. You said you'd hear from them sometime this week. I'd completely forgotten. Give me a moment while I get my things. We must celebrate! After all, this is something you've always wanted to do.'

When we were little kids and used to play after school or during the holidays my favourite thing was to act the English teacher. In those days I hardly knew any English. I used to make 'English' sounds, pretending to speak the language to my 'students', Kami and Parastou. The three of us had been friends since primary school. We were like the Three Musketeers, always taking each other's side no matter what.

Our families knew each other too, and we used to spend summer holidays together in rented villas up north. The whole region was covered with lush forests and waterfalls. It was paradise for Tehranis escaping the hectic life of the capital and seeking refuge in a tranquil and meditative environment. We'd drive there, three cars following each other in a convoy.

We did that every year until one summer six years ago, when I was nineteen. We were all coming back from another wonderful holiday on the Caspian coast when my parents had an accident. They were alone in the car when it happened. I was in the Vaziris' car playing cards in the back seat with Kami. I remember the radio was on. Mâdar was with Mr and Mrs Parspour and Parastou. My parents were leading, the Parspours were following them and we were the last car. My father was a good driver and always very careful. Haraz, a winding road up the Alborz Mountains, was the most scenic route, but it had a sting in its tail and had become something of an accident black spot. During the summer, drivers got lazy or fell asleep from heat and humidity; in winter, avalanches killed several people every year and blocked the road for days.

Mâdar had witnessed the moment when my parents' car collided head-on with a lorry that was overtaking on a bend. Their car was pushed over the cliff and down into the valley below. She watched her last surviving child fall to her death. She never spoke about it, nor did she ever visit the Caspian again. My parents' sudden deaths reduced our family to a small unit of two. It took Mâdar and me a few years before we could bring our shattered lives back to any sort of normality.

Parastou returned with her handbag. 'Let's hit the town and have fun. We have a fabulous excuse,' she said. She was jumping up and down like a little girl.

Kamran put on his shoes and told her to calm down. 'Girls are all crazy, aren't they?' he said looking at me.

Parastou playfully swung her bag at him and hit him on the head.

'Ouch! You with your flying dustbin,' Kami said.

'Flying dustbin' was the name we had given to Parastou's bags, all of them – from her school bags to her handbags. They always seemed to be full of everything you could imagine, and she liked to swing whatever bag she had with her that day.

As we left Parastou's front garden I decided to give them the whole story about the teaching job. I wanted their advice about how to break it to Mâdar. But I wasn't sure how they would take it either and I didn't want to spoil the good mood. I braced myself.

'The school they're sending me to is in Tabriz,' I said in one breath. I couldn't look at them.

My news broke to the accompaniment of a peal of thunder, followed by torrential rain.

'What?' Kami said. 'Are you crazy! You can't be serious?'

We had stopped dead in the middle of the footpath and were the only people not trying to get out of the rain. I didn't know what to say. I felt bad about spoiling their excitement. Parastou's mascara was running down her face.

I gave a little chuckle. 'You're beginning to look like a racoon woman!'

No one laughed.

'But why Tabriz? Do you have to go?' asked Kami. 'Can't you turn it down and wait a bit longer to get a place here?'

'You can't leave us,' said Parastou. 'We've always been together. If you go, you'd break up our little group.'

'But what about Kamran's plans,' I said. 'I'm only going to another city. This guy is planning to move to another country on the other side of the world! Isn't that going to break up our group?'

We were getting drenched now. We fell silent; no one seemed to remember what we were supposed to be doing. Then Kami looked me straight in the eye.

'What was Mâdar's reaction?' he asked.

I looked down.

'You have told her, haven't you?' he asked.

'No, not yet,' I said quietly. 'I don't know how! Come on, let's get a cab and get out of this rain.'

'She'll be devastated,' Parastou said. 'Will she leave her brother and come with you? You'll be putting her in an awkward position, you know. She'd have to choose between you and him, and you know how much she loves you both.'

'It would be better to tell her sooner rather than later,' Kami said.

I knew this, but deep down I knew that, at her age, the move would make her very unhappy. Her brother – *dâyi pireh* – was older than her and she worried about his health as it was. If she came with me to Tabriz, she would be all alone with no friends or relatives while I would be busy with my job and making new friends. To me it seemed more logical for her to stay in her own house in Tehran and just visit me instead. It was only a forty-five-minute flight; it wasn't that far away. I had a feeling she might disagree with my philosophy and decide to follow me, but I was determined to make her stay behind; I did not want her to sacrifice her life for me any more.

The three of us started walking again. At least the rain had slowed down. Despite their obvious disappointment, I felt sure they'd get used to the idea in time; they knew how much I'd always wanted to become a teacher. They would still have each other; I was the one who was moving away. Anyway, deep down we knew things could not stay the same forever, and soon Kami would be leaving us too.

The traffic in Pahlavi Avenue was still chaotic and after a while looking for a taxi we realised it would be impossible for the three of us to find an empty cab together. Parastou was the first one to get a cab, then Kami and I had to wait another ten minutes before we finally found one going to Valiahd Square.

I realised that this might be the last time the three of us would go to the movies for a very long time and decided to make sure we enjoyed our last days together. The plan was that whoever got to the cinema first would buy the tickets before they sold out. Fifteen minutes later, Kami and I were stuck in traffic only a few hundred yards away from the square.

'Come on, let's get out,' Kami suggested. 'It'll be quicker.'

He paid the cab driver. The taxi was in the middle of the road, surrounded by other cars. We opened the doors and squeezed out, running through the cars to the pavement.

The rain had stopped and the weather was cool. The fountains in the middle of the square, with spotlights projecting from the bottom of the shallow pool, were sending jets of water several feet into the air. Cinema Polydore's flashing neon lights were reflected on the surface of the pool. We were going to see *The Sting*, which we'd heard a lot about. It had been number one at the box office since its release the previous December in the US, and Parastou liked to see anything with Paul Newman in it – he was her dream man.

Just over two hours later when we left the cinema, I was full of popcorn and had the soundtrack to the movie playing on a loop in my mind. I loved ragtime.

"What lies ahead is an emerging Iran. In 25 years time we are going to be 65 million people, with a per capita income similar to the most advanced countries in the world. Our vital lifelines will go through the Indian Ocean … the Indian Ocean will be of prime importance to us.

"We are even thinking of creating some kind of common market in the Indian Ocean, between the northern and the southern countries of the Indian Ocean. That means Africa and Indonesia … and although Australia is not in the Indian Ocean it is a natural extension of it."

H.I.M. Shahanshah Aryamehr, *The Age*, September 1974

Chapter Two

A FEW WEEKS PASSED since I got the letter about my new job but I still hadn't found the courage to break the news to Mâdar about where the new job was. Tabriz is just under an hour's flight away from Tehran, six hours at least by road. I was supposed to report to the school there a week before the start of term. The city is the provincial capital of Eastern Azerbaijan. It is a mountainous region with mild summers but very cold winters. For over a thousand years Tabriz was the crossroads for caravans and travellers on the famous Silk Road, journeying from India and Central Asia on their way to Europe.

While Mâdar was out one morning, I rehearsed how I could broach the subject. I heard the front door open; she was back. It was time to say something.

She closed the door and carried her shopping bags into the kitchen.

'Why didn't you let me go and do the shopping for you?' I asked.

'I'm perfectly capable of taking care of us. I'm not crippled yet, dear!' She pulled a face that made me laugh.

I was taking the shopping out of the brown bags and putting

things in the fridge or in the appropriate cupboard when she asked me if there was a problem.

'A problem?' I said, trying to brush off her question.

'Is there something wrong with your job? They've not taken back their offer, have they? They can't, you know!'

'No, it's nothing like that,' I said as calmly as I could.

'I'll finish these. You go and wash your hands and I'll serve lunch.'

Relieved, yet cursing myself for not coming out with it, I went to the bathroom. I was so worried about how she would react. I took longer than usual to get back to the table and she called me, telling me to hurry up if I wanted my meal to still be hot.

She was sitting at the table and had already cut me a large slice of Koofteh Tabrizi. What a coincidence that we were eating a dish that originated in Tabriz. I quickly decided that the massive meatball would help me out. But she knew something was up.

'So what was it you were going to tell me?' she asked, looking worried.

'It's about my new school.'

'What about it?'

'It's not in Tehran,' I said, cutting a piece of Koofteh.

She raised her eyebrows.

'It's where this meatball comes from!' I added.

She looked down at her plate, then took another bite of her flatbread and a chunk of her meal with some of her famous homemade *Torshi* – pickled vegetables. The silence was killing me. I didn't know what was going through her mind.

'Well, say something,' I said eventually.

She took a sip of water and looked at me. 'Tabriz, Tehran or anywhere else, what difference does it make?' she said with determination. 'You're needed at a school there, so there you should be.'

Her reaction wasn't quite what I had expected. I suggested that I turn Tabriz down and wait for another position in Tehran.

'What do you mean?' She sounded cross. 'The ministry has found you a school where they need an English teacher. Do you want to make the students wait for another teacher while you're wasting your days here doing nothing? Anyway, what difference does it make?

Tehran or Tabriz – or anywhere else for that matter – they're all your home, aren't they?'

I should have guessed this would be her reaction; when there was a job to be done she believed you just had to knuckle down and do it. I thought another patriotic lecture was on its way. I admired her unshakeable dedication to her country. For her it was always duty before self. Had she been a man, she would have done well in the army.

Before I got the chance to say anything, she started to talk about the time when she was given the chance to teach. I loved it when she told me about her life, even though I had heard it all many times before. She went on and on about how my generation took things for granted and how difficult it was for her generation to live, let alone to study. There had been no electricity in those days and she had had to do her homework by the light of a small lantern in a smoky room filled with the rest of her family.

We continued eating while she talked about her past. Fifteen minutes into her sermon I realised I wasn't really listening to what she was saying any more. I was full of admiration for this old lady sitting in front of me; she was as strong as Mount Damavand.

Suddenly she banged on the table and shouted, 'You spoilt brats throw your government-subsidised meals on the floors of your university canteens in protest! What are you protesting for? Haven't you boys been pampered enough?'

How had we got to *that* conversation – from the bad conditions in Iran in the old days to the pampered students of today?

She carried on: 'No one protested in the days when they had to pay for their study. But now that universities are free and open to all – not just the rich – you protest? They even cover your living expenses and subsidise everything. What else do you want? Blood?'

'How did we get to talking about this? The protest,' I told her, 'was about the lack of freedom – political freedom.'

I knew she would disagree. She was from a generation that had been born with nothing, no proper housing, no sanitation, no schools, no roads, not even hospitals. Iran was bankrupt, and the nation was ill and miserable. In 1974 all she saw was new developments and construction sites everywhere. Mâdar's generation believed politics should be left to politicians.

A few years earlier she had shouted at a student friend of mine who had come home with me so we could study together. I recall it as if it was yesterday. He had spoken of students needing to bring about a proletarian revolution to free the chained and oppressed masses. She overheard him referring to people as 'masses'. She was furious! 'You talk about the people as if they are herds of animals and you are their shepherd,' she had yelled. 'Do you have any idea what poverty means? Have you ever lived it?' I had kept quiet; I was a bit embarrassed with her outburst. I had had to listen to the two of them argue for over an hour.

'Do you know what lack of freedom really means?' she began again now. She went on to point out that the total political freedom the students were demanding was the result of their high level of education and the reasonable standard of living the country provided them with. She did not disagree with aiming for democracy and a multi-party system, but she thought that this would inevitably happen. She believed that all we as a nation had to do was be patient and learn to walk before we could run.

'So what will you do when I go to Tabriz?' I interrupted her. 'Will you come with me or would you rather stay in Tehran?'

She gave me no direct answer. Instead she told me to do what I had to do and not to worry about her.

'But I need to know whether you'll come to Tabriz or not,' I replied. 'If you are coming, we'll need to make preparations.' At the very least I had to find a place to rent and needed to know whether I should look for a two-bedroom or a one-bedroom flat, or even just a room for myself.

'I'll let you know,' was all she said.

We had finished lunch, but I had been so consumed by the conversation that I couldn't remember what I ate or how it tasted. She left the kitchen and went to the sitting room. Soon I could hear Delkash's voice from the radio. She loved her songs and when I looked in on her she was humming along while flicking through her favourite women's magazine, *Zaneh Rouz* – Woman Today.

I phoned Kamran. Mrs Vaziri answered and told me that he wasn't in. She had sent him out on an errand while she and Parastou were busy preparing a surprise birthday party for him that evening.

'Don't be late!' she scolded. 'How is Mâdar? Can I speak to her?'

I called Mâdar to the phone and said goodbye to Mrs Vaziri, then went and got ready for the party. When I returned to the sitting room to tell Mâdar I was going out, she was still on the phone, enjoying her conversation with Kami's mum.

I left the apartment and, though I was in no rush, jumped down the steps two at a time. I'd done that since I was very young; it was a habit and sometimes I did it in public without realising. I had got a package from Richard, my English pen pal, that morning and I took it with me on my way out.

Since Kamran was determined to leave Iran at the end of his degree, he was busy preparing himself for the E'zam exam. Students had to pass this in order to receive a government scholarship that would cover their university fees and living expenses abroad. Every year, thousands of Iranian students found their way to the best universities around the world. Not all our politicians were happy about it; some argued that young people educated in European and American universities would have high expectations when they returned to their own country, expectations that could not be met. Yet the government couldn't afford *not* to send them abroad either. We had a shortage of skilled people and our universities could not meet the demand for qualifications and training. We needed specialists and trained personnel in every field imaginable. We had a long way to go to catch up with the industrialised West. Failing to meet our young people's expectations would bring disappointment and damage their faith in their own government. Nevertheless, many of those students had returned home and taken up some of the best positions in important organisations and now enjoyed a comfortable lifestyle.

I remember Richard mentioning, in one of his letters, that Oxford and Cambridge universities had a large number of Iranian students, apparently all very successful in their various fields of study. American universities had become more and more popular in recent years, and an increasing number of Iranian students graduated every year from prestigious institutions such as Harvard, Yale and Massachusetts Institute of Technology.

Richard, who studied law at the London School of Economics, had written to me about Iranian students in British universities who actively protested against the Iranian imperial government. He had met and apparently knew some of the members of the Confederation of Iranian Students at University College London. They were part of a larger group organised internationally by Iranian communists who opposed the Shah. None of this was published in our own newspapers, but Richard used to send me cuttings about it from the British press.

None of my friends were political. We each had our own opinion, of course, but we were by no means politically active. We were the middle-class youth of Iran who enjoyed what our society offered. Our parents were not rich, but they were a generation who had survived a difficult childhood, graduated from high school and found work easily. They had been able to provide a reasonable life for their families. We were behind many of the advanced nations in the world, but we were far better off than our immediate neighbours, Turkey and Iraq, not to mention the Soviet Union, Pakistan, Afghanistan and the Middle East in general, a fact the authorities failed to remind the nation of.

Western European and American lifestyles had become models for us. The affluent population in the cities had increased steadily over the past decade, but by the mid-seventies a fast-growing middle class had emerged which formed the majority of the nation. As more people were able to afford to travel abroad, disappointment and resentment increased at home. They wanted Iran to catch-up with Europe and America overnight, forgetting that it took those nations centuries of hard work and political stability to get to where there were today. Opposing the rush to catch up were the conservatives and religious classes of society. They considered the Western influence to be immoral and damaging to our traditional way of life. That view often made them oppose all government policies.

By 1974 in Iran education was free and compulsory for every child, and a new national healthcare system had been introduced giving patients free access to doctors and hospitals, even in villages. But in many respects Iran was still a very traditional country. The sudden influx of income from burgeoning oil revenues had turned our land into one massive construction site. With finance guaranteed, our government felt confident about introducing ambitious development programmes in all walks of life. The constant chase after progress, pushed by the Shah and backed by the increasing flow of petrodollars, could be seen throughout the country as every city and town got a major facelift, from gigantic nuclear power stations in Bushehr on the Persian Gulf to a sophisticated naval base in the once-sleepy port of Chahbahar on the Sea of Oman; from technologically advanced agricultural projects in Dasht-e Moghan in Azerbaijan and Qazvin to mining facilities in central and Eastern Iran. Factories and industrial plants mushroomed all over the country revealing our severe shortage of skilled manpower. Rapid industrialisation brought villagers from the rural areas to Tehran and other major cities. The cities offered them a new life and a new beginning, but the cities weren't equipped to meet this sudden invasion.

Many believed the changes taking place were happening too fast for us to adapt and adjust to and feared that sooner or later everything we had achieved would burst like a bubble. At family gatherings, some people complained that the country had become immoral – that there was too much Western influence. But others, including myself, believed that we could make it. 'Although it might get tough,' I used to say, 'we've already achieved so much. What could stop us?' I thought we needed to go full steam ahead.

'We're now in a transitional period,' I said to a middle-aged man I met at a party. 'This is a dangerous time for any traditional society to pass through on its way to modernisation and industrialisation.'

But he felt uneasy. He believed that the Shah was pushing us too much, too soon. 'His Majesty wants to see the changes happen during his lifetime,' he said, 'but it's impossible.'

I had disagreed. I thought it was entirely possible. 'There's no reason why he won't see the fruit of his leadership,' I said with total conviction.

We were definitely living in an exciting time in our country's history.

Shah offers plan for Indian Ocean

The Shah made it clear that the purpose of a 'military understanding' would be to reduce the presence in the Indian Ocean of the United States and the Soviet Union, replacing their naval power with that of such nations as Iran and Australia.

The New York Times, September 1974

Chapter Three

I HAD BECOME SO preoccupied with my thoughts that I had forgotten where I was supposed to be going. I had about three hours before I had to be at Kami's house for his party, so I decided to take a walk. I wanted some peace and quiet to read Richard's letter.

I headed back up Amiriyeh Street, past our apartment and the shops that were closed for the afternoon. At the junction with Sepah Avenue, an old beggar had fallen asleep on his mattress in the shade of an old ash tree, a few coins lying in a hat in front of him. Eventually I reached the park at the old Marble Palace. I can remember my grandmother bringing me there often as a child. I used to pedal from the house on my little burgundy tricycle and race around the large ornamental pool with the other kids.

The palace hadn't been used since the late fifties. It was small, rectangular in shape and had a dome in the centre of the roof. The marble walls changed colour from white to pale green depending on the intensity of the light. If you peered through the windows you could see parts of the interior. There was a large carved wooden wardrobe with a brown leather suitcase on top of it. Was it the Shah's? As a child I had always wanted to find out what was inside it. Mâdar, younger in those days, used to walk with me for hours or she would sit on one of the benches in the shade of the tall trees reading a book or one of her magazines.

I sat down on a bench under a giant oak tree and set Richard's package on my knee. It was unusually thick. I opened it without ripping it, careful not to damage the stamps as I collected them. Inside was his letter plus a few pages of newspaper articles and a recent picture of him that he had taken with a few of his classmates on a weekend trip to Brighton. There was also a book – André Gide's *The Immoralist*.

His friends in the picture looked like my own. With the exception of a blond-haired chap and Brighton Pier in the background, the picture could have been of a group of Iranian students, although there probably would have been more guys with moustaches or beards. But the fashions and hairstyles were exactly the same.

Richard wanted to come to Iran to meet me and visit the country. He had suggested coming the following summer, once he had finished his exams. He also mentioned that he might bring an Iranian student friend with him.

I glanced at the press cuttings he'd sent. One was an article in *The Times* dated 12th July 1974 – eight weeks previously – about the sale of Iranian paintings in London. It read: 'Two exceedingly rare seventeenth-century full-length Persian court portraits, in oil of exotic charm, were sold at Christie's yesterday for £150,000 and £85,000.' I wondered how these paintings from Shah Abbas' period had ended up in Cotterstock Hall, near Oundle in Northamptonshire. Apparently they had been there until 1823, when the widow of Sir George Booth, sixth and last baronet, left them to a Margaret Maskelyne of Basset Down in Wiltshire where they remained until her descendants sold them.

What a romantic journey it must have been, I thought – from the court of Shah Abbas in Isfahan to Northamptonshire, then Wiltshire. The article said that an Iranian, Mr Mehdi Mahboubian, had purchased the paintings at the auction. It was good to know that they belonged to an Iranian again. I knew there were thousands of Iranian treasures scattered throughout the world. I just wished we could bring them all back to their birthplace.

Another press cutting was even more interesting. *The Times*, dated 23rd July, was a speech by Mr Healy, Chancellor of the Exchequer, delivered in the British parliament:

> The Imperial Iranian Government has offered to provide the United Kingdom with a line of credit of $1,200m, to be drawn on in the form of three separate loans by public sector bodies within three years from now.
> I know that the willingness of the Iranian Government to enter into an arrangement of this kind reflects the concern of His Imperial Majesty the Shah of Iran over the difficulties facing the world economy and his constructive attitude to the problems at present facing the international monetary system, and I believe that the House will join me in welcoming this development.

I felt proud when I read that. I couldn't remember having heard about it in our own newspapers. The fact that we were lending money to countries such as Great Britain was a sign to me that we had 'made it'.

Before sunset, people from the surrounding neighbourhood came to the park for a late afternoon walk before heading back home to prepare dinner. Children gathered around the ice cream van and fought over who was to be served first, mothers pretended to chase their children around the trees, young couples in love walked hand in hand, old men sat alone reading the afternoon papers or with their wives chatting.

It was getting busy in the park, so after glancing through the press cuttings and the book, I got up and headed off towards Kami's. On my way there I stopped at Abraham Lincoln's English bookshop opposite the American embassy on Takht-e Jamshid Avenue to buy Kami a copy of Jane Austen's *Sense and Sensibility*. Then I got a cab to his place.

There were about fifty young men and women at his house when I got there. Some were relatives but they were mostly mutual friends and a few people I hadn't met before. I was the last one to arrive before the birthday boy got there himself. I walked into the house searching for people I knew. The music of the Bee Gees and ABBA filled the large reception room. The doors onto the balcony were open and the scent from the manicured garden – roses and jasmine – created a heady mix with the smell of cigarette smoke, aftershave and perfume and gave the party an exotic ambience.

Parastou saw me from the far end of the room and pushed her way through the guests, disappearing and reappearing, until she was standing right in front of me. She looked radiant. Even though she was more like a sister to me, I thought she was definitely the most attractive girl at the party. We kissed on both cheeks and she told me to follow her to the bar.

'Has Kami arrived?' I asked. 'Did I miss his big surprise?'

'He should be here any minute,' she said, searching for something behind the bar. 'Let me get you a drink. Then go and turn the music down or he'll hear it from the street. Don't want to spoil the surprise.'

I left my gift and rucksack behind the bar, then asked her for a gin and tonic. She passed me a glass with a few cubes of ice, a shot of gin and a slice of lemon in it and told me to help myself to the tonic. At that moment Ardavan, Parastou's younger brother, came out of the crowd shouting at Parastou, 'He's coming!'

Parastou turned the music off and jumped up on a chair.

'Quiet, everyone!' she shouted. 'Shhhh, he's here. Somebody switch off the lights. Quiet, please!'

It took a few seconds for the chatter to quieten down to complete silence. We heard the front door slam. He'll smell the cigarettes, I thought. Then he opened the door to the reception room, turned on the light and everyone screamed 'Surprise!'

The music and commotion started up again as Kami did the rounds of the room, saying hello to his friends and relatives. It took him fifteen minutes to get to the bar where I was waiting for him with Parastou. We embraced, I wished him a happy birthday and gave him his present. He thanked me and put the present behind the bar with all the others. I decided to go outside for a bit of fresh air and left Kami and Parastou to mingle with the guests.

On my way to the garden I bumped into a few old friends, some of them from our old high school. We chatted a little, but I had to excuse myself – I could no longer cope with the smoke. There were a few couples outside on the balcony and on the steps leading down to the lawn. They were too busy kissing to notice anything going on around them. Another couple were in each other's arms, holding onto their drinks while gazing silently at the stars. They were in a world of their own, carefree, happy and content.

I recognised a few of them from university. Some were still studying; one had returned home for summer holidays from Paris where he studied at Sciences Po. Other friends of Kami's were scattered all around the garden. A group were having a heated discussion about a movie; one guy was sitting on a decorative rock at the back of the garden making rings with his cigarette smoke.

Parastou found me and asked me to dance. While we danced to Demis Roussos we gossiped about the guests and how much Ardavan had grown up – he was dancing cheek to cheek with a pretty girl on the opposite side of the room. Kami seemed to be enjoying his surprise party, mingling and dancing with his favourite girls.

It must have been around two or three in the morning when I finally decided to head home. The party had died down and the guests had either left or had dozed off in each other's arms. Kami was busy with one of his female friends, so I found Parastou and told her I was leaving. She came to the door with me.

'You hardly danced with anyone tonight,' she said.

'I danced with you.'

'You know what I mean!' She gave me a hug and we said goodbye.

When I stepped outside, Queen Elizabeth Boulevard was silent. The streets were deserted and it was unlikely that I'd find a taxi at that time of the morning. The air was cool and the moon full; thousands of stars were sparkling in the dark sky. So I decided to walk for a bit.

The party had brought back so many bittersweet memories. It was two summers ago that I'd broken off the only long-term relationship I'd ever had with a girl. We met on campus at Tehran University and over the next three years Faranak and I had spent most of our time together. We became like one soul in two bodies. We visited different parts of the country together and shared so many dreams. Everything seemed perfect, as if we were made for one another. I thought we had a future together. Then one summer afternoon, not long after the end of term, Faranak had to attend a family gathering, so I decided to catch-up with one of our classmates. We'd spent many days at his apartment revising for our exams. His place had become a second home; we even had our own set of keys if we needed a refuge to study in peace and quiet. That afternoon, as I turned the key in his door I heard Faranak's voice. I stood still and listened. Then I heard my friend's voice too. The last time I saw them they were making love under the shower.

Since then I had been with no other girls and I wasn't ready for anything serious. I wasn't sure if I ever would be. I missed the companionship, but the fear of being betrayed and hurt again was stronger than my yearning.

The dustmen were clearing the rubbish bins on Queen Elizabeth Boulevard and their vehicle was noisy in the otherwise silent night. I heard music approach, getting louder and louder until a white Buick sped by with its roof down, its passengers laughing and shouting over the music. The sounds faded away as the car disappeared from view.

When I was young, the only things to do on weekends were to visit friends and family or go to the movies. Nowadays, we were spoilt for choice – nightclubs, cabarets, amusement parks, restaurants serving food from every continent, ice-skating rinks and bowling alleys. There were lots of new sporting facilities too. The city was awake twenty-four hours a day.

By the time I got home it was just after four. I was absolutely exhausted and my legs were killing me. I let myself in quietly, went straight to my bedroom and fell fast asleep with all my clothes on.

The next day I woke up with a splitting headache. Mâdar was out shopping. I made myself some tea and sat at the kitchen table. Half an hour later she came home and went straight to my bedroom, knocking on the door and shouting, 'Pedram, Pedram, get up, it's almost noon!' I went out to the hallway.

'Sssssh,' I said, frowning at her. 'I've a sore head.'

'Oh, there you are! I'm not surprised. It was very late when you got in.'

'Did I wake you up?' I asked.

'No,' she replied. 'You know I don't sleep properly when you're out.'

I gave her a hug. We sat at the kitchen table and I poured her some tea.

'How were Old Uncle and Auntie?' I asked.

'They're both fine. They asked about you. I told them your good news and they were both very pleased. But listen, I wanted to tell you that I've thought about your move to Tabriz and I've come to a decision.'

Suddenly my headache seemed to disappear. I wasn't quite ready for this. I'd thought it would take her longer to make her mind up.

'And?'

'I have been with you all your life' – she ran her finger around the rim of her teacup – 'and I think it's best for you and about time that you live by yourself. I won't always be around and if you learn to live without me now, it'll make it easier for you when I'm gone.'

I hated it when she spoke about death. My parents were dead and they didn't have any brothers or sisters, so Mâdar was the only one I had left.

'I've decided to stay in Tehran, but not here,' she added.

'What do you mean, not here?'

'I want to sell this place and move to a smaller apartment uptown' – she paused and looked around the kitchen – 'near where some of my friends live.'

My parents and I had always lived at Mâdar's. We owned an apartment but never lived there; it was always rented out. After their deaths I inherited the place and the income from it covered my expenses. But my home was always where I lived – at Mâdar's.

'I want to live in a better part of town now,' she went on. 'We've lived here as long as I can remember. I have nothing against it, but the air is cleaner in the northern suburbs and the city is better managed and more modern there.'

This was all a bit sudden for me. I hadn't expected her to follow me to Tabriz, but I'd never imagined her selling our home. It held too many memories, and the thought of strangers living here was just unthinkable. I could still see the lines my father had drawn on my bedroom wall every year marking my growth.

'It's time we moved on,' she said. 'It's not healthy to live in the past. The future is always better, and that's where we should look.'

She was right, even though I didn't want to admit it to her face. Since my parents died, the apartment had become like a mausoleum. Except for their clothes, which Mâdar gave to a charity, nothing else had really changed. We'd even held onto our old wooden-framed Schaub Lorenz television set and never considered getting a new colour set.

'So do you have a place in mind?' I asked.

'Yesterday I mentioned it to Mrs Vaziri and she said she'll ask the managing agent at Saman Towers where she works. And, of course, they live only a couple of blocks away.'

'But can you afford those apartments?'

'Well, we'll see. I have to go and negotiate,' she said.

Over the next two days, Grandma went to see several properties but in the end preferred the one Kami's mum had found her at Saman Towers. Meanwhile, I said my goodbyes to my friends and was almost ready to head for Azerbaijan to teach.

The weather was getting cooler, and even though the leaves were still on the trees and the city squares and boulevards were full of flowers, you could smell that autumn was on its way.

On Sunday morning I went with Mâdar to see the apartment at Saman Towers. They were located on Queen Elizabeth Boulevard, opened by Her Majesty Queen Elizabeth II on her last state visit to Iran. It was bursting with colour from the yellow jasmines that lined the boulevard, and the narrow canal in the middle was full of goldfish that people had thrown in from their Nowruz's Haft Sin over the years.

We were a little early for our appointment, so Mâdar suggested popping into Bank Bazargani on the ground floor of one of the towers to say a quick hello to Mrs Vaziri – Kami's mum – who was the manager there. What an impressive building! The walls and floor, as well as the giant columns bearing the weight of the twenty-two floors above, were all made of black marble. We walked past the tellers and turned right at the end to get to the branch manager's office. Light bulbs were suspended from the high ceiling on long chains, and the large windows facing the boulevard let in huge columns of light.

Mrs Vaziri stepped out of her office as soon as she saw us and with her usual warm welcoming smile hugged my grandma and me and kissed us on both cheeks.

She said, 'Come in, Roudie *joon*' – all Mâdar's friends called her Roudie, short for Roudabeh – and invited her to take a seat, pointing to a chair in front of her desk. I sat down beside Mâdar. I thanked Mrs Vaziri for the fabulous party on Thursday.

'Don't mention it,' she said. 'Now, I'll just call for some tea.'

A young girl in her twenties appeared and was asked to bring us some tea. A few minutes later she returned with small glasses of tea and a dish full of biscuits and left. Mâdar and Mrs Vaziri talked a little about the properties and Mrs Vaziri asked if Mâdar needed any financial help from the bank. But she didn't. The sale of our old apartment would cover the cost of the new one. A few people had seen our apartment and one had already made a good offer. When we'd finished our tea we said goodbye and left for our appointment.

The entrance next door to the bank took us into the black marble lobby of one of the twin towers of Saman. A smart porter greeted us with a smile as we approached his desk, but then someone called out 'Mrs Hakimi?'

A man in his forties, who had just walked out of the lift, stretched his hand towards Mâdar. He was dressed in a light-blue designer Italian suit with a pocket handkerchief that matched his tie, and he was carrying a small leather bag. He was tall and clean-shaven, with straight, thinning black hair brushed back off his face, and looked more like a distinguished diplomat than a property dealer. We shook hands and after a brief introduction followed him to the lift and up to the apartment on the seventeenth floor; higher up were duplex apartments and a few penthouses.

We walked out of the lift into a large but dimly lit landing. The apartment we were being shown was on the left next to the fire exit.

After trying several different keys the estate agent finally managed to open the door. My first impression was WOW! It was smaller than our current apartment, but it was new and very modern. A short wide corridor led to a sitting and dining area. The walls at the entrance to the sitting and dining room were red. I never imagined that red could be a suitable colour in a house, but here it looked magical. The dark wooden parquet floors complemented the warm red on the walls.

Three huge windows on one side of the room opened to the north and east, and the views from the windows were out of this world! My beautiful Tehran was spread out beneath us. The sunrise from this room would be spectacular. The other tower, situated diagonally to the north-east, didn't block much of the view. The window in the dining area, with the bedrooms next to it, faced the snow-capped majestic Alborz Mountains.

The bedrooms were a good size and had built-in wardrobes with mirrors on the doors, which made the rooms seem even more spacious. Neither the kitchen nor the bathroom had any windows, and the black marble flooring and navy-blue tiles were a bit overpowering. Nevertheless, I could see the satisfaction written all over Grandma's face.

The estate agent explained the service charges and other amenities in the area. We could make use of an underground car park and there was a small shopping centre with its famous Saman supermarket below the two towers. Super Saman, as it was known, was one of the most fashionable supermarkets in Tehran at the time.

I was admiring the mountains when Mâdar called me to leave. She liked the place and had decided to make an offer, hoping to get possession of the apartment before the end of the following week. I could see she was very pleased. On our way home she opened her handbag to search for her sunglasses. I teased her, telling her that she would soon be an uptown girl!

'I don't know about you but I am starving. Aren't you?' she asked, just before we reached Valiahd Square. 'Fancy a chelo kabob?'

She took off up the street, laughing. She was clutching her handbag with one hand and holding her skirt down with the other, fighting the afternoon breeze. I couldn't keep up with her. She looked good in her elegant suit. She was always well dressed. Her dresses were not necessarily expensive – she made most of them herself – but she liked to take care of herself and considered it part of her freedom and social position.

Since the death of my parents, Mâdar had become my entire world. I never knew whether she just pretended to be happy when I was around or if she was truly happy. She never mourned the loss of her daughter in front of me. Aside from the time leading up to the funeral and the customary gatherings for the deceased afterwards, she made me accept that life had to go on and I admired her strength and determination. Now we were both about to start new lives. I felt as if I was missing her already.

She yelled for a taxi and one skidded to a halt in front of us. We jumped in like two schoolkids full of excitement and she instructed the driver to take us to Yâs in Abbas Abad, the best chelo kabobi in Tehran.

After our meal, I wanted to pop into the university and check out a few things in the library; Mâdar wanted to head home. I asked our taxi driver to go to Shahreza Street and then to Amiriyeh. For once, we were the only passengers. We apologised for having onion breath.

'Been to Yâs?' the driver asked.

'Yes!' my grandma replied.

'I'm starving – can't wait to get home,' the driver commented.

'Why haven't you eaten yet? It's late in the afternoon,' Mâdar said.

'I haven't had the chance,' he replied. 'I've been up and down this city all day. Every time I've said to myself this is the last customer before heading home, but then I've picked up another one that took me in a different direction. This is no life! I even dream about driving and curse other drivers in my sleep.'

Further along the road he drew our attention to the banners hanging from the lamp posts.

'*Now* they tell us it's better to have fewer children,' he said, looking at Mâdar in the rear-view mirror. 'It's a bit late for me!'

We asked him how many children he had.

'Six,' he said with a sigh. 'Back then, no one told us to have less.

Now that we have them, they're talking about the advantages of not having so many. I have to work from five in the morning till midnight to feed eight mouths.'

'What does your wife do?' Mâdar asked him. 'Where does she work?'

'With all due respect, madam, she's a woman! If she goes out to work, who'll look after the children? Who'll cook and get the house ready?'

I thought his reply would infuriate Mâdar.

'How old are the children?' she asked calmly.

I wasn't fooled; I could sense one of her inquisitions on its way. She was always searching for solutions for everything and everyone.

Four of the driver's six children were attending the same school near Jaleh Square; the other two were still too young for school.

'Why don't you let your wife find a job at the school where your kids are and she can take the young ones with her?' Mâdar suggested.

I decided to keep out of it while Madam Hakimi – Mâdar – reshaped the taxi driver's life. She took his telephone number, telling him that she used to be a teacher and could find colleagues who would probably know somebody in the same school. They might be able to find a position for his wife in the school canteen. The driver seemed a bit uncomfortable with the idea of his wife being out in society.

'You see' – Mâdar leaned forward from the back seat – 'if your wife works, your income will be doubled. She can afford to pay for the kids and you can take care of the rent. Together you can run a better household. And, please, do not plan for another child.'

The cab driver laughed and turned his attention to me in the mirror. 'This mother of yours is a very wise lady. Does she plan your life too?'

'She's actually my grandmother, not my mother,' I replied.

Mâdar gave me an evil look. 'Don't listen to him,' she said. 'I'm actually his girlfriend.'

The driver, still laughing his head off, said, 'Madam, four of my kids were accidents. There wasn't much planning involved.'

'Then make sure you have no more accidents, sir,' Mâdar said a little sarcastically.

By this time we were opposite the university's main entrance at Shahreza Street. I tried to give Mâdar some money to pay the cabbie at the end of the journey, but she told me I ought to be ashamed of myself. I kissed her goodbye and thanked the cab driver.

'Don't let her bully you,' I said to him.

Later on Mâdar told me the driver wouldn't accept payment for our journey. In return she had promised to be in touch once she had spoken to her friends at the Department of Education. I knew she wouldn't rest until she had sorted something out for the taxi driver and his family.

The Asian Games have come to an end leaving us in second place, next to the Japanese. His Imperial Majesty, the Shah was pleased by this coincidence since he holds that, of the continent's more advanced nations, Japan should lead in the East and we in the West.

Asadollah Alam, *The Shah And I: The Confidential Diary of Iran's Royal Court, 1968–1977*, September 1974

Chapter Four

In less than two weeks Mâdar had sold our home and had her offer on the Saman apartment accepted. Everything happened so quickly, as if it was meant to be. We were so busy with packing up, Mâdar's legal affairs, my hunt for somewhere to live in Tabriz, and saying our goodbyes that the days between visiting the apartment and moving out of our old home flew by in the blink of an eye. I thought it was good we were busy – it gave us no time to think about *our* separation.

It took my friends and me two full days to move all Mâdar's stuff to the new apartment. I decided to leave some of my stuff with her, taking the bare necessities with me on my first trip to Tabriz. But we threw out or gave away to charities more than we actually took with us. It was time for her to leave her daughter's memory behind and start a new life in new surroundings.

On our final morning, while Grandma was checking her bags and chatting with Parastou, I decided to take one last tour of the place before leaving it for good. With all the furniture, the Persian rugs and the pictures gone it looked so much bigger. Every scratch and mark on the walls inside the apartment brought back memories.

Out on the balcony, I took in the view one last time. As a child I used to stand there looking down on Amiriyeh Street, naming the makes and models of all the passing cars to the amazement of my parents' friends and relatives. It was the only way Mâdar could keep me in one place long enough to finish my food. She used to have to chase me around, and if I was on my tricycle, she'd follow me around, pretending the spoonful of food was an aeroplane and asking me to open my mouth so it could land.

Like a lot of Tehranis living in apartments, on hot summer nights we used to sleep out on the large flat roof. I'd put my head out of the mosquito net that rose above us like a white see-through tent and try to count the stars. On clear nights they seemed so close that you could jump up and catch them. When I was five I used to sit for hours in a corner of the roof, fascinated by the revolving red, blue and green lights radiating from the control tower at Tehran's Mehrabad International Airport. One of my older cousins told me that the lights were to guide the aeroplanes in to the airport at night. It all seemed mysterious and captivating to me.

I looked down from the balcony into the alley and recalled the days when, with the other kids from the neighbourhood, we would ride our bikes up the middle of the alleyway after the rain to see who could make the water splash the furthest. And God knows how many times our plastic football landed in people's gardens. We used to buy them for five rials. They came in blue, green or red with white stripes and were so soft that after a good kickabout we had to push the dents out. Sometimes angry neighbours would puncture our ball or never give it back as punishment for ruining their flowers. It seemed serious at the time, but looking back it was all so innocent. Many of those boys and girls had already left Hoor Alley. Some had got married; others went to universities abroad or to other parts of the country. I was the last of the old gang to leave Koucheyeh Hoor behind.

I saw a taxi pull up and Kami got out, so I headed back downstairs. He was coming with me to the bus terminal. I didn't want Mâdar to come. I knew she would cry, and I wasn't strong enough to cope with that. Parastou was going to help Mâdar unpack and stay with her until she settled into her new apartment.

Kami, his eyes still puffy, apologised for sleeping in.

'You worked hard last night packing and taking the last boxes to Saman,' Mâdar said. 'You needed a good night's sleep.'

It was time to go. We hugged and said our goodbyes once we were out of the house. Mossayyeb was standing on the corner next to his heap of cucumbers; he looked so sad. Mâdar had told him that the house was sold and we were moving out. I pointed to Mossayyeb and suggested that we go and say goodbye. Mâdar used to stop and chat with him when she passed him and his display of cucumbers. Lately, he'd brought his son during school holidays to look after his stand for him while he either took a rest or did other chores. After so many decades of living in the same district you get to know most of the neighbours and shopkeepers.

Mâdar stretched out her hands towards Mossayyeb and he burst into tears. Then he grabbed her hand and kissed it.

'Madam, this street – this neighbourhood – won't be the same without you. You were a mother to all of us, a pillar of the community.' He let go of her hand, took a clean handkerchief out of his pocket and wiped his face with it.

She thanked him for his kindness. There was a catch in Mâdar's voice too.

'Keep us in your prayers, *khânoum bozorg* – grand lady,' Mossayyeb continued. 'Don't forget us.'

'I'll only be a few roads away,' Mâdar said. 'It's not as if I'm leaving the city. It's this young man' – she pointed at me – 'who is leaving. I don't know how I'll get used to his absence.'

Soon other neighbours came out to bid us farewell, some of them bringing bowls of water to splash behind me, an Iranian custom to wish the traveller a safe trip.

I had three suitcases; all Grandma had was her handbag and a couple of small bags which Parastou carried. We kissed and hugged. Tears were rolling down Mâdar's powdered face. I told her to come and visit me in Tabriz, and reassured her that I would be back in Tehran in six months' time for the New Year. I had a lump in my throat. Both of us were leaving our home and each other, heading into the unknown.

By the time Mâdar had got into her taxi and Kami and I were in ours, a small crowd of neighbours and children, as well as a few of the old shopkeepers, had gathered to wave us goodbye. It was all very emotional. Memories of the past twenty-five years flooded into my head as we left, our cars driving away in opposite directions. I turned around to take one last look. A few of the neighbours were throwing water behind us. I already felt homesick.

We were running late for my TBT coach to Tabriz, and on our way to the terminal neither of us said a word. I was so late for the coach that my farewell to Kami was very rushed – probably a good thing.

'I'll write to you as soon as I get settled,' I shouted to him through the window, but my words were drowned out by the sudden loud noise of the engine as we set off.

The coach was almost full. I had a window seat a few rows behind the driver. Next to me sat a smart young man who looked to be a few years older than me. It didn't take us long to introduce ourselves.

'He must be your best friend,' he said, beginning a conversation that was to last the rest of the eight-hour journey.

'Yes, he is,' I replied.

'I'm Kasra,' he said.

We shook hands and I introduced myself.

'Are you from Tabriz or just visiting?' he asked.

So I told him about my new teaching job in a school there. He had come from Switzerland to visit his parents in Iran for a while before heading back to start the new term at university in Basel. He had lived there for a few years and was about to begin his specialisation in medicine.

As we travelled on, our conversation turned to more personal subjects. We talked about our lives, our hobbies and ambitions. Kasra hoped to teach at a university in Iran after his graduation, so teaching became a topic of mutual interest.

'By the time I come back to Iran you'll be a well-established teacher,' Kasra said. 'You may have a few tips for me.'

'When will you finish your studies?' I asked.

'I should finish in about four years' time,' he said. 'Have you ever thought of going abroad – to study I mean?'

'No. I wouldn't be able to afford it, even if I wanted to, and as far as the government grant goes … well, you see I have a grandmother who's alone and I wouldn't want to leave her behind. It's already hard leaving Tehran, let alone the country. I'm almost the only one she has. We've always been together. Sometimes I think of her more as a friend than a grandmother.'

'What about your parents? Can't they look after her?'

'No, they're dead.' I looked out the window.

'I'm so sorry to hear that,' he said, sounding a bit embarrassed.

I asked him about his parents. He told me that his mother was a housewife and his father, a doctor. He seemed like a really nice guy – extremely courteous for a twenty-eight-year-old man. His pale skin and clean-shaven face gave him a very European look, or maybe it was because, having lived in Switzerland for a while, he had lost the constant tan that comes from being exposed to the sun for a good part of the year in Iran.

We drove past the Shahyad Tower, opened just a few years previously. It was a very modern construction and looked nothing like our other buildings or monuments, yet there was something very Persian about it that I never could put my finger on. Perhaps it was its narrow bands of turquoise tiles. Once our bus hit the Tehran-Karaj Freeway, heading west, the magnificent Aryamehr Stadium came into view. The Seventh Asian Games had been held for the first time in Iran – or for that matter in Western Asia – and to host the games we had built the sports complex. Naturally the conversation with Kasra moved into sport and the games that the nation was currently enthralled by.

Before the stadium was built that area had been nothing more than a dusty piece of barren land. Now it was a magnificent landmark on the Tehran horizon. The stadium was built like a bowl scooped out of the earth and resembled an ancient amphitheatre. The surrounding hills had been transformed into a massive man-made forest, and nearby a seventy-acre lake had been created in the middle of the desert for nautical sporting events and for Tehranis to enjoy during the summer months.

Further up the freeway was the Imperial Pavilion where every year the Shah attended the annual military parade on 21 Azar (12th December) – Resistance Day – better known as 'The Liberation of Azerbaijan'. During the Second World War the Allied forces ignored my country's neutrality and invaded Iran. The British came from the south, the Soviet forces from the north. The newly established Trans-Iranian railway and our roads were needed by the Allies to supply ammunition and provisions to the Soviet forces fighting what seemed at the time a losing battle against the Nazis on the Western front. The occupying powers promised to leave Iran within six months of the end of the war. While the British kept their promise, the Russians remained and occupied the north-western province of Azerbaijan in the hope of annexing it to the part we had already lost to them during the earlier Qajar period. But the newly established United Nations passed a resolution ordering Soviet forces to leave Iran and respect our national sovereignty. The Russians had always dreamt of having access to the warm waters of the Persian Gulf, and on the eve of their departure they set up a puppet government, proclaiming the territory the Democratic Republic of Azerbaijan. However, with international support and recognition of our territory, the Iranian army, commanded by the Shah himself, was despatched to liberate Azerbaijan from the traitors who had divided our nation.

We had been on the road for an hour or so but our conversation had travelled further. I felt quite comfortable chatting with Kasra, and the topics we discussed – from our own lives and families to the latest album by Kourosh Yaghmaei and the Asian Games – shifted with the scenery. The flat, open space west of Tehran gave way to the cultivated lands of Qazvin, then skirted the Alborz Mountains before entering Azerbaijan. As the road gained altitude so our tête-à-tête became more intimate and friendly.

Just before we got to Miyaneh, a town about a hundred miles south-east of Tabriz, we saw Pol-e Dokhtar (The Girl's Bridge). The bridge had no middle, but its remaining brick arches were an impressive sight. Not far away and almost parallel to it stood a modern flat metal bridge. As a child I had travelled this route several times with my parents and used to beg my dad to tell me again the story of the broken bridge. I could remember looking at the old bridge through the back window of the car while I listened to him, trying to visualise what happened.

I asked Kasra if he knew the history of the bridge and when to my amazement he said he didn't, I began telling him about it, just the way my dad told me.

'It was blown up by the Russians during the Second World War. Up to that time it was still used by travellers – you can still see the old Tehran–Tabriz road on the other side of the river.' I pointed out the window at a dusty road a few hundred yards from us. 'When the Russian forces were retreating they blew the bridge up in order to stop the Iranian army from reaching Tabriz. When the imperial forces got to this point they laid down that metal bridge you see over there, so our soldiers were only delayed by a few days before they were able to reach Tabriz and push the Russians further back.' In my mind I went back to when I was seven or eight years old and would try to imagine the shock our soldiers must have felt when they first encountered the blown-up bridge.

'The Russians were not welcome here and we managed to get them out. That's all I cared about when I was a boy,' I said to Kasra. 'I was too young to understand the international diplomacy involved. All that mattered was that Azerbaijan remained ours and I could go there on holidays. Now I'm on my way to teach its children.'

The coach continued on, up and up the winding road, past rocks as big as our bus. In the valley on the other side of the bus, the river meandered through tall poplar trees. The air was fresh, and much cooler too. It seemed like a different land.

* * *

It was early evening when we entered Tabriz. The sun had set but the sky was still bright. The bus stopped at the terminal just outside the city and Kasra and I decided to share a taxi. It would drop me at the intersection of New 25th Shahrivar and South Shahnaz Street before going on to Manzariyeh, an affluent and relatively new district of the city where Kasra's family lived.

On the way I stared out at the city. Through a friend of mine

I had managed to find a one-bedroom apartment within walking distance of both the centre of Tabriz and my school. I wondered what it was going to be like.

'You're very lucky to have found a place so reasonably priced in such a central district,' Kasra told me in the taxi.

'Really? You're making me anxious. Maybe there's something wrong with the place.'

'Well, let's hope that you're just lucky!' Kasra said with a smile.

Banners welcoming the Seventh Asian Games to Iran were visible on the city's streets, just as they had been in every other town and city we had passed through on our journey. Shops and restaurants were open and people, refreshed from their afternoon *chort*, were going about their business in the busy streets of central Tabriz. We drove down the 6th Bahman Boulevard, a beautiful wide boulevard lined with tall poplar trees on both sides and a central reservation crammed with thousands of colourful dahlias. It was Kasra's turn to explain the sights on the route to the city centre.

'There's our best hospital,' he said, pointing to a grand building sitting slightly higher than street level on our left as we entered the city. '6th Bahman it's called – fully equipped with the latest medical technology. My father works there. It's one of the hospitals where he carries out operations.' His voice was charged with excitement; you could hear his love for his city. 'The road you saw going up the hill on our left when we entered the city goes to Shahgoli. A little bit further on we'll reach Tabriz Archaeological Museum.'

As we neared Town Hall Square the traffic got heavier, and the cab driver took several shortcuts in order to avoid the busy Shahnaz Junction. Then, after cutting through numerous alleyways, our taxi stopped at the corner of a crossroads.

'There you are,' said Kasra, nodding towards a building across the road. 'That must be your apartment.'

The cab driver got out and unloaded my suitcases. I was about to pay for my share of the ride when Kasra jumped out and spoke to the driver. I didn't understand a word he said – he spoke Azeri to him – but I assume he was telling the driver not to take my money.

Kasra then pulled the banknote out of the driver's hand and shoved it back into my jeans' pocket.

'You are in my city and you are my guest, at least while I am here,' he said.

He promised to visit me within the next few days and left in the cab for Manzariyeh. I stood there as his taxi drove away, and then crossed the road with my heavy suitcases to the front of the building.

The building was at the corner of South Shahnaz and New 25th Shahrivar Street. It looked new, and every apartment had a balcony overlooking the intersection. Mine was the very last one on the third floor. I rang the bell and seconds later someone pressed the buzzer and the door opened.

'Mr Azad, is that you?' The voice, calling from the top of the stairs, echoed in the empty hallway.

'Yes, it is,' I called back.

I heard footsteps coming down the stairs. We met halfway.

'Hello, Mr Azad. I'm Akbari.' He stretched his hand towards me and gave me a pleasant smile.

I put my suitcases down and we shook hands. My landlord was a short, chubby man in his mid-fifties with salt-and-pepper hair who reminded me of characters in Italian movies.

'Let me help you with them,' Mr Akbari said and immediately picked up two of the suitcases.

I thanked him and told him I had another suitcase and a few small bags at the entrance. I ran downstairs to fetch them.

When we got to the top floor the apartment door was ajar.

'Please, do go in.' He pushed the door open for me and stood aside.

The moment I walked in I felt good about the place. It had white clean walls with a new grey carpet throughout. The rooms were a good size and all the windows faced north. The balcony ran along the sitting room, the bedroom and the kitchen, and there was access from each of them. It was furnished with everything I could possibly want – a television set, a couch and two armchairs, a coffee table and a bookshelf in the sitting room; a double bed and a cupboard next to a wooden desk and a chair in the bedroom. The kitchen had a gas cooker, an Iranian Arj fridge, a sink, a few cupboards and a table with four chairs.

'What do you think, Mr Azad? Do you like it?' Mr Akbari asked, beaming with pride.

The place had turned out to be much better than I'd expected. I walked into the bathroom and saw the washing machine.

'It's perfect!' I exclaimed.

He showed me where the meters were, gave me the details of when and how the building was serviced and when the rubbish was collected. We agreed that I would take the rent to his shop in the bazaar on the first day of every month. He then left two sets of keys and gave me his business card. I thanked him once again for the apartment and for helping me with my luggage.

So there I was, in my first home, alone. As soon as Mr Akbari left I rang Mâdar and we had a long chat. She and Parastou had spent the day sorting out her new apartment and she had then taken Parastou and Kami out for dinner. I wished I could have been with them.

By the time I finished unpacking, it was nine o'clock and I was absolutely starving, so I went round the corner and found a small sandwich shop. The owner was an Armenian man who ran it with his wife. He was pleasant and courteous and had a strong Armenian accent when he spoke Persian. I bought two sandwiches – a smoked ham and a Mortadella – and a bottle of cold Canada Dry and came back home.

I went straight to the sitting room, sat in front of the television, ate the sandwiches as quickly as I could and drank my fizzy orange drink straight from the bottle. I was too tired to sort out my clothes. I just took out the bare necessities, brushed my teeth and had a quick shower before going to bed. Even though the windows were closed I could still hear the traffic, and I wondered how noisy it was going to be during the hot months with the windows open, but I fell asleep almost immediately.

When I woke up the following day, it was a sunny Friday with a nice cool breeze in the air. I shaved, got dressed and decided to go out to do some shopping. Just across the road there was a bakery; I could smell the fresh bread from across the road. I joined the queue. There was a young lady in front of me with a four- or five-year-old boy in shorts. I said hello to the little boy. He immediately hid behind his mother's chador but she said good morning to me. When it was my turn to be served, the guy behind the counter said something in Azeri. I felt embarrassed and apologised for not being able to speak Azeri.

'No problem, my son. How many Lavash breads do you want?' he said in Persian with a strong accent.

He must have been in his early sixties but his face was so wrinkled he could easily have passed for ninety. I asked for four, paid two tomans and walked across to the apartment.

I had eaten almost half of one of the hot, freshly baked Lavash breads by the time I got to the top of the stairs. I made some tea with the Lipton teabags that Mr Akbari had kindly left me, finished the bread and headed back outside again. This time I took my coat too in case I didn't come back until later in the evening.

I crossed the road and walked up Shahnaz Street. With it being Friday, most of the shops were closed and the streets were deserted. But it gave me the opportunity to inspect my new city in peace. I knew my school was somewhere in the city centre and I wanted to find it. I arrived at an all-girls high school called Parvin. A short distance away I saw the spire of a church. Could that be my school? I wondered. I asked a young man who had just passed me.

'No, you need to keep walking. The church you see there is Noor Primary School's church and it is Assyrian,' he informed me.

Further down the road a sign attracted my attention: 'The Armenian Central Caliphate of Azerbaijan' – something I had not heard of before. Tabriz was a relatively religious city compared to Tehran, and had a large Armenian community that mostly lived in Baron Avak, a street in the centre of the city. There were more women wearing the chador here than in Tehran, but what chadors! In Tehran the chadors were black and enveloped women's entire bodies, showing only their face and hands. Here they were made from transparent material or netting and revealed everything underneath. They wore miniskirts, no tights and open-neck blouses under it. This was their version of the Islamic hijab! I was fascinated that the women of a religious city had managed to push the boundaries of its strict, macho culture to such an extent. The chador for Tabrizi women seemed to be more of a fashion statement or an accessory than a demonstration of their faith.

The street was getting busier the further I walked. I kept smiling at people, hoping they would acknowledge me and welcome me to their city. Mostly they smiled back; some even greeted me as we passed each other. I got to the Shahnaz–Pahlavi intersection and asked a young pretty woman for directions to the Anoushirvan Secondary School. She pointed across the road and told me to go down Miyar Miyar alleyway, next to the hotel and Cinema Asia.

'The school is behind Pahlavi Passage,' she said. 'Walk to the end of the alleyway, turn left and then right. You'll come out right in front of its gates.'

So the school was literally about fifteen minutes' walk from where I lived. Other than the cafés and a few liquor stores that did not look very nice, there was nothing else near the school. I was quite surprised to see one of Tabriz's best schools hidden in such a location, nestled among the hotel's fire exits and the delivery entrances to the shops on Pahlavi Avenue.

Anoushirvan was an all-boys secondary school run by the French Catholic priests who partly owned it. I walked through the half-open gates. In front of me stood a huge brick church very similar in architecture to the Catholic churches of France. It must have been at least sixty or seventy years old, I thought. A few minutes later a slim, tall, balding man wearing a T-shirt and faded blue jeans appeared from round the side of the church. He gave me a broad smile and asked me something in Azeri.

'Good morning,' I said in Persian, walking towards him. 'I'm the new English teacher.'

'Oh, our new English teacher! Do you speak French?' he asked in Persian with a very strong French accent.

'No,' I replied, 'unfortunately not.'

He introduced himself as Père Lazar. 'Teachers and students call me Mon Père.'

We shook hands.

From Fall to Spring

'I am Pedram Azad. I only arrived yesterday from Tehran. I thought I should see where I would be working.'

'Come with me,' he said. 'I can show you. You have come at the best time. There is nobody here, so we can chat and have a cup of coffee if you wish. Let's begin with our church, shall we – if you're interested, that is.'

I was about to say that I was when he continued: 'Anyway it's best to know the history behind your workplace. You never know – one day a student might ask you questions.'

I found it fascinating to learn about old foreign communities in Iran, like the Polish one that had settled in Tehran at the end of the Second World War. I wondered how this tall French missionary felt about living in this provincial city.

I found Mon Père very pleasant. He was in his mid-forties and his Persian was quite good, though he claimed that his Azeri was better. As he began telling me the history behind my new school I marvelled at the commitment of the French Catholics. After all, Iran was by majority a Muslim society; it must have been difficult for a French Catholic mission to thrive here for so long.

'I find it interesting to see European missionaries like yourself in Iran,' I told him, as we were about to enter the church.

He stopped and looked at me.

'Have you ever had any problems?' I asked. '… with the Islamic clergy, I mean.'

'No. Why should we?' he replied bluntly. 'Religious minorities have never had any major issues living in your country, particularly since the Pahlavis.'

We stood outside the church, Mon Père pointing here and there. The church was actually called La Vierge Puissante, though the locals referred to it as Anoushirvan. It had been financed and built by a rich Frenchman in 1910.

'The architecture is Gothic,' Mon Père informed me. 'Unlike most churches around the world that are built in the shape of a cross, ours is a rectangular and all built with red bricks.'

He drew my attention to the entrance, a beautifully carved door made from walnut. Above it was a delicately carved stucco panel depicting the Virgin Mary surrounded by ten angels. It had been created in 1923, he told me proudly.

The cool air and stillness inside the church was pleasant and made me no longer feel like an intruder in this sacred place. In the entranceway, above us, the church's square-shaped spire rose heavenward. It opened out into a large hall with seven white marble columns on each side; towards the front was the gallery for the choir. Behind the altar were three stained-glass windows.

A large oil painting attracted my attention. It depicted angels on clouds riding through the sky.

'Various French painters painted it in Paris in 1895,' Mon Père told me, 'so this is, in fact, older than the church.'

I felt proud. Why, I wasn't sure, but I felt privileged to be there with a personal guide, and wondered how many in Tabriz were aware of this hidden treasure.

'And the statue of the Virgin was made in France too, in 1921,' he added, and he went on to explain that the other paintings and statues were all French and had been made between 1900 and 1926. 'You seem to be enjoying our little tour,' he said.

'I love it! I feel so proud to be here. This is the first time for me – being in a Christian church, I mean.'

He smiled and invited me to look around the rest of the school.

To the east side of the church was the schoolyard. The larger part was for the students, and white lines on the ground marked out basketball and volleyball courts and football pitches. There was also a small car park close to the church.

'Let me show you our quarters,' Père Lazar said, directing me up the path to the west of the church. 'You'll see the classrooms in a week's time when you begin work, so I won't bother taking you there.'

The path led us into a small well-kept garden, behind which stood an old rectory. After walking through the ugly alleyways this beautiful garden was an oasis in a jungle of concrete and rubbish. It was enclosed by high white walls and one side had a covered walkway that took you round to the veranda in front of the rectory. Leafy rose bushes were in full bloom, their red, yellow and pink flowers filling the air with scent. Vines twisted around the posts of the veranda and beautiful white grapes hung like small lanterns across the entire front of the porch. A small fountain in the middle of the rose bushes attracted thirsty sparrows.

Mon Père invited me inside for coffee. As soon as I stepped through the door I felt as if I was in rural France – not that I had ever been there, but it had a foreign feeling. Old Persian rugs, antique wooden furniture, oil paintings depicting Christ at the Last Supper and other biblical stories combined with the scent of incense that hung in the air and seemed to seep out of the walls lent the room a calm, spiritual ambience.

An old lady appeared and asked Père Lazar if he would like her to bring us some tea or coffee, and a few minutes later she appeared with two cups of freshly brewed Turkish coffee and a bowl of Qurabiya, a pastry speciality of Tabriz. Mon Père went over to a record player and asked if I like classical music.

'Yes, I like it very much,' I replied.

He put on Berlioz's *Rêverie et Caprice* and turned the volume down low.

'How long have you been living in Iran, Father?' I asked.

'I arrived almost ten years ago. But my senior priest, Père Corentin, a French Breton who is now in his mid-eighties, has lived in Iran – in the same church – for nearly half a century. He's not here at the moment. He's in Rome attending to some business.'

'Half a century!' I said in disbelief. I apologised for almost shouting. 'That's unbelievable.'

'Yes, indeed.' Mon Père smiled. 'He would tell you that it was Persian literature and history that attracted him to your country.'

Mâdar would have loved him, I thought; they'd talk literature for hours.

'Père Corentin told me that when he was given the choice of going to Baghdad or coming to Iran he chose the latter because he considered it more civilised and romantic.'

'When did Catholic missionaries begin coming to Iran?' I asked.

'Oh, European Catholic missions have been in Persia, as it was then called, since the thirteenth and fourteenth centuries, when the Mongols were at the height of their influence. Dominican and Franciscan emissaries sent by successive popes, although they were unable to achieve much, laid the groundwork for more successful Catholic missions in the future and we've been here ever since.'

'I had no idea!'

'But we came to Tabriz in 1840 when Eugène Boré, a staunch French Catholic, founded four schools in Persia, two in Tabriz and Isfahan for the Armenians, and two in Rezaiyeh and Shapour for the Chaldeans. The schools were then passed to the Lazarists to run, and they were joined later by the French Sisters of Charity. Father Fornier was the first Catholic missionary to come to Tabriz. I hope I'm not boring you, Mr Azad.'

'Not at all. I'm really enjoying this.'

'Please do drink your coffee before it gets cold.' He picked up the dish of Qurabiya and offered me one. 'So there you are. Now you know a little bit about your school's history.'

I was enthralled. He asked me various questions about my family and myself, my ambitions in life and so on. The time flew by so fast that I didn't realise I had been there for over two hours. I had to get some groceries; I didn't want to have sandwiches again for dinner. I thanked Mon Père for the coffee and the pleasant conversation and said I'd see him in a week's time.

The next day I woke up to a beautiful sunny Saturday morning. I wanted to go sightseeing on foot, and decided to give Kasra a call to see if he was free to come with me. An hour later he rang the bell and I went downstairs to meet him. I went to shake his hand, but he put his hand on my shoulder and gave me a kiss on the cheek.

'Where would you like to start your tour of the city?' he asked, putting on his Ray-Ban sunglasses.

'You're the guide, so it's up to you,' I said.

We walked up Shahnaz Street and turned into Pahlavi Avenue.

'I want to take you to the Arg, and I'd like you to see the opera house too, if it's open. Did you know the stucco work on the ceiling of the opera house is a copy of Moscow's?'

'There's an opera house in Tabriz?'

'Yes, of course. Russian artists were brought in to work on the ceiling. It's one of a kind – one of the finest you'll find in any building in Iran.'

I was thrilled to be able to see it for myself. The opera house just took my breath away.

'Its gigantic crystal chandelier is a work of art in itself,' Kasra whispered once we were inside.

The opera house was owned and managed by Shir-o Khorshid Sorkh, as was the Arg (the citadel) behind it, Kasra told me. Shir-o Khorshid Sorkh (Red Lion & Sun Society) was the Iranian equivalent of the Red Cross.

The citadel was probably the most impressive building I had ever seen. It was a remnant of a fortress built in the thirteenth and fourteenth centuries. In the early days it had been used as a mosque, but during the Qajar era it was transformed into a military post and weapons store. It was the tallest building in the city; you could still see the damage caused by artillery shells during the Constitutional Revolution of 1906. Kasra was a great narrator; the way he described the history of the place made it really come alive.

We left the Arg and headed towards Sa'at Square where the town hall is. I had caught a glimpse of it from the taxi the night we arrived; it had looked quite European. On the way I told Kasra about a book I had read on Tabriz's historic buildings and monuments a few years earlier.

'Oh, so I've been wasting my time telling you all about the citadel and the opera house!' he said, laughing.

'No, not at all. I was making sure you knew the history of your city well.' I gave him a cheeky grin.

'You haven't started teaching yet and you're already testing me?'

Once at the town hall Kasra admitted that he knew nothing of its history. So it was my turn to lecture him.

'It was built in 1933 by the mayor, Haj Arfa Al-Molk Jalili, on the site of an old cemetery,' I told him. 'It's also known as the Clock Building because of the four clocks in the tower. The building is designed in the shape of an eagle with its wings spread. German architects designed it when the Nazis were in power and incorporated their symbol into the building.'

'You're kidding,' Kasra said.

I felt proud that I knew more about Tabriz than he did, and carried on. 'Hence two German eagles on the side of the building, above the round window that represents the earth.' I pointed to the window.

Funny enough I discovered years later that many people in Tabriz didn't know about the eagles. It was the building's secret, I thought – visible yet not noticed by many.

I wished I could share my sightseeing experiences that day with Mâdar. Though I had only left Tehran less than forty-eight hours earlier, I missed her a great deal – far more than I thought I would. I was used to having her company. We often went to the movies and restaurants together. It seemed like a strange relationship to most of my friends, except Parastou and Kami. Since I'd lost my mum Mâdar had become my new mother, and I think that in me she somehow found the presence of her daughter.

Later that day Kasra and I returned to my apartment for some drinks, and before he went home I invited him over on Monday to watch the closing ceremony of the Asian Games broadcast live from Aryamehr Stadium.

The Shah, on a visit to Australia, told the National Press Club in Canberra that Iran was willing to negotiate an international treaty tying the price of oil to 20 to 30 other commodities, such as food and other basic materials.

'If the prices of these commodities go down, our oil will go down,' he said. 'We are ready for serious talks on that subject.'

But, he said, 'nobody can dictate to us, nobody can wave a finger at us, because we can wave back.'

While it was 'absolutely vital' for Iran to stay friendly with the United States because of their 'arsenal of nuclear arms,' he said, Ford's remarks criticizing the upward spiral of oil prices were 'not at all acceptable to Iran.'

'We will be ready to provide our energy resources against the Westinghouse and General Motors and General Electrics and all the other generals they have,' he said.

Columbia Missourian, September 1974

Chapter Five

ON THE LAST DAY OF summer, the day before my first day teaching at the school, I woke up to the sound of thunder and heavy rain. Today, Kasra was taking me to a chelo kabobi – the best one in town – for lunch. We were meeting at noon and I had a couple of hours to spare before he was due to turn up at my place. Since I'd arrived in Tabriz we had met up every day, Kasra proudly showing me around his city and helping me to feel more at home.

The sky was getting darker and darker and by the time I finished shaving it felt as if it was the middle of the night. The rain was so heavy that I could hardly hear the running water when I stood under the shower.

When I finished in the bathroom I was quite hungry. I was tempted to have something for breakfast but instead I made some tea and switched on the radio; I did not want to spoil my appetite for later. Hayedeh, our Iranian diva, was singing on the radio, and it made me think of Mâdar. Hayedeh was her favourite singer, and although I liked her too I thought no one could beat Googoosh – she was simply the best. I picked up the phone to have a little chat with Mâdar but it kept ringing, so eventually I hung up.

I lay on the bed and started to read Daniel Defoe's *Robinson Crusoe*. I'd read it in Persian when I was at school, but I'd never got round to reading it in English. I'd bought the English edition a few days earlier in a bookshop I stumbled across on Shahnaz Street. Once I was inside, I knew I had found my sanctuary in Tabriz. The books covered a wide variety of subjects, but the shelves dedicated to English novels were all I was interested in.

Moments after I came in, the owner had appeared through a door at the back of the shop. He looked like an old-fashioned gentleman, dressed in a dark blue suit with a watch chain hanging from his waistcoat. He wore round glasses and had a bow tie, something you didn't often see in Iran. We had only exchanged a few words when he invited me to join him for a cup of tea. He was a middle-aged man who was pleased to see young readers in his shop.

'What do you mean by that?' I had asked. 'Are you trying to say that young people don't read?'

'Yes. It's unfortunate but that is exactly the conclusion I have come to.' He poured a cup of tea for me and asked me to take a seat near his desk. 'You see, two years ago I had exactly the same reaction when a friend and a former colleague of mine, a professor of social sciences here at Azarabadegan University, made such a statement. I decided to run my own survey and finally last month, after exactly twenty-four months, I realised he was right.'

'I'd like to hear about your survey,' I said.

'Well, I registered the number of people who came into the shop. Then divided them into different categories: men, women and students. Then I broke them down further into subcategories by age. The majority of those who walked out of my bookshop with a book fell into two age groups – retired men and women, and children up to the age of thirteen or fourteen. I am worried about the big threat this poses. I believe that books are the only weapon we have against ignorance, and I'm deeply disappointed in our youth for not reading enough.'

While he spoke, several people had come into his bookshop and I watched to see if they bought a book and roughly what age they were. But no one purchased a book. My curiosity was piqued by his choice of words – 'the big threat' – and I wanted to know what he meant by that.

'Iranians don't know anything about themselves,' he had explained. 'We don't know or learn enough about our history and our cultural heritage. That's why our youth are so ignorant of their identity.'

'Yes, I see your point.'

'Can you also see the danger?' he asked. Without giving me the chance to reply he continued, 'When not enough time and effort is spent on educating our young people about their own country and making patriots of them, any charlatan can abuse their innocence and turn them against themselves without them realising it.'

What a fascinating man he had been! In all, I spent about an hour with him that day, and promised I'd stop by another day to carry on our interesting chat over a nice cup of his freshly brewed tea.

I'd got a few chapters into *Robinson Crusoe* when the doorbell rang. I looked at my watch. It was Kasra – I'd completely lost track of time! I buzzed him in via the intercom and opened the apartment door, stopping on my way down the hallway to check my appearance in the mirror. I quickly went to the bathroom and splashed on some more aftershave, by which time he was already standing in front of the door knocking.

'Hi, come in,' I said when he appeared at the door. 'Sorry, I was reading and didn't realise the time.'

'No rush. There's no reservation or anything. Take your time.'

'Let me just go and get changed,' I said and told him to make himself at home in the sitting room. But he followed me to the bedroom, chatting away while I put on my jeans and a shirt. I liked it that he felt so at ease with me.

'I'm ready,' I finally announced. 'Let's go.'

But he didn't move. 'Go? There's no hurry.' His voice sounded different.

I suddenly felt shy for some reason and pushed past him into the hallway, laughing as I grabbed my jacket.

'But I'm starving,' I said. Nothing could have been further from the truth. My stomach was all butterflies and I had no idea why.

By this time the weather was bright and sunny after the earlier storm. In Baron Avak, the main throughway in the Armenian quarter, we went up some narrow stairs. Chelo kabobi Asia was a small, unpretentious restaurant on two separate floors, one for families and the other for single men. Most restaurants, particularly those with less of a modern or Western ambience were like this; if single women wanted to dine, they could use the family area. The irresistible aroma of Persian rice with butter melting on it, together with skewers of chargrilled barbecued lamb and chicken, tempted every hungry customer to order more than they could eat. Its great food and its location in the downtown area had turned this small restaurant into a big success. Soon after we got our table the queue was down the staircase and out into the street. It was lunchtime and many people from nearby offices filled the place. You could see people were in a rush and the service was fast, courteous and efficient.

Over lunch Kasra did most of the talking while I ate and listened. It was just before two o'clock when we left the place. He insisted on paying, saying that it was his idea to go out for lunch in the first place. I thanked him and we walked down the narrow stairs out into the warm afternoon sun. The streets were busy and people were bustling about. Kasra put on his sunglasses.

'Where shall we go?' I asked him, seeing only my own reflection when I looked at him.

'It's too hot to go anywhere at this time. Shall we just go back to your apartment?' he asked.

I agreed and we strolled along on the shady side of Shahnaz Street under an awning of leafy green trees. Every day just before sunset these trees were a favourite spot for sparrows. They packed into the branches and began their deafening chirping. You could hear them but not see them, until you walked underneath and got your clothes and hair decorated. On the way back we went to an ice-cream parlour called Momtaz and I bought two large tubs of Akbar Mashdi ice cream and we headed back home.

The apartment was hot and stuffy. I opened all the windows while Kasra took his shoes off. I switched on the television, grabbed a couple of small bowls from the kitchen with two small spoons and a large one to scoop the ice cream out and gave them to Kasra to serve up while I went to the bedroom to change into my shorts and a T-shirt. When I got back to the sitting room, Kasra had already served the ice cream and was licking the back of his spoon. He was sitting comfortably on the armchair and I sat on the couch facing the television, stretching my legs.

'Have you been to Shahgoli Park?' he asked.

I had not. He suggested that we go there some day as it was the hang-out place for most Tabrizis.

We spent the rest of that afternoon watching television, talking about our lives and eating more ice cream. I was happy to have him around – it helped me feel less anxious about my first day at school. I wanted to iron some shirts and have an early night, so Kasra left after sunset.

On Monday morning I woke up at 6 a.m. The first day of the month of Mehr – 23rd September. The day when schools throughout the country open after the long summer break had always had a special place in my heart. I used to look forward to seeing my old classmates as well as meeting new ones at the beginning of every school year. But this year I was nervous and it got worse as time went on. Then when I was in the shower the phone rang. I grabbed a towel and rushed to answer it, dripping wet.

'*Bidâri?*' said the voice.

'Hi, Mâdar! Yes, I am awake. How are you?'

I immediately felt calmer when I heard her voice. Yet again my guardian angel had come to help me in my time of need. She was always there, as if she sensed my every mood.

'I'm fine, darling. I just wanted to wish you good luck on your first day at school,' she said.

'Thanks, Mâdar. Listen, I have to rush, but I'll call you tonight. Okay?'

'Don't worry. I'll call you tomorrow night. I'm out with a few friends tonight – going to the opening of a new gallery and then to dinner. It'll be too late to call you by the time I'm back home.'

We said goodbye and, after a light breakfast, I left the apartment and set off for Anoushirvan Secondary School.

A middle-aged man greeted me at the school and asked me who I was looking for. I introduced myself and told him that I was the new English teacher.

'Oh! Welcome, sir. I'm the caretaker here, Parviz Marandi – the school's baba for the past fifteen years.'

In Iran, school caretakers are usually referred to as baba, meaning 'father'. They are the first ones to arrive and the last to leave; in some cases they may even live with their family in the school. School babas are often a favourite of all the students and are respected by everyone. They are jacks of all trades and can fix almost everything, and they tend to the school grounds. They also keep an eye on the main gate to make sure there are no intruders and that the children don't leave without permission.

Parviz was not married and had a room in the priests' quarters, he told me. I shook his hand and thanked him for welcoming me to the school. While I was still chatting with Parviz a car drove in through the gates.

'This must be Mr Bushehri, the principal,' said Parviz. 'Have you met him?'

'No, I haven't,' I replied. 'I came here a week or so ago and only met Mon Père Lazar.'

'Oh, so it was you!' Parviz said as we walked. He was ushering me towards the principal. 'Mon Père mentioned that a new teacher had been here. I'd gone to Marand that day to visit my family.'

By the time we reached the car park, Mr Bushehri had got out of his blue Paykan and was coming towards us.

'Good morning, sir!' shouted Parviz. 'Here is your new member of staff, Mr Azad, your new English teacher.'

Mr Bushehri greeted us with a smile, shook my hand and then Parviz's.

'You're early, Mr Azad. Do you always rise so early? Let's go to my office and have a little chat before all hell breaks loose!' He gave a big laugh.

Parviz wished me good luck and went back to the gate as the headmaster and I walked up the stairs.

Anoushirvan School was an L-shaped building, with all the

classrooms located on the first floor. Below them, on the ground floor, were the liquor stores that fronted the alleyways and a mezzanine that served as a small drinking area; our classrooms sat right above them. Behind the liquor stores, in a corner of the schoolyard, was a laboratory with a workshop in its basement. The main entrance to the building was a staircase that led up to the classrooms and the principal's office, a large room that was also used as the teachers' common room. It had a balcony that overlooked the schoolyard and from it, speeches and announcements were made.

We walked into Mr Bushehri's office. His desk was right at the end of the room facing the door and hanging on a wall behind was a picture of the imperial couple. Mr Bushehri invited me to take a seat as the telephone rang. I had a look around. A map of Iran hung on a wall between two mahogany bookshelves, and he had a marble bust of Ferdowsi, the tenth-century Iranian poet, on his desk flanked by our national Lion and Sun flags. An old Persian rug was spread in the middle of the room and ten to fifteen chairs were placed around it.

As the headmaster finished his phone call, a voluptuous woman with pale skin and dark hair peeping out from under her silk scarf came in carrying two cups of black tea and some cubed sugar. Mr Bushehri introduced the school's tea lady, Parvaneh Khânum.

When she left, Mr Bushehri gave me a short history of the school. He had spoken to Père Lazar, so he knew I'd already heard some of it. As time went on the noise of students gathering in the schoolyard below became louder. Teachers had started arriving and Mr Bushehri introduced me to them as they came into the room. It was hard to remember their names and what each of them taught, but with the exception of the sports teacher, everyone else seemed much older than me.

The students had lined up in the yard below according to seniority and faced Mr Bushehri's balcony where all the members of staff had gathered. At 8:15 a.m. sharp our national anthem played on a tape recorder while a senior student carried the flag to its pole. The whole scene – the unfurling of our flag while hundreds of pairs of eyes followed it slowly up the pole – made me quite emotional. Some students and teachers joined in singing the anthem as the flag fluttered in the morning breeze, but at the end all the students sang the last verse together: '*Iranians continuously happy, May God protect HIM forever*'.

Then a student appeared next to us on the balcony and read out in Persian the customary prayer thanking God for our beloved country and sovereign, and asking him to protect Iran against her enemies and keep the imperial couple safe that they might remain our guiding lights. After that, Mr Bushehri made a brief speech to welcome the students, old and new, as well as his staff and reminded everyone that the school opened at 8 a.m., followed by the daily anthem and prayer at 8.15 at which all students must be present, and that classes began at 8.30. When he dismissed them, the students rushed towards the noticeboards searching for their classes while we went back to the principal's office to pick up our own timetables.

Some of the teachers wished me luck as they left the office to go to their allocated classrooms. My schedule was to teach the first-grade students, most of whom were learning English for the first time.

Most schools in Iran do not teach a foreign language during the first five years of primary school. English classes start at secondary school and are compulsory until the end.

The first week of every academic year is usually chaotic. Thursdays are a half-day and school finishes at lunchtime; we're also closed on Friday, the Iranian weekend. But because we were a Catholic school we also benefited from a half-day on Sundays.

Having a short week ahead of us I decided to spend the time getting to know my students, introducing the subject to them and talking about the importance of learning a foreign language, especially English.

My students, having just left primary school, were also new to the environment. The classroom was located at the end of the wide corridor facing Mr Bushehri's office and right above one of the liquor stores. The temperature was still in the low twenties so the windows were open and the noises from the alleyway drifted up. When I walked into the classroom with the register and my schedule under my arm, I remembered my own schooldays when, together with my friends, we gave hell to those teachers we didn't like. If the spirits of those teachers were still around, I thought, now would be the time for them to take their revenge on me. It was time to pay for my sins!

The classroom door was open and students were roaming about, pushing the seats around and arguing about where to sit. The noise died down as soon as I walked in. I knew they were scrutinising this young teacher, obviously new to the school himself, who they would have to put up with for at least the next nine months. I comforted myself with the thought that the kids were also new to the school and, other than those who shared the same primary school, they wouldn't know anybody else. I dropped my papers on my desk and stood in front of the class until the last murmur faded into silence. I introduced myself, and instead of following the usual procedure of reading names out of the register I asked them to introduce themselves one by one. According to my list I had forty-five students to take care of. They all seemed tolerable, but I knew I had to watch out for those who sat in the back row. They are usually the ones who believe they don't need to pay much attention during lessons because they know it all. But it was too early to pass any judgement.

The introductions took about half an hour and went fairly smoothly, with a few giggles and face-pulling here and there. By asking them to introduce themselves and to tell me a little bit about themselves I had put them in the spotlight, so they had to concentrate. I now had an hour with them, so without further ado I began by asking them why they thought they should learn English.

I picked one of the lanky lads in the back row.

'Because then we can pickup girls easier, sir,' was his answer.

The class burst into laughter, and I smiled.

'That's probably true,' I said, 'but you must speak it well, otherwise the girls, who are known to be better at their studies than boys, may answer you back and laugh at your expense if you can't continue a conversation in English.'

That wiped the grin off his face and the whole class went silent. It was my first show of authority. Teachers usually silenced students by shouting at them, so it was new for them to hear a reasonable reply to their comment – it made them think.

Another chap with freckles raised his hand. 'We need to learn foreign languages, especially English, because it's an international language, and in order to communicate with the rest of the world we need to be good at it,' was his wise answer.

Next, a small boy near the front said, 'I don't like the English and I don't like learning their language. Why should we? Do they make an effort to learn ours?'

Suddenly the classroom erupted again, the students shouting out their personal views. The whole thing was in danger of getting out of control, but I was determined not to shout at them.

'You all have valid points!' I said above the din. 'We need to learn foreign languages, especially English, because it has become an international language. We also need to know it well in order to translate books into Persian for the benefit of those who have not learned English so they can learn about foreign cultures, literature, science and technology. We need to know English in order to understand the modern world. And finally' – I paused for dramatic effect – 'you need to learn it because it's in your curriculum.'

I told them that I expected them to take their lessons seriously and that I didn't care whether they liked it or not. 'There are many things in life that we may not like but we still have to do them.'

I explained that we might not get much done that week but from next week they would need to work as hard for their English class as they did in maths and other subjects. Before I finished my sentence the school bell rang and they suddenly rushed out as if they'd seen a snake in the classroom.

'Slowly!' I shouted at them. 'Walk out like human beings, please.'

Mr Bushehri was outside the door, and the students behaved better as soon as they noticed him.

'Not easy, hey?' he said, pointing at the kids.

'No, but they're fine. It'll take a couple of weeks for us to get to know each other.'

'By the way, there is someone waiting for you at the gate,' Mr Bushehri said as he was about to head back to his office. 'I asked Mr Marandi to invite him in to my office but apparently he wanted to wait for you outside.'

I couldn't imagine who it could be. I didn't know anyone in Tabriz, except my landlord and Kasra; my landlord wouldn't show up here and I had seen Kasra only yesterday. It was just after ten in the morning and I had the rest of the day off. I was quite happy with my timetable and the way my classes were spread out. My busiest days were Saturdays and Tuesdays. I only had one class on both Sunday and Monday mornings with the rest of those days to myself; on Wednesdays I had a free morning and a class in the afternoon; Thursdays, the last day of the week, I had two lessons in the morning.

When I got to the gates I saw that it was Kasra who had called for me. He smiled and gave me a hug.

'What are you doing here?' I asked.

'I didn't know your schedule but I was in town and thought you'd appreciate a familiar face after being tormented by the kids,' he said.

'It's a nice surprise,' I said. I told him I was free for the rest of the day and if he wanted, we could go and grab something to eat.

The clouds had gathered and by the time we got to the restaurant the sky was completely grey. This restaurant was a traditional one next to the bazaar where they only served Dizi, a type of stew called Abgoosht that is made with lamb, chickpeas, white beans, potatoes and various spices, together with dried lime in a nice tomato sauce. It was another favourite of mine. Over lunch Kasra told me that he would be flying to Tehran the following week to catch his flight for Switzerland. I got a sudden rush of homesickness and loneliness mixed together. Once Kasra had gone I would have no one to spend my free time with in Tabriz. He had become the person I spent my free time with in my new town. We had met on the bus only a week ago, but it felt as if we had known each other for a long time.

'We must keep in touch, Pedram.' he said. 'I'll be back for Christmas for about three weeks.'

'That would be nice. I'll look forward to that.'

'Maybe you could come and visit me.'

'Where? In Switzerland?'

'Yes. Why not? All you need is to get a ticket.'

'And the money,' I added sarcastically.

'Oh, don't be silly. It's not that expensive. You could do it if you really wanted to come and visit me. You only need to buy your ticket. Once in Basel you can stay with me and I'll take care of you.'

An extremely skinny waiter with a Hitler-like moustache interrupted us when he put our Dizis on the table. '*Nousheh jân,*' he said – bon appétit – and left.

'Anyway, when I come back in December, I want you to come with me to Yam slopes so we can go skiing together,' Kasra said.

I had never skied before. Parastou and Kami used to go almost every weekend during the winter months in Tehran, but I had only ever joined them for après-ski. I smiled at Kasra and assured him that we would do that. We were both quiet while we ate. I was thinking about my social life once he was gone. Who would I call? How would I meet anyone? I wondered. I had an urge to call Mâdar and hear her voice, but I couldn't do that until I was back home.

Kasra and I left the restaurant and walked a little through Qiyam Square. But it was packed with shoppers, so we hurried across in the direction of my apartment. We hardly exchanged a word with one another, each of us deep in our own thoughts, and got to my place much sooner than I expected. He stopped outside the front door to the block.

'Aren't you coming up?' I asked.

'No, I better go,' he said. He seemed to be very preoccupied. I couldn't figure out what was wrong with him, but something obviously was.

'Will you come to my place on Friday?' he asked. 'Mum and Dad would like to meet you.'

'Okay, thanks. That's very kind of them. But I don't have your address.'

'Oh, don't worry. I'll see you before then. I'll call you anyway,' he said and left.

He is strange, I thought as I climbed the stairs to my apartment. Only a couple of hours earlier we were going to spend the day together and then he'd suddenly changed his mind. But then I hardly knew him really. What was it – a week, ten days since we'd met? I didn't know much about his friends in Tabriz, or if he even had any.

I had an urge to speak to Mâdar when I got in the door. I threw my jacket on a chair next to the phone and dialled her number. But there was no answer – again. The feelings of loneliness got worse. Kasra had abandoned me, Grandma wasn't home and as for Parastou and Kami, I had no idea what they were up to. I hadn't heard from them for over a week. They were probably busy with their studies and hadn't given me a second thought. I missed everyone. I went to my bedroom, took my clothes off and lay on the bed. I found myself thinking about my parents. I was sure my mother would have come with me to Tabriz to stay until I was settled. I mulled over the day's events. After all, it had been my first day teaching. I could only remember a few faces, and definitely no names.

I must have fallen asleep at some point as the sudden ring of the telephone woke me up. I rushed to the phone and, assuming it was Mâdar, blurted out, 'I rang, but you weren't in!'

'I just walked in. I had a few things to do and then came home. I just rang to make sure you weren't upset with my sudden disappearance.' It was Kasra.

I was happy to hear his voice, maybe more than Mâdar's because he was someone nearby. I was extremely homesick.

'No, I'm okay. Why did you change your mind though?'

'I suddenly remembered something I had to do. Mum's been asking me if you have confirmed for Friday lunch, so I thought I'd call to make sure you're coming.'

'Sure. Thank her for me, but you have to give me your address.'

'Oh, don't worry. I'll pick you up at ten.'

'At ten? But I thought it was for lunch.'

'I thought you might like to go to the American consulate beforehand,' Kasra said.

'If you're thinking of getting me a visa, they're closed on Fridays, you know.' I laughed.

It turned out that Kasra wanted to take me for a dip in their fantastic swimming pool. 'Then we'll have lunch at my place and later in the afternoon we can go and play tennis. Do you know how to play tennis?'

'Wow! Swimming, lunch, tennis – you've it all worked out. Well, I'm not good at tennis at all, and as for swimming, I'll have to look for my swimming trunks.' I wasn't sure I'd brought them with me.

'I'll teach you tennis and you can wear a pair of my trunks if you can't find yours.' It seemed he had it all under control.

The next few days went by pretty fast. In the evenings I was either busy correcting homework or preparing lessons. In the blink of an eye, it was Friday morning. I had a quick breakfast, had a shower and ironed my shirt. I had bought a box of pastries and a nice plant to take to Mrs Arjomand. At the stroke of ten, the doorbell rang.

'Are you ready?' Kasra asked when he reached the apartment. 'The weather's great – still warm enough for a dip.'

'Do you want a cup of tea before we leave?' I asked.

'No, no! Grab your bag and let's go.'

We headed out and walked down South Shahnaz Street towards the American consulate. This part of the city was completely new to me.

The consulate building sat in the middle of a large garden. Its entrance was an iron gate with an impressive arch above it from which hung the US coat of arms. It was a very grand entrance for a provincial city. At the gate Kasra presented an American soldier with his membership card for the club. The soldier opened the gate and we walked into its well-tended gardens. The swimming pool was surrounded by manicured trees, pruned rose bushes and a lawn cut to perfection. The building itself was an impressive blend of modern yet traditional Persian architecture.

'The building was designed by the American architect Edward Larrabee Barnes,' said Kasra. He had obviously done his homework as a tour guide, I thought.

The grounds were busy with families and young men and women enjoying the first days of autumn while the summer warmth still lingered. There were two pools: a small one for children right next to a bigger one where more serious swimmers were doing lengths. A few hundred yards away two Iranian couples were playing tennis doubles, while others were sunbathing or had taken refuge under the giant elm trees to read or to have a nap. Kasra didn't seem to know anyone but everyone seemed very relaxed and friendly.

He'd been to swim there every day since he'd returned from Switzerland. In this garden of peace and tranquillity the only noises to be heard were the chirping of birds, the splashing of water and the laughter of children as they played. There were people from almost every nationality there, which was very new to me. Most foreigners in Tabriz were Italians. They had been invited to work at Tabriz's oil refinery, and about fifty Italian families had relocated to a corner of the newly developed district of Manzariyeh, where Kasra's parents lived. But there were also many Americans, British, French and Turks in the city. The Turkish consulate was just across the street from the American's. In those days, you only needed a visa to travel to the Soviet block, so embassies and consulates were used mainly for trade delegations which were pouring into Iran in ever-increasing numbers, or by diplomats keen to befriend a nation that was spending its oil revenues in the rush to catch-up with Western industrial giants.

After we'd had a swim we were both starving, so we had a shower and got changed. In the shower area, an American guy about the same age as us, blond and well built, said hello to Kasra. They chatted briefly but Kasra didn't introduce us and seemed in a hurry to get away. It took us less than ten minutes to get to Kasra's house from the American consulate. I was pleasantly surprised with their district. The entrance to the suburb had a chain stretched across it, and a middle-aged security man in a dark blue uniform welcomed our cab driver. On recognising Kasra, he said a polite hello and dropped the chain on the road for our cab to cross. I was quite excited. It was another part of the city I hadn't been to before, and it wasn't the kind of place I would have been given access to had I not known someone who lived there.

Manzariyeh was being developed by a private construction company, a subsidiary of Bank Bazargani. It was so very different from anything else I had seen in Iranian cities. It had the air of a private village, very like some of the private resorts on the Caspian. At the time only about fifteen two-storey houses and a few bungalows had been built, many of which were already occupied by Tabrizi middle- and upper-middle-class families. Kasra told me that the neighbours all knew and socialised with each other. The gardens around the houses were built differently too; the houses could be seen from the street. They only had fences around them, whereas most other properties in Iran were surrounded by high walls to keep the family secluded from the outside world.

When we got out of the taxi in front of the Arjomands' house, the gates and the front door were wide open as if there was no fear of intruders or unwelcome guests. Kasra called out for his mum. A dog began barking its head off when it heard Kasra's voice and came rushing out of the house. I held on firmly to the box of pastries and the Boston fern I had bought for Mrs Arjomand. Kasra introduced me to their little black-and-white Lhasa Apso, Poppy. She was the cutest dog I had ever seen. Having heard her bark, I was not expecting her to be so small.

Mrs Arjomand appeared at the door and gave me a lovely welcoming smile. 'Hi! How nice of you to come.'

'Hello, Mrs Arjomand,' I said, and we shook hands.

'Kasra hasn't stopped talking about you since you two met. You've made a strong impression on my son. He's not easily impressed,' she said.

She invited me in and I gave her the plant and the pastries, thanking her for the invitation. Just as we were about to go in, a car stopped outside. A tall, handsome man who looked very much like Kasra walked into the front yard. Poppy began barking again.

'You didn't all have to come to the door to welcome me!' said Mr Arjomand as he turned to me and shook my hand. 'It's good to meet you, Pedram.'

'Thank you, sir. The pleasure's all mine,' I said politely.

I was shown into the family sitting room where I chatted with Kasra and Mr Arjomand until Mrs Arjomand came in with some tea and the pastries I had brought, nicely arranged in a crystal dish. She told me to help myself and she disappeared into the kitchen as we continued our conversation. Kasra's father was very keen to know about my family and my decision to choose teaching as a career. Soon, Mrs Arjomand called us for lunch.

Kasra's dad led me to the dining room and we took our seats around a long, white dining table. The table was set with simple but elegant china and silver cutlery. In the middle stood a pale pink crystal vase with a few stems of tuberoses, their scent filling the room. Kasra's mum had gone to a lot of trouble and had prepared several dishes. The food was delicious and we concentrated on eating; for a while, all you could hear was clinking cutlery. Eventually Mrs

Arjomand asked me if I had settled in Tabriz.

'I'm getting used to it,' I replied. 'It was a blessing meeting Kasra, though.'

'It's important to have friends your own age. I'm sure you'll make other friends soon. Unfortunately,' she continued, 'I don't think any of Kasra's friends are left in Tabriz. Most of them went abroad to university. I think only one is here, but he's at Tehran University. Isn't that right?' She turned to her son.

'Yeah, otherwise I would've introduced you to them,' Kasra said.

We talked about places of interests in the city and about which ones I'd visited. I told them about the French paintings in my school's church. They hadn't known its history. I was starting to feel more relaxed in their company. They seemed like a loving family who respected one another. It was nice. For a moment I saw my parents at the table and Kasra as myself. Again, I wished they were still alive.

'Have you heard about it, Pedram?' Mr Arjomand's question brought me back from my reverie.

'I'm sorry?' I asked, embarrassed to be caught out.

'You youngsters are too busy having fun nowadays,' he said, laughing and taking a piece of bread. 'You hardly pay any attention to what is going on around you.'

I wasn't sure if he was referring to my lack of attention to his question or to something totally different.

'I'm sorry, Mr Arjomand, but I have to confess that Mrs Arjomand's lovely food and my rumbling stomach distracted me for a moment from what you were saying.'

'I was referring to the new development on Iran–US relations,' Mr Arjomand said. 'One of my colleagues at the hospital is fully supportive of the Shah's strategies. Although I understand His Majesty's intentions, I cannot stop worrying about its consequences.'

'I'm sorry, I'm totally at a loss,' I said, looking from him to Mrs Arjomand and to Kasra. 'I do follow the news, but I'm not sure what development you are referring to.'

'I was talking to one of the surgeons over lunch a few days ago about what the Shah had told President Ford last Thursday, that "No country can dictate its oil prices".'

'Oh, that! Yes, I read about it,' I said.

'I am impressed! I thought you guys just think of having fun all the time and nothing else.' He smiled.

'Oh, come on,' said Kasra's mum, 'you can't assume such things.'

He turned to me and asked what I thought about it.

'I must admit I didn't read too much into it. It was nothing to me but a casual conversation between two world leaders,' I replied.

'Have you been following the Shah and the Empress's state visit to Australia?' he asked.

I had not. I knew they were down under but I hadn't seen anything on television or read about it. I had never been interested in politics, but once he began talking about it I was rapt.

'You must have heard about the I.O.E.U. – the Indian Ocean Economic Union,' he said.

I was chewing so I couldn't reply straight away, but he didn't seem bothered and carried on.

'His Imperial Majesty was the mastermind behind the concept. You see, Pedram, this is partly the reason for Their Imperial Majesties' state visit to Australia. The Shah wants to create a common market for the Indian Ocean countries – first, the countries to the north of the ocean and later push its boundaries further south to include the African countries that border it, as well as Australia and even New Zealand at a later stage. He is all for regional cooperation. He has spoken of the creation of a neutral bank, through which the oil-rich states might help developing countries with funds to overcome their problems and feed their projects.'

I was fascinated. 'It's such a grand gesture,' I said. 'An organisation bringing these countries together like that could in effect guarantee peace and progress in the entire region, something very similar to the European Economic Community.'

'But I wonder if the EEC nations would allow such a thing to happen,' he said.

Mr Arjomand had hardly touched his food. He was very animated and obviously very excited and passionate about the subject. But I did not quite understand what he was getting at. Mrs Arjomand and Kasra both looked bored out of their skulls. Luckily, the conversation changed to English literature as Mrs Arjomand had just finished reading Dickens's *Great Expectations* and was keen to hear what I thought of it.

After lunch I thanked Kasra's mum for the lovely meal; I hadn't eaten so well since I left Tehran, I told her. Kasra then took me to the Italian quarter of Manzariyeh to play tennis. The houses had been designed by an Italian architect, and their red gable roofs made them look very European. Outside virtually every house was a Citroën 2CV; Kasra explained that their employer, the National Iranian Oil Company, had supplied them. They had their own playground and swimming pool, and a strange tennis court – a huge white-and-green tent that was pumped full of air and looked like a half-buried Zeppelin. My fascination with it kept Kasra amused all day.

After our game of tennis we went back to Kasra's house, a mere ten minutes away, where I said goodbye to his parents. Mrs Arjomand asked me to keep in touch and contact them if I needed anything. She said I wasn't to shy away just because Kasra wasn't there.

'You are just like Kasra, Pedram,' she said. 'So I expect you to come and visit us whenever you're free.'

I thanked her and she gave me a hug and kissed me before I left their house. Kasra said he hoped we'd see each other before his departure next week, but in case we didn't we hugged and said our goodbyes.

'Are you going to walk all the way back?' Kasra shouted after me. 'You'll not find a taxi here. Let me walk with you to the main road where you can find one.'

But I pretended not to hear him and kept walking. He was being a bit too intense and it made me feel strange. I resolved not to see him again before he left.

* * *

Soon the class timetables became fixed. I had one hundred and thirty-five students in three classes across three different grades.

In the first few weeks at the school, I was more worried about my class management than my teaching. The textbooks laid out everything for teachers and if you were one of many who just stuck to the syllabus then you had an easy job, but as my only experience had been of teaching adults at the language college in Tehran I was slightly nervous. There, my students were keen to learn and had made time to attend language classes. Here, it was part of the syllabus and it was compulsory.

Kasra had left Iran the week before and, as I expected, I hadn't heard from him. As it turned out I didn't miss him either. I was enjoying my job very much. I connected easily with the students; I think they saw me more as an older brother than as a teacher. I treated them as adults and was less formal with them, which somehow established an atmosphere of mutual respect.

I wanted to introduce something new to the classroom, something that had never been done before. I decided to discuss my idea with Mr Bushehri. I took my opportunity when I saw him walking across the schoolyard one day and called out to him.

'Is there a problem?' he asked.

'No, no, not at all. Quite the opposite,' I replied loudly while hundreds of noisy pupils ran about.

'What is it that you would like to discuss?' he said, walking with his hands clasped behind him.

'Mr Bushehri, I know that I'm new and young and may be considered inexperienced, but …' I searched for the best words to express myself.

'But what, Mr Azad?'

It came out in a rush. 'Could I teach my classes and run them the way I like?'

'Give me more details of what you mean exactly.'

'Would you object to me introducing other topics in my classes while, of course, covering the syllabus stipulated by the ministry? From other sources, I mean.'

'What sources?' He stopped walking and turned to face me. 'On what topics?' Without waiting to give me a chance to elaborate he continued, 'Don't tell me you're one of those new graduates who thinks he can change the world and that the world we live in is heading for disaster.'

'No, sir! Not at all! All I'd like to do is make them see that the future could be brighter for them.'

'Okay. That sounds good, but may I ask how you're going to achieve that?'

'First of all I'd like to help them understand what learning English can bring to their lives and future careers. I want them to really feel it, not give them the usual list of benefits.'

'That's fine with me,' he said.

'But I would like to introduce other texts – for example, English novels that have been simplified for foreign students.'

I assured him that I would cover the syllabus too, but that I wanted my students to broaden their minds beyond what was expected of them, to see more of the world without leaving the classroom.

Mr Bushehri seemed slightly uncomfortable with the idea. He didn't want me to do anything that would antagonise the Ministry of Education. He was even more hesitant when I told him that I wanted my pupils to call me by my first name. In the end he agreed that I could give it a go, but he asked me not to mention it to any of my colleagues.

Mr Bushehri was a very intelligent, experienced headmaster. He had graduated from Tehran University with a degree in philosophy and was an avid reader himself. He was often to be seen with a book, whether he was in his office taking his tea or walking in the school grounds. All the staff respected him, and his gentle, calm demeanour made him a very approachable man. He was more like a father figure to us all, rather than our boss. In the years that followed, we were to become closer, spending many hours talking about all sorts of things.

When I told my classes that from that time on I wanted them to call me Pedram and I would address them by their first names, a deafening silence fell on the classroom.

'I don't think we understand what you mean, sir,' one student piped up.

They looked round at each other with wide-eyed wonder as if they had just heard the most astonishing thing in their lives.

In return I asked them to study hard, respect the class and not take advantage of my relaxed approach. I told them that I wanted us to be friends, the difference being that, as they had to pass their exams, they needed me more than I needed them. I told them that fifty per cent of the responsibility for their success in their final exams rested on my shoulders, but that the rest depended on how hard they worked.

The secret between Mr Bushehri and I did not last long. The students mentioned our arrangement to the other teachers who confronted me, warning that such relaxed rules would only lead to disaster in the long-term. 'You can't treat twelve to fourteen-year-old kids as adults,' one colleague said. 'They're pupils who should be obedient and in some cases tamed.'

I was amazed at how threatened my colleagues felt.

I believe in the maturity of my people and their terrible intelligence – I mean terrible in the sense of something good. They can learn so quickly. With their hands they are like monkeys. They are more individualistic than the Swedes. Nevertheless if they did not work together we could not have achieved what we have achieved.

H.I.M. Mohammad Reza Shah Pahlavi,
interview with *TIME*, November 1974

Chapter Six

SHAHGOLI IS A BEAUTIFUL park in a suburb of Tabriz. It has a restaurant and nightclub situated in the middle of a vast man-made lake. It was a cold but sunny weekend when I went there for a walk. It was mid-November and the weather had become much colder, especially at night. Tabriz is in a valley, which is why the city is usually windy, and I was not looking forward to the blizzards and freezing temperatures that were only weeks away. Shahgoli's beautiful gardens were the main attraction for most Tabrizis in the summer, but now that cold weather was on its way the entire park looked a bit naked. There were no leaves on the trees and all the flowers had been transferred to the greenhouse.

I was walking around the pool when I saw three of my students walking towards me, chatting and laughing together. Iraj, Babak and Mehran were inseparable; I had christened them the Three Musketeers. They reminded me of my friendship with Kami and Parastou. I assumed the boys knew each other from primary school: while the other students tried to make new friends, these three were less bothered about it. Iraj said hello and they stopped. I just asked how they were and let them go on their way. When you are new in a city, it's nice bumping into familiar faces, but I didn't want to spoil their fun.

Mrs Arjomand had called me a couple of times and we talked about Kasra, although I hadn't heard from him myself. She insisted that I visit them, but I was always busy preparing for my classes or marking test papers. I promised her I would visit them soon.

I was getting used to my new life in Tabriz and to being away from Mâdar. Our phone conversations had reduced to once every other day. She seemed to have got used to my absence too and spent more time with her friends. She promised to visit me in Tabriz but it was unlikely she would come before spring.

Homesickness and loneliness were disappearing fast as I got more involved with my work and my students, especially the Three Musketeers. They sat next to each other in class, arrived and left school together, and socialised very little with other students. Having seen them in Shahgoli together, I knew they spent outside-school hours together too.

I was preparing end-of-term exam papers when Mrs Arjomand rang. I felt guilty for not contacting her. She told me that Kasra might be coming back during his university's Christmas holidays. It would be good to see him again. She invited me for lunch on Friday, 6th December and this time I accepted. I was desperate to have a face-to-face conversation with someone other than my work colleagues. Since classes began I'd kept myself busy with work, books, walks and television. With the exception of a few visits to my bookseller friend, I spent my time alone, so I was looking forward to seeing Mr and Mrs Arjomand and marked the day on the calendar on the kitchen wall.

The Christian schools were getting ready for the short Christmas and New Year break, and I badly felt the need for a short holiday myself. Once the state schools open in September, there are no holidays until Nowruz, the Iranian New Year, on 20th March – the vernal equinox. But religious minority schools enjoyed extra days off for their own festivities. I was therefore happy to be teaching in one where I had Christmas, New Year and Easter off.

On 6th December I turned up just before noon but discovered that

Mr Arjomand had left for Tehran to attend an international medical conference. So my hopes of playing backgammon with him vanished into thin air. Instead, Mrs Arjomand had invited her best friends for lunch. She introduced me to Mrs Jaleh Omidvar, a housewife with a degree in sociology whose husband was a carpet merchant, and Mrs Simin Pouya, a forty-nine-year-old heart surgeon married to a rich industrialist twenty years her senior. She was a colleague of Mr Arjomand's at Sixth Bahman Hospital and also lectured at the Faculty of Medicine at the University of Azarabadegan.

The three ladies were modern, educated Iranian women who were almost the age my mum would have been had she been alive, but I felt a bit out of place and wished that either Mr Arjomand or Kasra were there. Mrs Arjomand, noticing my uneasiness, insisted that I relax and not be so formal. She asked me to call her by her first name, Azar, as did the other ladies, which meant that by the end of the afternoon we were chatting away like four old friends and having a lovely time together.

Simin, in particular, seemed eager to get to know me better and I spent most of the time answering her questions about my life – past and present. We realised that we were both fond of European literature. She had completed her medical studies in France and was drawn to French literature while I was more familiar with English and American literature.

'You're the first person I've met since leaving university that I can speak to about European literature,' I told her.

'That's very flattering,' she said, leaning forward. 'I know exactly what you mean. I could spend hours talking about Zola, Balzac and, of course, my all-time favourite, Flaubert.'

A couple of times Azar tried to get Simin to change the subject. 'You're boring Pedram,' she said.

'No, no,' I said. 'There's no need to worry about me. I'm glad to have found someone to talk to about my passion.'

The telephone rang and Mrs Arjomand left the room to answer it, on her way out saying, 'I bet this call is for you, Pedram.'

'Have you read any of their works?' Simin asked me, ignoring Jaleh's efforts to change the subject.

A few minutes later Azar joon shouted, 'Come! Come, Pedram! I told you it would be for you, didn't I?'

I excused myself and as I left the room I heard the two women bickering in hushed tones.

'Thanks, Azar joon,' I said as I took the receiver. 'It's Kasra, isn't it?'

'Oooh! So it's Azar joon now!' Kasra said when I put the phone to my ear. I could hear him laughing.

'Well, it's very new,' I said. 'Mrs Pouya and Mrs Omidvar are here too. How are you doing?'

'I'm fine,' he said, still laughing. 'How are you getting on with your work and the school? What are you doing among those women?' he asked.

'Actually I'm having a lot of fun,' I said. 'Both here and at school. But tell me, what are you up to? I hear you may be coming home for Christmas.'

He said he still wasn't sure whether he'd be coming or not and we chatted for a little while. He promised to either call me or write.

I had a lovely time at the Arjomands. It was nice to see Mrs Arjomand again and to meet her friends, even though there was a big age difference. Thinking that the ladies might want to spend some time alone together I decided to leave early.

'Can I give you a lift?' Simin asked.

'That's very kind of you, but—'

'No buts,' she said. 'I have a few things to take care of, so I was thinking of leaving anyway. I can drop you on my way.'

I said goodbye to Jaleh and Mrs Arjomand and we left. On our way to my apartment Simin and I chatted some more about novels we had read.

'I live right there,' I said, pointing to the building a few hundred yards away. 'If you hadn't got things to do I would have invited you in for a drink and we could have continued our conversation.'

'I'd love that, thanks,' she said without hesitation and pulled into a parking space.

'But didn't you have errands to—'

'Oh, no! That was just an excuse to get out of there.' She looked into my eyes and smiled, then patted me on the leg. 'Don't get me wrong, I love them both to bits. They're my oldest friends.'

She had already turned the engine off, so I asked her if she would like to come up for a drink. She accepted without a second thought.

I apologised for the state of the apartment. 'I left this morning in a bit of a rush and didn't have time to tidy up after last night.'

'Did you have a wild party then?' she shouted across as I went to the kitchen to get our drinks.

I came back into the room with two glasses of ice and a bottle of Johnnie Walker Black Label.

'No,' I said, laughing.

'No need to be embarrassed,' she said. 'I know you young stallions have to get all that trapped energy released somehow.'

I didn't know what to make of her comment, but I didn't want her to know that, so I decided to go with the flow to see what would happen. I gave her a wink as I passed her a glass with a double shot of whisky.

'*Be salâmati!*' she said, raising her glass.

'Cheers,' I said. 'To your health too.'

I took a sip of my whisky, but she finished hers in one go. I filled her glass again and offered her some pistachios.

'What's that?' she asked, pointing to my glass on the table. 'Don't tell me that's how you're going to drink with me. Come on, you can do better than that.'

I picked up my glass and drank it all. She refilled my glass.

'Hoooo!' The whisky burned everything on its way down.

'So tell me, what was the last risqué book you read?' she asked. 'Have you read *Madame Bovary*?'

I had not.

'No? Oh, I had forgotten. Excuse me, sir!' she said in English, trying to put on a posh English accent. 'I'd forgotten you were an anglophile!'

She made me laugh. I had never considered myself an Anglophile.

'So are you a Francophile?' I asked.

'You must have read *Lady Chatterley's Lover* then,' she said, suddenly sounding very serious.

As a matter of fact I hadn't, which astonished her and made her fill my glass again, this time almost to the rim.

Before I knew it half the bottle was gone. Next thing I remember she was sitting on my lap and we were kissing. It felt good and, after a little initial hesitation, we lay down on the couch and made love.

In the days that followed I was busy with the end-of-term exams. I couldn't wait to get them over and done with – I was anxious to see how my students would do on their tests – but I was also glad to have something to keep my mind off my sexual escapade.

Kasra decided not to return during the Christmas break. I was a bit disappointed, but at the same time I was relieved. Every time I thought of the Arjomands I thought of Simin and shuddered. What if she had told Kasra's mother about our one-night stand? I felt embarrassed and mortified.

In the end, the results of the exams cheered me up no end. Most of my students, including Hamid whose reason for studying English was to improve his ability to charm the girls, had scored above average. Mr Bushehri congratulated me and it made me feel proud. I had not let him down; it also showed that my new teaching method worked despite the other teachers' warnings.

On the last night of 1974, Tabriz was bitterly cold, so cold that the air penetrated your skin even through a thick jumper. I went out onto the balcony of my apartment to breathe the fresh winter air but I wasn't able to stay out for long.

There were special programmes on television for New Year's Eve. The religious leaders of the Armenian and the Assyrian churches had appeared earlier on delivering messages, in their own languages but subtitled in Persian, wishing their respective communities the best for the new year and our country, a prosperous future. After their broadcasts I watched *The Song of Bernadette*, the black-and-white movie starring Jennifer Jones, which was shown every year around this time. It was the story of a peasant girl from Lourdes, in France, to whom the Virgin Mary appeared on a cold day in February 1858. I had watched it countless times over the years, but this year I saw it through new eyes and wanted to discuss the story with one of the priests at school.

In major cities around Iran, especially those with large Christian communities, restaurants, nightclubs and discos were fully booked on New Year's Eve, mostly by the Muslim Iranians. Armenians used to joke about it, saying that others took all the tables at clubs and restaurants, leaving none available for the Christians. For the first time in centuries, we – the middle classes – had become better off and were able to afford the time to enjoy ourselves. Iranians are also by nature the type of people who look for any excuse to gather together, mostly after dark when the air is cooler, to eat, drink and dance.

Armenians do not celebrate Christmas on 25th December but on 6th January – Epiphany – when the three Persian wise men, or Magi – the Zoroastrian priests – arrived in Bethlehem and found the newborn Jesus. Armenians have been part of Iran's history for centuries, but it's only since the Pahlavis ascended to the throne that Iranian citizens, irrespective of their religion, have been treated equally. Armenia and Iran have a lot of shared history. In ancient times, Armenia was either part of a federal Persian empire or a protectorate. Iran has been a safe haven for thousands of Armenians escaping Turkish massacre and, later, the Bolsheviks. The fact that they celebrate Christmas on 6th January, the day our Persian priests arrived, signifies for me a strong tie between our two ancient peoples.

So a few days after New Year there was another Christmas celebration. I was at home on my own that night too. I always kept my curtains open. Rooms with closed curtains made me claustrophobic – they still do; I enjoy the light and space and openness – and I was watching the snow falling outside. I was neither sleepy nor tired, so I decided to go to Baron Avak, the Armenian district of Tabriz, to experience the celebrations on that special evening.

I dressed up warmly and went down to the quiet streets. The trees at Shahnaz Junction where the noisy birds had made conversations inaudible just a few months earlier were silent now, with only a few lonely birds jumping from branch to branch.

Baron Avak Street was lively though. I saw smartly dressed men with beautiful women, young and old, hand in hand walking down the street. The scene looked like an English oil painting from the Victorian period. I stood under the canopy of an Armenian patisserie and gazed at the passers-by. They all seemed to be heading in the same direction. I wondered where they were all going. So I followed them. They led me down a narrow alleyway where I found myself outside the Holy Sarkis Church. I stood there for a while watching people go into the churchyard. They seemed friendly; those who knew each other greeted one another with kisses and hugs.

One lady on her way to the church slipped on an icy patch, but I caught her before she hit the ground. As I helped her up, she was giggling like a child. I began to laugh too.

'Are you okay, miss?' I asked.

She was still laughing. Once she had dusted the snow off her coat and had stopped laughing, she managed to get a few words out.

'Yes, thank you. I'm okay. Sorry for laughing. I always laugh at people who fall down. I can't help myself. I think it's funny, even when I'm the one falling down.'

'Someone who can laugh at herself in public must have a good sense of humour,' I said.

'I'm waiting for a friend,' she told me. 'She's always late.'

I gave her her hat, which had come off when she slipped, and she tidied her hair.

'How rude of me!' I said, taking off my glove and putting out my hand. 'I'm Pedram.'

'Nice to meet you. And thank you again,' she replied, shaking my hand. 'I'm Armineh.'

She was a slim, pretty girl with the most beautiful black eyes and dark shoulder-length hair. She brushed the snow from her hat and put it back on, and greeted a few people who passed her on their way into the church.

'Are you waiting for someone?' she finally asked.

'No, I'm not,' I said. 'I just like walking in the snow, which was why I left my apartment. Once I got to Baron Avak and saw people out and about I just followed them and ended up here. You see, this is my first winter in Tabriz.'

'Oh! So you're new in town,' she commented.

'Yes, I came here at the beginning of September. I'm an English teacher at Anoushirvan Secondary School.'

We chatted for a few minutes more before I decided to leave; I couldn't think of anything else to chat about.

'Have you been to a service at an Armenian church?' she asked as I was about to say goodbye.

'No!' I replied excitedly as if she had invited me in and I had already accepted.

She laughed again. 'Well, would you like to attend our service?'

I was embarrassed at being so obviously desperate. But it looked like my lonely evening was about to turn into a night of friendship blessed by the Armenian Archbishop of Tabriz.

'Aren't others going to ask you who I am?' I said, hoping she wouldn't change her mind.

She chuckled and told me she didn't care. Her friend was late and the service was about to start, so we made our way into the churchyard. Just before we went in an out-of-breath voice called from the alleyway.

'There's madam! She's finally decided to show up,' Armineh said, pointing to a well-wrapped-up girl coming to a halt in front of her after what must have been a long run.

'*Shnorhavor Surb Tsnund*,' the girl said in Armenian.

'*Shnorhavor Surb Tsnund*,' Armineh replied.

I assumed they were exchanging Christmas greetings. The breathless girl glanced at me and gave Armineh a look of curiosity, then turned to me and said, '*Barev*.'

'This is Pedram,' Armineh said in Persian.

'Oh, I'm sorry,' the girl said. 'Hello! I thought you were Armenian.' We shook hands.

'I could be for a night,' I said.

She couldn't control her wicked smile.

'We've just met,' Armineh told her. 'I've invited Pedram to come with us to the service. Pedram, this is my best friend, Gilda, who is always late.'

'I'm sorry about that—' Gilda began.

'Leave your apologies for later,' Armineh said, dragging her by the sleeve into the church. 'Come on. We don't want to be the last ones in, do we?'

Inside, the light from hundreds of candles and the smell of burning incense, mingled with ladies' perfume gave this lovely old place of worship a warm and welcoming ambience. We took our seats in the back row on a wooden pew near the aisle; Armineh sat between me and Gilda. The burning candles and the large chandelier hanging from the centre of the high dome gave the paintings of the Virgin Mary, Jesus Christ and his Apostles that hung on the walls an imposing presence. There were other paintings of Armenian saints and religious leaders. As if by magic all of them seemed to have come to life.

Everything had happened so fast and with such ease. I had only come out for a walk in the snow and now here I was, sitting among Armenian worshippers not understanding their rituals or their language. At the same time I felt warm and safe. It was as if I'd walked into a dream, another world, where I knew no one yet everyone seemed familiar. I loved the fact that they had welcomed a stranger into their church.

The service began and I followed every move the two girls made. I stood, sat and knelt with them, and during prayers I kept quiet and listened to their beautiful language. When the service came to an end I waited in a corner while Armineh and Gilda spoke to their friends and relatives. Nobody seemed to ask them about me and no one questioned me.

Before we left Armineh wanted to show me the churchyard. The snow had stopped when we got out and everything was white. It was a beautiful moonlit night, and the air was cold and crystal clear. The churchyard was lit by a few light bulbs hanging from lamp posts. It looked so romantic, so magical.

There were a few graves behind the church. Armineh was taking me to see the grave of their famous priest Hakop Gharapetian when a stone carving under an arch with a carved cross attracted my attention. The inscription underneath was written in Armenian.

'What does it say?' I asked. 'This can't be a grave. It's more like a plaque.'

She sighed. 'This is to commemorate all those Armenians who died for freedom. These are some of the most famous ones.'

She began reciting their names to me – 'Meghredich Jalalbegian, 1896, Arshak Barsamian, 1896, Missagh Danjevian, 1909, Ardem Razmik, 1908' – her voice echoing in my head while I tried to decipher the alphabet on the stone. Why had they 'died for freedom', I wondered. I had never heard of Armenians fighting for freedom.

She was still reading aloud – 'Mardirous Charoughchian, 1909, Gharou Ardames, 1909, Stoua Sighssi, 1909, Georg Ghiraghoussian, 1909, Petros Anderiazian, 1912' – and when she stopped, I noticed that her cheeks had turned rosy from the cold.

'Who are all these people?' I asked. 'What's this all about?'

Before she could answer me, Gilda called us. She was standing near the church's main entrance.

'Where did you two suddenly disappear to?' she asked when we caught up with her.

Armineh replied to her in Armenian while I listened. I assumed she mentioned the stone plaque.

Then she said, 'I have to say goodbye to the *derder*,' and went over to the priest standing by the gates.

When she came back I thanked her and told them how lovely it was to meet them. I suggested it would be nice to meet again for a drink. Though I was addressing both of them, Armineh was the main focus of my attention. I took a small notebook out of my pocket, wrote down my phone number and passed it to Armineh. I offered to walk them home, but they thanked me and politely turned down my offer.

On my way back, I went over the events of the evening in my head. It had all happened so fast, and my encounter with Armineh had been so pleasant. Everything was so simple, friendly and innocent. I wondered if anything would come of our meeting. Most girls I'd gone out with during my schooldays or later at university had been hard work and, with a few exceptions, difficult to feel relaxed with. But tonight had been very different.

At two o'clock in the morning I was lying awake in bed and thinking about her. Was I in love? I wasn't sure. Although I kept thinking about her, Simin kept popping into my mind too. Strangely enough, I no longer felt guilty about what I had done and would have loved to have had her in my bed right then.

The next day I slept in past noon. It was a Tuesday, which meant a heavy schedule, but luckily my first class wasn't until 1.30 p.m. I rushed to get ready, not knowing what to do first. While blaming myself for going out and getting to bed so late, I was trying to shave, get dressed and look as decent as possible. But the mirror told a different story. My eyes were puffy and my hair was sticking out all over the place. There was no way I could avoid raised eyebrows. As it turned out, no one said anything; there were a few funny looks from both colleagues and pupils, but they were too polite to pass comment.

Two weeks after I first met Armineh I had heard nothing from her, but she was constantly on my mind. She hadn't called me and I had no way of reaching her. We had definitely hit it off – at least, that was my impression. I began searching for her in crowded streets every time I went out, hoping to bump into her. But I never did.

Mâdar hadn't contacted me either for at least ten days. I'd become so entangled in my own daydreams that I'd forgotten to call her. But why hadn't she called me either? I wondered. I was busy with my weekly shopping at Gajil Gapisi one Thursday evening when all this was going through my head. How could I have forgotten to call her! I hoped the reason she hadn't called me was simply because she was sulking with me for not having phoned her.

I rushed back home with various scenarios going round in my head. What if something had happened to her? Every time the cab stopped at traffic lights or was slowed by heavy traffic I could hear my heart pounding. I tried to reassure myself that nothing bad had happened – someone would definitely have contacted me if it had.

As I dragged my shopping up the stairs to my apartment I bumped into my neighbours from the first and second floors. Mrs Oskouie and Mrs Niroumand were smartly dressed for the evening. We greeted each other and paused on the landing for a chat. They were on their way out to the opera. Mr Niroumand was away on business and Mr Oskouie had agreed to cook dinner and look after Mrs Niroumand's children until the ladies got back.

'It's their turn for a change,' said Mrs Niroumand. 'Changing roles in a household from time to time is very healthy. Don't you think so?'

'Couldn't agree more,' I replied as Mrs Oskouie's laughter echoed round the stairwell.

'We have to rush now,' Mrs Oskouie said and turned to her friend. 'We'll have to invite Mr Azad over one evening for dinner or at least for a drink.'

Mrs Niroumand agreed and assured me that she would give me a call as soon as her husband was back from his business trip in Tehran. The two ladies carried on down the stairs and out to the busy streets of Tabriz.

By the time I got up to the apartment my anxiety had subsided. I sorted out my shopping and changed into something more comfortable before calling Mâdar. But the phone kept ringing and ringing. I began worrying again and decided to call Parastou to see if she knew how Mâdar was. Ardavan answered and after a little chat he passed the phone to his mum.

'You have just missed Parastou, darling Pedram,' she said. 'No more than ten minutes ago Kami came over and picked her up and they left to meet some friends somewhere.'

I asked about my grandma and explained why I was worried. Mrs Parspour had spoken to her that very morning and reassured me that she was fine. She scolded me for not contacting her more often.

On Friday morning I was awoken by the phone ringing. It was Mâdar.

'Good morning! Were you still in bed? It is almost ten!'

'Mâdar! Where have you been?' I was so happy to hear from her.

'Where have I been? That's the question I should be asking you. I thought to myself, he must have found new friends and completely forgotten his old granny.' She could be so sarcastic.

She asked me about my classes and my days at the school. She was proud that her only grandchild was following in her footsteps. I told her about the Three Musketeers, how they had great ambitions. Iraj wanted to become a diplomat; Babak loved plants and wanted to revolutionise Iran's agriculture; Mehran wanted to join the Iranian Armed Forces. So we talked about them for almost an hour. Before I hung up I promised to go to Tehran for Nowruz – 20th March – and spend the festive season with her.

Not long after my conversation with Mâdar had ended the phone rang again.

'Could I speak to Mr Azad, please?' said a soft, gentle woman's voice.

'Yes, that's me. Who is this?' I asked.

'Pedram?'

'Yes.'

With a sudden burst of liveliness she said, 'Hi! It's Armineh. Remember me?'

'Of course I do,' I replied. 'I thought you'd completely forgotten about me. How are you? How's Gilda?' I must have sounded like an excited machine gun, shooting aimlessly until she stopped me.

'I'm fine and so is Gilda.' She laughed. 'How have you been? I never heard from you either!'

'Well how could I? You never gave me your number.'

'Didn't I?'

'No! I gave you my number so you could call if you were interested.'

'Oh, I'm sorry … And all this time I thought you had my number.'

So we chatted about what she'd been doing and my work and my students.

'Fancy going for a coffee?' I asked. 'I know this cute café in Valiahd district. Can you make it next Thursday at five o'clock?'

It was a date!

Monarchs with the Mostest

Iran's supremely confident Shah and his beautiful Empress Farah clearly qualified as "monarchs of the year." To the West's dismay, the Shah kept oil prices sky-high. With his new riches, he made massive loans and investments in Europe and America and stepped up his drive to transform his country into a modern industrialised state. As the Shah saw it, Iran was well on its way to becoming a major global power.

Newsweek, January 1975

Chapter Seven

IN THE SECOND TERM, my students seemed to be enjoying their English classes even more than before. A few days earlier Mr Bushehri had called me to his office to tell me that one of my students had thanked him for having me as their teacher. A rare occasion, I thought, in the history of education. I found it hard to imagine any pupil, even if they were happy with a teacher, making the effort to express their gratitude to the school's principal. Later on I discovered that the student was Hamid, the very one who on the first day of the school year had been sarcastic about learning English. Looking back at his test marks I noticed he was among the top ten in a class of almost fifty students.

In spite of my busy teaching schedule I had not forgotten my rendezvous with Armineh. The thought of it was like a breath of fresh air in my stuffy mind that was constantly preparing for classes. I had been choosing extra topics for my students with a lot of care not only to make sure they were suitable but also to keep them awake. I picked articles about Iran's economic progress that were covered by the Western press and sent to me by my British pen pal, Richard.

By the end of the week I was exhausted and really looking forward to my date with Armineh. On Thursdays this term, my only class was in the morning and I was home by eleven. I had plenty of time to get ready for the evening, so I watered my plants, did a few chores around the apartment and, after lunch, took a nap. Afterwards, I shaved and took a long bath. By four o'clock I was dressed and ready. I left the house and jumped in the first taxi that was going to that part of the city. Taxis in Iran have their own rules: the drivers choose the routes they are willing to drive, and they'll only take you if you happen to be going their way.

The roads were getting busy. People had finished work for the weekend and were getting ready to hit the town to shop or party. Valiahd district, where I was going, was a newly developed part of Tabriz and had modern shopping areas and some of the best boutiques in the city. Trendy restaurants and cafés, too, had become the hangouts for boys and girls to meet and socialise. My taxi had been stuck in traffic for part of the journey and I was anxious to get to the café before Armineh, but I still managed to get there five minutes early. The café was almost full but I found a table in a quiet corner.

The café was L-shaped with the bar running along the long side of the L and a cosy nook at the back round the corner. There were rows of booths – tables surrounded by high-backed seats covered in lush scarlet velvet – above which hung red lights that caught the swirls of smoke as they drifted up towards the ceiling and gave the place a cosy, relaxed atmosphere.

The air was filled with the smell of beer, strong Turkish coffee and cigarettes, as well as a cocktail of rugged aftershaves and perfumes. Other couples were chatting away, drinking and smoking; laughter and serious discussions were going on in various corners; guys with moustaches or immaculately trimmed beards were in jeans and shirts, girls were in miniskirts or flared trousers. The music playing hardly complemented the ambience. Telly Savalas had spent two weeks at number one by just talking his way through 'If'. In my opinion, that song shouldn't have been in the charts, let alone at the number-one slot, but at least it didn't last long!

The waitress came to take my order. I told her I was waiting for someone and asked her to come back later. She smiled and cleared away a few cups and bottles left on the table, then restocked the fridge behind the bar with bottles of 7 Up.

Armineh was running late. Perhaps she wouldn't show up, I thought, or maybe something had happened. The bartender must have noticed me checking my watch every few minutes. He came over and, as he emptied the ashtray, said, 'The traffic's heavy tonight. She'll be here soon.'

Taken aback, I asked if he knew who I was waiting for.

'Sure!' he said with a grin. 'A girl.'

'But do you know the girl I am meeting?' I asked.

'How the hell would I know?' he said, and turned his attention to the end of the bar where a couple were waiting to be served.

I was feeling a bit pissed off with his tone when I heard Armineh's voice.

'I'm so sorry for running late,' she said, slightly out of breath.

I got up and gave her a kiss on the cheek. She sat down in front of me and put her jacket and hat on the seat beside her. 'It's unbelievable out there,' she complained. 'The whole city seems to be coming this way.'

She looked absolutely stunning. It was only three weeks since we first met but I had forgotten how beautiful she was. I felt butterflies in my stomach. She ran her fingers through her hair and her dark eyes sparkled.

We placed an order with the barman who had hung around our table like a vulture since Armineh arrived. After the initial niceties we began finding out about each other. We hadn't been able to do that when we first met.

Turkish coffees were put in front of us together with some small Persian pastries. Armineh was easy to talk to and we chatted about lots of things – our ambitions, our families and friends, everything was discussed thoroughly. The coffees kept coming and we continued talking; it seemed as if there was almost nothing we *didn't* talk about. We spoke about our dreams for the future. I told her about my ultimate ambition: to move up in the Ministry of Education to a position where I could introduce various changes to the educational system.

'Maybe one day I'll become the Minister of Education in Iran,' I said, laughing.

'Sure! And why not?' she said. 'Nowadays everything is possible. There's nothing to stop you. You can achieve whatever you want.'

Armineh wanted to improve the justice system with particular attention to women's rights. Women were already active in all walks of life in Iran at that time. Mrs Dowlatshahi was our imperial ambassador to the Royal Danish Court; Mrs Farrokhroo Parsa was the Minister for Education – my boss. There were dozens of women in high positions in the government. Even Iran's imperial armed forces prided itself on its women officers. By the mid-seventies many women had set up their own private enterprises, helping our economy.

Our ambitions and dreams weren't impossible; all we needed was time and patience, coupled with hard work.

Suddenly it was seven o'clock and time to leave. Armineh had to be home in time for dinner, so we grabbed a cab together. She got out at Baron Avak to avoid her parents and nosy neighbours from seeing us together. She wanted to meet up again and we agreed not to leave it so long next time. She promised to call.

Before I knew it, it was almost the end of the second term. I was preoccupied again with preparations for my students' exam papers. Nowruz was nearing, too, and I was planning a surprise visit to Tehran to see everyone. Despite our promise, Armineh and I didn't find time to meet again. We had spoken on the phone many times but never managed to find a slot in our schedules that suited us both.

I had received a few Nowruz cards from friends in Tehran; Richard had remembered too and sent me a card together with a long letter and pictures and press cuttings from British newspapers and magazines. I was a little ashamed: I hadn't written to Richard once since I'd moved to Tabriz to tell him how it was going in my new job.

I called Armineh just before I left for Tehran. She told me that she was setting the Haft Sin table. I'd never heard of Armenians celebrating Nowruz, but she reminded me that Nowruz was an ancient New Year rite that belonged to all Iranians. We weren't the only people honouring Nowruz; there were millions of Afghans, Tajiks, Parsees in India, Kurds in Iraq, Syria and Turkey, and Iranian and non-Iranian Baha'is all over the world who celebrated the rebirth of life at the spring equinox, so I included Armineh on my list of those I had to send a Nowruz card. She was staying in Tabriz for the holiday season as her family had visitors coming from Isfahan. I said goodbye to her and, for the first time, told her that I loved her. The phone went silent; I couldn't even hear her breathing. Perhaps I should have kept my feelings to myself. Eventually, all she said was 'Have a safe trip' and she asked me to call her once I got back. I was relieved – at least she wanted to hear from me again.

I left Tabriz on the eve of Nowruz, 19th March, with a suitcase packed with presents for Mâdar, Parastou and Kami. I had decided to fly; I didn't want to waste time travelling by road. This was my first time on an aeroplane and I was very excited about it. Tabriz Airport was busy and the flight was packed. Men in suits, ladies in the smartest fashion; even children were wearing their best clothes. In those days people used to dress up when they flew somewhere. Many passengers seemed to know each other and they exchanged polite pleasantries on the forty-five minute flight. Iran Air's stunning stewardesses were most courteous as they attended to our every need. Having always travelled by road, it was amazing to see our beautiful country from the sky.

Not long after we finished our meal and drinks we landed at Tehran's Mehrabad Airport, which was a hive of activity as thousands of Iranians arrived home from all parts of the world to spend the New Year with their families. Tourists, too, had come to enjoy the festive season. The weather was warmer here than in Tabriz, and the smell of spring was in the air. I was so happy to be back in the city I was familiar with, the city of my childhood.

I happened to share a cab with a young American couple who had chosen Iran as their honeymoon destination. The cab driver took me to Saman Towers in Queen Elizabeth Boulevard before dropping them off at the Royal Tehran Hilton Hotel in the north of the city. The whole place was decorated with tiny, colourful lights, like bubbles sparkling in a glass of champagne. I tipped the driver extra, as is customary at New Year, and wished my American travellers a joyous stay in Iran.

I was excited to see Mâdar. I knew she would be at home because I had told her I would phone; I'd told her I couldn't get a seat on a flight, so she wasn't expecting me to arrive on her doorstep. I could hear the disappointment in her voice, but it would be worth it when I surprised her. We always sat together at the Haft Sin table for the New Year, and she thought she would be alone this year, the first time ever.

The porter, smartly dressed in his uniform, opened the tall glass entrance door for me and welcomed me in. Not knowing who I was, he politely asked me to sign in as a visitor before he called Mâdar to announce me. I explained that I was paying a surprise visit to my grandmother and told him to follow me up if he wanted but not to call her. After a little hesitation he agreed to let me go up on my own and helped me with my suitcase to the lift.

Standing outside the door to her apartment, I could hear her singing along with Hayedeh. I waited a while, wanting her to get to the end of the song before disturbing her. As soon as the music stopped I rang the bell. I could hear her coming towards the door.

'*Kiyeh?*' she asked before she opened it.

I got the giggles when I replied, '*Amu Nowruzeh!*' He's the equivalent of Father Christmas for Iranian kids. She opened the door, asking again who it was and then she saw me.

She squeezed me so hard I could hardly breathe. I was so happy to see her, but she was on cloud nine. She kissed me all over my face and pulled me into the apartment so quickly I just managed to grab my suitcase. I was glad I'd decided to surprise her.

'Why didn't you tell me you were coming?' she asked, hugging me some more. 'What a wonderful thing you've done. You are truly a present from *Amu Nowruz*.'

The whole apartment smelled of the hyacinths she had bought for her Haft Sin. Tulips and roses were arranged in various vases all around the apartment. I took a look at her beautifully laid Haft Sin in front of the window. The table was covered with her most precious tablecloth, a beautiful Balouchi embroidered cloth she had inherited from her mother on her wedding day, and on it were placed a large bowl with two little red goldfish wiggling around in it, a large mirror with candles on each side, a dish of green wheat grown especially for Haft Sin, and photographs of my parents and of me. There were coloured eggs representing fertility, garlic to chase evil spirits away, coins to bring wealth and, of course, the hyacinth trumpeting the arrival of spring. It was very pretty.

There was less than twelve hours until the New Year, the exact time when the vernal equinox took place. Mâdar had already had her dinner but I was hungry, so she served me the leftovers from her meal, which made me realise how much I had missed her delicious food. My cooking was okay, but nowhere near her standard. We chatted about my life in Tabriz and I repeated my invitation for her to come and visit.

'I'm fed up with my cooking,' I said. 'I need you to come and feed me – even if it's for a short time.'

'Is that the only reason you want me to come?' she said, pulling a face. She was laughing. 'You want me as your maid?'

It was so good to see her.

* * *

I forced my eyes open to check the time. I would have liked to stay in bed longer but I had to get ready as there were only a few hours to the end of the year. Mâdar was already up; I could hear her radio. Before leaving for Tehran, I had paid a visit to Sormeh, an exclusive boutique for Tabrizi upper-class ladies where the owner knew his customers by name, in order to get Mâdar a present. As soon as I walked into the shop the scarf grabbed my attention. The shop assistant laid it out on the counter for me to see. It was exquisite. Its pattern in bright tropical colours made me think of Gauguin. It was perfect for her.

Grandma never wore a scarf as a scarf. She either used it as a shawl or let it hang over one shoulder. Even on windy days, when most women wore something to protect their coiffed hair, she refused to wear it. As far as she was concerned she had come out of the hijab and no force, even the wind, could persuade her to go back in it. For her, the wind blowing through her hair was a reminder of the freedom that Iranian women like her had achieved over the years.

Minutes before the countdown to New Year on television we sat around the Haft Sin. We were silent and avoided looking at each other as we thought of my parents who we both missed so much. Nowruz was the occasion when we felt their absence most.

The presenter announced, 'Thirty seconds to the New Year' and a clock ticked loudly, setting the pace for all our hearts. Mâdar and I smiled at each other and joined in the countdown.

'Ten … nine … eight …'

With the firing of an artillery gun, the customary way to herald in the New Year since time immemorial, the year 1354 was announced, followed by the usual Nowruz anthem played on an oboe and a dohol, a type of Persian drum. It was a wonderful way to seal the end of winter.

We hugged and kissed and wished each other good health and a happy life for the year to come. Then came the time to exchange presents. Mâdar had bought me a fantastic leather briefcase, which I badly needed for work. She had remembered that I was still using the same bag I had had at high school, faded and battered with age. I gave her the scarf and, just as I thought, its vibrant colours suited her perfectly.

Once spring had been officially declared, it was time for the annual imperial Nowruz broadcasts by the Shah and Empress Farah, followed by our long-standing prime minister, Mr Amir-Abbas Hoveyda, conveying the government's message to the nation. Mâdar never missed the three speeches. She considered them important to begin the New Year. It was a briefing by the leaders of the nation on what we had achieved and where we were heading.

Mâdar had prepared the traditional herb rice and fish dish for our New Year's meal. As we sat together having our lunch I felt so happy to be with her again.

She looked at her watch, then at me and said, 'You gave me a great surprise last night by turning up at the door. Now it's my turn.'

I wondered what she meant, but she wouldn't give me any clues.

She said I would find out as soon as we had cleared the table. I helped her with the dishes and tidied up the kitchen. Just then the doorbell rang. Giving me a big grin, Mâdar sent me to answer the door.

'There you are – your surprises are here,' she said.

And what a surprise! It was a double surprise. There at the door stood the Vaziri and the Parspour families. I was over the moon. The two families, thinking that it was Mâdar's first Nowruz alone, had decided to visit her before going to see their own families. When we saw each other, the initial Happy Nowruz words and kisses were suddenly transformed into screams of joy. I hadn't expected them and they hadn't expected to see me. Kami, Parastou and I had a lot of catching up to do. There was so much to tell them. However, I decided not to mention Armineh – either to them or Grandma. Nothing had happened yet; our friendship had not become a relationship and I didn't want to jinx it.

I was staying in Tehran for ten days. Kami and Parastou wanted me to stay until the thirteenth day of Nowruz for the traditional picnic, but I needed to be back in Tabriz to get ready for my classes, so we promised to call and arrange to get together again before I returned.

The weather was mild and pleasant in Tehran for the rest of the holiday. Deep blue skies, warm days with cooler nights and occasional spring showers that lasted no more than a few minutes were melting the remaining signs of snow in the city. Most boulevards and squares were carpeted in yellow daffodils and pink hyacinths – the very smell is a strong reminder that Nowruz has arrived and it was in the air everywhere. But it was very different in the Alborz Mountains. Kami, Parastou and a few of their university friends had rented a chalet for the weekend in Dizin. Although I had never skied, I welcomed the opportunity to try and learn.

The air was crisp when they picked me up on Friday morning in Kami's Jeep. They had their skis strapped onto the roof rack and had hurled a collection of ski poles into the back of the vehicle. Kami had brought his old skis for me and I had everything I needed to give it a go. Above the city, a panorama of snow-covered peaks, crowned by the perfect cone of Mount Damavand, beckoned us as the Jeep climbed the foothills. The winding mountain roads were still icy, although a roaring creek below us signalled that the spring melt had started in the high country.

The Alborz range is higher than the Alps and is on the same latitude as the Rockies; its mountains boast powder snow comparable with any that can be found in Colorado, so it's not surprising that skiing has become one of the most popular sports in Iran.

I had a wonderful two days at Dizin. Every muscle in my body was aching, but I enjoyed it immensely. The bumps and bruises from falling countless times were worth it once the sun set and we joined the others for après-ski in front of the fire at the chalet. The resort's bar, restaurant and small disco were the meeting place for everyone after a hard day of skiing. I had a great time with Kami and Parastou. It could only have been more perfect if I'd had Armineh by my side.

Back in Tehran, Mâdar and I spent our days shopping and visiting friends and family. All too quickly the holidays came to an end and it was time for me to pack and leave for Tabriz again.

Iran to get eight US nuclear power plants

The United States and Iran signed a trade agreement today which Dr Henry Kissinger, the Secretary of State, described as "the largest of this sort that has ever been signed between two countries". It provides for American exports to Iran of $15,000m (£6,000m) over the next five years.

The most striking is eight nuclear power plants, which are in addition to the four plants Iran is already buying, two each from France and West Germany.

The Times, March 1975

Chapter Eight

I wasn't supposed to call Armineh – her parents knew nothing about our friendship – so I had to wait for her to call me, but a chance encounter put us in touch sooner than expected. The day after I got back to Tabriz I was shopping in Tarbiyat Street, looking for a new pair of shoes, when I saw her walking towards me with someone I assumed was her mother. Not sure what to do, I kept going until her eyes met mine. With a subtle acknowledgement we passed each other without exchanging a word.

That evening she rang.

'I'm sorry I couldn't introduce you to my mum,' she said. 'I still haven't told her that I have a boyfriend.'

She called me her boyfriend! With those words I realised that our friendship had become something more meaningful. That was what I had hoped for, so why did it make me feel anxious?

Over the next few months we spent all our free time together, either at my place or in our favourite hang-out, the coffee shop in Valiahd. Gilda joined us from time to time; she was a fun person to spend time with.

Spring was in full bloom and my students were preparing for

their end-of-year exams. Contrary to my expectations, my experience with my students had been very good. We had established a good understanding among ourselves based on mutual respect. They had begun to enjoy English and I introduced them to a different way of learning other than the monotonous world of their textbooks. My idea of encouraging them by introducing topics that interested them had been extremely successful. Almost all the students at some point talked over their future academic plans with me; Mr Bushehri told me that I was the only teacher with whom the students discussed their problems. I became more confident in myself, and Mr Bushehri was delighted that my unorthodox methods had proven productive.

When the results of the exams were released at the end of June, my students had the highest pass rates in the entire school. That not only made me proud but also made my life easier as I didn't have to prepare for many to retake their exams in September.

On the very last day of the academic year, when my summer holiday was about to begin, I was meeting Armineh at our usual café in Valiahd. I really loved that part of the city. It was young, vibrant and forward-looking, a place where my happy-go-lucky generation liked to enjoy our free time with our girlfriends and boyfriends. I was running late, and Armineh and Gilda were already there when I arrived. There was also a young chap sitting opposite them, his back to the door so I couldn't see his face.

I walked towards their table and bent down to kiss first Armineh and then Gilda. The guy stood up and Gilda introduced him to me. He was Vartan, her boyfriend. He was tall with black hair and very good-looking. We shook hands and I sat down next to him. A waiter took our order.

'Vartan is in my class at Azarabadegan University,' Gilda said, looking at her boyfriend with much affection. 'I'm sure Armineh has mentioned him to you. We've been together a few months now.'

Vartan pulled her hands towards him and played with her fingers.

I said I was sorry that he had to put up with her in class as well as outside and everyone laughed. Gilda pulled her hands away from Vartan's, slapping them gently.

'Hey, you two! I'm not that bad!' She glared at us in mock

innocence, somehow looking like a girl who probably gave her parents hell when she was younger.

I was a bit annoyed that Vartan and Gilda were there. I'd been looking forward to spending some time alone with Armineh, but it turned out to be fun. As the evening drew on, we suggested going for dinner. Armineh wasn't sure; she hadn't told her parents she would be out this late. Gilda suggested she gave them a call and tell them that she'd be spending the night at Gilda's place. I found out later that Gilda's parents were away and that her brother was off doing his national service, so Gilda was having the time of her life.

We decided to go to Shahgoli's restaurant and nightclub and have dinner there. Gilda preferred the rooftop restaurant and discotheque at Tabriz Airport, but Shahgoli won out for its proximity. Vartan had an orange BMW 2002, a trendy car that every young man wished to own and impress girls with. Armineh and I squeezed in the back. Vartan turned out to be one hell of a driver, as if he was channelling Stirling Moss. He and Gilda were laughing their heads off, the music was loud and I could hardly hear anyone speak. But it was there in the back of Vartan's orange BMW that I held Armineh in my arms for the first time and, as she looked up at me, I kissed her. I hadn't felt so happy for a long time, and the fact that she had reciprocated was a reassuring sign. I'm not sure if it was the loud music, Vartan's non-stop smoking or Armineh's lips that made me feel giddy.

Gilda noticed us kissing. 'Heeeyyy, enough! You're suffocating my friend.'

We broke off our heady embrace and burst into laughter.

'What are you, jealous?' I said. 'Vartan, don't you kiss her enough?'

Gilda might be cheeky and funny, but my comment made her blush, which was kind of sweet; under that façade of mischievousness there lay a shy, warm-hearted girl.

Shahgoli's was an old Qajar palace that sat in the middle of the park's huge man-made lake, with access via a long jetty-like avenue. The building faced a hill, from the top of which a waterfall, illuminated at night by multicoloured lights, poured down to an underground passage.

By the time we arrived at the restaurant it was still too early to have dinner, so we asked the waiter to reserve us a table while we had a few drinks at the bar. The waiters were rushing about preparing the tables for the evening and the band was rehearsing and tuning their instruments. Vartan and I ordered two Shams and the girls stuck to their usual gin and tonics.

We were tipsy by the time our table was ready. The place was getting busy and the band was playing slow music, Persian as well as Western. Families and couples, young and old, were ordering drinks and meze before their main courses. There were tourists among the clientele too. There was a campsite in the forest overlooking Shahgoli where low-budget European travellers settled for a few days before heading off to explore the rest of the country.

At that time, Iran was truly a bridge between the Orient and the Occident, between East and West. It catered for both sun worshippers and snow skiers. Tourists could swim in the warm waters of the Persian Gulf and then fly to Tabriz or Tehran to ski from December to the end of March. Since 1971, when we extravagantly celebrated twenty-five centuries of Iranian empire, millions of tourists had converged on the country to discover that this ancient sleeping beauty was actually a young and vibrant society steaming towards modernity and prosperity.

After we had our meal, we watched a few young couples and two little kids who had got up on the dance floor. The two children, a boy and a girl of about eight or nine years old, were completely unselfconscious about their dance moves; it was so sweet and innocent. When the music changed, I asked Armineh to dance.

Once on the dance floor, I pulled her into my arms and held her tight. I could feel every curve of her body; her hair smelled of her perfume and her hands were wrapped around my neck. I was nervous, excited and happy all at the same time.

Suddenly, I caught a glimpse of a face I didn't want to see there. It was dim in the nightclub; perhaps I'd been mistaken. Was it Simin? I wondered, hoping I was wrong. Unfortunately I was not. She was sitting at a table right behind ours with an old gentleman who I assumed was her husband. Slowly, without showing any sign of panic or alarm, I swung Armineh to the other side of the dance floor.

How was I going to get out of this awkward situation?

The song ended and Armineh wanted to go back to our table, but luckily another slow song followed. I asked her for another dance, which bought me some time to think. I was completely unaware of my surroundings until Gilda tapped me on the shoulder.

'If you two don't mind, the music has changed, you know!' she said. Sure enough, the dance floor was heaving to the rhythms of a much-faster track.

'Come on! Let's boogie.'

Armineh and I, embarrassed, let go of each other and the four of us danced together, Vartan with his cigarette hanging out of the corner of his mouth, the smoke going straight up into his eyes. We continued dancing but it was getting hot. With every flash of the lights, I felt the temperature rise. I made my excuses and went to the bar for a glass of cold water. The tired-looking barman had obviously had enough for the night.

The three of them continued dancing and the odd Armenian word drifted in my direction. I wondered if they were talking about me. I watched them from the bar, smiling and trying to relive the slow dance I had had with Armineh. I really had been on another planet.

Simin was still sitting at the table with her husband. They didn't seem to be talking to one another much. They looked more like two spectators who had come to watch a game. I made a decision. When the music stopped I walked onto the dance floor, took Armineh by the elbow and guided her towards our table. But instead of sitting down, I led Armineh to the next table and stood smiling in front of Simin and her husband. I said hello to Mrs Pouya. I was impressed by her calmness. She must be an expert, I thought.

'Oh, Pedram, what a nice surprise!' she said and brought her face forward for me to kiss her cheek. She introduced her husband. 'Pedram is a good friend of Kasra's,' she told him. 'He's the one I told you about.'

I wasn't sure what she had told him, but surely not what he should have known in an ideal world.

'I'd like to introduce you to my girlfriend,' I said, looking pointedly at Simin and stepping back for Armineh to shake hands with them.

'Oh, what a lovely young lady you've got for yourself,' Simin said. 'Take good care of him, my dear. He is just the best.'

I felt a bit uneasy, but I was glad I'd had the courage to speak to Simin rather than try to hide.

The family with the children had left hours ago, but there were still a few occupied tables, although most people were on the dance floor swinging the night away. Iranians are people of the night. It must be the heat in most parts of the country that makes us come to life as the sun sets. This wasn't even the weekend, but the place didn't seem in a hurry to close.

It was almost one thirty in the morning when we left Shahgoli's. It was wonderful to walk out of that smoky nightclub into the clean, fresh air. I closed my eyes and took a deep breath. Armineh shivered and I put my jacket around her shoulders and pulled her close. Vartan and Gilda had walked on ahead. The car park wasn't far away.

I was worried about Vartan – if he was sober enough to drive – but he seemed all right. The walk in the fresh air did the trick. We got to the car and I was about to get into the back seat with Armineh when Gilda held me back and said she wanted to sit with her friend. I sat up front next to Vartan. I didn't mind too much because it meant I could keep an eye on him.

Vartan said he would drop me off first before taking the girls home, but I suggested he left me to last. The girls were whispering away in the back. I couldn't hear what they were saying, but it seemed like a serious conversation.

In the end Vartan decided to drop me off first. When we pulled up outside my apartment, I thanked him and got out of the car.

'Wouldn't you guys like to come up for a coffee?' Armineh said, pushing the front seat forward and getting out of the car.

Gilda and Vartan made their excuses.

'Well, I think I'll come in with you, Pedram. I'd love a coffee,' Armineh said and she linked my arm.

This was the first time Armineh had been at my apartment so

late at night. I wasn't sure how I felt about it – nervous mostly, and a little curious.

That night lingers in my memory. Armineh fell asleep in my arms afterwards and I lay there looking at her. She was so beautiful, but the experience itself hadn't been what I'd expected.

The Shah of Iran: A rise from poverty to work power

The Shah now sees most of his ambitions for Iran either achieved or entering the realms of possibility, and those who had demeaned his country made aware of their own faults. He took particular relish this year in warning Britain it faced bankruptcy if it did not work harder and continued to tolerate a permissive society. The wheel had turned full circle.

Port Arthur News, Texas, July 1975

Chapter Nine

I HAD THREE MONTHS of holidays ahead of me and so many plans. I was going to Tehran to see Kami before he left for the US, Richard was visiting from London, Mâdar was coming for a visit and best of all I had my new girlfriend to spend time with. Soon Kasra would be on the scene as well.

Early July I received a call from Richard. We had never spoken on the phone and I was excited to hear his voice. He wanted to confirm the details of his trip to Iran. He would be staying with me in Tabriz, and with my grandma when we were in Tehran. He was arriving in the second week of August. I told him to book his return ticket with either Iran Air or British Airways and leave the domestic flights for me to take care of.

'I've already booked my ticket with Iran Air,' he said, 'but I couldn't believe it when the lady at their office in Piccadilly asked me what time I'd like to fly. I didn't understand what she meant at first. I thought she meant which day. But it turns out they have twenty flights between Heathrow and Tehran every week, some of which are via Frankfurt, Paris, Geneva, Athens and – listen to this – Moscow!'

I laughed. 'Boy, you're in for a shock when you get here. What do you think we're like?'

We had been writing to one another for quite a few years now and our letters covered all sorts of things, including Iranian society and culture, but he still talked about the trip as if he was travelling to a third-world country. I was happy to hear how excited he was. It was his first time travelling abroad.

'Will you be coming to the airport to meet me?' he asked.

'Of course! I won't leave you there. I'm going to Tehran for a couple of weeks before you arrive, so I'll be there to pick you up at Mehrabad Airport,' I assured him.

That evening Armineh and I came up with an itinerary for Richard's visit. She would be joining us when we were in Tabriz. I really wanted to show Richard the very best of my country, so we made a list of places to see in Tehran before going to Isfahan, Shiraz and Persepolis. Then we'd fly to Tabriz to spend a week here before his departure for London.

I flew to Tehran on 26th July, the day before the anniversary of my parents' deaths. Mâdar and I always visited their grave at Behesht-e Zahra, the cemetery in the south of Tehran. My two weeks in the city passed pretty uneventfully. I went to the movies with Kami and Parastou and for walks after sunset with Mâdar in Farah Park. She was a great fan of Norman Wisdom, so one evening we went to see one of his old films at Cinema Polydore in Valiahd Square.

I was much more excited than I'd expected about Richard's visit. I borrowed Mâdar's car and got to the airport an hour early. The international terminal was busy; Tehran had become one of the hubs for intercontinental flights. The weather was particularly mild and pleasant, but you could smell the jet engines.

The Iran Air flight from London was on time, and at last Richard appeared. We had exchanged photographs, so it wasn't difficult to recognise one another. I wasn't sure whether we should shake hands or hug, but he stretched out his hand and I shook it warmly. It was wonderful to welcome him to my country. He was travelling light; all he had was a rucksack. By the time we were leaving the airport car park the sun had set and the city was glittering with the lights from the street lamps and the shops.

'Wow, it's beautiful!' was Richard's reaction when he first saw Shahyad Tower.

I was so pleased. He had complained already about the crazy driving in Tehran, and the tower and massive square seemed to take his mind off it – at least for a little while. Every month, different-coloured spotlights flooded the Shahyad Tower with light; this month it was pale yellow. The lit-up fountains on its huge lawn made the place look like an oasis of calm in the middle of the vibrant metropolis. Richard was too absorbed taking it all in to make conversation. He seemed overwhelmed by what he was seeing as we drove along.

I parked the car at Saman and we took the lift up to Mâdar's apartment. I could smell her wonderful cooking as soon as we stepped out. Mâdar welcomed Richard as if she had known him all her life. She kissed him on his cheeks, as Iranians do, and ushered him in. I had never heard Mâdar speaking English before – I didn't even know she could. She managed pretty well and I was impressed. Over dinner we discussed our plans for the following days. Richard was excited about arriving in Tehran but he was tired and we decided to stay in that night.

The next day Mâdar told us that she would be staying with a friend of hers for a few days and they were driving to the coast. It would be her first trip back to the Caspian since my parents' accident.

We were having breakfast when Kami rang to find out what we were doing. I told him that I was taking Richard out for the day but we could meet up that evening. I'd decided to take Richard to the old part of the city – downtown Tehran. Although Mâdar had left us her car, it was easier to take a cab; finding a parking space was always a nightmare. So we squeezed into one of our famous orange taxis and shared the journey with strangers. It was a most amusing experience for Richard who had come from a capital where the spacious black cabs might only be carrying one passenger at a time.

We got out at Bagh-e Melli so I could show Richard our early twentieth-century architecture, built when Reza Shah the Great began his modernisation plans. Bagh-e Melli – The National Garden – is a government compound of various ministries and museums, accessed through a beautiful imposing brick gateway. In the garden we visited the Iran Bâstân Museum. Its name translates to 'Ancient Iran' and it houses some of the finest artefacts from ancient sites such as Persepolis and Susa. Richard was very interested in ancient civilisations and spoke about the Iranian rooms at the British Museum. He told me how excited he was when he saw the much-talked about Cyrus Cylinder, the first declaration of human rights.

When we left the cool shade of the museum, the midday heat seemed to be too much for Richard, and since it was already lunchtime, I took him, on Mâdar's recommendation, to Yâs for a chelo kabob.

That evening, we met up with Kami and Parastou as we'd arranged. We decided to go to Chattanooga for dinner, a trendy, modern restaurant-cum-diner on Pahlavi Avenue. It was a night I'll never forget. Naturally we talked about life in Iran. Richard told Kami and Parastou about his views on Iran before he arrived in the country and how he was pleasantly surprised.

'I never expected Iran and Iranians to be so modern,' he told us. 'I've only been here a day and from what I've seen, it seems like a country of extreme contrasts, but which you've managed to harmonise well.'

'I'm so glad you're enjoying yourself,' said Parastou.

'So you think what we have here is good?' Kami said, looking at Richard as if he had just said something wrong, and gave a wry laugh.

I didn't understand what Kami was getting at. Suddenly Parastou seemed nervous and fidgeted in her chair. Their behaviour unsettled me a little but I put it to the back of my mind.

'Well, yes, I think you do,' Richard replied. 'Why? Don't you?'

'You are the ones who have it all. Here, what you see is just appearance.' Kami sounded agitated. 'Some have it all and others absolutely nothing.'

'You sound just like some of the Iranian students I know in

London,' Richard said, turning from Kami to me. 'They're members of the Iranian Students Confederation. They have left-wing ideologies and believe that things should change in Iran. It's from them that I get most of my information about your country.'

'Where did you visit today?' Parastou asked in an effort to change the subject. 'What did you do?'

As Richard told her about our sightseeing that morning, I thought about what Kami had said.

'Are you okay?' I asked him quietly in Persian while Richard was speaking to Parastou. His sharp reply bewildered me.

'Never better!' he replied in English.

'How's uni?' I switched back to English too.

'Yeah, good.' He took a sip of his cocktail. 'I've made a few new friends in the past year since you've been in Tabriz.'

'Great! What are they like? Are they nice?'

'Of course they are, but above all they're interesting. They're intellectuals,' he added, emphasising the last word with a nod.

'Well, most students, especially towards the end of their degree, feel like intellectuals,' I said.

'No, these are real intellectuals – not like the ones who waste their time reading rubbish. These are the type who care about the masses, who read books by great writers – real writers, you know.'

'I don't follow you,' I said. I was beginning to understand but I wanted him to confirm my fears. Although Richard was still chatting to Parastou about his sightseeing, I could see that her attention was not with him; she was listening to our conversation.

'No, I didn't expect you to understand what I meant,' Kami said in a condescending tone. He suddenly turned to Richard and said, 'I'm talking about Dostoevsky's *Crime and Punishment*, Gorky's *Mother*, Turgenev's *Fathers and Sons* …'

An awkward silence descended. I just couldn't process what was happening to my friend. He was speaking in a way that I never expected he would.

Parastou rescued the situation by explaining to Richard that we were talking about literature and that Kami had recently become an avid reader of Russian writers.

'But I thought most of them were banned in Iran,' Richard said, looking from Kami to me and back again.

'Oh, yes!' Kami said. 'They're all banned in our country. The government is scared that we'll read about the truth and learn from these books.'

'I'm not quite sure you can call them *the truth*,' Richard said. 'If they're the truth, they can only be true about a country at a certain time in its history. They're simply novels portraying a society and its people. But they don't necessarily reveal a universal "truth" applicable to everywhere else.'

Our evening was turning out to be a strange one. No matter what topic we spoke of after that, somehow the conversation turned political. Richard didn't seem to be bothered about it. Outside the restaurant he told me he was surprised to meet a communist who so openly spoke about his beliefs, not only to his friends, who don't seem to share his ideas, but also to a total stranger.

'Is he not fearful of the SAVAK?' Richard asked.

I felt uneasy when we left Chattanooga. It felt as if I'd worked the whole night in its busy kitchen rather than enjoying an evening out with mates. It was all too much. Gorky, Dostoevsky, masses, SAVAK, authoritarians … the words rang in my head.

Parastou and Kami went home, leaving Richard and I to walk back to Mâdar's apartment.

'Why were you so distressed back there?' Richard asked, lowering his voice. 'Were you afraid?'

'Afraid? Afraid of Kami? Why should I be afraid?'

'No, no, I don't mean afraid of Kami – afraid of what he was saying. You know, talking against the regime in a public place. You never told me he was a communist. I suppose you were afraid of mentioning that in your letters.'

'I'm not afraid of anything or anyone.' I stopped walking. 'Please get all this rubbish out of your head. I suppose your Iranian friends back in London are like those who've somehow managed to brainwash Kami.'

'Sorry, Pedram, I didn't mean to upset you,' he said.

'No, you haven't. Let me finish. I couldn't believe that nonsense coming out of his mouth. The guy we had dinner with tonight is not the guy I used to know. If I never told you he was a communist, it's because I didn't know he was.' I shook my head. 'I couldn't believe what I was hearing in there.'

We were wandering the streets without paying much attention to where we were going.

'I didn't think he was serious,' Richard said. 'I thought he was winding you up.'

'I kept asking myself why he was behaving like that in front of you. I still don't think he meant what he said. I don't know what's going on, but I'm going to find out.'

'But why are you so upset by this?' Richard asked. 'I have many friends who are socialists, even communists, in London. It doesn't bother me.'

'You don't understand. Here it's different. Communism is not a threat in Britain, but for us here, with clandestine groups and organisations carrying out terrorist acts, assassinating, murdering and kidnapping and so on, the story is very different.'

I couldn't stop worrying about Kami. I dug into the depths of my memory trying to think of anyone I knew at Tehran University who could have befriended him and made him think this way. There was no reason why I might know such a person, but I was keen to discover the source of this change in my childhood friend.

The following morning as we were about to leave Mâdar's apartment the telephone rang. It was Parastou.

'Have you spoken to Kami since last night,' she asked.

'No, I haven't, but I will. What the hell was wrong with him? What's got into him?' I was shouting at her as if it was her fault.

'It's a long story. That's why I called. I want to speak to you about him before you see him again.'

I told her that we were about to leave to go to the Imperial Crown Jewels Museum.

Richard guessed that my conversation with Parastou was about the previous night and interrupted to tell me that he wouldn't mind going to the museum by himself if I wanted to meet up with Parastou. He was so insistent and I was so eager to find out what was going on with Kami that I took him up on his offer.

Parastou said she'd come over because it would be easier to talk at my place than in a public café. I began preparing tea for her arrival, thinking over the conversation of the night before. It was very puzzling. Less than half an hour later, a few minutes after Richard left, Parastou arrived.

'I just bumped into Richard in the lobby,' she said. 'Was he okay to go out by himself?'

'Yeah, he wanted to go to museums. He said he'll be fine.'

'How are you?' she asked as she handed me her jacket.

'I'm fine,' I said, 'but is Kamran?'

'Pfft, I don't know what's going through his head.' Parastou threw herself on the sofa.

'You don't? But I thought you knew what was going on! Is there anything going on or was he just being stupid? I'm very angry with him.'

'Stop! Stop!' She put a hand up to her forehead. 'Calm down! Get me some tea first, then we'll talk.'

I passed her tea to her and set mine in front of me on the low table while I sat cross-legged on an armchair. Parastou always drank her tea in a large glass, black with no sugar. She took a sip.

'How is Mâdar?' she asked.

I rolled my eyes.

'Okay, okay!' She raised her hands. 'Kami is who we're talking about. No need to be so impatient.'

'You're making me nervous the more you drag it out.'

'Okay, when we started the new term at university he met these guys who are communists.' She took another sip of her tea.

'What type of communists?'

'What do you mean what type of communists? Just communists. I don't exactly know – some of them are Tudehis, a few Mujaheds – all sorts really.'

'How involved is he?' I asked. 'Does he go to their secret meetings? What do they do exactly?'

'We don't talk much any more, but he spends a lot of time with them.'

'Well, that was obvious from last night.'

I was angry with him for allowing himself to be manipulated. I wondered where he was right at that moment. Who was he with and what were they up to?

'Have you done anything to stop him, Parastou?' I asked.

She exploded. 'Do you think I haven't tried? Do you think I had to wait for you to come back and tell me what to do?'

I suddenly realised the pressure she must have been under all this time trying to deal with this on her own. I sat next to her and put my arms around her.

'I've tried.' She was crying. 'I've tried a lot. I've talked to him night after night, day after day but they seem to have brainwashed him. Little by little they've managed to separate him from his real friends. We hardly see each other now, let alone go out as we used to when you were around. First you left, and now he's disappearing from my life too. I'm almost non-existent to him now.'

I pulled a tissue out of the box on the table and passed it to her.

'Come on, stop crying. Look at you! You look like a freak with your mascara running down your face.'

She gave me a weak smile. I had to joke to lighten the atmosphere. She went to the bathroom to clean her face.

Minutes later she came back. 'What do I look like now?' she asked.

'A freak with no make-up on,' I said.

She punched me playfully on the arm and sat down to finish her tea. Neither of us said much. I got up and put a cassette on, then stood at the window looking over the roofs of Tehran. Pars Hospital, next door to Saman, had an ambulance in front of it from which the emergency team were rushing someone into ER.

'You should speak to him, Pedram,' Parastou said. 'He still respects you. You've always been like an older brother to him.'

'Not much older,' I said.

I really felt for Parastou. She had tried every way she could think of to talk some sense into Kami and she'd run out of ideas.

'I'll speak to him but don't get your hopes up. One thing that might save him is his imminent departure to the US.'

'His departure to the US?'

'Yes, to do his masters,' I said. 'That's partly why I'm in Tehran now – to say goodbye.'

Parastou remained silent, fixing her eyes on me. Then she lay back on the sofa and closed her eyes. 'I have to stay here, because there is a lot to do,' she said, imitating Kami. 'That's what he's been telling me.' She opened her eyes and looked up at the ceiling.

I reassured her that we'd sort this out, and told her not to mention it to anyone. 'You haven't talked about this to anyone, have you?' I asked.

'Of course not! What kind of fool do you take me for?'

'The fact that I'm not here shouldn't stop us. We can help him snap out of this. We have no choice.'

Parastou gave me a look that said she knew my efforts would result in nothing. She had to go. I promised her I would speak to Kami before I left for Tabriz.

After she left, I lay on the sofa thinking about Kami and the people he had got involved with. Kami was the last person I would have expected to become political. In 1970's Iran, like elsewhere, it was fashionable to call those who had read a couple of political books written by foreign theoreticians or who had become ardent communists overnight, intellectuals.

Years later I remembered His Majesty being interviewed by a British journalist. The journalist had begun: 'Your Majesty, all your dreams for the future of Iran lie with your investment in Iranian students who are supposed to run that future.' The Shah had confirmed this. But then the journalist went on: 'But how can Iran ever become a powerful industrial country when most of its students are communists?' To the reporter's astonishment the Shah replied, 'We have no communists!' When the reporter said, 'But it is a well-known fact that most of your students, particularly those abroad, belong to leftist organisations,' the Shah responded in his usual calm manner: 'Of course, students at university become communists! It's natural! Once they graduate and realise that their country provides them with jobs, housing, family and medical care, and so on, they all forget they had ever been communists.'

So many of them I knew personally had followed exactly the same path.

* * *

Richard had left over eight hours earlier and not yet returned. I began to worry that he had got lost. It was almost six o'clock in the evening when he finally showed up looking tired but excited.

'Where have you been?' I asked.

'All over the place,' he replied. He took his shoes off and threw himself on the sofa, panting, as if he had run up the stairs. 'You've no idea how much I walked today.'

'Why didn't you get a cab?'

'No way! The streets were too busy, and I wouldn't have seen everything.' His voice was charged with excitement. 'After visiting the Crown Jewels I had no particular place to go, so I just wandered from one street to another and I loved it – absolutely loved it.'

Hearing he had enjoyed himself, I felt less guilty for having let him go alone, but I still apologised for not having taken him around myself.

'What for? You'd probably have slowed me down.' He laughed. 'The Imperial Crown Jewel Museum. Wow! The wealth sitting there is beyond me. And I only realised today that, unlike what's said about the Pahlavis abroad, all that luxury and glitter doesn't actually belong to them. Did you know that?'

'Of course it doesn't,' I said.

'I spoke to the tour guide at the museum who had perfect English and he explained to me that the imperial jewels, as well as the palaces and most of their contents, are state properties.'

I laughed out loud. 'Well, every idiot knows that!'

'Well, this idiot didn't!' he said, smiling. 'Not everybody knows that. Back in the UK, we've been made to believe that the Shah is even richer than our queen, but far from it.'

'What do you mean, *been made to believe?*'

'Well, the media doesn't always talk favourably about the Shah. Most of the time they do, but then there are people who don't.' He sat up on the couch.

'Who are these people?' I asked. 'Are we talking about Iranian students' communist organisations?'

'Well, yes and no,' he said. 'There are those groups, of course, but there are also politicians who are against the Shah. Every now and then you hear the MPs in parliament opposing your king's policies, internationally as well as domestically.'

I was all ears. This was the first time since we'd met that we had talked about politics. I suppose I owed Kami for having started it all. I was very keen to learn what was said about us abroad, especially in Britain. In Iran, the British have a reputation for being cold people who are politically savvy, people who will manipulate anything and everything in order to get their way. They are always looked upon with suspicion.

'Tell me more. I'd really like to know your views,' I said.

'*My* views? … or our politicians' views?'

'Well both, especially if yours differ. I'd be interested to hear yours too.'

'Remember last year, last summer, when your government lent us – I can't remember the exact figure – millions of pounds?'

'Not especially,' I replied.

'Well, sometime last summer the Iranian government offered financial help in the form of a loan to our government,' Richard explained. 'Economically we weren't doing so well. We had the miners' strike – and high petrol prices, thanks to you guys!' He smiled. 'It made life quite difficult for us Western Europeans – in particular, us Brits who had all sorts of other social and economic problems to deal with at the time, including Northern Ireland.'

I sank back in my armchair, listening to him carefully. I vaguely remembered something.

'Of course, we needed financial help,' he continued, 'but taking it from a country not considered an equal partner was probably difficult for some. After all, there are still many who believe in the British Empire and don't count Middle Eastern countries as anything but oil-rich deserts where our politicians and soldiers once exercised influence and control.'

Everything was becoming clearer for me and made me believe more in my 'Third-Option' theory. As a young Iranian man who had never travelled abroad, I had a naïve picture of Iran. But during our conversation that day I realised we were treading on dangerous ground. Iran was like a lion cub that wanted to be a lion and didn't realise it took time to grow. Our media gave the impression that the West supported us almost unconditionally, even though we knew nothing in politics was unconditional, while the West insisted on calling us the 'Gendarme of the Persian Gulf'. We believed they couldn't afford to lose us.

Richard did most of the talking, sketching out a political world in which different political factions or politicians were divided for and against us. Little by little the blurred picture I started with became clearer. By the time Richard had finished, I had a pretty good idea of how our country was perceived in England.

'So within the British government there are two divided camps as far as Iran is concerned,' I said, 'both of them maybe unhappy with our newly achieved financial and regional dominance because it marginalises the UK. But there are those who would rather support the Shah, despite the many things they don't like about him, than disturb the balance of power in the Middle East.'

'Yes, you're right,' he said. 'That's exactly how it is.'

'But have you ever thought that one day the West may decide to have the Shah removed, no matter the cost, in order to have him replaced by a man or even a new system that's easier to manipulate and so regain influence in this region?'

'You make it sound very devious now!' he said.

'Well, it's a fact – politics is a dirty business. It's said that if you want to succeed in politics, you must keep your conscience well under control.'

We fell silent for a few moments.

'So are you going to elaborate on your Third-Option theory?' Richard asked.

'Sure, but first – show me what you bought today.' I nodded at his shopping bags.

I found it difficult to express my own political views then. I was much more comfortable listening to others talking about theirs. Over the years that Richard and I had corresponded, it was only he who spoke about politics, making comments about the press cuttings he sent me. During my years at Tehran University, a university that always played a pivotal role in the country's political moods, several students had tried to attract me to their political organisations but I'd remained neutral. That didn't mean I supported our government's policies wholeheartedly, like Mâdar did, but I was neither against the regime nor supported it blindly. But for some years I had begun developing my own political ideas, which I'd never discussed with anyone. That day, with Richard drawing a clear picture of how Iran was perceived in the West, was a great opportunity for me to share my ideas with a neutral person and it was exciting. But I still needed a bit more time.

Richard opened one of his shopping bags.

'I got this for us tonight,' he said.

He took out a bottle of red Shiraz. 'I tried your wine once before in London at a friend's place but couldn't remember what it was called to save my life! So I thought we could try this one.'

Then he took out a beautiful large handcrafted silver dish.

'I bought this for your grandma, just to say thank you for letting me stay at her home. The man said it was the work of Isfahani artists.'

He must have paid a fortune for it. I thanked him and assured him that Mâdar would love it.

I had bought some nice meat, chicken as well as fresh Persian Gulf king prawns, for dinner. Richard prepared the salad while I set the table and heated the oil for fondue. We had a nice meal, even though the fondue was not the right choice for a hot summer night in Tehran, but it went very well with the delicious red Shiraz that Richard had bought.

'Okay, this Third-Option of yours. I'm all ears,' he said.

'What about it?' I said, feeling suddenly shy.

'Tell me about it. I want to know.'

'It's nothing intellectual, so don't get all excited.'

'I don't care. I'd still like to hear about it.'

I felt a little embarrassed at first, but once I began talking I felt more confident.

'You see, in Iran we have two factions. One is the so-called National Front, which supports the former prime minister, Dr Mosaddegh, who died about eight years ago, and the other is composed of reactionary groups from both the right and left camps. I believe the Shah has named them quite appropriately "the reactionaries of the red and the black".'

Richard had read about Mosaddegh and was well aware of the Iranian oil nationalisation movement and the British involvement in that affair. He knew quite a bit about Iran's political history, partly, I assumed, through the Iranian students in London but also because of his legal studies.

'I can understand your dislike of, or objection to, the Islamic fundamentalists and the communists,' Richard said, 'but what I'd like to know is what you think about the Mosaddeghists?'

'I was getting there.'

'Don't you think their theory of constitutional monarchy would suit Iran better?'

We had finished our meal and, before answering Richard, I offered him some brandy. We left the table and went to the sitting room. Richard wanted to continue with the wine, but I poured myself a double shot of Courvoisier before making myself comfortable in the armchair.

'We need a new party—' I began.

'A new party?' Richard said, jumping in before I'd finished. 'I thought your king only believes in a one-party system now and at the moment that happens to be Rastakhiz. Has it been a *resurgence* in reality?'

The Resurgence Party, formed in March 1975, had been the Shah's idea as a way to represent all social levels and all opinions together in the one party. He believed that by eliminating an opposition party, he could enlist the help of the best politicians without concern for party politics. However, many people, myself included, did not share this view.

'What I would have suggested to His Imperial Majesty,' I continued, 'was that instead of creating a single-party system at a time when we needed all the support we could get, domestically as well as internationally, it would be better to create a multiparty system, keeping the existing parties, creating a new National Front or maybe a liberal national party, and inviting the old elite to join in, thus bringing about a truly democratic system loyal to the constitution.'

Richard was listening carefully. 'Go on!' he said.

I poured some more wine for him and finished the brandy left in my glass.

'That's it. By creating loyal part*ies*, plural, not just one, we could disarm all the negative publicity and propaganda against the regime, gather support for our attempts in laying the foundation of a democratic system and, while the Shah is still supervising such an important and historic exercise, we, the people, can learn how to walk democratically before deciding to run.'

'Bravo!' Richard began clapping, which snapped me out of my serious mood and made me smile. I wasn't quite sure if he meant it or if, under the influence of the fermented Shirazi grapes, he was being sarcastic.

'You've chosen the wrong path, Pedram,' he said. 'You should have joined the political arena instead of the Ministry of Education.'

Not long afterwards we went to bed, but I was too excited by my own speech, and it was a while before I could fall asleep.

The next day I took Richard to the bazaar and we visited the Ethnological Museum at Golestan Palace. In fact, I was so busy with my guest that I didn't get the chance to speak to Kami alone before we left Tehran. It's something I regret to this day.

Soon Richard and I left for Isfahan and Shiraz. We had a great time together. It was so satisfying to see Richard enjoying his holiday. He marvelled at the beauty of Isfahan and fell in love with Shiraz, particularly Persepolis and Pasargadae. Then we were to meet Parastou and Kami at the Caspian, but that didn't go quite as planned. Kami made some excuse and pulled out – I knew he was avoiding me – and Parastou fell ill with a bad cold and couldn't join us either.

During Richard's visit having the use of Mâdar's car made our trip north more pleasurable. We drove to Ramsar, a few hours from Tehran. The mild, clean but humid air of the Caspian was a welcome change from the dry, hot, polluted air of Tehran.

We decided to rent a small shack near the beach. The past two weeks had given us enough time to get to know each other better. As my father used to say, 'to know a friend thoroughly you must go on a holiday together. It is on a trip that the true nature of a person reveals itself.' I had expected Richard, as an Englishman, to be very reserved in terms of expressing his thoughts or feelings, but he had proved me wrong. I got the impression that the English, no matter how rich or poor, were more satisfied with what they had than Iranians were. In Ramsar he told me that the biggest lesson he had learned from his trip to Iran was never to believe what you hear until you see it for yourself.

We spent our days visiting the nearby towns and villages, having lunch in remote eateries and swimming in the Caspian in the afternoon when most people were having their afternoon *chort*. In the evenings, after dinner, we headed back to the beach and set up a campfire and spent hours chatting. One night, Richard and I were talking about my job and school, and we were both surprised when our conversation turned to salaries. I discovered that Richard's cousin had begun teaching around the same time as me. She was at a school outside London and had an annual salary of £1,400, giving her a monthly take-home salary of about £80. My monthly salary after tax and converted into sterling was roughly about £62.

'Why do you look so surprised?' Richard asked.

'I thought your income would have been far greater than ours here.'

We were also offered various other perks by the ministry, such as food subsidies and even low-cost teachers' accommodation – newly built apartments that were sold on favourable terms to teachers. Richard didn't think such extras were available to teachers in the United Kingdom.

Once Richard and I returned from our trip to Ramsar, I decided to tell Mâdar about Armineh. She was so happy when she heard that I had a girlfriend at last. She was determined now to visit me in Tabriz. I teased her, saying she was coming to Tabriz not because she wanted to spend time with her grandson but because she was nosy.

A few days before our departure for Tabriz, Parastou, Richard and I went out for a drink. Parastou was angry with me for not talking to Kami as I'd promised. That wasn't strictly accurate. I had tried to get hold of him, but either he was never in or when I did get to speak to him he somehow avoided the subject. So I gave up.

Towards the end of August we left for Tabriz. I invited Mâdar to come too, but she promised to pay me a visit once Richard had returned to England. I was really looking forward to seeing Armineh again. I had spoken to her almost every other day since I'd left, but it would be so good to hold her in my arms.

At Tabriz Airport, the sky was grey and the air felt humid; there was bound to be a shower on its way. Richard remarked that it felt like the Caspian, but Tabriz was never that humid. Armineh knew what time we were arriving, but I hadn't expected her to meet us at the airport. Seeing her at the terminal was such a wonderful surprise. We embraced one another for a long time and for a moment I forgot about Richard altogether.

During Richard's stay in Tabriz, Armineh and I took him to see the usual sights. Even though this was his first trip abroad, he didn't seem to feel strange or even foreign. I told myself it was because the British, with their history of empire, had interacted and lived with so many different people in the world that they were used to it. But the Iran of those years was not a typical Middle Eastern country either. The changes that had taken place throughout the country, which most foreign journalists referred to as westernisation, was really just modernisation. After all, we had by no means lost our culture or traditions, although there were some traditions I wished we had dropped.

Travelling with Richard around Iran gave me a new perspective on my own country and allowed me to see the changes it had undergone over the previous decade. Wherever we went, new construction projects were under progress in cities, in the desert or in the northern forests. It felt as if the whole country was on the move. The rise in oil prices had generated enough of an income that the government could realistically envision a prosperous future for Iran. If every aspect of life in Iran was revolutionised, the government said, we could be rubbing shoulders with the most advanced nations on the planet. We had come a long way already, although naturally there were problems that any country taking a giant leap from a feudal system to a modern, industrialised society in a short period of time might face.

When the end of Richard's trip was near, I was surprised by how emotional he was. Throughout his exploration of Iran he had hardly shown any sign of emotion. The sites of Persepolis and the beauty of Isfahan had dazzled him, of course, but he never came across as an emotional person. Armineh, who had visited London on holiday, had told me that the English were cold people. But I thought they were just too reserved to express their feelings. Richard was to prove us both wrong.

On his last day in Tabriz, before heading back to Tehran to catch his flight to London, he became a bit moody. And it intensified on the way to the airport. Armineh was driving and I was sitting in the front talking away when she noticed in the mirror that Richard was wiping tears from his eyes. She tapped me on the leg and drew my attention to it. We decided to say nothing. But once we got to the airport it was impossible to ignore. He grabbed us both and cried.

'I'll miss you both,' he said. 'This was the best holiday I've ever had.'

Now Armineh and I had become teary too. I told him we were happy that he had enjoyed his stay. I was delighted to have finally met him.

'Don't forget, Ardavan – Parastou's young brother – will be meeting you at the airport in Tehran,' I said as he was about to head off for the gates. 'He'll take you to the international lounge, so you don't have to worry about anything.'

'Thanks for everything, Pedram. You must both visit me in London. And next time I come back I want to see the other parts of Iran. Bye!'

We bid farewell but waited for him to pass through security before leaving.

* * *

Over the course of the next two years, Armineh's family and mine met on several occasions and I spent a lot of time at Armineh's parents' place. They were very kind to me. Mâdar and I, our own small family unit for so long, became a proper family with Armineh's parents. Mâdar visited me at least once a year and stayed a couple of weeks with me. Once we all celebrated Christmas together at Armineh's parents. I knew Mâdar missed me – I missed her too – but I could also see that she had turned her life around and enjoyed it more at her new apartment and spent more time with her friends.

My job, too, was going well and I had a great relationship with my pupils. I had the smallest number of student failures, and students who had not been interested in learning English grew to love it and took it seriously. Iraj, Babak and Mehran, my Three Musketeers, had moved on to high school but they still kept in touch. Even Hamid, the reluctant student who had mocked the idea of learning English in my very first class, had enrolled in the Iran–America Society and was taking evening classes to improve his English.

Kasra returned to Iran every summer and Christmas. We wrote to each other in between times and he phoned on my birthday. We always made time for each other during his visits, and I looked forward to seeing him very much. He had almost finished his degree and his family expected him to return home soon.

As for Kami, he left for the US after weeks of reasoning with his family and Parastou. He had received a grant from the Iranian government, the very government that he wanted to bring down, and had gone to study in Washington. As Iranian students abroad only paid ten per cent of their annual return airfare to Iran, I assumed Kami, like Kasra, would return regularly for holidays.

Parastou remained in Iran and we saw each other every time I went back to Tehran. Ardavan, her younger brother, just a teenager when I left Tehran, had grown into a fine young man.

After three years living in Tabriz, I still didn't have that many friends. My world revolved around Armineh, the ever-humorous Gilda, and Vartan. I especially enjoyed Vartan's company; he had become a good friend, one with whom I could discuss politics, life and the future in general. Even though I spent a lot of time with Armineh, Gilda and Vartan I had hardly learned any Armenian. My Azeri, however, had improved. The students told me that I still had a strong Persian accent but I could understand them better.

Mr Hekmat, my friendly bookseller, still invited me in for cups of tea and kept me informed about new releases on his shelves. He was my intellectual companion. Our conversation covered a wide range of topics and, despite our age difference, we had grown close. Usually the conversations moved from a book to an article that had appeared in a newspaper or a magazine, then to life in general.

I remember him telling me once about an article he'd read in an Iranian scientific magazine called *Daneshmand*. The article was about the use of gigantic solar panels in the Iranian desert as a new, clean source of energy. It was a fascinating project, expensive to set up but well worth it in the long run. Such energy was 'God's gift to man,' he used to say. 'It abides by our ancient religion too.' Zoroastrianism, our way of life before Islam, considers water, air, earth and fire as sacred; therefore, polluting them is forbidden. That's what he was getting at – that taking advantage of solar energy would reduce our dependency on oil and help our environment.

In the summer of 1977, I began teaching evening classes at a language centre, which put me in a much better financial position. During the summer break I worked full-time, teaching students who just wanted to improve their English as well as the ones who had failed the subject at school. Hamid enrolled and even brought a few of his friends. He joked with me that it was my fault that, where in the past he had been quite content spending his summer breaks doing nothing, now he felt guilty if he stayed at home. I also began tutoring a few students privately. I enjoyed it immensely. The private lessons were far less formal than those in the school, and I taught the pupils in their own homes, which allowed me to get to know them better.

That summer we also had a big celebration. Armineh graduated from the Faculty of Law and was now ready to practise her lifelong dream. She had specialised in criminal law and was thinking of setting up her own practice. She hoped to join with a couple of her friends, Jamshid and Bahman, to set up a law firm in Tabriz.

Meanwhile, Mâdar kept dropping big hints about other big life events. I was twenty-eight years old and she thought it was about time that Armineh and I got married and started a family. Armineh talked about it too and I got swept along in the excitement of it all and planning our future together.

Part II

Rioting Kills Six in Iran

Six persons were killed and 125 others were injured in weekend rioting when demonstrators shouting pro-Communist slogans set fire to schools, banks and other businesses in the northern city of Tabriz, the official Pars News agency reported Sunday.

The agency said police and demonstrators calling themselves Islamic Marxists clashed Saturday in Tabriz, 300 miles north of Tehran, capital of this conservative, oil-rich state.

The report did not explain how the six were killed, nor did it identify them. The agency said 11 policemen were among the injured.

Colorado Springs Gazette Telegraph,
February 1978

Chapter Ten

SATURDAY, 18TH FEBRUARY 1978 is a significant date in my mind. With hindsight I know why. It marked the beginning of the end.

That day, I dragged myself to school even though I felt unwell as I had to set a test for one of my classes. Armineh had spent all of Thursday and Friday looking after me, making soup and keeping me company while I burned up with a high fever.

Scattered clouds hid the sun every now and then, and capillary-like frost had formed on the lower parts of the windows. There were patches of snow on the rooftops and corners of the street where the sun had not reached. It was a comforting thought that I didn't have a long day; once the test was over I could take the papers and go home.

As I walked through the school gates, huddled in my long coat, its collar pulled up round my ears, I bumped into Mr Marandi, the caretaker, who was having a conversation with Mon Père. I said a quick good morning.

'You should have stayed at home in this cold weather, Mr Azad,' Mon Père said. 'You don't look at all well.'

On my way up the stairs I came face-to-face with Mr Bushehri. He asked me if I was all right. But before I could answer, he said,

'That's a silly question, isn't it? Look at you! You could have called and let me know you were sick. I could have arranged for someone else to take your class.'

'That's very kind of you, sir,' I said, 'but I had to come in as I'm setting a test for one of my classes today.'

'Even easier then,' he said. 'Anyone could have handed out the papers to those devils and invigilated the session. Go back home. I can see to this.'

I turned down his offer but thanked him. I thought there was no point in going home now that I was at school; the test wouldn't take that long anyway.

It seemed quieter than usual. The students were probably doing some last-minute revision. As I walked in, they fell completely silent. I wasn't sure if their worried faces were due to the test or because I looked so ill.

As they began their test I sat at the front of the class and read my copy of *TIME* magazine. That week's edition had a special report on computer society. I was fascinated by the new technologies taking over our daily lives. Computers were revolutionising the way we lived, and Western technology was seeping into our traditional way of life faster and faster. A couple of my students gave up on the test and handed in their papers not long after it began. I glared at their work; they'd hardly written anything – one had even forgotten to write his name. By the time I'd finished reading the article the test was over. When the school bell rang, I collected their answer sheets and asked the class to leave quietly, a request that never seemed to work.

I tidied the papers, put an elastic band around them and put them in my bag, then headed for Mr Bushehri's office to tell him I was going home. But he wasn't there. One of the other teachers told me that I might find him in the schoolyard. And indeed I did, but he seemed rather anxious.

'Have you finished?' he asked as I walked towards him.

'Yes. I was thinking of going home.'

'Good. But you'd better hurry up.'

Puzzled, I pulled my collar up and walked out into the alleyway.

Why had he said that I should hurry up? At the end of the alleyway I stopped at the newspaper kiosk to look at the front pages of some of the papers.

Suddenly I heard a rush behind me. I turned around and saw about nine or ten policemen running, batons in hand, to Shahnaz–Pahlavi junction. I wondered what had happened but didn't take too much notice. I couldn't make my mind up what to buy.

'Hurry up,' the man in the kiosk said. 'I have to close now.'

Thinking he was a bit rude, I paid for a copy of *Daneshmand* and put it in my bag. Why was everyone suggesting I should hurry up? What was going on? It was still morning and the streets were as busy as always, but something was different.

The clatter of the kiosk shutters coming down startled me a bit. I turned around. I could not believe my eyes. All the shops on the other side of the street were closed, people were scurrying around; more policemen were rushing towards the junction and turning into Pahlavi Avenue.

I stood there, baffled by the events unfolding in front of me. I had no idea what to do. Everyone was running. I wished I knew where. There were no cars on the streets at all, therefore no taxis to catch. Bewildered, I simply couldn't move an inch.

Suddenly someone grabbed my arm and dragged me back into the alleyway.

'Are you crazy, standing there like a statue? Can't you see everyone is running away?' he shouted as he pulled me into a building and towards a flight of stairs.

'Mr Arjomand! Hello, how are you, sir?'

He rushed me up the stairs, ignoring my question; someone slammed the front door behind us.

'What's going on?' I asked. 'Has everyone gone mad?'

Mr Arjomand had been in Betty's barbershop, on the second floor of the building, and had seen me from the window. He ushered me into the barbers where a few terrified customers were sitting half shaved with towels around their necks or with unfinished haircuts. I found out later that shops and businesses were not supposed to have opened that day at all.

Everything happened so fast I didn't have time to absorb it all. It hadn't been more than fifteen minutes since I'd left the school. Now I realised why Mr Bushehri and the newspaper man downstairs had told me to hurry up, but I wondered how they knew that something was going to happen.

Betty had pulled the blinds down in order to appear closed. But we peeked through the blinds and watched the street below. Young men, most of them in their twenties, were attacking shops, especially the liquor store across the street, breaking the windows and ripping open the metal shutters. They brought bottles of alcoholic drinks out of the shop and smashed them in the street. I was confused, to say the least. I'd never seen such madness in all my life; I was watching people destroy their own city. Then flames sprang out of the liquor store. It all looked like a movie set below us. Everything was out of control. There were no policemen anywhere – just people allowed to run wild, burning tyres, vandalising shops and anything else that crossed their paths.

By now, everyone who worked in the offices in the building had gathered in Betty's for a better view of the riots. Hotel Asia on the other side of the street had all its windows smashed. It wasn't long before ambulance and fire-engine sirens filled the thick, smoky air. Cinema Asia beneath the hotel was set on fire. Soon hundreds of guests were rushing out looking for safety. Later I learned that many of them escaped into my school's courtyard.

As the hooligans burnt and destroyed the city centre, we heard their shouts: 'Death to the Shah'. I was shocked. I couldn't believe what I was hearing. I asked Mr Arjomand if he knew what was happening. He explained that about forty days ago some riots had broken out in the holy city of Qom – the equivalent of the Vatican for the Shi'a branch of Islam – in response to a newspaper article that ridiculed a religious leader. As a result a few people had been killed and several injured. Shi'a tradition dictates that there must be a commemoration forty days after someone's death. Today's riots in Tabriz marked the fortieth day after the deaths in Qom.

How come I hadn't heard a thing about this? I read the newspapers, I watched television and listened to the radio. What was going to happen now? I wondered. There were bound to be casualties today too.

Then army units appeared in the street below, trying to restore order of some kind in the city. They must have been taken by surprise or they would have been there earlier. Whatever happened in Qom had not been taken seriously by people in other parts of the country. After all, I had read and spoken to many people over the past forty days and nothing was mentioned about it.

Suddenly my thoughts went to Armineh. She was at my apartment. I asked Mr Betty if I could use the phone. The other customers were worried about their families too and I had to wait my turn. Armineh answered the phone on the second ring.

'Oh, thank God you're okay. Where are you?' she asked. 'I rang the school and they told me you'd left over an hour ago! I've been worried sick.' She burst into tears. 'What's going on?'

'I don't know. It's all a bit crazy. Don't leave the apartment. Just call your parents,' I told her. 'Would you give Mâdar a call and tell her that I'm okay? I'll be home …' I didn't know what to say '… as soon as I can.'

Mr Arjomand, who had seen the riots of the 1950s over the nationalisation of Iran's oil industry, kept saying that they had been different, that their purpose had been clear. What engulfed us today appeared so well organised, as if a bunch of paid hooligans and opportunistic anarchists were on a mission.

We were trapped like hostages, and had no idea when it would be safe to leave our sanctuary.

'Are they communists?' I wondered aloud.

'Who knows!' Mr Betty said.

It just didn't feel real. The next time I looked out, there was a Chieftain tank roaring up North Shahnaz Street, behind it an army personnel carrier and a Jeep. I started to laugh, which made the others turn to look at me. It was nervous laughter and I couldn't help it. I didn't even try to apologise for it.

'What is this?' I said. 'Who would bring tanks into the streets? Are we at war? Is this another Lebanon?'

My questions were met with silence.

Then scattered gun shots were heard.

The phone suddenly rang. Mr Arjomand, who was sitting closest, answered it.

'Mr Betty,' called Mr Arjomand. 'It's Betty, your wife.'

We all burst into nervous laughter. I think it dawned on all of us at the same time that we didn't know the barber's real name. He was a man well into his forties, one of the best-known barbers in town, and he'd always been known as Betty to all his clientele.

'Let's call the Central Police Station,' said Mr Arjomand. 'We need to find out what's happening. Everywhere seems deserted. I wonder if they're aware that people are stranded in their shops and businesses.'

A silence descended on us like a parachute when it lands as we listened to Mr Arjomand's side of the conversation with a policeman. When he hung up he told us that we could leave so long as we drove very slowly but warned us that we might be stopped by the police or army who would want to see some sort of identification.

When we left the building we were all nervous, not knowing what to expect. It was mid-afternoon and absolutely silent. Betty offered to give one of his clients a lift as they lived in the same part of town. I went with Mr Arjomand.

I wondered about the kids at the school. Were they safe? Should I go back? was a question constantly hammering in my brain.

'No matter what happens remain calm, Pedram,' Mr Arjomand said as we walked to his car parked right outside in Miyar Miyar alleyway.

'Sure, but what can happen?' I asked.

'God knows!'

That wasn't the answer I'd hoped for.

We saw close up the burning hotel and Cinema Asia across the alleyway. It made me think of my dad and a story he had told me when I was nine or ten years old. During the Second World War he had gone onto the roof to throw his slippers at the Russian aircraft bombing Zanjan, hoping it would make them go away. I remember thinking how exciting that must have been.

Mr Arjomand slowly drove off. There was broken glass and debris everywhere; the public telephone boxes had been vandalised. I could not believe what I was seeing. In a matter of hours the tranquil city I had lived in for four years had turned into an ugly battlefield.

We couldn't go down Shahnaz Street, so we had to make a detour to get to my apartment. We were stopped several times by police and soldiers who checked our identification and asked where we'd been and where we were going. A journey that on a normal day would have taken me less than five minutes by taxi took us well over half an hour.

It was strange to see the empty streets of this usually bustling city, a city that since time immemorial had been on the Silk Road route for travellers from the east and the west. The devastation we witnessed in just a few hours was unbelievable. Whatever the rioters objected to, I thought, they had no right to hold it against ordinary people who had to work hard and earn a living.

Before I could turn the key in the lock, Armineh opened the door and threw her arms around me.

'Thank God you're okay! What's going on? Is this the response to the riots in Qom and that article in the paper?' She wiped a few tears from her eyes.

I kissed her and took my jacket off.

'What article?' I was hopeful that I would find some sort of explanation for this madness.

'You know, that article we talked about.'

'What? The one about the Ayatollah? What about him? You know more about these Shi'a religious leaders than I do.'

'He's asking for an end to the Shah's rule.'

I decided to leave it at that; I didn't want to continue the conversation. For the next few hours we didn't say much, just watched a bit of television, hoping for some reassuring news. But the tension and the stress of the day eventually got the better of me and early in the evening I started to feel ill again.

The events of that day, which allegedly left six dead and many injured, became the only topic of conversation among friends and relatives. That day marked a beginning, a beginning to a dark passage of history that sucked many in without their realisation.

Government spokesmen later said that the death toll in Tabriz had risen to nine, while an underground opposition religious party claimed that more than one hundred rioters were killed in clashes with the police. Having been a spectator in the middle of it I realised that exaggeration on the part of the rioters was going to be a weapon used against the government.

Kami kept coming into my mind. I asked myself what his reaction would be to the recent events. I hadn't heard from him for some time and every time I spoke to Parastou she didn't have much news either. We assumed he must be busy with his new life in the US.

The government kept blaming the 'red and black reactionaries' – the communists and the Islamic fanatics – for the recent events in Qom and Tabriz. We were always very sensitive to communism. The border with our huge neighbour, the Soviet Union, covered nearly fifteen hundred miles along our entire northern frontier. Their puppet political party, the Tudeh, had been outlawed since the mid-fifties but their agents had always been active in Iran. Less than a month before the riots, an official from the Ministry of Education, a member of the Tudeh Party who was to be executed by the firing squad for selling Iranian secrets to the Soviet Union, got lucky and had been granted a reprieve by the Shah.

Then foreign opinion started to turn against us. Up until 1978 we had enjoyed the respect of all the nations in the world, but that year it was as if a collective decision had been taken and country after country turned their backs on Iran.

* * *

Iraj, Babak and Mehran, my Three Musketeers, who were now at high school, had kept in touch. In fact, I was teaching Babak privately during the summer break. Since they'd left school, I'd become more of a friend, an older brother, with whom they shared their dreams, their ideas and their secrets, which were mostly love related.

Iraj wanted to become a diplomat, representing the Shah abroad. Babak, on the other hand, hated the idea of a life away from his home and family. He was so attached to his friends and even to the street he lived on that the thought of being away had never crossed his mind. His great passion was agriculture; his motto was 'Plant Iran From Corner to Corner'. Looking back, I can see that he was our Green Party activist. His faith firmly rooted in our ancient Zoroastrian religion, he believed in protecting the soil, water and air from pollution, the fundamental principle that he said everyone should respect.

Mehran was the most serious and the most patriotic one. Once, when I was defending freedom of speech in one of our many long heart-to-hearts, he agreed with me, adding 'so long as it wasn't damaging the country's sovereignty'. An ardent anti-communist, he wanted to join the military cadets in Tehran when he finished school. All his life, his hobbies and free time revolved around military history, the army and anything to do with wars and weapons.

My Three Musketeers, whose lives and education I had taken a particular interest in, were my hope for the future. I was counting on their generation, the first that had grown up in a peaceful country where jobs were abundant, security was guaranteed and a prosperous future lay ahead.

Nowruz seemed to come round faster and faster every year. That year, as in previous years, I gave in to Mâdar's wish to celebrate the New Year in Tehran. She wanted to observe Nowruz in her own home, sitting next to her Haft Sin. She enjoyed family and friends visiting her and she wanted to spend some time with her brother and his wife. The three of them – and their generation – had 'seen it all'. Every wrinkle, every fold of their skin proclaimed the hardships they had endured in the early years of their lives. But they were comfortable now; unlike their own parents, their retirement was far easier and more peaceful. Once again I left Armineh behind to join my other favourite lady. Our Nowruz ritual was the same as always: preceded by a visit to my parents' grave.

The country seemed to go back to some sort of normality after Nowruz, though the riots left a bitter aftertaste. No one spoke about it any more, at least not among the company I kept. Had it all been a flash in the pan? Unfortunately not.

In May, a fresh series of riots broke out in Qom and Tabriz. More people got involved this time, raising their voices against the Shah. By the second week of that month a group of demonstrators in the Tehran bazaar district came face-to-face with police who used tear gas. Many were injured.

I was getting worried again. I had witnessed the riots in Tabriz first-hand and it didn't look like something that had just happened spontaneously. It seemed well-orchestrated, well organised and disciplined, unlike riots and demonstrations elsewhere in the world. The rioters knew exactly who to target, what do to and how to go about it.

Another academic year was drawing to an end and I felt relieved. The country was tense and I was worried for the kids who had to travel every day to and from school. At least with the summer holidays ahead of us, our responsibility for them was lifted from our shoulders for three months. But I couldn't help wondering what the students might get up to in their free time. How susceptible were they to being recruited by the rioters? Everyone seemed concerned, but the students themselves were excited. One of the boys in my class said he thought it sounded like fun!

As the days passed the government kept changing; new prime ministers followed one after the other, ministerial cabinets got reshuffled but still the riots continued. As anti-government demonstrations increased in number, the police and the army tried to fight off the crowd with tear gas and plastic bullets. It had become a fruitless, demoralising battle, while the government failed to find a way to either resolve the differences or simply put an end to it.

Little by little it became obvious that nothing was going to quell the unrest.

Shah of Iran Forbids Royal Family To Make Profits on Business Deals

The Shah of Iran has issued discreet orders to bar members of his royal family from business deals in which they stand to benefit, and a private 'code of conduct' is to be imposed on them.

The New York Times, July 1978

Chapter Eleven

As the Americans celebrated their independence on 4th July, we seemed to be losing ours. The country was definitely in a different mood; even the Shah felt it. In the end he decided not to fight his own people. On 4th July he banned members of the imperial family from any business deals from which they might profit. It was the beginning of a string of concessions to the demonstrators, in the hope of appeasing those who, in reality, had no clear idea of what they wanted.

I didn't think for a second that the demonstrations expressed the nation's frustration with the regime. There were those who didn't agree with the way things were done, of course, but there were professional agitators too behind the whole operation, encouraged by foreign governments who stood to gain from the collapse of the Iranian imperial government. Oil concessions, instability and wars in the Middle East promised lucrative rewards for the West who would be the sole beneficiaries by selling weapons to the region.

People were becoming increasingly concerned about new tragedies and events taking place almost every day somewhere in the country. One day late in July, just before I left for Tehran, I bumped into a colleague. He talked about the next academic year beginning with 'uncertainties'. I didn't take much notice of his predictions, and when he said there would likely be strikes throughout the Ministry of Education, I laughed out loud.

'What are you talking about?' I said. 'Why would teachers go on strike? What could possibly be our excuse?'

I still had two months of holidays ahead of me and I didn't want them ruined by worrying about something that probably wouldn't happen. I wanted to relax and spend as much time as I could with Mâdar. I was due to fly to Tehran on 26th July for my usual summer, but a few days beforehand Armineh surprised me by saying she wanted to come with me. She had mentioned several times before that she'd like to come; she especially wanted to visit my parents' grave. Luckily, Armineh knew someone at Iran Air and was able to get a ticket at the last minute.

I rang Mâdar to tell her that Armineh would be accompanying me to Tehran. She was very excited and said she would pick us up at the airport.

The night before our departure I hardly slept a wink. I was toying with the idea of proposing to Armineh while we were in Tehran. I'd been thinking about it for some time but found it hard to commit to the idea. Money wasn't the issue. The extra I'd been earning from my private tutoring and from summer school meant I had been able to set some aside. I knew that it was expected of me; Mâdar's hints were becoming less and less subtle.

On the morning of our flight, I was on my way to pick up Armineh when I bumped into my neighbour, Mr Niroumand. After the initial greetings, the conversation quickly turned to politics.

'How do you feel about this mess, Mr Azad?' he asked.

'Frankly, I haven't thought too much about it recently. Yes, there have been disturbances here and there, and, yes, the government has changed a few times, but I don't think the situation is that critical.'

But he didn't share my optimism. 'I think we're giving in too easily. The demonstrators are getting away with everything, despite their bad behaviour. They ask for what they want, not even politely, and we meet their demands.' He gave a hollow laugh. 'I'd say it's crazy, not to mention risky. We can't let them get their own way all the time.'

I didn't have much time to chat, so I suggested we get together and discuss it over a drink when I got back from Tehran. He thanked me for the invitation and said he would look forward to it.

His comment, 'it's crazy, not to mention risky', lingered in my mind. I had complete confidence in our government and in the Shah. I couldn't envisage a situation where they failed to reach an amicable agreement with the demonstrators so that peace and harmony could be restored. After all, we had pushed the Soviets out after the Second World War and put an end to the crises that arose from nationalising the oil industry in the 1950s. But now, in this current crisis, we seemed to be without the support of the international community. Previously, 'we' had meant Iran as a nation, but now for the first time cracks were appearing on the surface of our national unity.

All the way to the airport while Armineh talked non-stop I was preoccupied with what Mr Niroumand had said. Had I placed too much confidence in our politicians? Should I question their loyalty and patriotism? Perhaps I had been too busy with my own life and completely missed the significance of the things that had been happening all around us. In our country we had hardly ever fought to achieve anything. From the liberation of women to land reforms, from the reformation of our civil and secular laws to free education and national healthcare, everything had been handed to us on a silver plate. The idea that the people really wanted to uproot all our traditional and modern institutions and replace them with a backward, reactionary system was simply laughable. I couldn't believe that after all we had achieved people could still be so blind and gullible.

'Where are you?' Armineh asked, sounding a little cross. 'Have you been listening to anything I've said in the past twenty minutes?' She turned away and watched a group of veiled women pass by on the pavement as our taxi sped towards the airport. 'Is it just me or are there more veiled women nowadays in the city?' she asked quietly, all anger gone.

We ignored the driver on our way to the airport; instead, the driver had to listen to us discussing politics between ourselves. On the plane, Armineh expressed her concerns more fully. Her father was apprehensive about the situation and didn't know what to do.

Mr Israelian was a successful businessman and was worried about a communist takeover if the regime collapsed. His family had run away from the Bolsheviks during the Russian Revolution and he remembered quite clearly the horror stories his grandparents had told him as a child. His great-uncle had made his fortune from an ammunitions factory that supplied the Tsar's army during the First World War. His opposition to the workers' strikes during the revolution was one of the charges brought against him by the Bolsheviks, and Lenin had personally ordered his execution.

Unlike the atheist revolution that ousted the Russian imperial family, our demonstrators expressed their inclination towards Islam more and more with each passing day. Surprisingly, even our atheist communists seemed to be going against their own ideology and, together with the National Front, showed a bizarre solidarity with an ayatollah who led the mass hysteria from Iraq.

Three years earlier the Shah had managed to bring the de facto leader of Iraq, Saddam Hussein, to the negotiation table where he had finally signed a peace and friendship agreement. But many people thought that Ayatollah Khomeini, who had lived in Iraq for almost fifteen years, was being used by Saddam, backed by the Soviets, to bring chaos to Iran, and that communism would then be introduced as the only means to control the situation. When this conspiracy theory became prevalent, the Iraqi president offered to 'take care of' the Ayatollah in order to prove his friendship towards Iran. Unfortunately, His Imperial Majesty the Shah declined Saddam's offer.

Forty-five minutes after leaving Tabriz our plane touched down at Mehrabad Airport and, as if by magic, our gloomy mood gave way to upbeat anticipation of the great time we were going to have in Tehran.

Mâdar was awaiting us at the terminal. There were joyful hugs and kisses all round and then we went to her apartment for dinner. She had prepared a feast: Iranian caviar and champagne, followed by leg of lamb with vegetables and salad and finishing with my favourite ice cream, Akbar Mashdi. It filled me with joy to see my two favourite ladies get along so well, chatting, joking and laughing together.

The following day at the cemetery, standing at my parents' grave, Armineh became quite emotional. She cried a lot and I held her in my arms to comfort her. Mâdar stood silently at the graveside as always. We didn't stay there long; it was tense in southern Tehran, where the cemetery was, and we didn't want to hang around longer than we had to in case trouble broke out.

A few days later, anti-government demonstrations in ten Iranian cities resulted in seven deaths and the arrest of one hundred and fifteen people.

The following Thursday, 3rd August 1978, Armineh and I went for a walk in Jamshidiyeh Park in the fashionable northern district of the city. I found a quiet spot in a corner from where we could see the entire city spread out below us. We sat down on the bench under an old weeping willow.

'I have something to tell you,' I said nervously, looking into her eyes and holding both her hands in mine. 'Well, as a matter of fact I've something to ask you.'

'Ask me or tell me? Which one is it?' she said, smiling.

'We've known each other for quite some time now,' I said. 'Even our families have met.' An old couple walked past, greeting us with a soft 'good evening'. I continued: 'You've finished your studies and have set up your new practice.'

She was frowning a little and her eyes searched my face.

'I was wondering if you would consider marrying me.' I reached into my pocket, took out a tiny box and opened it.

All I could hear was my heart pounding. She stared at the ring without saying a word. I searched her eyes, trying to anticipate her answer.

'Wow, I didn't see this coming! You've caught me completely off guard,' she said eventually. Then she threw her arms around my neck and said, 'Yes. Of course I'll marry you!'

That day in August I vowed to focus on what was expected of me. Even though we'd been together for a few years already, this was the moment that really made us a couple.

On our way back to the apartment she asked if Mâdar knew that I was going to propose. I told her that no one knew and no one had seen the ring. That made her even happier, and she immediately wanted to tell all our friends about our good news.

Armineh walked into Mâdar's apartment holding out her left hand. 'Mâdar, look!' she exclaimed.

Mâdar was confused for a moment. Then she spotted the ring and looked from me to Armineh and back.

'Pedram proposed today,' Armineh said, full of excitement.

Tears began to roll down Mâdar's face and she grabbed Armineh in her arms, kissing her on both cheeks. Then she gave me a hug and, holding my face firmly in her hands, she kissed me on my forehead.

'Then let's celebrate!' she said.

She disappeared into the kitchen and came out a little while later with three crystal flute glasses and a cold bottle of Moët et Chandon.

'I always keep a bottle in the fridge,' she said proudly. 'One should always be ready for celebrations.'

We had a great evening together. While Mâdar prepared a delicious supper, Armineh rang her parents who congratulated us both and gave us their blessing. We ate, laughed and drank until the early hours of the morning.

Our new happiness discouraged me from thinking about the political climate in Iran. Iranians were not very political as a nation – at least, not until the late seventies. We lived, worked and laughed and liked nothing more than to have fun. We looked for any excuse to get together to eat, play and dance.

By mid-August Armineh and I were back in Tabriz. A few days earlier, at a press conference in Nowshahr on the Caspian, the Shah stated that his plan to restore free political activity, starting with elections in June 1979, was irreversible, even if violence resulted. The newspapers reported anti-government riots in Tehran, Isfahan and Shiraz. Martial law was declared in Isfahan after the rioting lasted all day. The Ministry of Information announced that four people had been killed and sixty-six injured. Orthodox Muslims, protesting against the government's liberalisation programme, led the riots.

Unrest broke out in Tehran again when the religious-dominated Shopkeepers' Association closed the bazaar. Troops were brought into the streets to try to restore order and some sort of normality.

Dariush Homayoun, the Minister of Information at the time, said in a press conference that the troubles were extremely well planned, with rioters being moved from city to city by private transport, and that Palestinian extremists were involved.

The demonstrators were demanding a rigid enforcement of Islamic laws and the closure of cinemas, bars and nightclubs, which they considered symbols of Western decadence. They also opposed television and the emancipation of women. What I couldn't understand was that women, and not only the veiled religious ones, took part in many of the demonstrations. How could they want to go backwards? How could they not support the modern, civil laws that had been introduced over the past five decades and which gave them all the freedom that had been unimaginable only a generation before. Mâdar was outraged. People's behaviour shocked her more and more. She kept repeating that this was not *our* nation committing such crimes. She was convinced that foreign mercenaries had been brought in to agitate the masses, especially after Homayoun's press conference had claimed the involvement of Palestinian terrorists.

Sunday, 20th August 1978 was a terrible day. In Abadan, at the heart of Iran's oil industry, Cinema Rex was set on fire during a film. The exit doors were locked from the outside imprisoning the audience, and just over four hundred people were burnt alive. Images of the charcoaled, unrecognisable remains of loved ones, broadcast from Abadan cemetery in the evening television news bulletin, shook the nation; some buried up to eleven members of their family. The opposition was quick to blame the government. It was an absurd accusation and many of us found it preposterous. However, months of unrest had weakened the morals of those who were not even part of the opposition. Everyone seemed confused and no one knew who to believe any more. Later on the culprits were arrested and the involvement of revolutionaries, with direct orders from Ayatollah Khomeini in Iraq, was proven. But the damage had been done. The imperial government took no action. Instead of bringing those responsible to public trial and thereby reveal the evil intentions of Ayatollah Khomeini and his gang, the government did nothing.

Up until that day the demonstrations and opposition to the regime had been carried out with a relative absence of violence. The Shah had turned down numerous requests from his generals to use live ammunition against the demonstrators, and, as a result, our protests were still fairly bloodless compared to riots and demonstrations elsewhere in the world. Although there had been occasional clashes with the police and a number of people had been injured or killed, the situation had not yet become uncontrollable. The Cinema Rex tragedy changed all that, plunging the country into a state of mass hysteria.

On 27th August, the Shah replaced Prime Minister Jamshid Amouzegar with Jafar Sharif-Emami, who had been prime minister in the early 1960s. The regime relied on his close links with the religious leaders of Qom and his reputation for personal integrity to pull them through. He was in office just over two months, and made concessions to the demonstrators in an attempt to calm the country. He gave priority to Islamic traditions in the hope of convincing the religious leaders that Islam had a place in determining the country's future, replacing the recently introduced imperial calendar with the Islamic calendar and announcing the closure of all casinos, gambling halls and nightclubs.

On a Friday afternoon in early September, a few days after a terrorist attack on a police station in Tehran in which a policeman had been killed, I was having that promised drink with my neighbour, Mr Niroumand. Armineh had gone to help her mother entertain a few guests for the evening, so Mr Niroumand and I decided to have a gentlemen's evening in my apartment. We drank and chatted, putting the world to rights – especially our small part of it, over half a bottle of fine single malt Scotch whisky and a large bowl of pistachios. The radio was on in the background playing traditional Persian music.

Most of our conversation was about the previous day's demonstration in Tehran where the crowd apparently reached one hundred thousand. Mr Niroumand was furious about the new policies that Prime Minister Sharif-Emami had introduced.

'More concessions again?' he said angrily. 'They might as well just hand over the country now. It's like witnessing a slow, painful death. If it carries on like this we're going to lose everything, but no one's taking firm action and doing anything about it.'

'What do you mean by "taking firm action"? Shooting people in the streets isn't going to solve the issue, is it?'

'No, but there needs to be some kind of plan. If this situation continues, even His Imperial Majesty the Shah will lose his nerve. Can you imagine what would happen to this country if he suddenly decides to leave?'

'He won't leave!' I laughed.

'He did it once before,' he replied. 'But if he does it again, it won't be the same. Do you understand?'

'So what do you suggest?' I asked, getting up to open the windows to clear the fog caused by Mr Niroumand's chain-smoking. 'Are you considering a military coup?'

Just then, the radio fell silent and it brought our conversation to a halt. We looked nervously at the antique radio Mâdar had given me, its two dials staring back like a pair of eyes. A chunk of ash from Mr Niroumand's burning cigarette fell on the carpet. We didn't say a word.

Minutes later the radio burst into life with an announcement that Tehran and eleven other cities were under martial law.

Mr Niroumand got up and paced the room, puffing away on yet another cigarette.

'Martial law could help to calm the country,' I said. I didn't sound convincing even to my own ears.

'I doubt it,' he said. 'We'll just have to wait and see now.'

The telephone ringing startled us so much that we burst into nervous laughter. It was Armineh, checking to see if I had heard the news.

What we later found out was that, despite the announcement of martial law, Khomeini had ordered his followers to ignore the curfew and come out into the streets. Jaleh Square in Tehran, where thousands of demonstrators had gathered, was the scene for another of the Ayatollah's evil plans. The crowd, which hadn't heard about the imposition of martial law, suddenly found itself face-to-face with the military.

Although the Shah had stood firmly against the idea of ordering the imperial forces to shoot, Khomeini had no fear of bloodshed; he claimed that blood was what the revolution needed in order to grow and bear fruit. Under his direction, the so-called Shiite clergy hired Palestinian terrorists and that Friday, while demonstrators gathered in Jaleh Square, the Palestinian mercenaries, positioned on rooftops behind the army, opened fire on the crowd, making it look as if the gunfire was coming from the military. In the confusion that followed, people attacked the security forces who, in order to protect themselves, started to shoot at the crowd. Up until then, no one claimed that the demonstrations were a nationwide movement demanding the fall of the monarchy. But the mayhem on that day, which left many dead and injured, guaranteed an end to twenty-five centuries of kingship in Iran.

* * *

The school holidays were almost over. I had finished my summer tutoring and the students resat their exams. Armineh and her business partners finally moved into their new offices in Tabriz. We were both ready for new starts, but that year proved to be very different from anything we could have anticipated.

On 17th September, a week before the schools were due to reopen, an earthquake shook the central desert town of Tabas, killing more than ten thousand people. The Shah and the Empress went to the devastated area, their visit caught by television cameras. Hordes of villagers threw themselves on the Shah; grieving women mobbed the Empress, wanting her to share their pain. The images beaming out around the country showed the special bond – a bond of mutual affection – between the nation and their sovereign. But then the revolutionaries' powerful propaganda and rumour machine began blaming the Shah for the earthquake. The red and the black reactionaries – the communists and fanatic Islamists – claimed that the US had dumped their nuclear waste in the Iranian desert and that was what had caused the earthquake. From then on, anti-American slogans, condemning the US for its support of the Shah, became the new theme of the demonstrators.

The night of the earthquake I rang to speak to Mrs Arjomand, Kasra's mother, who was from the Tabas region. She sounded pleased to hear my voice. Luckily, no one from her family was from Tabas itself. After a while our conversation moved to Kasra. She had told him not to return to Iran that summer because of the unrest. My heart sank; I had been looking forward to seeing him. Now I wasn't sure he would even come home for Christmas. I promised her I would call again and visit them together with Armineh. She was excited to hear the news of our engagement and promised to tell Kasra our good news. She hoped the political situation would improve so that Kasra could attend our wedding.

Saturday, the first of Mehr, 23rd September, the schools opened in Iran in a sombre mood. Just like every other year, the national anthem was played, our flag was raised and prayers were said to protect our country and our 'Crowned Father'. But the atmosphere was different. It all appeared artificial; no one put any heart into it.

I carried out my duties as usual. The teacher who had predicted a strike when I'd bumped into him a few months previously saw me in the corridor. He smiled and passed by without saying a word. Had he known something then that none of the rest of us knew? I was beginning to feel paranoid. I stared into peoples' faces – at school and in the streets – feeling suspicious of them all. What's he smiling at? I would wonder. What does he know that I don't?

At the end of the first week of the academic year, I was walking back home, my mind miles away, when familiar voices broke my train of thought. I turned around and there were my Three Musketeers, Iraj, Babak and Mehran, running behind me shouting, 'Mr Azad! Mr Azad.' By the time they reached me they were all out of breath.

'You don't seem very fit!' I joked.

I always felt pleased to see them. They were growing into young men so quickly, and even though we were able to have a laugh together now, they always remained respectful. I could see they felt closer to me since they had left Anoushirvan Secondary School.

As we walked along, Babak suggested we go for a coffee; they had an important issue to discuss and valued my opinion. I was intrigued. Maybe Babak has fallen in love again, I thought. I suggested going to an ice-cream parlour, but Iraj said we needed to be alone.

'It sounds serious,' I said.

'It is, Mr Azad – at least to us,' Mehran said with a sense of authority.

I couldn't think of anywhere in the vicinity where we could go and have a private chat, so I invited them to my apartment, which seemed to be what they had in mind from the beginning.

I told them to make themselves at home while I prepared some tea. Mehran suddenly announced that he would be back in a minute and, before I got the chance to ask where he was going, he had disappeared out through the door.

'We forgot something, didn't we,' Iraj said to Babak.

While I was serving the tea, Mehran came back, slightly out of breath, carrying some ice cream. The four of us sat around the coffee table drinking our tea and chatting. But after ten minutes they fell silent. They clearly wanted to talk about something but didn't seem to know how to broach the subject. I decided to serve some ice cream and help them get to the point.

'I'm sure we're not here for tea and ice cream. Why don't one of you tell me what this is really about.'

The three pals looked at each other. Iraj, the young diplomat-to-be, spoke first.

'You see what is happening around us, Mr Azad. We're very concerned.' His voice was sombre, as if he was about to confess to a crime.

'We all are,' I said.

'Please, hear us out,' he said. 'It took us a long time to come to this decision and you're the only person we could think of who might understand our argument.'

I handed them each a bowl of ice cream.

'Fine,' I said. 'I'm all ears.'

'You know our parents, Mr Azad,' said Babak.

It was true. I'd met them during our private tutoring sessions at their homes.

'Our parents aren't rich,' Babak went on, 'and you know that they know each other. Well, recently we found out that they've been talking about sending us abroad to continue our studies.'

'That's not a bad idea,' I said. 'Is that what you call a problem?'

'But we don't want to go,' Mehran said angrily. 'We've decided not to go. That's where the problem begins.'

I could understand their parents' worries. The boys had definitely grown up; even their mannerisms and speech had changed. They were just the kind of young men who might get caught up in the violence of the demonstrations.

'We were wondering if you would speak to our parents – see if you can talk some sense into them,' Babak said.

I didn't want to contradict their parents, so I flat out refused. That was taking my duties as their old teacher too far, I thought. I told them it was up to them to make up their own minds and suggested that they discussed it with their parents. I suspected that, deep down, the main reason they didn't want to leave Iran was because they didn't want to be separated.

Had I known what was to come, I would have backed their parents one hundred per cent and encouraged them to leave Iran at once. To this day I curse myself for not doing so.

Iran riots

At least five people were killed and more than 18 wounded when police opened fire on teachers and students demonstrating against Government in Hamadan, 380 kilometres west of Tehran, press reports say. The clashes took place after the demonstrators ignored the police warning and began setting fire to banks and government buildings.

The Canberra Times, October 1978

Chapter Twelve

ALTHOUGH TEACHERS' SALARIES and benefits were quite adequate, they were nevertheless used as a pretext to begin a nationwide strike. The real reason for the strike, however, was that many teachers felt compelled by their religious beliefs to follow the instructions of Ayatollah Khomeini: to go on strike in order to bring the Shah's regime to its knees.

On 1st October, a commander of a police station in Mashhad was assassinated while taking his son to school. The following day the government declared an amnesty for all persons engaged in 'anti-state' activities, even students abroad and those in exile, including Ayatollah Khomeini. It shocked me beyond belief. Mr Niroumand, my neighbour, was in a rage!

By mid-October the strikes in the Ministry of Education had spread across the country, and despite the Shah's declaration, at the opening of the new session of parliament, that progress towards democracy would 'certainly continue', that the liberalisation process would be extended and that the government would meet in full the demands of striking workers, the rioting continued in most towns and cities throughout the country.

Schools closed their doors; whether you wanted to be on strike or not, no classes were held. This was a golden opportunity for Khomeini to bring the students out of schools and into the streets. The demonstrations had gained momentum after the massacre in Jaleh Square back in September, the government appearing to condone it rather than condemn it by failing to arrest and bring the Palestinian culprits to justice.

The imperial government abided by the law and paid us our full salaries and benefits, according to our terms of employment, while we stayed at home. But some teachers took advantage of the long holiday at the state's expense and joined the demonstrators. I remember one day coming back from shopping while thousands were marching in orderly fashion in the streets and seeing a colleague in the crowd. He left the crowd and came to say hello. I was shocked, almost speechless. But when I asked him what on earth he was doing among the protestors, he told me not to get the wrong idea.

'How can you expect me not to?' I said.

'You know I'm not part of all this. Look, there are a few others.' He pointed to the crowd and I spotted two other teachers from the school waving at me. 'We're off and have nothing to do, so we meet up for tea and then take a walk with the public for the exercise. No harm done.'

I felt like punching him. How could they be so stupid, so gullible, I asked myself. Did they think it was all a game? Since the massacre at Jaleh Square the demonstrations had become a daily ritual, encouraged indirectly by the government, which had given orders that no resistance or force was to be used to stop or disperse the demonstrators.

I discovered that a few of my other colleagues who weren't into 'having tea and taking a walk with the demonstrators' took advantage of the situation by starting their own businesses. I found it very disturbing. I had nothing against people becoming richer; I liked the idea, too, of entrepreneurship and using your own initiative, but it troubled me greatly that while the stability and economic security of recent years had given Iranians the best lives they'd had since the collapse of the Sasanian Empire in the seventh century, all they seemed to care about was financial gain.

Mr Fava, the physics teacher, a short, stocky man with a narrow moustache, had set up an electrical repair shop while the maths teacher had opened a mini supermarket. Both shops were centrally located, and I visited them every time I was downtown. With each visit, I felt more and more disappointed by their attitude. These were the men entrusted with our children's futures.

'I've always loved repairing electrical appliances, especially radios and televisions,' Mr Fava told me, sitting behind the counter in his shop. 'It's always been a hobby of mine. Now I do repairs as well as sell appliances. I've never made so much money in my life. Not that as a teacher I suffered financially. Like many of us, I had my salary from the ministry and I taught privately too. My wife is a headmistress at a girls' high school just down the road and together we earn enough to be able to send our son to a boarding school in England where he'll eventually go to university.'

I'm not sure how he expected me to react. He seemed to think it was all perfectly normal.

'I spend all my time here and at the end of the month my salary from the school is like a bonus,' he blithely went on. 'Now that the schools are closed, many parents are concerned about the education of their children, so I have a few private pupils too. If the strikes continue, I may pay off most of my mortgage, if not all of it, in the very near future.'

I used to get so mad with his attitude that I'd nearly lose my temper and kept promising myself that I'd never go back to his shop, but every time I passed by, he saw me and would call me in for a chat. I rarely managed to escape. He didn't think the people running around destroying public property would ever make a difference. To him they were stupid people just seeking excitement in life, using their new-found freedom of expression to let off steam.

Eventually, I crossed to the other side of the street to avoid him.

I thought carefully about what Mr Fava said and could not agree with him. Sure, after a few years of single-party rule the government had opened up to allow other voices to be heard, but the reforms proved to be too late and badly introduced. The riots and demonstrations were becoming more violent and the demands more extreme. It wasn't democracy the demonstrators – or rather their organisers – wanted. As time went on, I believed that the plan was to stop Iran from becoming democratic and halt our progress as an industrial nation. A religious government with its head in laws and beliefs belonging to fourteen centuries earlier was the best way to achieve that.

The other teacher, Mr Rossva who ran a small supermarket, believed that civil servants in Iran should enjoy the same standard of living as those in the US and in Western European countries. This was a new line of thought emerging as a result of our recent economic boom. Although he had never visited any of those countries, he believed that because of Iran's wealth from oil and our other natural resources, we should have as easy a life as those in the West. I wondered how he had got this information on European teachers' standard of living and how he was so convinced that they were financially better off than us.

My conversations with these two blinkered gentlemen – and many others who I spoke to and argued with in the months since the first disturbances had broken out – revealed a terrifying facet of Iranian people.

The rapid progress we had all experienced in the country led to a rise in people's purchasing power, and this, in turn, raised expectations. But it was unfeasible for the nation's aspirations to be realised in such a short time, and people were feeling frustrated and disappointed in their government.

But what bothered me the most was the vast gap between what the ordinary people complained about and the demands being made by the revolutionaries in the streets. The Shah realised that democracy and strong governmental structures were the vital foundation for a successful and prosperous nation. He also wanted his son to inherit a stable country with a sophisticated society that could match Western secular democracies while at the same time holding on to its national traditions.

However, the sophisticated civil society the Shah was so keen on developing seemed to have chosen a different path. Little by little, the big issues were no longer pay rises, freedom of expression or freedom for political prisoners; once the floodgates were opened the avant-garde – the intellectuals and those who had read a few books – began asking for an Islamic society. The so-called intellectuals of our community, who for years had complained and nagged like pampered kids, demanded the first theocratic government in our history.

During those months of paid strikes, Armineh's business took off and she was busy with her work; the disturbances didn't seem to affect it at all. As for me, I had nothing to do. Otherwise I spent my days reading books or with my old bookseller friend Mr Hekmat. I watched television, followed the events in the newspapers; reading *TIME* magazine became my weekly ritual. It always had something in it about Iran. Much of the world's media was focused on us, a country that in a matter of months had turned from the fastest-growing economy into the most chaotic one.

Between October and the following February, when the strikes finally came to an end, I went to Tehran every month and spent at least a week with Mâdar. On each occasion, I found her more anxious than before. She worried all the time and was extremely nervous about what was going on in the country. We took many long walks along the tree-lined Pahlavi Avenue, and sometimes we drove to Darband, the fashionable northern district of Tehran, where we parked the car and walked in the mountains.

On almost every trip she repeated stories I'd heard millions of times before. 'I know you probably have heard this many times,' she'd begin, but I always let her go on and never interrupted. Each time I listened patiently, and even questioned her as if it was my first time hearing it. I could feel her apprehension. She was not the serene, calm lady that she had been a few months previously. I had never seen her like this before. She had lost all her fun and optimism. She was seventy-four, and for the first time, I think, both of us came to accept the fact that she was no longer a young woman.

That autumn, Mâdar and I walked many miles in the foothills of the Alborz. The sky was grey, the wind gusted through the naked trees and all we could hear was the occasional chirping of birds left behind by their migrating flocks and the Darband River as it crashed down the rocks on its way to the city. It provided a sombre, melancholic backdrop to our conversations; I couldn't recall ever having such gloomy talks with her before, not even when I lost my parents.

When I returned to Tabriz I kept in touch with her on a daily basis. But every time we talked she sounded drained, not like the energetic woman I had always known her to be. I couldn't remember her once complaining about the arthritis she had suffered from for almost twenty years, but in the weeks leading up to the end of that year she complained every time we spoke.

Armineh saw how worried I was and kept telling me that I should stay in Tehran and keep Mâdar company while the schools were closed. But Mâdar objected, insisting that she was fine and reminding me that I had my own life with a fiancée to take care of. She was easily irritated and often moody, which was uncharacteristic of her.

On a wet and stormy morning in November the postman delivered two letters, one from Richard in London and one from Kami in Washington. Strangely, both letters had similar themes and touched on the same issues: the political situation in Iran.

Richard was worried that the disturbances would not have a positive outcome and that he might have to cancel his plans to visit again the following year. Kami, too, was concerned that the situation might worsen in the coming months, but to avoid openly discussing political matters in his letter, in case it was checked, he had used metaphors, referring to the country as his family and the Shah as his father who would eventually leave them and who had failed miserably. His true message was very clear.

Kami wanted to come back once his studies were finished and when Iran was 'liberated', he wrote.

'Liberated?' I said to Armineh who was also disappointed with his choice of words. 'He talks as if we are under foreign invasion. Who are we going to be liberated from? From those who are paying for his education in the United States?' I was furious with him.

Armineh pulled the letter from my hands to read Kami's words for herself.

'He's either losing it completely' – she raised her eyes from the letter – 'or the US media is taking sides with the Iranian revolutionaries. That's what makes him feel so confident about what he's saying. Kamran hasn't got over his earlier madness. If anything, it seems to have become deeper.'

While Armineh read Kami's letter I drifted off to think about Kasra. By that time I knew for sure that he would not be visiting Iran that winter. It made me sad. I think I would have been more positive and optimistic had he been around.

Since the strikes began, I couldn't remember talking about anything other than politics. It was heartbreaking to see so many intelligent men and women who with the best of intentions – at least, that seemed to be the case for most of them – were blindly letting a few charlatans quash their dreams for a democratic society.

I learned from Mrs Arjomand that Mrs Omidvar, one of the ladies I'd met at her place, had decided to leave the country. Apparently she'd sold all their belongings in order to finance a new life in London. Then Armineh told me that her father had said he would take the family abroad if the situation got any worse.

That was when I became conscious that the riots and strikes, by this time recognised as a revolution, were beginning to reshape my life too, whether I liked it or not. Mr Israelian's idea of leaving the country could split Armineh and me up.

When Armineh told me of his plan I said nothing, although I sensed she expected me to say something. When she brought it up again, I realised we needed to discuss it seriously. It wasn't going to go away on its own.

I suggested going for a coffee to our usual café in Valiahd district. We had spent so much time in that cosy little coffee shop, often with Gilda and Vartan, that it had become like a second home. It might be a more comfortable place to discuss uncomfortable things.

Saied, the owner, was sitting bored behind the bar, staring outside. There was only one other couple in the coffee shop.

'What have you done to your customers?' I shouted across to Saied, grinning.

He turned to us and shrugged.

'I suppose they're all out there asking for an Islamic society,' I said loudly.

Armineh prodded me in the ribs and put a finger to her lips.

'Here's to their Islamic society,' Saied said and farted loudly.

The other couple had paid no attention to us up until then, but Saied's fart had us all laughing.

When we got our coffees, we became serious again.

'Dad is worried,' Armineh said, holding her cup with both hands. 'He believes the Shah will leave the country soon.'

'Oh, come on, the Shah won't leave us.' The very idea of it sounded outlandish to me. 'Leave us and go where? He and Iran belong together.'

'Please, Pedram, don't get patriotic on me. Now isn't the time. Let's just talk about ourselves.'

I took a sip of my coffee. I was going to have to face the facts, open my eyes and see what was really going on. Armineh told me that her dad had sold the property they owned in Tehran a few days earlier and was seriously planning to leave the country.

'And what about you?' I asked. 'Will you just follow your parents? You're a grown woman, not his little girl any more. You have just started your own business. It's your career, your future. Our future. Have you thought about that at all?'

'What do you take me for?' she replied angrily. 'Of course I've thought of all that. It's a big thing for me. I'm still trying to work it out in my head. But Dad is thinking of all of us. You're part of the family too, you know! He knows we want to get married.'

I decided to say nothing and let her tell me everything she had to.

'He's thinking of us all moving abroad together, and no' – she paused to order another coffee – 'he hasn't forgotten Mâdar. He wants to discuss the matter with you, and he'll invite Mâdar over too so we can all decide what might be the best thing to do.'

Up to that point, leaving Iran, the country I had lived in all my life, had never even crossed my mind. I had hoped that once we were married and Armineh's business was fully operational we could visit a few European capitals, do some travelling. But the idea of living in a foreign country was not my cup of tea. I couldn't keep quiet any longer.

'If your dad wants to meet with Mâdar, it can be easily arranged. But I can tell you now, I'm not leaving Iran, nor would she. If you want to give up so easily on everything we have here and leave, well, that's your decision. Personally, I think you're all panicking a bit.'

I couldn't help feeling disappointed with her. I thought she would have had more guts and wouldn't have been so shaken by the situation in the country. Yes, many people had begun to leave Iran, but the Shah was still in power.

That day at the coffee shop we could not agree on anything.

The workers' strike at the world's largest oil refinery in Abadan was followed soon afterwards by the resignation of Mr Sharif-Emami, the prime minister. His government had failed to come to an agreement with the opposition, despite the concessions made to the rioters.

Soon we had a military government, headed by an army general. The Chief of Staff, Gholam Reza Azhari, proved to be the worst military man we could have chosen to lead the world's fifth non-nuclear power at the most critical point in its history.

A few days after Azhari's appointment had been agreed by the Shah and endorsed by the parliament, Mr Niroumand appeared at my doorstep. I invited him in but he seemed to be in a rush.

'Have you heard?' he said nervously, both hands deep in his pockets. 'They're all mad! Even the *Emperatour* has lost it!'

Armineh's head appeared over my shoulder.

'The Emperor?' I asked, smiling. I couldn't remember anyone ever calling the Shah the Emperor, although its Persian equivalent *Shahanshah* was widely used. I put my arm around Armineh and Mr Niroumand repeated himself: 'They're all losing it.'

'What's happened, Mr Niroumand?' I asked calmly. 'Who are you talking about? What do you mean, the Shah has lost it?'

'Why don't you come in?' Armineh said.

'Our new military government, our last hope,' he replied. 'This idiot of a general has just ordered the arrest of almost thirty officials, including the former prime minister Amir-Abbas Hoveyda, *on charges of corruption*. How ridiculous is that?'

Armineh and I looked at each other, puzzled and bewildered.

'How can the prime minister order the arrest of a man who had been our prime minister for thirteen years?' I said. 'Besides, the Shah would never allow such an order to be carried out, especially against Mr Hoveyda.'

'Oh, for God's sake, Pedram, stop being so reasonable!'

Mr Niroumand had never called me by my first name before, let alone scolded me.

'Don't you believe me?' he said, his voice becoming more high-pitched. 'Don't you watch or listen to the news?'

Then he turned angrily and rushed off down the stairs.

'What was that all about?' Armineh said, looking stunned.

She went straight for the television and switched it on. Mr Niroumand was right. A list of prominent personalities, key supporters and long-serving figures, including Mr Hoveyda, was being read out by the newsreader. They were now under arrest, put behind bars by the very regime they had been part of. To further please the fanatics, the so-called military men of our country who had taken over most of the ministerial posts ordered an investigation into members of the imperial families' assets. More concessions, again.

For the first time, I felt that the end was near. Mr Israelian's idea of leaving the country flashed through my head.

'Lashing out at your own soldiers and public servants in order to appease your enemies is a last desperate act,' I said. 'It will only make the opposition more confident in their demands.'

We looked at each other in silent desperation.

'He's right,' I said with a deep sigh. 'They are losing it!'

I missed my teaching and my students. I hadn't seen my Three Musketeers for quite a while either and I wondered what they were up to. I had come to Tabriz to teach, and although I still gave private tuition and taught in a language school, that was no substitute for the atmosphere of a real school. For several nights I dreamt that I was back at my own school.

That evening, Armineh and I were going to dinner with her parents and we both knew what the topic of conversation would be. The news of the arrest of our prominent politicians had shaken us all. Her dad was incensed at the new developments. He kept telling us that Iran was finished.

'Look at the situation,' he said. 'Vandals are roaming the streets while our government, which I hoped would bring the whole drama to an end with a military coup, is arresting their own comrades and putting them behind bars.'

I had never seen him so angry. He kept shouting, 'What's wrong with the Shah? Can't he think straight any more? Azhari? For God's sake! We have top generals in this country – Aryana, Oveissi, Rahimi – these are men who can save Iran. Who the hell is this wimp of a general?'

Armineh's mum, too, who had never talked about politics before, expressed her anxiety. 'Who's next to be arrested on the Shah's order?' she said softly, 'the Empress?'

I remained silent for most of the evening. Her dad, once he'd calmed a little, suggested again that we should all look into leaving the country. He knew how I felt about it. I could see his point but I could not see myself living in exile, so we didn't reach a mutually satisfactory decision that night.

Throughout December 1978, despite the presence of the military government, demonstrations increased in frequency and the numbers attending rose too. Millions reportedly protested in Tehran, Mashhad, Isfahan, Tabriz and other major cities.

A harsh and extremely cold winter had set in. Due to the strikes, oil production was slow and there were queues of up to a kilometre in some places as people lined up for kerosene for their homes or petrol for their cars. Every day the weather got colder; the refinery workers' strikes meant that it was going to be even colder. Each day General Azhari gave in to more of the opposition's demands; our so-called military government even went so far as to declare that future laws would not be drafted in the parliament unless a Grand Ayatollah had confirmed its compatibility with Islam. Every dawn the sun shone darker on Iran's political and social landscape.

According to Mâdar, who had decided to take a short break in the warmer climate of the Persian Gulf coast to get away from the madness in the city, Tehran Airport was packed with people leaving the country with or without their belongings. She was angry with the people who didn't support the revolutionaries but instead of fighting them ran away. She thought they didn't care and were giving up too easily.

The mass exodus had begun.

The military government, the weakest of all previous ones, ordered the release of most of our political prisoners, among whom were some of the well-known terrorists who later occupied high positions in the revolutionary regime and in the Islamic Republic. The military government was not losing it, as claimed by Mr Niroumand; it had already lost it.

By this time Mâdar seemed to be suffering from depression, which only got worse after her return from the South. We never had long phone conversations any more. When I invited her to Tabriz she accepted, but she didn't sound excited. It was as if she had given up and couldn't care less. While Mâdar was in Tabriz, Armineh's mum kept her company and tried everything she could think of to raise her spirits.

Mrs Israelian invited us for dinner the first weekend Mâdar was in Tabriz and we got dressed up for the occasion. On our way to their house, Mâdar bought a nice basket of flowers for our host. Mrs Israelian gave us a warm welcome and hugged Mâdar. Mr Israelian, being the gentleman he always was, greeted Grandma by kissing her hand. Armineh's mum placed the flower basket on a round marble table in the middle of their entrance hall, a prominent position where the flowers could be admired by all visitors.

'Hello!' said Armineh as she came down the stairs.

Mâdar's face lit up with happiness at seeing her future granddaughter-in-law. They hugged and kissed; Mâdar wouldn't let go of Armineh's hand as we walked to the sitting room. For the first time in months, I saw Mâdar smiling. We took our places in that lovely room where there was always at least one large vase of fresh flowers. I can't remember that room without flowers.

Armineh hovered around us playing the hostess, serving tea and cakes, offering fruit and nuts; she was very attentive. Soon Mrs Israelian invited us to take our places in the dining room. She had really gone to a lot of trouble. She had laid out her best Wedgwood china plates, expensive crystal glasses and newly polished silver cutlery on a well-starched ivory tablecloth. A small vase of pink roses in the centre made us forget it was cold and windy outside. She had cooked enough to feed an army.

We were halfway through our main course when Armineh's dad brought up the topic we had gathered to discuss – leaving Iran. In what appeared to be a planned and well-rehearsed speech, Mr Israelian first talked about 'our children's future union and the family they hoped to have.' He thought it was important for his grandchildren, and Mâdar's great-grandchildren to grow up in a stable society where they would be safe and free. I noticed that Armineh seemed a bit uneasy when her father spoke about the children we might have. I had never seen her feel shy or embarrassed.

Then he went on to analyse briefly the current situation in the country and then proceeded to list every reason and motivation he could possibly think of to support his plan to leave Iran. Mâdar remained quiet throughout, politely listening. Little by little I could sense her warming up to the idea.

'You are so sweet, both of you,' were her first words once Mr Israelian finished his spiel.

She was smiling and relaxed. I was relieved when I saw that she understood and, more importantly, agreed with Mr Israelian's assessment of the situation. I had never been in favour of leaving Iran, but imagining all of us together in some other country didn't seem so bad now after all.

But it turned out that we had underestimated my grandmother.

'You are all very sweet to think of an old woman like me,' she said.

Mr Israelian lifted his glass and toasted her health. We took a sip of our delicious red wine and wished my grandmother a long and healthy life.

'Thank you! I wish you the same,' she replied. She took a sip and patted her lips with her white napkin. 'But I am not leaving this country, no matter what happens.'

We were all shocked and exchanged glances.

She continued: 'But I raise my glass and drink to the future of Iran.'

We raised our glasses. We were all feeling a bit grim and said nothing. No one dared to push her or try to discuss the matter further. In my short moment of happiness, I had fooled myself. Picturing all of us living in another country had made me feel good, even if it had been a passing moment. But in imagining that, I had gone against my principles and my upbringing in which she had played a pivotal role. I was a little ashamed by my gullibility. How could I have been such a fool to think she would leave her country? How could I have allowed myself to forget who she was?

My grandmother, a woman of propriety and good manners, sensing the heavy atmosphere quickly changed the mood. She raised her glass and toasted Armineh and me, wishing us health, happiness and prosperity for our future life together. I could see disappointment written all over the Israelians' faces. What I also saw was the one thing I wished I did not – they seemed determined to leave, especially if the Shah left the country. All I wished for Iran was for His Imperial Majesty to stay.

That evening it dawned on me that it may very well be impossible for our wedding to take place the following summer. There was no such thing as normality in Iran any more. You could feel the tension in the air no matter where you went to escape. If the Israelians decided to leave the country, it would definitely be before next summer, thus leaving our wedding in limbo.

We were all being forced into a world of uncertainty and the unfamiliar. Every day, a little bit more of the life we knew faded away and the unknown crept in by stealth. We had to be careful when we spoke in public. Women from non-religious families had begun wearing more conservative clothing, especially in provincial cities where chador-wearing ladies had been on the rise since the disturbances had begun to take on a religious tone. Everything was changing so rapidly once again, but this time heading in a different direction – backwards, regressing.

Luckily Gilda and Vartan were still in Tabriz. We got together now more than before in our refuge, the coffee shop, and spent long hours chatting, getting quieter and quieter each time, in case someone heard us talking unfavourably about the revolution.

The situation had brought great fear with it. Those not involved in the revolution were losing control on a daily basis while the revolutionaries seemed more and more organised. Though the Shah was still in the country and the governing structure had not entirely collapsed, it felt like a slow death and only a matter of time. Towards the end of December, even my optimism, which had kept me going, was vanishing fast.

Another Christmas was just round the corner. But the events of that year left a bitter taste in everyone's mouths. Looking back to when Armineh and I first met on that snowy Christmas Eve, it felt as if we had time-travelled from a different era, like we had been beamed up from our familiar world to one that was utterly alien.

That Christmas everyone had more serious issues on their minds and there was less laughter in the air. It was bitterly cold. Snow had already covered most parts of the country, but its white blanket was not thick enough to hide the deepening cracks on Iran's face. She was thousands of years old, but it seemed only recently that she had aged so much. Rather like my grandmother.

At the Palace, Sadness and the Residue of a Domestic Life

At the palace gates, women were wailing and imperial guardsmen spoke sadly of their departed Shah.

The New York Times, January 1979

Chapter Thirteen

FIVE PAIRS OF TEARY eyes were fixed on the television screen at the Israelians'. You could hear a pin drop in a silence filled with anxiety and apprehension. The occasional sigh was the only thing to be heard, mostly from Mâdar. We huddled together feeling cold, the shortage of kerosene, thanks to months of strikes, had forced many families to ration their fuel consumption. We all pondered our uncertain future, which appeared to be increasingly despondent, gloomy and worrisome.

We watched the live broadcast of Their Imperial Majesties' departure from Tehran. The Shah and the Empress, the last members of the imperial family, were leaving Iran. The farewell ceremony at the Imperial Pavilion was short and simple. The newly appointed prime minister, Dr Shapour Bakhtiar, who took office after yet another failure by General Azhari's government to calm the situation, just made it to the airport to see them off after getting an official vote of confidence from the Majlis – the Iranian parliament. The images on television, for those of us who supported His Imperial Majesty and sought his protection, were too much to bear.

Large crowds of revolutionaries had gathered in the centres of most cities to celebrate the historic event by dancing in the streets. Cars had their headlights on whether the drivers wanted to be part of the celebration or not. The time to show sympathy or support for the monarchy was gone; it was too dangerous.

At the Israelians' house the mood was sombre. We wept behind closed doors, like many others, and were angry with the mobs. We expressed our sorrow in any way we saw fit, with the exception of Mâdar who sat up on the sofa with her legs crossed, motionless, continually straightening her skirt. Looking over the top of her glasses, she didn't take her eyes off the television. She showed no emotion while we expressed our sadness and anger. We kept taking a peek at her, waiting for some sort of reaction. Mrs Israelian's efforts to draw her into conversation were fruitless; Mâdar was determined to remain silent. Mr Israelian took the opportunity to bring up the subject of leaving the country again.

'We should leave too, Mrs Hakimi, as soon as possible,' he said, swallowing the lump in his throat. 'Our Crowned Father is leaving. We are orphans with no more protection. What is there to stay behind for?' He kept banging his fist on his right knee, a new habit he had developed in recent months.

Armineh refreshed Mâdar's tea countless times only for it to get cold again. Nothing seemed to stir her. The rest of us needed some kind of sign from Mâdar to break the feeling that we were caught in a bad dream since the beginning of the broadcast.

Out in the streets the cheering crowd's mood reached an unprecedented climax as the news of the Shah's plane taking off from Tehran's airport was announced. The clamour outside had a magnetic pull on me and I headed out to witness the scenes for myself. Despite our personal feelings about the Shah's departure, I wanted to witness this national suicide first-hand. Outside I was grabbed and hugged and congratulated for 'our' victory by total strangers. 'We have won! We are victorious!' they shouted. There I was being jostled by a horde that had seduced and bullied thousands of people onto a path that would eventually lead to carnage. Most perplexing of all was to see Armenians among the revolutionaries chanting for an Islamic Republic.

There was talk of Ayatollah Khomeini's return to the country. Though Dr Bakhtiar was officially still the prime minister and the imperial government was in place, the streets told a different story. The Ayatollah assured Iranian women that on his return the Islamic chador would not be compulsory, that freedom of speech would prevail and that the media would not be censored. He spoke of free electricity, water and gas, and promised that he would create a new society where people could use public transport without charge and even receive a monthly income from the country's oil revenues. There would be no dictatorship in an Islamic society, Khomeini claimed. Although the so-called intellectuals did not take his rhetoric seriously, the masses believed him. Our 'intellectuals' didn't believe the mullahs could take over. Their gullibility, and their lack of vision and in-depth understanding of international politics led them to be easily fooled by a bunch of fanatic criminals. In the end they paid the price, most of them with their lives or that of their children's.

There were numerous rumours that the government intended to close down airports in order to avoid Khomeini's return. Mr Israelian spoke to a couple of his friends who had recommended leaving the country before this happened. Despite his eagerness to leave, he didn't have a solid plan about where to go or exactly when. He had spoken about it for weeks but had not taken any action.

His desperation seemed unjustifiable to me. He did not hold a governmental post; he was not a business tycoon or a politician. His fear of being persecuted for his religious beliefs under an Islamic government was the only thing I could think of that might worry him. His family had escaped the Bolshevik revolution more than half a century before and now history seemed to be repeating itself in the country in which his father had sought refuge.

Later that January, Armineh's mother moved from Tabriz to rented accommodation in Tehran. Her father stayed behind, finalising the sale of their house. I did not speak to Armineh about her family's decision to leave the city. I waited for her to tell me in her own time. She knew that I wouldn't leave Mâdar behind, but I feared she would give up on us and our plans and follow her parents. I couldn't force her to stay, but every time I brought up 'us' and 'the future', she remained silent. She was under a lot of pressure. She had to choose between her parents and her future husband.

A few days after her mother's departure for Tehran, we were at my apartment when the phone rang. It was Mrs Israelian; she wanted to speak to Armineh. Once their conversation was over I knew I wasn't going to like what I was about to hear. Armineh stood for a long time by the phone, staring at the carpet. I just watched her from the sofa. Then she came towards me, sat on the floor in front of me and held my hands in hers. She put her head on my lap and wept. Tears began to roll down my face too, but I tried to tell myself to be strong and not lose hope so quickly. But how could I not?

'I wish you would leave with us – you and Mâdar,' Armineh said. 'I beg you to reconsider and come with us.'

'You know I'd love to, but I can't leave her behind. And you know she won't leave.' I stroked her hair as she wept in my lap. 'She has no one to take care of her.'

Before Armineh left the apartment she promised to call as soon as their situation was clearer. I held her tightly in my arms not wanting to let her go. We kissed and hugged again and again. I took deep breaths so I'd remember her perfume. Neither of us could stop the tears.

From that day on I began a purposeless life with no hope for the future. Not being in control of my life was excruciating. Feeling powerless was something I hadn't encountered before. I found it so hard to accept that there was nothing I could do to keep us together.

On 1st February 1979, Ayatollah Khomeini, the leader of the Islamic Revolution, returned to Iran after living in exile for fifteen years. He expressed no feeling whatsoever for the country and the very people who had helped to make his dream a reality. When asked by a journalist before his plane touched down at Tehran how he felt about returning home after such a long time, he replied '*Hichi*!' – nothing.

With Khomeini's arrival, major cities turned into battle zones between the revolutionaries and the forces loyal to the imperial government. The army, to everyone's surprise (even the revolutionaries), announced its neutrality. On hearing the statement announced on the radio, the young conscripts as well as the officers began deserting the barracks and their posts. Small pockets of resistance, mostly Guard-e Javidan (The Immortals), the Imperial Guard modelled on the ancient Achaemenian ten thousand immortals, was the last hope for the imperial regime, but that soon vanished into thin air.

Four days after the Ayatollah's arrival he said he would declare a Jihad – a holy war – if all attempts at a peaceful settlement failed. In response to his rhetoric, the prime minister, Dr Bakhtiar, said he didn't believe in a holy war of Muslim against Muslim, but if violence broke out he would answer a bullet with a bullet. Not long afterwards, mobs captured one police station after another, followed by radio and television centres. The ammunition warehouses were attacked and opened to the rioters, and armed teenagers roamed the streets terrorising everyone who crossed their path.

Little by little, street by street, in town after town and city after city, the new young, inexperienced soldiers of the revolution, most of them as young as my own students, took up arms, stopped cars and searched them.

I hadn't heard from Armineh since she left Tabriz. I had called Vartan several times but no one answered the phone. Gilda, my last hope of hearing news of Armineh, astonished me when she told me that she wasn't even aware of her departure. If there was one person who would have known where Armineh was, it would have been her. She said she'd ask around to see if she could get some information about Armineh, or her father, who we believed might still be in Tabriz.

On 11th February 1979, ten days after Khomeini's return to Iran, the prime minister went into hiding and eventually fled to France. Khomeini set up a provisional government, announcing Mehdi Bazargan as its prime minister. The riots continued, even though the army had left the streets and returned to their barracks.

The schools were still closed, and with Armineh gone I felt aimless and alone. One early afternoon in mid-February, there was frantic banging on my door and ringing of the doorbell.

'Mr Azad – Pedram, Pedram,' someone shouted.

211

I rushed to the front door thinking the building was on fire. There stood my neighbour Mrs Oskouie, crying and looking frightened.

'Calm down. Stop it!' I scolded her. 'What's the matter with you?'

'I'm going crazy!'

She was hysterical. I'd never seen anyone so terrified before.

'Where is Mr Oskouie?' I asked, inviting her in.

'They're killing people in the streets! I saw a man on my way back home just now. They lynched him in front of Cinema Diamond and then splashed some petrol on him and set him on fire. He was still alive! I felt sick and threw up. Then when the flames burned the rope ...' her voice dropped '... his charcoaled body fell to the ground.'

She fainted and luckily I caught her in time. I carried her to the sofa and rushed to the kitchen for the half bottle of whisky I had left on the windowsill. I opened the bottle and held it under her nose. That brought her round. I helped her to sit up on the sofa. She began crying again. Her long highlighted hair that was always beautifully styled was in a mess. I poured some whisky into a glass and passed it to her. After a couple of sips she became calmer but was still visibly shaken. She sat there silently, shaking her head and repeating 'Oh, my God. Oh, my God!'

I wasn't sure if I had understood her correctly. Maybe I had and just didn't want to believe it. She kept bursting into tears and then controlling herself, but it never lasted more than a few minutes. Eventually she pulled herself together enough to tell me about the horrors she had witnessed.

Less than a mile away from our apartments, the revolutionaries had got hold of men who were allegedly members of the former Organisation of National Intelligence and Security – SAVAK – and murdered them in any way they saw fit. Further up the street another man had been taken. Each leg had been tied to a separate van and they drove off in different directions. He was torn in two. I was shocked and petrified by what she was telling me. I couldn't believe my ears. I wasn't sure if she was telling the truth or if it was the work of her traumatised imagination.

The doorbell rang again; its unexpected sound threw her into yet another panic. Mrs Oskouie's eyes were almost popping out in fear and she started crying again. She fell on her knees and begged me not to open the door. I reassured her it was safe and told her there was no need to worry. Then she heard her husband's voice outside the door, calling for her. She rushed to the door and threw herself into his arms.

'Have you been out there?' I asked him and his face confirmed his wife's story.

I asked him in but he refused and said he would rather take his wife home. I watched them walk down the stairs together, Mr Oskouie's arms around his devastated wife. I closed the door and stood there with my back to it going over the nightmare in my head. Shocked and horrified, I wondered what sort of human beings could commit such awful crimes. Part of me wanted to go out: I needed to see it with my own eyes. I found it hard to accept that such atrocities could take place on our doorstep.

I remembered reading in Isak Dinesen's *Seven Gothic Tales*: 'What is man, when you come to think upon him, but a minutely set, ingenious machine for turning, with infinite artfulness, the red wine of Shiraz into urine?' At the time, I had felt proud that the wine of Shiraz was acknowledged by a Western author. Now, however, it seemed that in the land that gave birth to the wine, we had truly turned the best into waste.

News of the atrocities spread like wildfire throughout the city. Similar acts of brutality were carried out not only against SAVAK members, but against anyone who had held a position in the former regime. The lucky ones were sent to face the firing squads.

Days passed by, but the images that Mrs Oskouie had described kept me awake at nights, and I decided to leave Tabriz. If I was in Tehran I could look after Mâdar, I reasoned, visit Parastou and, above all, search for Armineh. I had no idea where to begin looking for her but I knew I had to find her. Searching for my love in the midst of rubble and bloodshed seemed the noblest act for a lover.

Though the provisional government was established and Bazargan, an old politician from the National Front, was prime minister, total authority remained in the hands of the father of the revolution, Ayatollah Khomeini. His orders were imposed by the revolutionary committees that mushroomed throughout the towns and cities.

In the name of 'the Islamic Revolution, Allah and the downtrodden', the palaces, museums, art galleries and the private homes of the wealthy were broken into, looted and destroyed. The mausoleum of Reza Shah the Great outside Tehran was attacked by an organised gang led by the new Chief of Islamic Justice, Ayatollah Sadegh Khalkhali, also known as the hanging judge. He dug up the grave to take out the mummified body of the late monarch only to find his grave empty. Then the mausoleum and its surroundings were destroyed. He also planned to destroy the ruined palaces of Cyrus and Darius the Great at Persepolis, but the brave people of Shiraz managed to stave off such madness. Self-destruction became a national sport. Annihilation of an entire country's history and disrespect for our heritage led by gangs of mullahs became the new laws of our land.

I remembered that article Richard had sent me about an Iranian who had purchased two sixteenth-century Persian paintings at Sotheby's. I wondered what had happened to them. I had always agreed with those who believed our ancient artefacts and antiques held by museums around the world should be returned to Iran. With the looting of museums, palaces and individuals' homes, I was relieved that such a campaign had not succeeded. Persian culture was safer in other countries.

I spent the first few days in Tehran at home with Mâdar. We only went out if the streets seemed safe and took short walks in Farah Park, which was a few minutes away. I called Parastou a few times every day but no one seemed to be home. I had no idea where to start looking for Armineh. Gilda told me that she had no more news, either about Mr Israelian or Armineh and her mother. Nevertheless, it was nice to speak to her and Vartan whom I'd not heard from for some time.

Before the winter came to an end, the strikes were called off and I had to return to Tabriz to resume teaching, disappointed at not finding Armineh and worried about leaving Mâdar alone. Teaching was the only thing that gave me hope for the future. But the poor school! The floors of most of the classrooms above the café and the liquor store had caved in as a result of the fires set by revolutionaries. Mr Bushehri spent all his time in a series of never-ending meetings and phone calls with the new officials at the Ministry of Education to sort out the problems and find a new location for lessons. The obvious choice was to move our students to our sister school, Avicenna, a French Catholic school for girls, only a few minutes' walk away on the main Pahlavi Avenue. But mixing with girls in the newly established Islamic society, that up until now had promised equality and justice, seemed laughable. Under the new arrangement, the girls' timetable was changed so they attended classes in the mornings and the boys in the afternoons. This arrangement lasted until we were finally told we could move back to our own school.

The school was not ready by any means. Classes took place in the gym, exam halls and anywhere else possible. My initial excitement at being back at school was met with the realisation that nothing was the same as before.

On the first official day back in our own school students gathered to hear the principal's speech. The Iranian flag was banned, as was the national anthem until new ones were devised for the new regime, so the ceremony, reduced to Mr Bushehri's somewhat sombre speech congratulating the Islamic Revolution on its victory and remembering the martyrs of the past year, seemed fake and pretentious. The new revolutionary government had decided that two thousand five hundred years of Iranian imperial history was to be banned, forgotten and ignored. The school's name did not escape the new revolutionary ideology either. From then on, the school that had been named after a king whose reign had awarded him the title of Anoushirvan the Just in our history was to be known as the Dr Hossein Fatemi school, named after Iran's foreign minister under Dr Mosaddegh's premiership of the 1950s.

The chaos that reigned in the streets infiltrated the schools. Students were disobedient and disrespectful; if a teacher tried to control his class, he was immediately accused of being anti-revolutionary. Initially I thought that the students' disobedience was rooted in the problems we faced at school, but that swiftly changed.

With half the academic year gone there was no way we could cover the entire syllabus. Then the new Ministry of Education ordered a new syllabus in which every reference to Iran's imperial history, together with chunks from each subject were eliminated in order to fit a year's education into the four remaining months. The students had just finished three months of summer holidays when the strikes began in October 1978. In the five months since then, authority in schools had passed from teachers to the students. In those early years of the revolution, you could draw parallels between Iran and George Orwell's famous novel, *Animal Farm*. The pigs in the novel and their lifestyle after having taken over the farm mirrored exactly what had happened in Iran since the Ayatollah gained power. Orwell's story became so famous among Iranians that all available copies of the book were sold out within weeks and new ones had to be ordered. Mr Hekmat, my bookseller friend, told me that in his entire life he had never sold so many copies of a book. Of course, once the Islamic regime found out what the book was about it was banned and ordered to be taken off shelves throughout the country.

In schools, the teachers' authority was met by student resistance, and many threatened to report teachers to the newly set-up revolutionary committees. Several teachers resigned before the end of the academic year. Those who had no choice but to put up with hooligan-like behaviour paid a heavy price during those first months under the Islamic Revolutionary regime.

I had missed my students. Soon after classes started up again I looked for the familiar faces. Many of my former students were not present any more. I knew many families had either sent their children abroad during those months of rioting or had all left the country together. The atmosphere at school was tense and it made me feel awkward; every day at work felt like a battle. Students had split into political groups: Islamic supporters, People's Mujahedin members, or Fadayi Marxists militias – everyone belonged to a clique. The friendship that used to bind groups in the schoolyard had been replaced by arguments and on many occasions physical attacks. The chaos continued until the end of the short term, which I eagerly awaited, counting down the days to Nowruz.

Just before breaking for Nowruz, which the new government insisted was to be kept a low-key event, I found Mon Père Lazar in a heated argument with one of the teachers whose fervent support of, and participation in, the revolution was well known to everyone. Mon Père, whom I had grown to know quite well, had shown a peculiar bravery – or perhaps stupidity – in objecting to the removal of the Shah's portrait from the classrooms. As far as Mon Père was concerned, the fact that we were still a French Catholic school meant that he was still in charge. He would not accept that the new government, which came to power promising democracy and freedom of speech, was not prepared to tolerate any ideology that differed from theirs. I tried to talk some sense into him, but I had to be careful not to appear too sympathetic towards him. Soon after that argument, the teacher reported him to the revolutionary committee, and Mon Père was arrested a few days later. After spending a few weeks behind bars in Tabriz prison, he was deported from the country.

The first spring under the revolutionary regime was officially called the First Spring of Freedom. Freedom for the fanatics maybe, but for those who had assisted in the downfall of the Shah, the new establishment soon proved to be the biggest mistake they had ever made. But that first spring the mood was jolly for thousands who were still drunk from their victory over the former regime. By the time they had sobered up, the flames of the fire they had lit caught up with them.

Executions, tortures, hangings and prisons had become part of our daily vocabulary and topic of conversations – quietly of course! Death, dying and killing had become the norm. Assassinations, too, had become a means to eliminate political rivals. Even our former boss, Dr Farrokhroo Parsa, the education minister in Hoveyda's cabinet, was executed. In order to denigrate her, the respected and revered Dr Parsa faced the firing squad with a famous madam of a Tehran brothel.

The coffee shop where we had spent hours every week over the past few years – our second home, so to speak – was burnt down by the mobs determined to eradicate public places where the youth of both sexes could meet. Such places were considered a Western institution that corrupted our good young Muslim men and women. Saied, its owner, had been imprisoned on the charge of 'Corrupter On Earth And Fighter Against Allah'. Similar charges had become a daily routine for many innocent people who faced the regime's henchmen in the six weeks since the establishment of the Islamic government.

I was packing to leave for Tehran to spend Nowruz with Mâdar and hoping I would find Armineh when Gilda rang. She wanted to see me at home, and when she arrived she was tense and seemed upset.

'Sit down and listen to me,' she said. 'There's something you need to know before you set off for Tehran.' She started crying.

'What's the matter?' I asked. 'Please stop crying and just tell me.'

'I have news from Armineh.'

I knew it! I fell back in my chair. I was shaking.

Gilda wiped her tears and told me that there was nothing to worry about. 'Armineh is safe, Pedram.'

Her words were like music to my ears. *She is safe*, I kept repeating in my head, over and over.

'Then why are you crying?' I asked.

'Armineh and her mother are safe and sound,' Gilda went on, wiping her tears with the back of her hand, 'but …'

'But what?'

'I wish I could say the same about her father. Mr Israelian is dead, Pedram.' Gilda burst into tears again.

'Dead? But he was a healthy man!' I said. Then I realised what she was getting at. 'Dead … or killed?' I asked. 'Nobody just dies nowadays. It's almost become fashionable to be killed.' But it didn't make sense to me. Why would harmless old Mr Israelian be killed? So I asked her again: 'How could he die? He was a healthy man!'

She took a tissue out of her pocket and wiped away her tears. 'Do you remember a few weeks ago when you told me about Mrs Oskouie's horrible day?' she asked.

I felt a shiver down my spine. I was horrified. All of a sudden I could put a name to the charcoaled body of the man she had witnessed burning to death.

'Why? What was his crime? Why did they want to kill him?' I began shouting. 'For God's sake, they burnt the man alive in public. Can somebody tell me what was his crime? What on earth could he have done to deserve such a death?'

I cried my eyes out once Gilda had left, and for the next few hours I sat motionless, not wanting to believe what I'd just heard, wondering if Gilda had made a mistake, but above all worrying myself sick about Armineh and her mother. Even though Gilda told me that they were okay, I couldn't imagine how anyone could be after such a tragedy. That day I missed my flight, but luckily I was able to get another ticket for the next day.

When I left for the airport in the morning I was still in shock and cried openly. Everyone stared at me, some wondering what was wrong, others guessing. I shed tears for a man who simply carried the wrong surname in the Islamic Republic, an honest Armenian man whose family had survived the horrors of the Bolsheviks and who had built a new life for himself and his family in Iran.

He had been dragged from his house and murdered, I learned later, not only because of his name but because he had been affiliated with SAVAK, the imperial regime's secret service.

Thousands of women in Iran have been demonstrating against the rule of Ayatollah Khomeini's government's moves to return women to their traditional subservient position in Iranian society. This week American feminist leader Kate Millett joined the women in their protests calling Khomeini a "male chauvinist."

Tribune Progress, March 1979

Chapter Fourteen

On the plane, I pushed back my seat, closed my eyes and gave some thought to Armineh's whereabouts. Gilda hadn't spoken to Armineh herself but had heard the news from a mutual friend in Tehran named Helen, who had met Armineh's mother. Gilda assumed that Helen would know more about them. When my plane landed three quarters of an hour later, I rushed to Mâdar's to call Gilda, hoping she had some more news for me.

Mâdar welcomed me at the door and I was struck by how vulnerable and fragile she was since the last time I'd seen her. Her arthritis seemed to be getting worse too. While Grandma made some tea, I called Gilda.

'I spoke to Helen,' she said.

'So? Where is Armineh?' I said. 'Did you get her number?' I grabbed a small notepad and pen by the telephone ready to write it down.

'No,' Gilda replied.

'No? Why not?' I put the pen down.

'Helen saw Armineh last week but …'

'But what?'

'Armineh didn't tell her much, but Helen got the impression that they were leaving the country. She thinks they may already have left.'

The borders were closed. No one could legally leave the country without the permission of the new revolutionary government. Of course that had not stopped those desperate to escape the new regime, but it was extremely dangerous.

'I have a feeling you have missed her, Pedram. She is not in Tehran any more,' Gilda said gently.

We both fell into what seemed like a long silence. I took Helen's telephone number; I wanted to speak to her myself. As soon as I finished my conversation with Gilda I rang Helen, but there was no answer.

Mâdar and I sat around the Haft Sin, waiting for the New Year. At the exact moment of the vernal equinox, when the new spring was announced, she turned the television off before Ayatollah Khomeini delivered his Nowruz message to the nation. She didn't seem to feel very festive.

'I can't bear listening to that mullah's garbage,' she said.

To lighten the mood I suggested that we should listen to the Nowruz message by our new imperial leaders. 'Afterwards, our new empress may address the nation. We have never seen an empress covered in a chador.' I laughed at my own joke.

But Mâdar didn't find it funny. She looked me straight in the eyes and told me to watch my language, which took me by surprise.

'The Empress is currently out of the country,' she said sternly, 'and I don't like people joking about it. Why don't you put your suitcase in the bedroom?' She pointed to it in the corridor as she made her way to the kitchen.

As if I was a little boy again I did as I was told and took my suitcase to my room. On passing her bedroom I spied a framed picture of the Shah and the Empress next to her bed. It had never been there before. I was startled, worried about the consequences of openly displaying imperial sympathies. Since the revolution many houses were broken into either by yobs or by the official thugs, the Revolutionary Guard, and searched. I thought I should warn her but I changed my mind – it wasn't the right time.

I tried Helen's number several times again that day, but there was no answer; nor was there on the following days, so I assumed they had left Tehran for the Nowruz break. Parastou and her family were away too on the Caspian coast, so I couldn't even spend some time with my only remaining close friend in Tehran.

I called to see other friends and family members where the conversation inevitably focused on politics, something I was definitely not in the mood for. During the second week of my visit, I finally got a hold of Helen. They had been away, staying with relatives in Isfahan. She sounded glad to hear from me and she said she had been expecting my call. We arranged to meet the following day at her place.

The situation in the country was very tense. In just over a month, the regime had created a suffocating atmosphere that no one could escape or find sanctuary in, not even in their own homes. Fear, threats and intimidation, and bad luck seemed to have crept into people's lives, even behind locked doors. Meanwhile, on a daily basis the media carried pictures of executions and stories of individuals, famous and unknown alike, who had at some point in their lives been connected to the former establishment.

I woke up early on the morning of my meeting with Helen and left the house without breakfast. I can't remember the route I took to get to her place; my mind was totally preoccupied by Armineh and what more Helen could tell me. My meeting with her, however, only lasted about half an hour. She had no idea where Armineh and her mother had gone, but she had told Helen that they had arranged to be smuggled out of the country. It was quite understandable that Armineh wouldn't want to give out too many details. Helen told me that Armineh had tried to contact me but every time she had called I had not been at home. Those were comforting words to hear, especially since I was powerless to do anything other than wait.

'She will definitely write to you, Pedram,' Helen told me. 'She said so herself. I'm sure she'll be in touch as soon as they have crossed the border and found a country to seek refuge in.'

But I knew it could be weeks, or even months, before I would hear from her.

At the end of the second week, I returned to Tabriz. Back in my own apartment, every time the telephone rang I jumped. The postman must have thought I was weird, as every morning I was waiting for him at the door. Every day, Gilda and I called one another in case one of us had heard from Armineh. But days turned into weeks where neither of us, nor Helen, received any news from her. Her disappearance, where they might be, whether they were alive at all or not, the uncertainty of it all was tearing me apart. My work – teaching, the school – usually my place of refuge, was no comfort at all. The atmosphere there was dire, and I always look back on those days as some of the worst in my life.

It was during those dark days that Mâdar lost her only brother and spent most of her time with her sister-in-law, one as depressed as the other. The end-of-year exams were just around the corner and I couldn't take any time off to be with her. I didn't want her to be alone, and I could have done with her company myself. But she refused to come to Tabriz, claiming that she couldn't leave her sister-in-law alone.

One night towards the end of June I was getting ready to go to bed. The weather was warm and though I was tired, I knew I wouldn't sleep. I was lying in bed reading when the telephone rang, breaking the night's silence. I rushed to reach the phone, anxious about who this could be calling at this time of night and hoping nothing was wrong with Mâdar. On the way I hit my toe against the door frame and screamed in pain.

'Hello? … Shit!' I had split my toenail and when I pressed it the pain shot up my leg. 'Hello?' I asked again, but all I could hear was the faint voice of a woman calling my name.

'Yes? I can't hear you well,' I shouted. I suddenly realised it was Armineh. I shouted 'Hello, hello' several more times but there was no reply and then the line went dead.

I sat by the phone in my underwear, sweating as if I was in front of a furnace, holding the phone receiver in one hand and my foot with the other. Was it her? I kept asking myself while hissing 'Shit!' every now and then from the pain.

I wanted to call Gilda but it was late. What could she do? I would only have worried her. Anyway, I couldn't be sure it was Armineh. Eventually I got up and went to the bathroom to wash the blood off my toe and put some disinfectant on it. I came back as quickly as I could and sat down by the phone again, hoping it would ring. It was when the room got lighter that I realised it was almost morning. I had done nothing all night but sit with my foot in my hand staring, almost as if hypnotised, at the phone. In a last effort to banish the uncertainty I called the operator who told me there was no way they could trace the call in order to find out where it had come from. I hadn't slept that night at all, and once the sun was completely up, I looked like death. I rang Gilda later in the morning and told her what had happened. From that day on I only left the apartment when I had to. The school exams were well over and I decided I was going to spend my summer holiday in my own apartment waiting for that phone call. I spoke to Mâdar every day and eventually she came to Tabriz so I could be at home as much as possible in case Armineh called again.

Late one morning in August, coming back home from Gajil Gapisi, my usual fruit and vegetable market, I bumped into my dear friend the postman. Even though he saw that my hands were full, he gave me five or six envelopes addressed to residents at my building. I put my bags down to open the main door to the building and the letters fell out of my hand. When I bent down to pick them up, I caught sight of a blue British airmail envelope addressed to me in Armineh's handwriting.

I rushed up to the apartment, dumped the groceries in the hallway and ripped the envelope open. How on earth had she and her mum made it to Britain? Inside was a single sheet of thin airmail paper.

My dearest Pedram,
   I am sure you have spent days, weeks and months being angry with me, feeling upset for all that I have done.
   Not a day has passed that you aren't on my mind.
   I am sure by the time you receive this letter, you'll have heard what happened to us, how destiny threw us about and destroyed us beyond belief.

Mum and I, although we are well in body, suffer deep in our souls every day. But we keep our pain to ourselves and try to be strong for one another. We are far from settled, but at least we are safe and things are looking better.

I would not beg you to come to me, as I know you would never leave Mâdar behind. I miss her too, so very much. I miss everything. Above all I miss you.

This is as much as I can tell you for now, but you would make me very happy if you wrote back. I hope life, somehow, brings us together again. I live and wait for it. Please don't forget me. Write back soon. I'll try to call you, but here is my number.

Yours forever in love

Armineh xx

I felt like I was being ripped apart. I was torn between two worlds, one that felt like a slow death but which I couldn't leave behind, and the other that offered me love and life but which I could not reach. I read her letter over and over, trying to figure out how I felt about her news. I could not breathe. I got up from the bed and opened all the windows. I needed air.

Mâdar stayed with me through July and August that year, while I merely existed, going about life like a robot, carrying out my daily chores with no aim and no plans, and certainly in no mood to see anyone. Depression took over as every day the impossibility of leaving Iran to join Armineh hit me harder. Mâdar told me she had called once and they had spoken for about an hour. But I, for some reason, which to this day I can't really explain, could not bring myself to hear her voice. 'What's the point?' was how I responded when Mâdar or Gilda and, from time to time, Vartan told me off for not getting in touch with her.

In September I began the new academic year without my former enthusiasm to teach. Education was the last thing on students', or the country's new leaders', minds. No matter what we taught, no matter how hard we worked it all seemed so futile. We had worked hard for everything we had achieved up to that point, so where had it all gone wrong?

Soon after the schools opened Mâdar lost her sister-in-law. I didn't want to leave her alone, so I asked the new principal if I could take some time off on compassionate leave. Mr Bushehri had been sacked over the summer break and Mr Mohammadi, a short man with a bulky beard and tons of religious credentials behind him, had taken his place. He was sent to us by the new Ministry of Education and promoted to headmaster for his 'revolutionary sacrifices'. He had been a low-ranking civil servant within the ministry with no experience or qualifications whatsoever to run one of the best schools in the country. Such absurd decisions had become standard in the Islamic Republic. He was a man who could barely read and write but who was feared by members of staff who were not zealous followers of Ayatollah Khomeini and his revolution. We all learned to tread fine lines every working day, and little by little it became unbearable.

Right from the start Mr Mohammadi seemed to have made his mind up about me, accusing me of not taking my revolutionary responsibilities seriously enough, and he made life difficult for staff who had not taken part in the riots of the previous year. He did not permit me to take any leave, so poor Mâdar attended her sister-in-law's funeral without me. Despite the fact that I respected his wishes and attended my classes, Mr Mohammadi made sure to show his dislike of me at every opportunity. I did not join the staff and students ordered to take part in regular demonstrations designed to show 'anti-revolutionaries' that the Islamic Republic was not to be messed with and, therefore, I was not considered a Khomeini supporter.

In November, a group of university students calling themselves 'Students Following the Imam's Line' attacked the American embassy in Tehran and held the embassy staff hostage, refusing to release them until the American government arrested the Shah and returned him to Iran. As a result, the American government froze Iranian assets in the US and brought us international condemnation, entrenching Iran's isolation and imposing an economic embargo that was to last for many years. It was no hardship for the people in power in Iran. While the Iranian people faced a far more difficult life than ever before in their history, the mullahs profited from various black markets through which they illegally imported all sorts of commodities, making themselves richer by the day.

Mâdar remained in Tehran and I could not visit her. My position at the school was extremely precarious, not just because I refused to condemn anti-revolutionaries. Teaching a foreign language, especially English, which was considered the language of imperialists, was not high on the new establishment's agenda. Several students whipped up with revolutionary fervour questioned why they ought to learn it at school.

I had got in the habit of marking the Armenian Christmas on 6th January, and that year was no different. Despite what had happened, it was still the anniversary of the day I met Armineh in front of the Armenian church in Tabriz. Over the previous five years I had visited the Holy Sarkis Church on many occasions; in particular, I enjoyed the midnight Mass.

I was not a Christian, but Sarkis still felt like a holy place to me. I loved the smell of the incense and the heavenly voices of the choir. Sometimes I went there just to be alone and to contemplate, to escape the world outside. Since the revolution, non-Christians were not permitted in the church; the Armenians were afraid of being prosecuted by the authorities for attempting to convert Muslims. But I was well known by the priest and many others in the Armenian community, so I was always welcomed there, especially since Armineh and I had spoken to the *derder*, the priest, about our wedding plans. Being among Armenians now I respected them more than ever for their support of one another and for working hard to keep their culture, traditions and ancient language alive. That year, as I joined the Armenians for their Christmas service, I felt very sad and extremely lonely. Memories of the time I spent with Armineh all rushed back. I felt that this would be the last time I would visit the church. Now that Armineh was not here with me, there was no reason for me to be either. After the service, as everyone was leaving the church, Gilda spotted me in the crowd and gave me a big hug.

'I'm so happy to see you,' she said, her sincerity touching me deeply. Seconds later Vartan, who I had not seen for quite a while, appeared and gave me an affectionate hug too. For a few seconds, it felt like the good old happy days. We agreed that we shouldn't let Armineh's absence distance us, and promised to keep in touch and get together as often as we could. Gilda excitedly suggested that we should meet up at Ararat, the Armenian Youth Club we had frequented in the past. Since the beginning of the republic, relationships between unmarried men and women had become more and more difficult. Many who walked in the streets together, whether hand in hand or not, were arrested and questioned. So, the thought of getting away from the Islamic vigilantes who roamed the streets of our cities like hungry hyenas was a refreshing idea. Gilda told me off again for not having contacted Armineh. It was almost six months since I'd received her letter. She had called and spoken to Mâdar; Gilda and Vartan had been in touch with her too. Only I did not have the guts to hear her voice. It appeared that I was being extremely selfish, even heartless.

I had not spoken to Armineh for nearly a year and there was no better time to contact her. It was Christmas, and it was our anniversary. Seeing Vartan and Gilda again brought back so many good memories. I was still hurt that she had left me behind so suddenly and with no explanation. But at the same time I knew why it had to happen that way. I probably would have done the same thing had I been in her shoes. She had contacted me eventually; I had not been man enough to face the reality of the situation around me.

I felt embarrassed and ashamed and regretted not taking action. Instead I had remained neutral. I should have put more effort into coming up with a solution. If only I had encouraged her family to leave before all this happened, Mr Israelian might still be alive and with his family now in safety.

What was wrong with me? Here I was, thousands of miles away from my closest friends. Why had I accepted what destiny had thrown at me without even trying to challenge it? What was I doing? What was my life all about? The career which I had wanted so much all my life had become a struggle with colleagues and students alike. Classes were a mess, and religion had become the focal point controlling everyone's life. Even the way we dressed was dictated by a mentality that considered shaving and wearing aftershave and ties a Western decadence. I had continued to wear my suit and tie to work until the day I was stopped by a Revolutionary Guard who insulted me for wearing a 'leash' around my neck, then violently pulled it off and cut it with scissors. I hated my life.

I had been home for a couple of hours, sitting all alone fighting my emotions and losing. It was late. Then I picked myself up. Perhaps it was not too late to fix things. The least I could do was to apologise for not doing my best. I decided to start with Armineh. I picked up the phone and dialled her number, but the phone just rang and rang and rang.

The next day, Mr Mohammadi stopped me in the schoolyard and politely warned me of my un-Islamic behaviour.

'A number of your students have complained to the school's Islamic Society that you have been making pro-American statements,' he said.

'What is that supposed—'

'As your colleague I only wanted to inform you before the matter reaches higher levels.'

Without giving me the chance to say anything more, he looked at his watch and said he had to go and pray before it got too late.

'Aren't you joining us?' he asked as he disappeared into the sports hall, which had been transformed into the school's prayer room and Islamic Society.

I stood there in the middle of the deserted schoolyard trying to figure out his intentions; what was he up to? A few of my colleagues had been sacked on various ridiculous charges. Little by little anyone who did not fit into the government's interpretation of Islam – a version alien to those of us who had been born and brought up as Muslims – were sacked from their jobs, or, if they were lucky, made redundant or offered early retirement so they could be replaced by teachers sympathetic to the Islamic Revolution.

I walked back home that afternoon without giving too much thought to his warning. I just didn't care any more. I was tired of the whole situation and no longer bothered if I lost my job.

As soon as I got back to the apartment I tried to call Kasra. He was the first person I thought of calling, but his phone just rang and rang and rang. So I decided to try Armineh. She answered on the second ring. There were so many things I wanted to know about her new life – what she was doing, where she lived, everything – but the question I mostly wanted answered was how on earth they had managed to reach the UK, but it was the one thing we couldn't talk about on the phone. I promised I'd write, and I gave her Richard's address so that she could contact him. I had not heard from him for a long time and since the revolution his letters had dwindled. I spoke to Mrs Israelian too. She couldn't stop crying. Hearing my voice brought back memories of her dead husband, something she just couldn't talk about at all.

From then on Armineh and I kept in touch by letter. It was the only thing that kept my spirits up. Other than that, I met up with Gilda and Vartan at the Ararat Club once a week, a refuge for many of us at that time. Named after the sacred mount that is a symbol of Armenians' past glory and national unity, the club reminded us of the tranquil, friendly society we once were. With its traditional Persian architecture, the club was our Garden of Eden, an oasis of peace and gentleness in the midst of terror and cruelty. Outside its walls fear took all our attention; we had no energy left to appreciate beauty. We spent many afternoons at the Ararat, sometimes staying on well into the night, chatting, playing games and cards or just listening to music.

I called Kasra's mother one day. Her excitement at hearing my voice on the phone really lifted my spirits; she invited me for lunch the following Friday. When I got to their house in Manzariyeh, it reminded me of the days when I had played tennis there with Kasra. But it looked nothing like the place I had visited before. Many of the residents had left the district, moved either to Tehran or left the country. The Italian families, too, had left long ago. It had turned into a ghost town, like many other places in Iran. The streets were dirty, and the Revolutionary Guard occupied the restaurant that had once been the crown of Tabriz's private clubs; its huge hall was now used for military training.

Over lunch our conversation inevitably turned to politics, and when we were having tea afterwards Kasra's parents informed me of their decision to leave Iran and join Kasra. He had finished his studies but because of the situation in Iran he had decided not to return. He would only come back if the Islamic regime was no longer in power. Like many of us, the Arjomands hoped for a counter-revolution. I asked Mr and Mrs Arjomand to promise not to leave without saying goodbye. So many friends, acquaintances and relatives had left without a word and it made me feel betrayed and irrelevant. When I said jokingly that in Switzerland they would have the same weather in winter as in Tabriz, they informed me that Kasra no longer lived in Switzerland.

I was taken aback. When had this happened?

'Following his graduation, Kasra found an amazing opportunity to practice medicine in Sydney. It's only a couple of months since he emigrated to Australia,' Azar joon informed me.

The thought of another close friend drifting further away made me feel lonelier than when I arrived at the Arjomands'. I knew I could not ask them about their plan, or even the approximate date of their departure. It was always a secret and no one questioned the traveller as to how he or she was planning to escape.

The borders were still closed. Passports were only issued for severe medical cases that, due to the US sanctions or lack of medical specialists, could not be treated in Iran. But those who were willing to risk everything in order to escape left in the most bizarre and secretive ways. Relatives and friends were only notified once they had crossed the border safely. Stories of individuals and entire families escaping on foot, or on horseback, or disguised as sheep and mixing with flocks that grazed on borders, or crossing with migrating tribes who had established a lucrative trade smuggling desperate people, had become a hot topic of conversation. I was amazed at the innovative routes some people had masterminded.

Late that afternoon when I said goodbye to Mr and Mrs Arjomand, I knew it might be for the last time.

A few weeks later, after several unanswered phone calls, I decided to pay them a visit one morning before going to school. The sight of a woman covered from head-to-toe in a black chador at their house scared the shit out of me. After the initial shock I enquired about the Arjomands.

'Are you a close friend?' she asked with a strong country accent.

'I knew their son at primary school, well over twenty years ago,' I said. It was safer not to give too much away, especially as I didn't know who this woman was.

I watched her eyes check me over. 'We didn't know them,' she said, total indifference in her voice. They were *taghooti* and their belongings were all confiscated, so we got the house free from the Bonyad. I think they've left the country. I don't know.'

She didn't give a damn. I thanked her and left immediately. *Taghooti* was one of those new terms taken from Arabic, meaning 'those who reject God's orders'. Since the Islamic Revolution, it was used to refer to those of us who were either connected with the imperial family or monarchist. In other words, I was also *taghooti*. The Bonyad was 'The Foundation for the Downtrodden', an organisation that little by little took possession of all Iran's cultural buildings, and people's property and businesses, while the Revolutionary Guard took possession of factories. None of the profits were ever spent on the so-called downtrodden.

I never did hear from Kasra's parents again.

For the first time I felt like a foreigner in my own country. People I knew, places I used to go to, activities that had been part of my daily life were all gone – closed, destroyed or banned. Meanwhile, the career that I had always wanted and the school I had come to love had turned into a nightmare.

My students still achieved the best marks, and although many were influenced by the mass propaganda, I still managed to run my classes more smoothly than my other colleagues. However, my hard work and effort and my dedication to my pupils, along with my reputation for being one of the most caring teachers in the school proved not to be good enough for the new system.

It was June 1980 and the last day of the academic year. I had finished marking the end-of-year exam papers when I was asked by the head of the school's Islamic Society to report to the principal. I walked into Mr Mohammadi's office and he immediately handed me an envelope emblazoned with the logo of the new Islamic Ministry of Guidance and Education of Iran. My heart sank as soon as I saw the logo – a promotion was hardly likely – so without further ado I opened the envelope. The letter was only a few lines long and got to the point straight away: 'The ministry does not see Mr Pedram Azad fit to guide or to educate students in our Islamic country.' One sentence terminated six years of teaching, just like that.

I looked up at Mr Mohammadi who couldn't get up from his desk quick enough. He walked to the window with his hands in his pockets and looked out over the balcony to the empty schoolyard. I noticed his shabby suit and his white shirt buttoned up to the top, hiding his short fat neck. I don't think I'd seen him in any other clothes. The trouser pockets were bulging from many years of carrying bunches of keys in them and pushing his fist down. The image of him silhouetted against the grey sky was a good representation of the Islamic Republic: full of suppressed rage, untidy and unfit for purpose.

'I am sorry, Mr Azad,' he said in a patronising voice, 'you have only yourself to blame. Had you cooperated better this could have been avoided. I warned you before.'

I burst out laughing, and in doing so I released all the stress and anger that I'd suppressed during the past year.

Taken by surprise by my reaction and annoyed by it, he turned to me. I moved towards him and, thinking I was about to attack him, he put a hand out to defend himself. But I stretched out my hand, grabbed his and shook it firmly.

'Thank you, Mr Mohammadi,' I said, pumping his hand violently and firmly. 'You have done me a great favour. I have no desire to be a part of a scheme you have the audacity to call education and guidance.'

Then I walked out.

On my way down the stairs, I could hear the laughter and shouts of my past students. I could see them bidding me goodbye; in my mind's eye I could see my Three Musketeers. Everyone I had met on my first day of teaching at the school seemed to be coming towards me.

I didn't choose my profession because it paid well; it was the interaction with the young people that brought joy and deep satisfaction to my life. Now, I only had a weight on my chest and a lump in my throat. Crying by this time was nothing to be ashamed of – it had almost become a past-time – so I cried.

As I got to the bottom of the stairs, Mr Marandi appeared through the door. This sweet man who had been there to welcome me on my first day at the school six years ago, stepped aside and lowered his head. I stopped in front of him. He was looking down at his shoes. I grabbed his hand and shook it. He looked up at me.

'Mr Azad, God is a witness. Things will not stay this way.'

I smiled at him without saying a thing.

He continued: 'One day there will be justice.'

I held his rough hand in mine, thanked him and walked out.

'God be with you,' he shouted after me.

I raised my hand and waved at him without turning back.

In less than two weeks I had said goodbye to everyone I knew in Tabriz, handed in the keys to my flat and headed back to Tehran.

As it turned out I wasn't in the slightest bit upset about the loss of my job. I was optimistic that in a bigger city with more opportunities I would stand a better chance of finding employment, either tutoring privately or at an independent language centre. Mâdar was more upset about it than I was, but she didn't know how much I'd lost interest in teaching at state schools. She was happy for us to live together again though, and I thought that the move to Tehran might somehow bring me closer to Armineh.

I hadn't seen Mâdar for a few months and she appeared feeble. She asked me about Armineh, and when I told her that we had finally established contact she was in high spirits.

'You should not discount the idea of joining her, especially now, Pedram,' she said.

'Oh, come on!' I replied, incredulous that she could suggest such a thing.

'What's that supposed to mean? You have to face reality,' she said.

'Reality? Is anything real any more?'

'What I am trying to say is that you should try to focus on your future. You've lost your fiancée to the country's political circumstances, now you've lost your job. If you are waiting for me to go—'

'Stop that! I don't want to think about that.'

'No, I won't stop,' she shouted. 'What are your plans for your future?'

I couldn't remember her ever having shouted so angrily at me.

'Do you think I am going to be around forever?' she went on. 'Are you waiting for the regime to change so that Mr and Mrs Israelian and Armineh can come back to Iran? Wake up, Pedram. This regime is going to be around for a long, long time.'

'Oh, come on. How can it?'

'I'm not saying forever, because brutality and dictatorships never last.' She had stopped shouting now. 'But you can't waste the best years of your life waiting for something to change so you can pick up the pieces and put them together again.'

'I know, Mâdar. No need to get angry,' I said calmly. I didn't want her to get excited; it wasn't good for her blood pressure.

'I'm not angry with you. I'm angry with the gods. I'm angry because all that hard work and suffering we endured to drag this country out of the poor state it had been in before the Pahlavis, it's all been for nothing. What we achieved is all gone. Everything. It's all gone.' She shook her head. 'We never thought that black veil we joyfully burnt decades ago could ever come back to enslave us again. We never thought, not even in our worst nightmares, that we could lose everything so easily to a bunch of hungry vultures.'

She began crying quietly.

I held her and let her shed tears for everything she had lost. How frail she had become. She gave me a little smile, as if she was embarrassed for having cried. I gave her a big hug and, in her usual fashion, she held my face in her hands and kissed me on the forehead.

I went to the kitchen to make us some tea. Later, we spoke about Armineh. Mâdar obviously thought the Israelians had all escaped to the UK and I wasn't going to tell her anything different. It was best she didn't know the truth. I asked her about Parastou and her family. I was looking forward to seeing her again now I was back in Tehran. I was also keen to hear any news of Kami. I hadn't heard from him for ages.

'Oh, yes!' Mâdar said. 'I was speaking to Mrs Vaziri the other day and she told me Kami has decided to pack in his studies in the US and come back to Iran.'

'What? What is the matter with that guy?' I said.

She just shrugged and said nothing.

Four in Iran Executed by Stoning

Four Iranians convicted of sexual offenses were buried up to their chests today and stoned to death, with the presiding judge of a revolutionary court casting the first stone.

The New York Times, July 1980

Chapter Fifteen

It didn't take me long to find employment. I returned to the language centre where I had taught while studying at Tehran University. The principal was of course no longer there and what once used to be the common room had been redecorated and changed into a prayer room. The staff was almost the same, with the exception of Mr Richardson, an American from Vermont, and the two British teachers, Miss Coombes and Mr Reilly. They had left the country when the revolution began.

On the afternoon of 27th July, Mâdar and I were driving at a snail's pace through south Tehran's heavy traffic on our way back from our annual visit to my parents' grave. It was very hot and Mâdar was suffering in the heat. The radio was on but we weren't paying much attention to it. Suddenly the radio fell silent. Mâdar and I looked at each other. The last time a radio programme had been interrupted was when the revolutionaries attacked the National Iranian Radio and Television station a few days before the collapse of the imperial government. The silence continued. We knew that the imperial army generals had regrouped in Turkey to form an Iranian Liberation Army. We lived for news of a counter-revolution. Suddenly the presenter came back on the air, his voice flat and emotionless: 'The deposed Shah died this morning in Cairo.'

Mâdar wailed and burst into tears. I controlled myself. It wasn't easy, but there were many people in the streets and it was important to seem as indifferent as possible. But Mâdar couldn't care less. 'What are we going to do now? What are we going to do now?' she kept repeating. I had no answers. I didn't know what the future held. It undoubtedly marked the end of an era.

Mâdar had always been my tower of strength, but that role seemed to have shifted to me since I'd returned to Tehran. I had to get her home before she made a scene and attracted unwanted attention.

She walked into the apartment and, throwing her bag to one side, rushed to the radio. It was time for the Voice of Israel's Persian programme. We spent the rest of the evening listening to various broadcasts by foreign radio stations airing news bulletins in Persian.

Mâdar massaged her arthritic knees while she listened to the news and shook her head in disbelief. She carried the small transistor radio around the house with her; it became part of her anatomy. She was in a different world. Several times she walked to the window and looked out at the lights of the city. She avoided any conversation with me. Her friends, having heard the news, phoned to check on her. I answered the calls but she shook her head and refused to speak to anyone.

It was midnight when all Persian programmes finished.

'I'm exhausted,' she said. She straightened her skirt and headed to her bedroom, but she suddenly stopped, turned to me and said, 'You know, the Shah is dead, but long live the Shah.'

She walked into her room. With those words she somehow sounded like the old Mâdar again. It was as if she had worked out some sort of a solution to the problem.

I had just got up from the sofa to clear the cups from the coffee table when she came out of her bedroom again. She pointed her finger at me.

'Now it's up to you and the younger ones to protect our young king and bring him back. I don't want you to forget your duty. You must promise me, okay?'

Has she gone mad? was the first thought that went through my head.

'Promise you?' I said. 'How can you expect such a thing? How can I make you such a promise? You think it's up to me? Mâdar, I think today's events have made you very tired and you're talking without realising what you're saying.'

'Don't be so rude! I may be an old woman but I'm not crazy. I'm telling you because I know you have always taken my advice seriously. You must never forget who we are.'

I got to my feet and faced her. 'Yes, you tell me! Who are we? Do we know any more? I feel like a stranger in my own country, that's who I am – a stranger.'

I had never shouted at her before. Something took over and I just let go. She stood there motionless and said nothing for a moment.

Then she pulled a chair out from the dining table and pointed at it, telling me to sit down. That night, the twelfth anniversary of my parents' death, the day our young crown prince took over his father's responsibilities, Mâdar told me her wishes in the event of her death.

She instructed me to look after Armineh and myself and lectured me about our heritage. 'We are the children of Cyrus and Darius the Great,' she said with an authority in her voice that was familiar. 'I want you to remember that we are a unique nation currently under siege. We have suffered a lot, Pedram. It's up to you and your generation, no matter how, no matter where, to fight for the liberty of this land and our people.'

Every time I tried to interrupt her she held her hand up.

'I'm not going to be around for too long,' she continued. 'It's a reality that you have to face, so listen – I may not have another chance to tell you this and you better listen carefully.'

I *was* listening carefully but I certainly didn't expect to hear what she was about to say.

She revealed that she was involved with anti-revolutionary cells inside, as well as outside Iran, coordinating various operations.

I burst out laughing. 'Oh, come on, Mâdar! You're too old for all that kind of thing.'

But that was just the point. Believing that no one would suspect an old woman of being involved in such clandestine activities, she had established contact with anti-revolutionaries outside and inside our borders. Together they wrote, printed and distributed newsletters that spoke out against the regime.

'This is crazy!' I said once she finished. 'Do you realise what this means? Do you have any idea what they would do to you if they find out?'

'That's none of your business,' she replied.

'Of course it's my business!' I yelled.

'Lower your voice, young man. I'm not prepared to carry on this conversation if you are not going to show me some respect.'

She got up from the table.

'It's you who is acting irresponsibly. It is you who is misbehaving,' I yelled at her again.

Suddenly she slapped me hard across the face.

'What is there to be afraid of?' she asked looking fiercely into my eyes. 'I'm a seventy-six-year-old woman. I have nothing to lose.'

We both fell silent. I was furious with her. This was pure madness, putting her life in danger. My face was smarting like hell.

'You can't expect me to follow in your footsteps,' I said.

'Well, I'll leave that to your own conscience,' she said. 'One last thing. When I die I want to be buried near my husband. That way I'll be close to your mum too. I have it all arranged. You won't have to do a thing.'

She walked to her bedroom and shut the door behind her.

We never discussed politics after that day and I never questioned Mâdar about her activities. But I began to notice the phone calls, and every time someone called the conversations seemed a little strange in some way.

A few weeks later Kami called from the States. I was excited to hear from him. I asked if it was true that he wanted to return home. I was shocked to learn that it was. In fact, that's why he had called: did I want anything from America? We always worried that telephone conversations were listened to, especially the international ones, so I couldn't say much. I just told him that I was disappointed that he had decided to return. All he said was, 'You don't understand.'

A few days before he arrived I met up with Parastou who informed me that Kami had continued his political activities in the US. We couldn't understand why a political activist would want to return to Iran at a time when the regime executed its opponents every day.

Kami was due to arrive on an early flight and Mr and Mrs Vaziri went to the airport to pick him up. Parastou and I decided to give him a day with his parents before visiting him, but later on that day I called the Vaziris just to say hello. There was no answer. Minutes after I put the phone down Parastou rang to see if I had spoken to Kami. We both thought it was odd not to have heard from him. Parastou had been calling the Vaziris all day but no one had answered; she assumed their phone was out of order.

The following day I rang again and there was still no reply. I called Parastou who said she was about to go to the Vaziris' house. I told her to wait for me so that we could go together. I took a cab, picked up Parastou, then went to the Vaziris. As our taxi approached their house, we saw them pulling up in their car. Mrs Vaziri looked exhausted and devastated. On seeing the two of us she burst into tears. We knew then that something was very wrong.

Mrs Vaziri held on to Parastou and kept saying something about Kami, but we couldn't make any sense of it. Mr Vaziri got out of the car and ushered us all inside. It turned out that they hadn't seen Kamran at all. He had been arrested at Mehrabad Airport as soon as he got off the plane. Their plea to the Revolutionary Guard got them nowhere. Eventually, after more than eight hours, they were told that he had been transferred for questioning.

I was angry with Kami. He should have known better than to come back. Mr and Mrs Vaziri had spent the entire morning driving from one Revolutionary Guard comité in the city to another searching in vain for their son. Mrs Vaziri was beside herself. Parastou tried to calm her down while I discussed various plans of action with Kami's father.

I decided not to tell Mâdar anything, but she knew there was something on my mind. I don't think I fooled her when I said it was because I missed Armineh.

Ten days passed and there was still no news of Kami. Mr and

Mrs Vaziri looked drained and ill. Parastou and I were in touch with them daily and visited them every other day. We were there when Mrs Vaziri received a phone call.

'Yes, Kamran is my son,' she said into the receiver.

Suddenly Mrs Vaziri's worried face broke into a smile and she assured whomever she was talking to that she would be there in less than an hour. Kami's father was at work, so as soon as she put the phone down she called him to say that she would be collecting Kami in an hour.

Mrs Vaziri was ecstatic. She ran about the house hugging and kissing us.

'It's a good omen that you are both here. Come with me. Let's jump in the car and go fetch him. I can't wait to see my baby after all these years.'

Parastou and I both gave a sigh of relief. Mrs Vaziri put on her black manteau and headscarf and we rushed to the car. I was a bit sceptical. Kami's mum had not really told us anything about the telephone conversation.

'So where are we going?' I asked. 'Where is Kamran? Where had they taken him?'

'We are going to Evin,' Mrs Vaziri said.

'Evin!' Parastou said in disbelief.

'Evin?' I repeated. 'Oh, my God! Are you serious? Is that where we're going? Is that where Kami has been all this time?' The palms of my hands started to sweat.

Parastou turned to me and I could see the fear in her eyes.

'Yes, we are going to Evin,' Mrs Vaziri repeated, confirming our fear. 'That's where the phone call was from.' There was hint of nervousness in Mrs Vaziri's voice. 'The man asked me to report to the chief prison officer who will let us collect him. They also said that we had to sign a few papers. Standard formalities, I expect.'

Evin was a notorious prison situated in the foothills of the Alborz where the Islamic regime tortured and executed political opponents. The fact that Kami had been under arrest in such a place made me very uneasy. I didn't dare ask any more questions. I just got more nervous the closer we got to the prison. That day was the only time I was glad of Tehran's heavy traffic.

During our drive up to north-west Tehran, I kept wondering what they had done to Kami. What had been his crime that he ended up in that nest of evil? We had all heard so much about the atrocities taking place at Evin. Since the revolution the prison had expanded below ground and into the hills behind it. The human rights violations taking place in the prison had been leaked to the international media and had shocked the world.

I was snapped out of my awful thoughts by Parastou shouting, 'Hey! Where are you? I was saying that it's good to have a man with us. You know how they are. They ignore women and don't look us in the eye when they speak. It really pisses me off.'

All I could do was give her a weak smile. I was filled with trepidation and couldn't say a word.

'You know what I'm talking about,' Parastou continued, 'the types who are so Hezbollahi they can't even look at women without thinking it's a sin.'

'Yes, yes, I know the type you're talking about.' I had raised my voice unintentionally. 'The ones who rape the virgin girls they arrest to make sure the girls won't end up in heaven, because they believe only the virgin ones would. Those are the ones you are talking about, no?'

Mrs Vaziri frowned at me in the rear-view mirror. I was ruining her happy day, but like an erupted volcano, my abhorrence of the regime had exploded and was pouring out of me. I just couldn't stop myself.

'They are the same guys who rape the boys they arrest and lash, torture and amputate them,' I went on bitterly.

Suddenly Mrs Vaziri shouted, 'Okay, okay! Enough! We've got the message.'

Parastou stared at me in silence. Kami's mum, angry with me, began cursing other drivers for their bad driving.

There was something in what Mrs Vaziri had told us, something in the phrase she used, that just didn't sound right. We had promised to call Mr Vaziri as soon as we'd collected Kami. He hadn't told his colleagues that his son had been arrested, as it would have created problems for him at work. Mrs Vaziri was not happy about going to Evin without her husband, but she had no choice.

We parked the car not far from the prison's main gate. As we walked towards the place where visitors had to register, I felt my legs tremble. I thought I was going to be sick. We joined a short queue along a wall. Every fifteen to twenty minutes the gates opened and they let the next person in. Eventually it was our turn, but when the gate opened we were not let in. We waited another few minutes wondering what was happening. Mrs Vaziri pressed the buzzer insistently. Seconds later a small shutter on the gate opened. An eye peered through and a voice asked us what business we had.

'My name is Vaziri. We received a call telling us to come and collect my son.' Mrs Vaziri's voice could hardly be heard. She didn't want others in the queue behind us to hear her name. 'Kamran is his name. Kamran Vaz—'

The shutter slammed in her face before she finished. We waited for a few minutes and nothing happened. The queue behind us was getting longer. The others, mostly women covered in a black chador or in a dark Islamic manteau and headscarf, had come to fetch or enquire about their loved ones. I had heard there were no visiting hours at Evin.

'Where did he go?' asked Mrs Vaziri looking nervously at Parastou and me.

She rang the buzzer again and banged her fist on the gate. I tried to stop her but she wouldn't listen. The walls were high and had barbed wire stretched along the top. Revolutionary Guards were at their posts on the watchtowers.

The little shutter opened again and what seemed to be the same eye appeared, asking what business we had. Mrs Vaziri repeated herself.

'You are the same woman, no?' the eye asked abruptly.

'Well, yes.' Mrs Vaziri replied. 'But you—'

'Wait!' shouted the eye.

We waited another ten minutes. I looked around and noticed the shops across the road. They must be owned by the Pasdars – the Revolutionary Guards – I thought. They must have said to themselves, 'Let's open a couple of shops here to sell food and drink while the families are kept queuing for hours under the scorching summer sun and the bitter cold winters.' Who else could possibly want to set up business in such a desperate place? About fifty yards from where we were standing I noticed a piece of blue-and-white-striped cloth caught in the barbed wire on top of the wall, fluttering in the breeze. Was it just a piece of cloth brought by the wind, or was it all that remained of a prisoner who had attempted to escape? I felt like I was on a movie set. As we discovered years later, Evin was no better than the Nazi concentration camps of the Second World War. Had the world learned nothing from Auschwitz?

Suddenly the gate opened and we were ushered inside. I will never forget the sound of the door slamming behind us. Anything could have happened to us in there and nobody would ever have known. Within the walls of Evin we weren't even a number.

A scruffy Revolutionary Guard in his early forties took us into a waiting room in the courtyard. The smell of sweat made me gag and I tried to cover my nose as discreetly as I could. The walls were bare, except for a poster of Khomeini whose evil gaze never left us. There we waited for another half an hour. Our anxiety levels were sky-high by this time. I retreated into my own thoughts once again while Mrs Vaziri and Parastou whispered to one another. As I sat on a metal chair a few seats away from them I thought of all those who, at that very moment, were being tortured. I began checking my watch every few minutes. I just wanted to get out of there as quickly as possible. The longer we waited, the more panic-stricken I felt.

At last the door flew open and three armed guards walked into the room. A breeze followed them in, and, with it, a few dried leaves – pale yellow and orange – swept inside dancing around their feet. I focused on the leaves until they settled in a corner.

Parastou and Mrs Vaziri had risen to their feet. My chair fell over as I nervously got up; the noise echoed around the room. Parastou fussed at her scarf, making sure it covered all her hair properly. Another two guards walked in. They were carrying a long, dark green bag, which they dumped at our feet. We all stared at this six-foot long bag in front of us. None of us moved or said a word.

'Here you are!' said a chubby man with a dirty beard. 'Here is your son to collect. You need to sign some papers and cover the costs.'

I managed to move fast enough to catch Mrs Vaziri as she fainted. Parastou screamed and threw herself on the body lying in the bag at our feet. The guards left, locking the door behind them. Parastou began throwing the chairs around, screaming and cursing. She had ripped her manteau. She looked like a wild beast, injured and trapped in a cage.

My head was spinning. The body of my best friend was in a bag on the floor, his mother had passed-out in my arms and Parastou had gone completely berserk. I couldn't understand what she was saying. What was I supposed to do? What was expected of me? I let her scream and shout in the hope that her rage would subside.

Now I understood why I had thought there was something wrong from the beginning. Mrs Vaziri had not been told to come and get her son, but to 'collect' him, as you do when you collect a parcel from the post office. That was what Kami had become – a parcel to be collected.

I was worried for Mrs Vaziri. I didn't know what to do. She seemed to be trembling; soon I realised it wasn't her who was shaking but me. I noticed a tap in the corner of the room. There was no sink under the tap, just a hole in the ground for the water to pass through. A copper goblet was tied to the pipe with a piece of dirty yellowish string. I dragged Mrs Vaziri across the hard floor to the tap and splashed water on her face. Her scarf fell back and her hair got wet. By this time Parastou was weeping over Kami, stroking the smooth surface of the body bag.

I couldn't say how long we were there when the door flew open again. The guards entered the room and one of them yelled at us.

Parastou, suddenly engulfed by anger, got up and rushed towards the guard pummelling him with her fists and screaming, 'You filthy murderers.'

I was terrified and shouted at her to stop it unless she wanted to be killed too.

Another Pasdar turned to me, laughing, and said, 'Who is going to dirty his hands on a whore like her?' He turned to Parastou and slapped her so hard she fell to the ground and her scarf fell off. 'Cover your hair, you bitch.'

'Get up, get up, you fucking bitch. We have a lot to do.' Another Pasdar kicked the scarf towards her. 'Cover yourself.'

'Yeah, you seem very busy,' Parastou shouted back. 'How many more are you killing today? Is that why you are in such a rush?' Her eyes were red; she looked like a wild dog ready to rip everyone apart.

'Shut up, Parastou! Just shut your big mouth!' I yelled at her.

Just then, Mrs Vaziri moaned and started to come round.

One of the Pasdars walked to the corner of the room, picked up a chair Parastou had thrown earlier and placed it behind the desk. He spread some papers out in front of him and told me to sign the documents. No one asked me who I was. I presumed they thought I was another son. I gestured to Parastou to come over and hold Mrs Vaziri. I felt nothing. I was on autopilot. I wished Mr Vaziri was there, but he wasn't, so it was up to me to do his job and take responsibility in this awful situation. The papers claimed that Kami had been executed on the charge of 'spreading vice on earth and acting against God and the revolution'.

I told the guard that I needed to see the body.

He called to one of the other guards. 'Unzip the bag for him to see it.'

I motioned for Parastou to shield Mrs Vaziri from the sight. I thought it would be better if she remembered her son as he had looked when he was alive. The Pasdar pulled down the zip and stopped just below Kami's throat. Some blood had dried on the side of his head and his cheek. I have never been able to describe how I felt at that moment. I did not even feel hatred towards the guards. I looked at them, searched in their eyes. There was nothing, no sign of life. I turned to Parastou and Mrs Vaziri. They were weeping in each other's arms. I wanted to see more than his face. I pulled the zip further down. One of the guards made an attempt to stop me, but his superior told him to leave me be.

'Let him see it. It will only teach the living a lesson, a lesson that they cannot mess around with the Islamic Republic,' he said.

I wanted to witness for myself what they did to the people of this country. I pulled the zip all the way down. I knew that what I was about to see was going to be hard to stomach, but I had to see it with my own eyes. Even if we do eventually forgive them, it would be a crime to forget, I thought.

Kami's slim body was covered with bruises and cuts. His thighs and groin were dark purple. The tips of his fingers and toes had been burnt and a few of his nails were missing. A bullet had ripped through his heart and the coup de grâce had left a hole above his left eyebrow. I grabbed his cold body in my arms but I didn't want to show any weakness in the face of their cruelty. I couldn't have cried even if I'd wanted to. But I couldn't suppress my anger any longer.

'You fucking bastards!' I screamed.

I felt a blow to my side that sent me sprawling. The other guard shouted at me to get up and finish off the paperwork. I caressed Kami's face before pulling the zip up.

The man in charge told me that I had to cover the cost of the bullets. Robotlike, I just followed the instructions. It was common knowledge that they charged families for the bullets used to shoot their children, so it didn't come as a surprise. Thank God I had enough cash with me. They wouldn't have let us take the body without payment and they only accepted cash. We were being charged by the murderous regime for delivering such first-class services as killing our loved ones.

Once the formalities were over I was told to drive straight to the designated cemetery without stopping anywhere. Plain-clothes police would be following us to make sure we found our way. We were all aware of its whereabouts. La'nat Abad, the Land of the Damned, was the name given to a cemetery the Islamic authorities had built where political prisoners were thrown into ditches; they had no burial rights. They were considered to be non-Muslim and therefore did not deserve any respect.

Before we set off I told them that the deceased's father needed to be informed in order to join us at the cemetery. They took me to a small room to phone Mr Vaziri while Mrs Vaziri and Parastou waited in the car. When I rang Mr Vaziri's office I asked to speak to one of his colleagues. Mrs Vaziri insisted that I let a colleague who happened to be a close family friend tell him. I felt sorry for this man who had such a heavy responsibility. Mr Amini was crying himself as he promised to drive Kami's dad to the cemetery.

At the cemetery of the Damned there were rows upon rows of heaped earth as far as the eye could see. No names, no clues, nothing. The only information provided to the families was a little metal plaque giving the row numbers. It looked like furrowed, ploughed farmland. We were met by a few dusty-looking Revolutionary Guards. The reward for their services to the revolution was to bury the executed. All day long they buried the dead without emotion; nor did they question why there should be so many.

The broken Mrs Vaziri, supported by Parastou, followed the two Pasdars who carried Kami's body to the edge of a newly dug furrow. I heard a car pull up behind the cemetery wall as we walked with Kami to his final resting place. I looked over and saw his dad wailing and stumbling towards us. The sight of this once-proud man in such pain broke my heart. I choked back my tears.

The burial did not take more than ten minutes. The lack of any form of ritual for the dead made it look more like we were dumping garbage into a dumpster. No ceremony, no burial ritual, nothing. Kami's body was thrown into the ditch, soil was pushed over it, and that was that.

Crying wasn't allowed at mass graves. We had been warned when we arrived to take our mourning home. But Mr and Mrs Vaziri didn't care about any of that, so on their knees they cried and held on to each other. Parastou stood by my side, sobbing with her head buried in her hands. After a little while I helped the Vaziris to their feet and we walked back to the cars. There was another family at the entrance begging the guards to let them in. They didn't have a body with them, so I assumed they had come to visit a grave, but the guards would not help them.

Mr Amini offered to drive me and Parastou home while the Vaziris left in their own car. As we got into the car I noticed that the two women we had just passed at the gates were now sitting in their black chadors on the dusty ground behind the gates weeping. The man with them stood leaning his forehead against the metal railings of the gate. There was a young girl with them, three or four years old who, too young to understand what was going on, walked around by herself, holding on to her headless doll. That scene has stayed with me to this day.

Mr Amini dropped Parastou off first and I asked him to drop me by Pars Hospital. I couldn't face Mâdar yet. I needed some space and fresh air. As I wandered the streets I came to a restaurant. I hadn't eaten anything all day. Lunch had been a cold dish of death seasoned with hatred. The restaurant was busy, but I paid no attention to anyone else as I sat at a table. I was in a daze. Chatter was just white noise passing through my head. I hardly touched my dinner and after some time I left.

The image of Kami's body kept flashing up in my mind. I missed all my friends beyond imagination, but thinking about them – all of them, wherever they were – was like taking a painkiller to soothe my pains; it lifted my spirits and raised my hopes for the future. I kept thinking about what Armineh might be doing right that moment in London or what the weather might be like where Kasra was.

Mâdar was asleep when I returned home, so I slipped into my room as quickly and quietly as possible. I had to be up early in the morning to attend my classes at the language centre, but I wished I didn't have to go.

I managed to keep the news about Kami from Mâdar. Parastou and I went to the Vaziris' house every day, despite the danger it entailed; we didn't care if their house was kept under surveillance or not.

The families of the deceased were not allowed to mourn in public or hold receptions at mosques or elsewhere. On the seventh day of mourning, Shiite Muslims usually hold a reception in honour of the deceased. Instead, the Vaziris had a few friends and relatives over to pay their respects. It was a very small, sombre gathering.

'I'm sorry that Mâdar has neither visited nor called you,' I said to Mrs Vaziri. I confessed that I had not told her about Kami's murder.

'Oh, God,' Parastou said, 'she doesn't need to know. It would only upset her. When she asks you about Kami, tell her he changed his mind about coming back to Iran.'

'Parastou is right, Pedram. Let her believe that Kami is still in America,' said Mrs Vaziri wiping her eyes. 'It isn't safe to be here anyway. They may be making a list of whoever comes. Perhaps you shouldn't be here either.' She put her hand on my shoulder. 'The last thing we want is to cause problems for you or Mâdar. You have already done so much for us.'

'Will you stop it! Please! Do you think if she finds out she would be worried about security?'

'But still, don't tell her.' Mrs Vaziri broke into tears again.

I held her in my arms and we cried together. While she shed tears on my shoulder she told me how much she would have loved to have seen her son get married, to have grandchildren and for him to carry on the family name.

'Now they have killed our family too,' she said.

During the Second World War many were aware of the existence of the Nazi concentration camps and the horrors that took place in them. In the Islamic Republic, too, we knew of the torture and the daily executions that took place, but unlike the genocide of the Nazi period, the international community ignored ours.

The War in the Oil Fields

Iraq invades Iran, putting the West's oil and the hostages at risk, and the big powers stay neutral.

Newsweek, October 1980

Chapter Sixteen

'We are all in the gutter, but some of us are looking at the stars.' Oscar Wilde would have reminded us of this had he been alive and witnessing the situation in Iran after the revolution.

I wouldn't have disagreed with him either. We were all in the gutter, but some of us didn't lose hope and kept looking up at the stars. I can't say that I was one of them. They believed, while I hoped, that eventually a day would come when the powerful rays of the rising Iranian sun would vanquish the long and painful night.

The end of September 1980 brought another disaster that consolidated the regime and made sure its roots took hold. The Iraqi dictator, Saddam Hussein, believed that, with the execution of most of our generals, our armed forces would be in disarray and that therefore it would be a good time for him to take over the oil-rich province of Khouzestan. He had dreamt of its annexation for years. Iraqi aircraft made the first attacks on major Iranian airports and oil installations on 22nd September 1980. Every day, major cities in western Iran, particularly Abadan and Khorramshahr, were pounded by Iraqi gunfire.

A few days into the war, Mâdar asked me to come to the sitting room. There was a broadcast on an opposition group's radio station in which they read out a message from the Shah's Private Secretariat. Our young Shah had sent a letter to the Islamic regime, offering to serve as a fighter pilot in the war against Iraq. We both felt proud and astonished by such a show of solidarity and patriotism. The news gave Mâdar another opportunity to remind me of my duties towards Iran and our new king.

Of course, the war provided the regime with an excuse to prosecute anyone who stood against it on the charge of collaborating with the enemy and standing against the Islamic Revolution. The Kurdish population, which had risen against the tyranny of the mullahs, were massacred in their villages by the regime's henchmen. The Islamic government also hired mercenaries to carry out assassinations throughout the world against Iranians who had joined opposition groups planning to bring about a counter-revolution. Our youth, who only two years earlier had been considered the country's future, were sent to their deaths on battlefields stretched along our Western fronts.

In the midst of all this Armineh and I stayed in touch. After the initial hardship of settling into a foreign country she had passed her bar exam and could now practice law in England. She had started work at a reputable law firm in the City of London and she was very excited. One of her concerns after the revolution had been that under an Islamic regime she might not be able, as a woman, to become a lawyer. Her fear was by no means baseless. Since the Islamic Republic had been established, women had become second-class citizens; for instance, the testimony of two women was needed in court to equal that of a man. In England, Armineh could live her life the way she wanted. I couldn't help but feel happy for her. She kept trying to persuade me to leave Iran and come to London, an idea that with every passing day became more appealing. She was not the only one urging me to leave Iran. Soon after the war began Kasra, now reunited with his family, wrote to me, begging me to consider leaving the country. In his affectionate letters he suggested he would do anything to get me to Australia. My only problem was Mâdar. The borders had opened again by then and the government had started issuing new passports, but not everyone was allowed to leave the country. Those who were permitted to leave were either regime officials, patients with recommendations from their doctors, or merchants with strong ties to the ruling clergy.

In the latter part of the seventies, when Iran's foreign assets and our economy had grown more quickly than any other developing country in the world, our citizens were welcomed and respected around the globe with no visa requirements. Presenting an imperial Iranian passport at any border had earned the bearer a welcoming smile and respect. Now, those once-proud citizens were queuing in their hundreds outside foreign embassies in Tehran or in the provincial capitals, camping in tents like desperate refugees. Many people had already left the country, through either legal or illegal channels, and for the first time in our history, Iranians were forming Persian communities in major European and American cities. The concern of most families, however, was for their eldest sons, especially if they were of conscription age.

Economic hardship, partly due to the sanctions imposed by the West and the ongoing war with Iraq, but mostly due to the ineptitude of those in charge, promoted to positions of power purely for their religious or revolutionary merits, brought shortages of everyday necessities. Basic living conditions around the time the war began went from bad to worse. Every day we wondered if it could get any worse, and with each passing day it did.

This was not a war in which national identity or sovereignty was at stake; it was a pointless war of revenge between two mad men. Inflation went through the roof and unemployment was rife. Poverty, which the ayatollahs had claimed to eradicate, reached new heights. Tens of thousands of Khouzestanis and others from the Western provinces bordering Iraq escaped their homes as the Iraqi army advanced. The war refugees from these provinces crowded cities in other parts of the country, cities that were already suffering daily Iraqi bombardments and numerous domestic shortages. Hospitals, clinics and medical centres throughout the country were inundated, with fresh casualties brought in daily.

The leaders of the Islamic Republic, who up to then had accused the Shah of wasting money buying the latest military technology and equipment, what they called 'useless metal scraps', admitted they were lucky to have inherited large quantities of first-class weapons and trained personnel. Despite the execution of most of our high-ranking officers, the Iranian army managed to hold its own against the Arab invaders and eventually push them back.

Ayatollah Khomeini, who had lived in exile in Iraq for fifteen years under the watchful eyes of Saddam Hussein, considered this the time for revenge and vengeance, and an opportunity to spread his Islamic Revolution to other Islamic countries in the region.

In a televised broadcast to the nation he stated: 'Islam and the revolution need more blood. Therefore, this war is a blessing, sent to us by God to irrigate the fields of Islam. Our people, especially the young ones, are welcoming martyrdom with open arms. More blood has to be shed.'

I watched his speech with Mâdar.

'Do you see the difference, Pedram?' she asked. 'The Shah used to say that every Iranian family should be able to afford a car, at least a Paykan, but the new leader is saying that each Iranian family must have a martyr.'

Every day the cities fell into darkness as soon as the sun set. No shops opened after dark since the war. Restaurants, cabarets, bars and casinos had all been banned; cinemas showed only censored films, mostly about war and misery. We were given instructions on the radio on how to recognise different sirens. 'Red, sounding like this … is to announce an immediate air raid. White … indicates an all-clear and you may come out of your shelters.'

'But what shelters?' everyone asked. Not everyone had a basement.

Whenever I had a moment to myself I contemplated my future. Financially I had no problems. Even though inflation had made everything more expensive, I still earned enough through teaching to support Mâdar and myself. I was worried that I might be drafted into the army if the war continued, but I never said that aloud. The Iraqis had taken many of our teenagers prisoners of war. In interviews on Iraqi radio, now broadcasting daily programmes in Persian, those kids cried and told their families that they missed and loved them very much. I couldn't bring myself to listen. Every young voice I heard ripped my heart open. They could have been my students. Then I wondered what my students were up to. It was not uncommon to see images on television of boys as young as twelve heading to the front, their task to walk over fields as minesweepers and getting blown-up so that the path was cleared for the army to advance. Many of my students were probably already in the army. I wondered how many of them might already be dead.

I did not allow myself to get involved in political activities or to know any of the people that Mâdar associated with. Since my return from Tabriz, I paid frequent visits to the bookshops in Shahreza Avenue – now called Revolution Avenue – where I used to go when I was a student at the university. But their stock of books was rapidly drying up as they weren't allowed to import foreign books. Parastou and I spent many hours together sitting on a couch in her bedroom talking about the future and reminiscing about our past. She kept running her fingers through her hair and looking out of the window. There was a spectacular view of the city from their house. You could see parts of Tehran through tall conifers that had grown over the years along the walls of the garden. I had noticed that recently many of us, myself included, spent a lot of time looking into the distance, as if with our present so unbearable and the past gone, we were searching the horizon for a better future. Mâdar did it more than anyone else I knew.

From the outset, the regime had targeted our Persian heritage, especially the Nowruz, trying to undermine it. But their tactics backfired and by the second year of their Islamic Republic we had forced the new authorities to respect it, even celebrate it with us. Little by little we learned how to live our new lives. Gradually the term *taghooti* with its negative connotations became a word that referred to anything good and modern, and we adopted it with pride.

One grey morning, when Tehran seemed more polluted than ever, I was queuing for a prescription for Mâdar next door at Pars Hospital when I saw a familiar face. I had to queue for over an hour before I got served. Drug shortages had meant empty shelves in most pharmacies, but luckily I had had no problem getting her arthritis medicine. As soon as I got the medication, I approached the lady. Dressed in a manteau and a matching headscarf she looked older than I remembered her.

'Hello,' I said, smiling.

Looking curiously at me at first, she suddenly said, 'Oh, my God, you haven't changed a bit! What are you doing here?' She forgot that we were in public and threw her arms around me and kissed me on the face. 'I am so happy to see you.'

Everyone was staring.

Holding my elbow, Simin guided me out of the hospital.

Come on, let's go and sit somewhere and catch-up. How long has it been? Five, six years maybe? You don't know how happy this makes me. It's been such a long time.'

'What are you doing here? In Tehran, I mean?' I asked.

'I live here!' she replied as we walked out of the hospital and into the front yard.

An ambulance pulled up and the ER nurses, dressed head-to-toe in white and looking like ghosts, pulled a stretcher out of the vehicle. We both stood watching them in action, paying more attention to the nurses' impractical Islamic uniform than to the patient on the stretcher.

'After my husband and I separated I decided to leave Tabriz,' she said. She looked at her watch. 'What are you doing here? Are you on holiday?'

'No, I live here too.' I pointed up to Saman Towers behind me. 'I'm back in Tehran living with my grandmother again.'

She gave me a satisfied smile. 'Listen, why don't we go and get something to eat. There's so much to catch up on.'

'Well, it would make more sense if you came up to the apartment. You can finally meet Mâdar too.'

'So what about your school in Tabriz? Are you teaching here now? Which school are you working at?'

'Yes, I'm teaching here now.' The sight of a mullah going past distracted my attention.

'I had no idea!' She touched my elbow, which shifted my focus from the clergy back to her.

'Yes, the school that I loved so much couldn't reciprocate, so I was "cleared out", as it's fashionable to say nowadays.'

Simin didn't come up that day after all, but she gave me her telephone number and made me promise to get in touch.

Gangs forming what was called the 'Morality Police' were roaming the streets of our cities, arresting young and old, men and women for not behaving according to their interpretation of Islamic code. Parastou was arrested on charges of not abiding by the Islamic dress code – she was wearing make-up and her scarf had slipped back, showing part of her hair. As a result she received eighty lashes. Religion was destroying the nation and, little by little, people had begun policing their own behaviour and checking themselves to make sure they weren't crossing any lines. But the lines were forever shifting and it wasn't easy to stay on the right side of them.

My solution to coping with this new life was to escape the city. I sought refuge in the valleys and mountains high above Tehran. I would sit under a rock reading a book, looking down on the city in disappointment. I had become so distant from its inhabitants that I couldn't connect with anyone. I was an alien, a feeling that many of us shared. When I was not teaching, I was not socialising either. Occasionally I met with Parastou and we spent most of the time indoors, sitting in silence or listening to pop music from the 'old' days. There wasn't much left to talk about. Persian and Western pop music was banned, the television had no programmes other than religious ones, men and women could not mingle outdoors, sport facilities were segregated (in some provincial cities swimming pools were closed down altogether because men's swimming trunks exposed too much of their bodies), and all cultural centres, bars and clubs had been shut down. Censorship meant that we had no access to the free world except through radio.

Almost two years after Kami's execution, a hole under a rock just a few feet wide on a mountain path above Tehran had become my refuge, a place I could run away to and meditate, read and just be alone. In the many hours that I spent there, a question I asked myself day after day, month after month was a simple one: why? Why did we let this happen to us? To this day I still have no answer.

Oscar Wilde was not the only notable figure I wished could visit Iran at that time. Sitting under my rock looking out at the horizon, I wondered what Nietzsche would have made of it. I think he would have agreed with me that God was truly dead in Iran. The kind and compassionate faith we had been taught and brought up with had been replaced with a brand of Islam none of us recognised and that was terrorising the world, including other Islamic societies.

* * *

I had a few weeks off in July, so I decided to take a trip to Tabriz to catch-up with Gilda and Vartan; I was also keen to get together with my Three Musketeers. I asked Mâdar if she wanted to accompany me, but she turned down my offer, saying that her days of travelling were well over.

By this time she spent most of her days at home and hardly left the apartment. I was worried about her but there was nothing I could do. Feeling lost, demoralised and defeated was how most of us felt, but for her it must have been worse. She had fought in every way possible all her life to uphold the values of women's rights in our country. Now, after all those years of hard work, she was being forced to regress and live under a medieval reactionary regime.

I made the trip to Tabriz, not knowing it would be my last. On the plane I read an article in a state newspaper that gloated about the execution of three teenage homosexuals. Looking at the images of their lifeless bodies hanging from cranes, I could not believe that people had gathered to watch as if it was a form of entertainment.

Vartan picked me up from Tabriz Airport in his old, and now rusting, BMW; the smell of the car brought back so many memories. It was good to see him. We drove to his apartment where Gilda welcomed me at the door. She had prepared a delicious Armenian dish and served it with an even better red wine.

'Wine! I have not seen a glass of wine for years,' I exclaimed.

'Well, you only have yourself to blame,' said Gilda. 'If you visited us more often, you could drink the wine we produce behind closed doors.'

That night I guzzled wine by the bottle and enjoyed a heady night of reminiscence, good conversation and … fun. It had been a long time since any of us had had some fun.

I woke up the next day with a foggy head but with plans to visit Babak, one of my Three Musketeers. I hadn't kept in touch with them but I hoped they were still in Tabriz. All three would have graduated from high school two years previously, but with universities about to reopen, I hoped they had managed to pass all their exams and were able to attend university. The government insisted that all students applying to university had to sit entrance exams, mostly on religious doctrine.

I arrived at Babak's and rang the bell. His younger brother answered the door and asked me who I was. His mother appeared behind him and, immediately recognising me, invited me in. It seemed no one else was at home, so I asked about Babak. Instead of answering my question she invited me to sit and told her son to get us some tea. In the sitting room a large black-and-white photograph of Babak on a shelf attracted my attention. His mother asked me how I have been and what I have been doing. I answered her questions quickly, then asked about Babak again. She lowered her face and I could see the tears rolling down her cheeks.

I immediately knew it was bad news. But it was worse than I could possibly have imagined. Babak, Mehran and my diplomat Iraj – all three of my musketeers – were dead. I had read somewhere that what does not kill us makes us stronger, but was it true? No matter where I went I seemed to walk into a disaster zone.

Babak, Mehran and Iraj had been conscripted together and were even sent to the front together. Babak was shot by the Iraqis; the other two were blown-up by mines. I didn't want to hear any more. Though Babak's mother was still speaking I couldn't hear her. I had stepped into another world, a world where my three best students, my Three Musketeers, were still alive and talking about their dreams. I felt agitated; I needed fresh air. I couldn't take it any longer. I got up while she was still talking, sharing her pain, and said, 'I have to go.'

She looked at me, puzzled and hurt by my sudden announcement.

'I need to see them,' I said.

She could see the distress and anxiety in my eyes. 'They are buried at Vadi Rahmat cemetery,' she said and gave me the address.

She asked if I'd like her to come with me to the cemetery – she was following me to the front door – but I told her I wanted to be alone.

Tears rolled down my face as I gave her a hug, and I kept crying as I walked back towards the city centre. I hated everyone who passed me on the pavement. The sound of muezzins suddenly rose from a newly built mosque nearby; it sent a shiver down my spine. I couldn't face a living soul, so where better to go than a cemetery. I yelled at the first cab I saw and asked the driver to take me to Vadi Rahmat. Less than half an hour later he dropped me in front of the gates.

'Shall I wait for you, sir?' he asked politely. He could see I was in a right state.

I shook my head and paid him. He headed back towards the city.

I took a deep breath and walked through the gates into what felt like a very quiet classroom. No one else was there. I went straight to the row and the plots where the boys were resting in peace. They were all together in death, as in life.

I fell to my knees and prostrated myself in front of their headstones. I wanted to grab them and hug them all. I called their names and shouted in anger.

'We need you, Iraj,' I said, running my fingers over his name on the headstone. 'My diplomat was not supposed to be killed in a war.'

'I'm sorry for having told you to be quiet in class,' I said to the headstones. 'I'd do anything for you to be able to speak now. Please, boys, my musketeers, speak up, speak to me. Ask me questions, please.'

I lost all sense of time and place. I must have been there for quite a while because when I next became aware of myself it was getting dark. An old man approached me and, seeing me in such a state, gently helped me up to my feet. He had to close the gates. He reminded me so much of Mossayyeb, the old, faithful cucumber seller across the alley from where we had lived in Tehran a lifetime ago.

'You should not upset yourself like this,' he said as we walked to the gates. 'Are those martyrs your friends or your brothers?'

I had come to hate that word, which once was held in high esteem. Martyred for nothing, I thought. I told him that they were my dearest students.

He shook his head. 'It must be very painful for you,' he said, holding on to my right arm. 'I'm touched to see there are still people out there like you – people who care.'

He took some tissues out of his pocket and gave them to me. I wiped my face and thanked him. I left the cemetery and crossed the road. I could hear the gates closing behind me and the old man put what sounded like a thick chain on the gates to keep them secure.

'Listen, my son,' he called after me, 'you're still young. Don't end up where your students are. Leave this country. Go!'

'Go?' I said quietly.

I turned around and walked back to the cemetery.

'Go where?' I asked him through the bars of the gate, desperation and frustration in my voice. 'Is there anywhere I can go to heal my pain?'

'Wounds will heal, my son. What will never vanish are the scars left on our souls. No matter where you go the memories will always be with you. But trust me, in time it will get easier. Little by little you will only remember the happy days that we once had.'

'You can't be serious? Do you have any idea what I've been through?'

I sounded arrogant, as if I was mocking his life. How could I say such a thing when I didn't know what he had been through. I quickly apologised. Then he opened his hands and showed me his palms. The thick skin and the cracks resembled a desert denied water for years.

'You see these hands, young man? They have washed so many men. They have buried so many young bodies. This place has grown tenfold in size since the coming of those who kill in the name of God. Just leave and go anywhere else, but don't stay here.'

'It's my country. It's my home,' I said, looking at the ground.

'I don't see a ring on your finger,' he said. 'It's easier for you to leave. Nobody knows what is going on here. You must leave in order to tell the world.'

I took his dried hands in mine and kissed them out of respect. Then I walked away.

I had visited Tabriz to find life; all I saw was death.

Plight of Iranians

Mr Gerald Kaufman, MP for Ardwick (Labour), speaking in the House of Commons, said: 'It is estimated that there are over 40,000 people in prison in Iran. In the six months after June, 1981 more than 2,500 people are known to have been executed; this is the number of announced executions, and it is believed that the true number is thousands more than this.'

The Times, July 1982

Chapter Seventeen

'I WANT TO GO BACK to Tehran today,' I said to Gilda and Vartan the next day.

'Why?' Gilda asked. 'You've only just arrived!'

'Come on, Pedram, I was hoping we could go out together. Stay at least for a few days,' Vartan said.

'We have to at least take you to Ararat,' Gilda said.

They won me round. Spending time with them was the best remedy, even though I was hardly in a mood to socialise. So I stayed for another day.

At the Armenian Youth Club I met a few old friends and we chatted and drank coffee together. Once they left I opened my heart to Gilda and Vartan and told them of what had happened the day before. They had heard a lot about my Three Musketeers; Gilda had even met them once. She began crying. I put my arm around her and we both shed tears. Vartan did his best to cheer us up but thoughts of my musketeers weighed me down. I found it such an effort to make conversation after that. I was glad I'd decided to leave the following day – every street in Tabriz seemed to remind me of Mehran, Babak and Iraj.

Next day, I took the last flight back to Tehran and I arrived just before it got dark. When I saw how exhausted Mâdar looked I decided not to tell her about my Three Musketeers.

The following morning I had nothing planned. I had a few more weeks of holiday remaining and had no private tuition to arrange. I got out of bed, had a shower and prepared breakfast before waking Mâdar up. She usually woke up earlier than me, but as she had been so tired last night I decided to let her rest. A little while later, once I had the breakfast ready, I knocked on her door. She didn't reply, so I went to have breakfast on my own.

About ten o'clock, the phone rang. It was Mrs Vaziri. I hadn't seen or spoken to her for quite a while. She wanted to come over later that day to visit us. I was looking forward to seeing her and I thought Mâdar would like it too. I knocked on Mâdar's bedroom door.

'Mâdar! Wake up!' I said gently, but there was no answer.

I slowly opened the door, but she was still sound asleep. Mrs Vaziri wasn't due to arrive for a while, so I let her sleep on. Meanwhile, I cleared the breakfast table, washed the dishes, tidied the apartment. I looked at the time; it was almost eleven. I changed the sheets on my bed and threw a load of laundry into the washing machine. When I'd finished the chores I knocked on Grandma's bedroom door and walked in.

'Come on, young lady!' I said and grabbed hold of her foot to tickle it. I had used this method to wake her up since I was a child.

But she did not respond. I stood by her side and gently called her. Still no response. Her back was towards me. I shook her gently. Her right arm fell loosely in front of her. I panicked. I rolled her on to her back and shook her vigorously.

'Roudabeh! ... Mâdar ... Oh, my God. No, no, please, God!'

I ran to the phone, but suddenly I couldn't remember any numbers to call. The doorbell rang. I hurried to the door. There stood Mrs Vaziri.

She was pulling her scarf down and about to give me a hug when she realised something was wrong.

'Oh, thank God you're here!' I said in a rush.

'What's the matter?' she asked. 'Are you all right?'

'Mâdar won't wake up.'

She threw her scarf to the side and rushed to the bedroom. I closed the front door and slumped down in the corridor, my back against the wall. Next thing I heard was the sound of Mrs Vaziri's gasp.

Mâdar was gone. My pillar of strength was gone. She was only seventy-eight. She had passed away in her sleep and from the look on her face, she had not suffered. She had slipped into her next life in peace and with dignity.

Her funeral went as smoothly as she had wanted. She had taken care of everything. She had purchased a plot near my parents' grave. Her lawyer revealed to me later that she had left the apartment to me; in order for me not to have the burden of inheritance tax she had changed the deeds to my name a few years ago without my knowledge.

In the days following the funeral I spent a lot of time thinking about Mâdar, going through her photographs, old, fragile, black-and-white images, her life unfolding in front of me like a silent movie. Mrs Vaziri helped me a lot during those tough days; we went through Mâdar's belongings together. Before her burial I had cut off a piece of her hair, which I kept in a small silver box. I wanted it to decorate my Nowruz Haft Sin table every year in order to feel her presence.

A few days after the funeral I rang Armineh. She had always spoken to Mâdar every time we called each other, but right from the beginning of our conversation she knew there was something wrong. I told her the bad news. She cried down the phone and I tried to comfort her.

As the weeks passed and the heartache became more bearable, I found myself, day after day, lying on the floor focusing on a spot on the ceiling. I needed to be truthful with myself. Mâdar was no longer around. I had only myself to look out for. Sometimes the thought was scary and lonely, but at other times it was exhilarating – I was free of responsibility for anyone but myself. I realised I could make decisions for me alone. No one was relying on me; no one had expectations of me.

One afternoon I had a yearning to hear Kasra's voice. Even though it was very late in Sydney, I called him. He was a good listener – kind and thoughtful. He was also challenging and confronting, asking me why I should continue living in Iran now that Mâdar was gone. Once again he suggested helping me reach Australia.

The following day I went to take a walk outside the city and headed up north to my rock. There were not many people on the path and I appreciated the calmness. I had taken with me my old copy of James Baldwin's *Giovanni's Room* to read again, but I could barely focus. I kept thinking about my conversation with Kasra.

For no good reason tears began rolling down my face. I felt so sorry for myself, emotionally destitute; no one in the world was as lonely as I was at that time. I had no one to talk to, no one who understood me. Even I seemed new to myself. What was going on? The Islamic Revolution had taught us how to keep lying to ourselves. But I couldn't do it any longer; it was killing me. It was Kasra I wanted to talk to, not Armineh. It was Australia I wanted to go to, not Britain.

That September the language centre opened for the new academic year and more than ever I looked forward to returning to my classes. They would give me something to focus on, but it became increasingly clear that I could not escape the reality of what was going on around me. I gave one hundred per cent to my students, but I wasn't as motivated as I'd once been. I still took pleasure in teaching, but the language centre and my private students were no match for the way I'd felt about teaching before the revolution.

I convinced myself it was because I was still grieving for Mâdar. I had lost the dearest person in my life, and people around me kept telling me I was handling my loss well. Personally, I thought I had become death-proof. Death had become such a big part of our daily lives that little by little our hearts became immune to it. The death of someone who had died naturally of old age was not considered tragic by anyone.

But there was more going on inside me than I was letting on. By the autumn of 1982, I was no longer a robot ticking a daily to-do list. Something within me had shifted. It all finally clicked one night when I decided to phone Armineh; I had not spoken to her since Mâdar's death. An English guy answered and said he'd tell Armineh I'd called. Forty-five minutes later she called me back.

'I'm so sorry I haven't had time to call you,' she said.

'It's okay, Armineh,' I said. 'Everything is fine. I am okay. I just thought you would tell me when you met someone special in your life.'

A silence fell on the line for what seemed like a long time.

'I don't know what to say. I am so sorry!' She genuinely sounded upset. 'We only met a few weeks ago.'

'It's absolutely fine. Things happen for a reason. Our relationship was always complicated.'

'Not always, Pedram,' she said.

'We have to face reality. We should have done this a long time ago but ...'

As a second silence descended, I felt ashamed. While she thought she had betrayed me, I felt nothing but relief.

'Listen to me, Armineh, you must believe me when I tell you that I wish you all the best that life can offer you, from the bottom of my heart.'

By this time she was sobbing.

'Please stop!' I begged her. 'I get enough of that here. Let's say goodbye like old friends. We will speak again at Christmas.'

That autumn the pain of Mâdar's absence eased a little, but I was so lonely and filled with despair. Yet, I chided myself, I was healthy, I still had a job and a few good friends. Things could be worse.

I pulled myself together, kept my chin up and my head down, and got on with it.

Part III

Iran reopens universities after 3 years

The speaker of the Iranian Parliament said last week that only those young people would be admitted who supported the ideology of the regime.

The Daily Telegraph, December 1982

Chapter Eighteen

I CELEBRATED CHRISTMAS 1982 alone, sitting at my desk looking at Mâdar's picture. Since her death I had turned her bedroom into my study. It was like a Victorian mausoleum with mahogany furniture and dark red walls, which I painted soon after. I removed the curtains so that nothing covered the windows. I could sit behind my desk and look out at the splendid Alborz Mountains. Most of the walls were lined with bookshelves, and in the only empty space I hung an old map of Iran that Mâdar had had since she was a student. I couldn't bring myself to throw away the picture of the imperial couple that Mâdar had kept by her bedside, even though it was dangerous. I also had beautifully framed pictures of Mâdar, my parents, and many of my students, one of which was of the musketeers taken on the day I bumped into them in Shahgoli. For a long time a clock on the wall had been set to London time, so I could imagine what Armineh might be doing. Looking at it made me realise it was time to be honest with myself even if I couldn't be with the remaining few friends I still had in Iran. I shifted the hands of the clock to show Sydney time.

Between Christmas and the New Year I thought of Armineh a lot, but in a totally different way. I still cared about her and hoped we would remain friends. I couldn't help getting nostalgic and remembering the wonderful times I used to share with Armineh and our friends in Tabriz. At the stroke of midnight on New Year's Eve in Sydney – 6.30 p.m. in Tehran – I picked up the phone and dialled Kasra's number.

I couldn't think of any other way to make that moment special. Although 31st December is not celebrated in Iran except among Christian communities, I knew it was a big deal in the rest of the world. When Kasra answered the phone, he sounded really pleased to hear my voice.

'Happy New Year!' I said.

'Oh, my God,' he shouted excitedly. 'Happy New Year to you too.'

'How are you?' I asked, making myself comfortable in the armchair. 'How's life?'

We carried on talking for I don't know how long – definitely more than an hour. His voice, so charged with kindness and caring, uplifted me. Without thinking, I blurted out that I missed him and immediately regretted it. What had I just said? How would he take it?

'Not as much as I've missed you!' he said softly. 'I worry about you, Pedram. You must leave Iran. You've no excuse any more. There is nothing keeping you there.'

'I know.'

'Look! Once you get out, things will make more sense to you. Life is so different out here. Honestly, it's hard to imagine until you experience it for yourself. No one judges you here. You're accepted for who you are. Let me look into it for you,' he said. 'I'll do everything I can to bring you to Australia. I realise this country might not be your first choice but at least you have someone here who can help you.'

It was so good to hear that someone cared about me. For the first time in a long, long time I considered myself lucky. His mum then took the phone from him.

'How are you coping, my son?' she asked. 'How is life, Pedram? So nice to hear from you, my dear.'

I got very emotional hearing Mrs Arjomand's voice for the first time in a few years but I tried to hide it.

'I can't complain, Mrs Arjomand. One can get used to anything,' I replied with a sigh.

'You sound beaten,' she said.

'The loneliness is the tough part,' I told her. 'I can handle everything else.'

'I know how it feels, Pedram.' She paused. 'Even though the three of us finally managed to reunite in this corner of the world, it was very tough at the beginning for Kasra's dad and me.'

'I can imagine.'

'It's really worth giving some serious thought to what you want to do with the rest of your life, Pedram. Get out of there before you are too old.'

Mrs Arjomand said her goodbyes and passed the phone back to Kasra. We promised we'd be in touch more often than before.

Afterwards, I felt elated. I missed them all very much, but the thought of being on someone's mind all the way across the globe made me feel much loved and less lonely. Mrs Arjomand's comment about getting out of Iran before I was too old gave my idea of leaving Iran a new impetus.

The next morning I woke up feeling optimistic and determined to change my life. Our conversation the previous night made it very clear to me that I no longer felt at home in my own country. It was like putting on a pair of prescription glasses for the first time; everything was surprisingly sharp and defined. My New Year's resolution became my only goal for 1983: to get myself out of Iran and perhaps to reach Kasra. The more I thought about it the more I liked the idea of living in Australia. I started to read about the country, its history and its people. Whatever book I could find about it I read from cover to cover. Captain Cook became my hero. I even placed a map of Australia under the glass top of my Chippendale desk to familiarise myself with its geography. I was completely entranced by the country. Yet I had no idea how I was going to get there.

Over the following weeks I began discreetly talking to trusted friends and acquaintances, trying to find out as much as I could about leaving the country. Those close to me knew that Armineh and her mum had ended up in the UK; therefore, they expected me to be trying to reach her. I didn't correct them. It suited me that they thought that. The less people knew of my true intentions, the safer I would be, I told myself.

Meanwhile, the ongoing war with Iraq had brought our country unimaginable destruction, and misery for many. There were shortages everywhere, from food to electricity, and all our cities remained pitch black after sunset. Inflation had reached new heights and salaries could not meet the daily needs of the middle classes, while those connected to the Islamic mafia which ran the country became richer by the day.

By this time there were black markets for absolutely everything, from alcoholic drinks and sugar to cooking oil. You could find pretty much anything you wanted; it was merely a matter of who you knew and how much you were prepared to pay for it. The state itself ran a lucrative black-market business selling the fuel ration coupons for high prices. A nation that was literally built on oil began importing petrol from other countries who were prepared to deal with Iran under sanction.

In the midst of the war, high unemployment rates and continual arrests and executions, I kept my focus trained on getting out of the country. A brief flicker of hope was a nationwide rumour that the regime was going to open its borders at the time of Iranian New Year in March and begin issuing passports. But that by no means meant that I would be able to get one and leave.

My world was constricting. The authorities, having closed every avenue to happiness they could find, were aware that many young people went hiking in the foothills of the Alborz Mountains to the north of the city. So the Pasdars – the Revolutionary Guards – took to roaming the hills searching for conscripts, splitting up young lovers and lashing them for their unlawful and un-Islamic behaviour. I had to forfeit my rock in the mountains and content myself with escaping in books.

20,000 held in mullahs' torture jail

A French surgeon operated yesterday on an Iranian refugee to save the rest of his toes, several of which had been 'amputated' through whipping in an Iranian torture chamber.

The Observer, March 1983

Chapter Nineteen

IT IS A COMMON EXPRESSION, I believe, in many cultures: 'Time flies when you're having fun'. We definitely had not had fun, but the four years since the coming of our Islamic tyrants had passed extremely quickly. During those years many individuals, for all sorts of reasons, political and financial, or even by mistake, had been banned from leaving the country. Then in February of 1983 the government felt secure enough to open the borders to the public and began the long process of issuing new passports. A long and arduous process awaited applicants; it could take up to a year for all the security checks to be completed. I stood no chance of getting one: I was single, had no dependants and had never done my military service.

Kasra's initial excitement at my decision to leave Iran turned into disappointment. On an intellectual level he understood the limitations, but he was frustrated that it was taking such a long time. For a while I toyed with the idea of escaping as others had, on horseback perhaps, or on foot through the mountains to Turkey or Pakistan. Once out of Iran I could contact an Australian High Commission and apply for an entry visa with Kasra's assistance.

Since my return to Tehran three years previously, I had two

students whom I taught individually: Mitra, a student from the language centre who I also taught privately each week at her house, and Ardavan, Parastou's brother. They both enjoyed learning English and were determined to take it further, and I took their progress seriously.

Mitra was an intelligent girl who had just finished her final year at high school. She wanted to go to university and do a degree in English literature. Her passion for the English language had transformed our teacher–student relationship into a friendship in which the nineteenth- and early twentieth-century writers played a major role. She loved the modern English language classics. Although I encouraged her to read some of the older canonical writers such as Austen and the Brontës, she stuck to her guns that Fitzgerald and Forster were more her style. She loved reading fiction. In novels, I believe, she found the missing parts of her life, whatever they were.

Ardavan had finished high school two years earlier and since then had stayed at home doing nothing. He had reached the age of conscription and had to either pass a university's entrance exams, the *Concours*, or join the armed forces. He could not get a job without his conscription completed or being exempted.

Over time I grew close to Ardavan and Mitra. They each treated me like an older brother, and, in them, I too found the siblings I had always wished for. During lessons, I encouraged them to talk about any subject they liked. We touched on social and political issues, as well as their ambitions and aspirations. We discussed books they had recently read and even chatted about who they'd fallen in love with.

Through me, they also heard a lot about one another, and Ardavan, in particular, was keen to meet Mitra. For some reason I never managed to make that happen. The safest way to do it would have been to invite them both over to my apartment, but in those days even liberal families were extra cautious about who their daughters socialised with. Mitra's grammar needed improvement, but her vocabulary was rich and colourful. All that reading had really paid off. Ardavan, on the other hand, had a good command of English grammar but a limited vocabulary. They were a perfect match!

One day in early April, Mitra told me about a member of her family who had recently escaped from the country. Her uncle, a successful businessman, had sent his wife and children to France before the return of the Ayatollah. He had planned to sell everything, convert the cash into US dollars and join his family as soon as possible. However, once the new regime seized power, her uncle was banned from leaving. He was stripped of his business and everything the family owned was confiscated before he could sell a thing. Mitra had talked about her uncle's numerous unsuccessful attempts to escape the country – through the mountains, bribing the custom officials and high-ranking individuals in passport control at Mehrabad Airport, with the help of smugglers. Having heard of his daring and persistent attempts, I cheered him on, impatient to hear that he had finally been reunited with his family.

I met him once, very briefly, in the front garden of Mitra's house. I had arrived for our usual lesson when he was on his way out; Mitra introduced us to one another. He had been among the first graduates from the famous London Business School after its establishment in 1964. He was very polite and seemed to be a very cultured man.

'My uncle came up with the most brilliant plan when he visited a cousin in Bandar Abbas,' Mitra told me.

I listened to her attentively. Mitra knew about Armineh and assumed that I still longed to be with her.

'A few weeks after his first trip,' Mitra continued, 'he returned to Bandar Abbas to put his plan into action. He got to know the locals, especially the fishermen, and purchased a small motorboat. Then …' she looked around the sitting room, as if someone might be listening in, and whispered '… he crossed the Strait of Hormuz and reached the Omani coast in less than an hour.'

'You're making this up, right?' I said, grinning.

'My uncle knew a few people in high positions in the Sultanate of Oman before the revolution,' she went on. 'His firm had carried out various construction projects there. So once in Oman, he was met by his former associates, who then arranged his departure to France.'

I realised this was not a joke. Sultan Qaboos of Oman was truly indebted to our late Shah. In the mid-seventies he had asked Iran for military assistance to crush a Marxist-inspired guerrilla war in Dhofar and to prevent his country from falling into the hands of the communists. Our imperial government, which saw communism as a major threat to peace and progress in the Middle East, had responded to the Sultan's plea. Since then, the sultanate had given favourable terms in contracts to Iranian firms carrying out various construction and development programmes in Oman.

When I got back from Mitra's that afternoon, her uncle's escape preoccupied my mind for the rest of the day. Our southern shores – on the Persian Gulf – had never occurred to me as a possible route to freedom. It was the first time I had heard of anyone going that way; the Turkish border or the border with Pakistan were the most common escape routes.

The following week Mitra informed me that her uncle had arrived safely in Paris. Although happy for his success, I couldn't help feeling sorry for myself and my dire situation. The fear of being conscripted and sent to the front was a good enough spur to find a way to escape. Up to now the regime had not searched private companies or institutions for men eligible to sign-up, but as time went by and the government became more and more desperate for soldiers it was inevitable that they'd snare everyone fit to fight.

Ardavan, too, wanted to leave, but his family was not prepared to have him smuggled out. He wanted to give it a go, but his mother and Parastou were afraid of him being caught and imprisoned or sent directly to the front. He was always working on some kind of a plan and joked that we should escape together. If it wasn't walking across the border on foot, it was befriending the security guards at Tehran Airport, who he believed could be bribed to let us through unchecked.

I told him about Mitra's uncle's successful attempt and it got him all excited. He was annoyed that he hadn't thought of it first. We talked about the logistics of it. We wondered how he had escaped the Iranian navy's patrol boats that kept a close eye on shipping traffic in the Strait of Hormuz. Obviously he had found a way, so it was up to us to devise our own tailor-made escape plan.

Each time after I came home from a lesson with Ardavan, I lay on the floor and thought about the ideas he had come up with that week. Ardavan improved his oral English by discussing escape plans with me. I didn't mind. His passion for the subject made him less nervous and he made fewer mistakes in English. If he hadn't cooked up a new plan he had usually heard of someone who knew somebody else who had managed to escape successfully. In time, the issue of whether to leave or to stay was no longer a decision that needed to be made. It was a no-brainer. There was no choice to be made between a life of apathy and fear and one of freedom and joy. Every time I thought about leaving Iran and being with Kasra, I felt rejuvenated and energised.

By the end of June the weather was intensely hot. The language centre had closed for a few weeks before the summer courses started, and I was happy to have the time off to relax at home, listening to music and reading novels.

I arrived home one afternoon hot and bothered after visiting my favourite bookshop, the one opposite Tehran University. I opened all the windows in the apartment – polluted air was better than the artificial air of the AC unit. I stripped off and stood in the shower, motionless, enjoying the feel of the cold water on my hot body. I must have stood there for a good fifteen minutes before getting out and drying myself off. I had just put on a large white linen shirt and a pair of cut-off denim shorts when the phone rang. It was Ardavan.

'At last! I have been calling you all day,' he said.

'Why? What's up?'

'I have to see you. I can't tell you over the phone. I've had a good idea.'

'Another one?' I laughed.

'This one will work, seriously. You have to hear me out.'

'Okay, well I've just got out of the shower. Where do you want to meet?'

'I was hoping to come to your place. I'm calling you from the public phone outside your building.'

Minutes later he was at the door.

'I've been waiting outside for the past three hours. I even called home and asked Parastou if she knew where you were.' He patted his forehead and neck with a tissue.

I went to the kitchen to get us cold drinks and came back with two bottles of non-alcoholic Islamic beer – Mâsha'ier. It was an acquired taste; when it wasn't ice-cold it tasted like piss.

'So, what's this new plan of yours? Are we going on a balloon across the Caspian to the Soviet Union?' I joked.

He nearly choked on his beer, laughing. 'Imagine that!' he said. 'What was the expression you used the other day? Fall out of the frying pan and into the fire?' He laughed again. 'No, nothing like that. Something much easier. Just hear me out.' He became serious again.

'I'm all ears!' I said.

'Yesterday I read an article in a newspaper about Iran importing coal from Australia.'

'Oh, yeah?' I couldn't keep the sarcasm out of my voice.

He continued: 'I managed to find the importing company's telephone number and I gave them a call.'

'Are we joining them?' I gave a little chuckle.

'We can.'

I burst out laughing. 'What? As partners or are we buying them out?'

'Listen! Huge bulk carriers bring Australian coal to the port at Bandar Abbas.'

'So?' I couldn't see where this was going, but the mention of Australia held my attention.

'I'm suggesting that the two of us take a trip south to check it out for ourselves.'

'Check what out, Ardavan?' I had heard so many 'fantastic' plans, none of which had been practical, and I found it hard to summon up any enthusiasm over this latest one.

'Don't you get it?' he said, sitting forward eagerly in his seat. 'We go there and find out how they operate.' He waited for me to say something but I just looked at him. 'This is the way to the free world,' he went on. 'No stopovers. Iran straight to Australia! From there you can go anywhere – to England to Armineh!'

He had a point. If we could get on one of those ships when it set off for Australia, we'd be free. Suddenly I was on the edge of my seat too. It was by far the most interesting idea he'd come up with yet.

And like he said, there was only one way to find out and that was to check it out for ourselves.

'It won't be too difficult for me to get away from home,' Ardavan said. 'But you must promise me you won't change your mind. You must accompany me on this expedition. In the meantime, don't say a word to anyone, including Parastou – especially Parastou.'

Listening to this young man boss me around somehow made me feel proud of him. I couldn't help comparing myself to him when I was his age. All my generation had been interested in in the late sixties and early seventies was how to have fun, chase girls, go clubbing, drink, listen to music, smoke weed. It was like a different planet. These kids had been going through adolescence under a medieval mullocracy and had no fun whatsoever. In a way, they had had no choice but to grow up faster, only to be bitterly disappointed by the bleak futures they faced in their homeland.

I promised Ardavan that we'd go together to Bandar Abbas on condition that he told his parents the truth. He left my apartment that day and I didn't hear from him until the following week, the day before we were due to have our English lesson.

He rang and told me to forget the lesson. 'Pack a small bag and come to our place early in the morning,' he said. 'We leave tomorrow.'

Even though it was short notice there was nothing stopping me from going. It was the wrong time of year to visit the south – the weather would be stiflingly hot – but I had to do everything I could to get out, even if the chance of success was slim.

The following day I showed up at the Parspours with a small bag and a rucksack. Mrs Parspour looked worried when she answered the door and invited me in.

'No, Mum!' Ardavan said from the other side of the room. 'We're going to be late.' He picked up his bag and came towards me waving two tickets in the air. He was fired-up and excited.

'You have bought us coach tickets to travel some nine hundred miles with no air conditioning? Are you crazy?' I pulled the tickets out of his hands.

'What's your problem? The heat or the distance?' Ardavan asked in exasperation.

'Neither. Can't you see! It's risky to travel such a long distance on roads where we know there are checkpoints.'

'So?'

'We could end up being drafted by any mad Pasdar who doesn't like our faces.'

Mrs Parspour suddenly began defending me, telling him off for not thinking it through. Since the disturbances in Kurdistan province had turned into a mini civil war, the regime was on high alert regarding people's movements in and out of the cities.

I suggested we forgot the coach tickets and flew instead; I would pay for the flights. After the initial polite refusal of my offer to cover their son's costs, the Parspours agreed and Ardavan's father gave us a lift to the airport. Mrs Parspour and Parastou waved us off, looking tense and anxious.

At the airport we managed to find two standby tickets on a flight that was due to depart in four hours' time. Mr Parspour parked the car and joined us for a cup of tea while we waited for our flight. Ardavan promised to call home as soon as we reached our destination and had checked in at a hotel.

Bandar Abbas in July is the place where God decided to create hell. On 9th July, after an hour and a half's flight, we landed at the airport. I could see the heat shimmering above the tarmac as we taxied towards the terminal building. When I stepped out of the aeroplane the full force of the heat hit me and I took a step back, landing on a lady's foot. I turned and apologised, but when I saw her I felt all the more sorry for her. How women survived in such heat under all those clothes was beyond me! Why did women have to be punished, in our strict Islamic society, simply because men could not keep their sexual cravings at bay?

In the taxi into town, Ardavan was as excited as a child at a funfair. This was his first trip anywhere away from home and he was enjoying his new-found independence. The windows of the cab were down, and it felt as if the hot, heavy, humid air was devouring our faces. It was difficult to breathe; the air was so thick you could have cut it with a knife. I remembered a news bulletin back in 1975 when Bandar Abbas had experienced snow for the first time in a hundred and twenty years. I mentioned it to Ardavan, who I didn't expect to remember it. But the cab driver did, and it started a conversation among us and made us all nostalgic about those years.

The taxi dropped us off at Homa Hotel, once part of the International Sheraton chain of hotels owned by Iran Air. It faced the sea on the southern side of the city, and its rose gardens, with numerous fountains, looked as heavenly as the Garden of Eden. We had no reservations, but summer was not the season for tourists in Bandar Abbas and the hotel was deserted.

We dropped our bags in our cool, airy room and headed for the city to do some sightseeing. Bandar Abbas didn't have much to offer. Old monuments were restricted to an abandoned Hindu temple with its characteristic conical roof; nearby was the bazaar with its covered streets reserved for small retailers. There was hardly anything pretty to be found in these tiny shops, some of them were no bigger than a cupboard. Many local women wore masks similar to those worn by Arab women across the Persian Gulf. They were hideous semi-rigid contraptions, surrounding the eyes and covering the nose and mouth. They reminded me of the Greek soldiers of antiquity; Ardavan said they were more like Batman. I learned later that the batoola or battoulah was a local fashion, a Persian-Gulf-type of niqab that had no roots in Islamic tradition.

After a couple of days of sightseeing, we headed out on our mission to the port. Before the war with Iraq, our main port on the Persian Gulf had been Khorramshahr, which lay further north on the Arvand River. But it had been destroyed by the Iraqis and now most of our imports came to Bandar Abbas instead.

The docks weren't open to the public and we could only look on from afar. Even from a distance we could see that the place was dirty and unkempt, with equipment and buildings that were rusting or falling apart. Ardavan had hoped that we could find jobs as crew on one of the vessels sailing between Iran and Australia. However, when we contacted the port authorities we were told that the only vacancies on the bulk carriers were for coal heavers. If we were interested, we had to show up the following day at seven in the morning. That evening we talked about it for hours and decided to give it a go.

There were twenty of us signing up next morning, all waiting outside the supervisor's office. Eventually a short, fat man came out, distributing pieces of paper. Ardavan and I thought he looked like Sergeant Garcia from the television series *Zorro*. We laughed out loud, which attracted his attention. He narrowed his eyes at us.

'Make sure you fill in this form correctly,' he instructed us all. 'Then we'll call you in one at a time.'

In the office the bored-looking supervisor went through our forms, confirmed our details and then took our pictures with a 1970s Polaroid camera. He seemed very proud of his camera, as though it was the latest thing in technology. I walked out of his office, my hideous picture staring back at me from my coal-heaver's permit card. We were supposed to carry the card with us at all times.

The job wasn't starting for another two weeks, which gave us time to return to Tehran and sort out a few things before we began our new lives as coal heavers. We kept joking about it. It was lucky for us that they were so desperate for labourers they didn't bother to check our conscription status.

We needed a place to live in Bandar Abbas too, and before our return to Tehran we managed to find a one-bedroom apartment in a part of the city not too far from the port. Soot from the coal lorries that travelled through on their way to the docks had blackened the whole neighbourhood. It was obvious from the beginning that our standard of living would have to change dramatically – the apartment was more like a hovel, with dirty walls and no carpets. Though I could afford to pay for a better place, we couldn't risk standing out from the locals or the other workers.

We returned to Tehran the following Saturday, 16th July. By this time, I was more optimistic about my young friend's plan. I decided to leave a set of apartment keys with Parastou who was going to contact an estate agent to rent my place out. She offered to keep all my belongings – books, furniture, clothes, pots and pans … everything – in their large basement for as long as I wanted. I also had to visit my boss at the language centre. He was a bit disgruntled but he took my name off the list of teachers who had volunteered for summer classes.

Before we knew it, Ardavan and I were heading back to Bandar Abbas, taking with us only our most treasured personal belongings. We spent all afternoon and most of the night cleaning the filthy apartment. Before going to bed, we agreed that we had to make sure we seemed eager to have the job and appear as genuine as we could – two single, unemployed guys desperate to make a living.

It was no joke. We couldn't talk about our backgrounds or our lives in Tehran to anyone, especially the other workers. No one was to be trusted; government agents were everywhere, and the Ayatollah had eyes at the back of his head.

Ayatollah fails in action for £37bn

A New York appeals court said yesterday that a $56 billion (£37 billion) action brought by Ayatollah Khomeini against the deposed Shah of Iran was rightfully dismissed.

The suit claiming that the Shah and his family operated an international network to loot the Iranian treasury was filed in November, 1979, 10 months after the Shah fled from Iran.

The Times, July 1983

Chapter Twenty

On 31st July 1983 at six o'clock in the morning the blazing sun had already raised the temperature to 22°C. We reported for work at the docks and getting through security checks. Security was far tighter at Shahid Rajaie than most other commercial docks. Due to the war with Iraq, it was treated like a military zone. While the other workers looked sleepy and sluggish, Ardavan and I were like two kids in a toyshop. For us, it was an important step towards making a new life in a new world.

We knew nothing about the job apart from the fact that we would be unloading the bulk carrier *Australian Progress* that had arrived a few days earlier from Australia. We were given neither instructions nor safety advice; we were simply given a shovel and told to get on with it. Most of those working with us were young men from smaller towns and villages who would have taken any sort of job in order to survive and to support their families. Ardavan and I must have looked so out of place. Not only did we look different, but our accents gave us away, even among the Iranian workers. It was also obvious that neither of us had ever done any kind of hard labour before.

We were taken to the ship anchored a few hundred yards away

and went on board holding our shovels. We were stationed at the first hold. It was a mighty scene on deck. There must have been well over a hundred coal heavers at work on deck, their skin blackened by the soot, and the noise of clanging shovels, together with cranes lifting cargo from the jetty was deafening. It made me think of the thousands of slaves who built the pyramids in Egypt. The coal shimmering in the sun and the swell of busy heavers made the deck look like it was being swallowed by a black monster.

With shovels barely bigger than the ones used on a building site, we had to lift the coal into wheelbarrows, which were then emptied into large square-shaped meshes made out of strong gunny sacks. The coarse sacking was then pulled up by its four corners, lifted by cranes and emptied into lorries parked alongside the bulk carrier on the jetty.

A few hours after we began work, Ardavan turned and whispered, 'Who else do you think is planning their escape?' We gave each other a knowing smile.

It was still early in the morning but I was already bothered by the heat and the temperature was rising by the minute. The ship was enormous. I couldn't imagine how long it would take to unload the entire cargo. I wouldn't have believed it had I not seen it for myself that there was no special mechanical equipment to do the back-breaking work of hundreds of coal heavers.

It didn't take long for us to turn black like the others. The soot went everywhere – up our noses, in our ears and mouths – into any nook or cranny it could find. The temperature had also reached its peak – it was 45°C. We were in hell. There was no way I could cope with this kind of work in such intense heat. I decided to tell Ardavan that we had to come up with an alternative plan. The thought of carrying on like that without having any idea of how and when we could escape made me doubt the whole project. We were only halfway through our first day and my entire body was in pain. I was also impatient to find out how the whole thing operated. After all, we weren't there to work, but to find out when the ships left Iran and explore the possibility of sailing with them. When Ardavan first suggested the idea, we thought we'd find jobs on board as crew members, not as coal heavers.

'I won't be able to do this for long,' I whispered to Ardavan.

His black face was streaked with sweat and all I could see were the whites of his eyes.

'I can't believe this!' he said, disappointment in his voice. 'We've only been here a few hours. Don't let your impatience get the better of you. We've come all this way. Stop being silly! Get back to work.'

He put his foot on his shovel and carried on digging like a real coal heaver.

Eventually it was lunchtime, not that I needed the klaxon to remind me; my stomach had been rumbling for over an hour and every muscle in my body was begging me to stop. I couldn't tell which pain was worse: the roaring of my empty stomach or my aching body.

The canteen in the port was a large warehouse that looked more like a hangar in an aerodrome. It housed the entire workforce from all the docks and jetties. Lunchtime was the only hour that we truly enjoyed and were able to relax. The food was good and abundant, and I heard that the menu changed every day. It was the only thing that no one complained about. Like the operations at the port, the canteen worked around the clock, providing breakfast, lunch and dinner. The whole complex – the harbour and various operational sites – was like a city in miniature, a primitive, dirty city full of filthy, tired men.

Ardavan appeared relaxed and untroubled by the heat or the hard labour. I had not expected him to have such stamina. He never complained. Whenever we had a moment to ourselves alone, he questioned me about Australia and what I had learned from the books I'd read. I could no longer see how working in Bandar Abbas was going to get us to our destination, but Ardavan got more excited as the days passed, as if we were already on our way.

Our first days on the job seemed to go on forever. Dehydration was the biggest problem and caused much of the exhaustion we suffered from. Hours of sweating under the unforgiving August sun sometimes caused rashes that looked more like third-degree burns. We were so tired that we hardly said a word on our way home. The majority of those who worked on the bulk carriers slept there, in the middle of all that noise. But they were so tired that they fell asleep as soon as their heads hit the floor.

Ardavan and I looked like two slaves from Zanzibar, brought to shore centuries ago when Bandar Abbas and a few of our islands in the Persian Gulf were under Portuguese occupation. We tried to see the funny side and joked about it, but it wasn't always easy. Almost everyone in the neighbourhood where we lived was involved in some sort of activity at the port. Most people we saw in the vicinity were covered in either soot or engine oil.

During the first weeks the soot irritated our skin. We felt uncomfortable and it wasn't an easy thing to get rid of. At the harbour, not far from the jetties where the workforce spent most of its time, there were public showers for the workers. They were so filthy that we never dared use them. The cubicles had broken doors and the walls were covered with scum. The water from the showers found its way into the harbour where it formed puddles of bacteria-ridden soup. The poor Afghanis, who had no places of their own and spent all their days and nights on the jetties or at the docks, had no choice but to use the dockside showers or remain smelly and dirty; often that was the wiser option.

In the beginning, we took a shower every evening back at the apartment. The cold water in the pipes was heated by the sun during the day and it was piping hot by the time we got home. We used so much washing powder on our skin – ordinary soap didn't get us clean – that Ardavan suffered from severe rashes and dry skin. At times the skin on our hands and arms cracked and bled. But little by little we got used to staying sweaty and smelly like the others. The only positive aspect of our hard labour was that it got us fit.

Even though we were lucky enough to have a place of our own, our living conditions were terrible. Ardavan kept saying that if his parents could see how he lived, they'd have dragged him back to Tehran. On several occasions his father wanted to visit us but Ardavan came up with all sorts of excuses to stop him from making the trip.

The port conditions weren't much better. At the old harbour, rats as big as kittens infested the entire district. The revolution that had brought the Iraqi war and other calamities upon us had also increased the numbers of destitute people, people who often sought comfort in all sorts of narcotics. It was difficult to ignore the drug addicts and their infected wounds we encountered on our way to work each day. I got them some disinfectant and penicillin from a pharmacy and tried to give them some basic medical care. They got to know me and used to shout across the road, 'Our nurse is coming.'

We didn't have a phone at the apartment, so we had to go to a telephone exchange centre to call home. Ardavan spoke to his family every other day to calm his mother's nerves – she worried that he might leave without saying goodbye – and I caught up with Parastou about my apartments in Tehran – Mâdar's and the one my parents had left me – in case there was anything I needed to take care of. Calling Kasra, however, required a lot of time, and I didn't want Ardavan knowing who I was calling. I had to go to the telephone exchange centre on my days off and wait, sometimes for a couple of hours, for an operator who summoned me into a booth once the connection had been made.

It was easier to keep in touch by letter. I wrote to Kasra every week without waiting for him to reply and he did the same. He told me about life in Australia, how friendly people were and how much the country had to offer. He also told me about his work and the medical system there, and promised to help me with my immigration case once I arrived. I was glad I was doing this with Ardavan who surprised me by turning out to be more mature than his age. The resilience I found in Ardavan earned my utmost respect.

In order to make the coal heaving work more bearable for the workers, the shifts were rotated regularly. We were eager to work the night shifts: not only did you escape the brutality of the sun but the shifts themselves seemed shorter. The night shift co-workers seemed to be in better spirits too; they were friendlier, and sometimes we sang together as we emptied the holds under the floodlights.

Ardavan never lost his sense of humour or his determination to leave Iran; indeed, he kept me buoyed up. Every time I felt down he told me to think of the freedom I would eventually enjoy in England. He was a godsend. Sometimes I spurred myself on by pretending I was preparing for a difficult exam which, if I passed, would give me the key to my future happiness.

'What would you like to do when you are in Australia?' I asked Ardavan one evening back in our apartment.

'I've no idea,' he said. 'It must be so different there. I can't decide that until I get there. I don't know what's possible.'

We became friendly with the kitchen staff, which was to prove vital in the future. They let us eat with them in the kitchen, and gave us all sorts of fresh fruit, sometimes even chocolate. Every now and then when they brought food for the crew on the ship, they invited us to join them. We took advantage of this, as it gave us the opportunity to learn more about the ship's routine and departure date. We also made friends with other coal heavers, but if they asked too many questions about our lives we would change the subject. They told us that it took roughly forty days to empty the coal from bulk carriers before they returned to Australia. But Ardavan and I weren't prepared to wait for the next carrier; we had to make sure we were on board *Australian Progress* when it was ready to sail. According to our calculations the ship would be emptied around the second week in September.

We decided to investigate how we could sail with the crew to Australia the next time we had lunch with them. That's when we made the disastrous discovery that no coal heavers were needed on board for the journey. We had assumed that at least some of us would be drafted to travel with the carrier to fill the ship's holds at the other end. This discovery had a devastating effect on our entire plan, and it meant we had to come up with an alternative plan quickly before we lost our chance.

That evening back in our lodgings, I had an idea and talked it over with Ardavan: we could stow away on the vessel.

On 3rd September, while we were busy sweating buckets working in Hold No. 2, the supervisor called for Ardavan. He turned and frowned at me, then climbed up the ladder to the deck. A few minutes later I heard my name being called. I was filled with foreboding as I dropped my shovel and climbed up. When I stepped out onto the deck I saw Ardavan crouched in a corner, crying his eyes out, tears running down his soot-covered face. He handed me a piece of paper. It was a short telegraph from Parastou which read: 'Dad is dead. Return to Tehran.'

I took the rest of the day off and accompanied him to the telephone exchange centre. He rang home, but most of the conversation consisted of the three of them crying over their sentences. I spoke to Mrs Parspour and conveyed my condolences. Parastou could hardly talk. Their dad had died the night before in his sleep; he had had a severe stroke. Broken, depressed and mourning his father, Ardavan left Bandar Abbas that evening, making me promise to go ahead and escape. I wanted to go back with him, but I couldn't get the time off. I would have loved to have kept the family company, at least until the funeral and the ceremonies were over.

Once Ardavan left I was lonely and I began to lose my confidence in a project that had always been his baby. I was devastated; I had lost the driving force behind our plan.

My job on the bulk carrier finished on Thursday, 8th September. I had a few days off before the next vessel was due to arrive, so I returned to Tehran to see the Parspours and finalise the sale of the two apartments. My few days in Tehran went very quickly, during which time I completed the sale of both apartments and exchanged the proceeds for US dollars at black-market rates. I had to carry wads of cash back to Bandar Abbas with me.

Most of my belongings remained at the Parspours. I called round to see them towards the end of my holiday. Parastou said she would sell my stuff in a garage sale for me; we'd decide what to do with the cash at a later stage.

'Aren't you supposed to be going back soon?' Ardavan said. 'I can't remember but wasn't the next cargo arriving on the fourteenth?'

'Yes, it's due to anchor tomorrow, and we have to be there for the start of working day on Wednesday.'

'We?'

'Well, yes! Of course, we.'

'I'm not going back, Pedram. I can't leave Iran now.'

I was shocked. It never occurred to me that he would change his mind once his father had passed away. I tried to convince him to come back with me; even his mum tried to persuade him, but he said he couldn't think of leaving the country when his mother and sister would be here alone. I knew that once he had made up his mind nothing would change it. I had never thought of taking the risks all by myself. Now I was on my own.

I returned to Bandar Abbas and on 14th September began working on the *Motahari*, an Iranian bulk carrier that had anchored a few days earlier. All the time I shovelled coal I was thinking about my escape, planning and scheming, trying to anticipate all the things that could go wrong.

We had been given a tour of the *Australian Progress* and I vaguely recalled its layout. This Iranian carrier was different in size but seemed to be similar in design and structure. There were many parts in the ship that hardly anyone visited unless there was a mechanical problem. And so I began a smuggling operation under the cover of darkness after my daytime shift was over. At the port's gates only our work permit card was checked. I could enter the port complex any time I wished; they never checked to see if I was on duty or not.

Each night for the next forty nights I brought in what I thought was vital for the journey hidden under my clothes or in my rucksack. While the night shift worked like ants up in the holds, I took containers filled with fresh water down a forty-step ladder below deck and placed them next to a shaft where the ship's engines were. I needed to calculate everything carefully in order to survive the twenty-three-day journey. Also on my list was: a knife, penicillin powder, torches, spare batteries, light bulbs, candles, electrical cables, tissues and a screwdriver. I believed I could survive hunger, thirst was a different matter. I always brought water every night. There couldn't be enough water. Bit by bit, night by night, matches, towels, soap, rope and clean clothes were added to my stock below deck.

My deafening heartbeat on every trip I made reminded me of the dangers I could face. Eventually I had stored nearly seventy litres of water, sufficient for the duration of the voyage. There was no toilet down there, so I would have to make do with plastic bags and empty water containers. It was also dark, and though I was bringing candles with me, it would be impossible to live day after day burning candles in a space with little ventilation. For food I had thirty tins of tuna, beans and stew each, and biscuits, and I stored thirty fresh Lavash breads at the apartment to take with me on the last day, courtesy of my dear friends in the kitchens.

When I surveyed my stores below deck or stopped to think about the whole plan, I couldn't believe what I was planning on doing. The plan seemed to be nothing but utter madness. I never thought for a moment that I would succeed, but I had gone too far to change my mind. The possibility of seeing Kasra again was motivation enough to keep me going. Had I been caught during those smuggling operations I would have been arrested, given many lashes and thrown in prison for a long time. That is, if I were lucky. Most likely, I'd end up at the front or executed.

We were well into October by this time. Since the beginning of fall, the weather had changed for the better. The fresh autumn breeze was pleasant and dried the sweat on our bodies. The days were getting shorter too, making the daytime shifts easier to handle.

My work on *Motahari* was coming to an end. The night before the ship was due to leave I came home to clean up and pack the bread. I needed to be back on board and in my hiding place before the last shift signed off. But there were a few things I wanted to do first. After all, it was my last night in my own country. Like a lover who is leaving on a long and dangerous trip, I needed to say my goodbye to it. I went down to the beach, which was deserted and silent. There was a gentle breeze, and little waves gently washed the beach. A flock of migrating birds arrived from the north to take advantage of the milder winters on the Persian Gulf. Not a soul could be seen on those golden sands.

I stood by an empty plinth, marking the spot where a proud statue of modern Iran's founding father, Reza Shah the Great, once stood. It was from that very place on the beach that he had boarded the British steamer *Bandra* on 27th September 1941, forced into exile by the occupying powers. He took with him a handful of Iranian soil, and was buried with it three years later in Cairo. I always associated Reza Shah the Great with Mâdar, who was so proud of him. I thought of her now. I wished I could tell her, 'Look, I'm on my way, too, to my own exile and from the same shores as Reza Shah.'

What could I take with me to remind me of Iran? I had lots of memories, of course, but there was no room to take even one of my precious family albums. The only thing I had that never left my side was a piece of Mâdar's hair. If something happened to the ship, no one would ever know my story.

It was time to leave. My stomach was in knots. The streets seemed strangely quiet, as if time was standing still. Even the stars seemed to have stopped twinkling as I made my way to the harbour.

I had a half-empty penicillin bottle in my pocket. Suddenly an idea for a keepsake came to mind, something that no one could put a price on, something even more precious than our Darya-ye Noor diamond. I emptied out the remaining penicillin and ran down to the beach. I pushed the bottle into the sand and put the top back on. My eyes filled with tears. With the bottle of sand in my fist I raised it to the stars and prayed to Ahura Mazda, the ancient God of Iran, to protect me on my voyage.

I had to rush. I didn't have much time left. I got to the dock without seeing anyone on the way. I stood before the bulk carrier, thirty-five thousand tons of metal and steel. The *Motahari*, named after a mullah who had been assassinated at the beginning of the revolution, was waiting to take me to freedom. I loved the irony of it.

I walked on board. It was almost the end of the shift and there was a lot of coming and going. Hardly anyone noticed me. By this time I was absolutely calm – no emotions, no second thoughts. I was heading to my future.

It was three o'clock on the morning of Monday, 24th October 1983. I opened the hatch to my home for the next few weeks, quietly closed it behind me and descended the ladder into total darkness.

Beirut blasts kill US and French troops

At least 146 American marines and 27 French servicemen have been killed after two separate bomb attacks on military headquarters in the Lebanese capital Beirut.

Two lorries containing 4000lb (1.4 tonnes) bombs exploded when they hit the buildings, the US Battalion Landing Team headquarters and the French paratroopers base which are situated just four miles (6km) apart.

The death toll is expected to rise to more than 200 as people remain trapped inside the collapsed buildings.

The US Secretary of Defence, Caspar Weinberger, insisted there was 'strong circumstantial evidence' that Iran was behind the attacks but did not rule out possible Syrian and Soviet involvement.

BBC, October 1983

Chapter Twenty-one

DOWN THE LADDER, in the bowels of the bulk carrier, I had set up camp in a chamber off to one side. This would be my home for the next twenty-three days.

I hunkered down in my spot. It was silent. Nothing would happen for at least another three hours; the crew would only board after sunrise. Time moved sluggishly as I sat in a corner in total darkness, waiting. The only thing I could see was the fluorescent dial of my watch. The more I looked at my watch the slower the time seemed to pass. Over the past few days I had been so anxious that I hardly slept. I had gone over and over my plans, checking every step. I just hoped I had everything I could possibly need. I had checked my list so many times. I couldn't afford to forget something vital. Now, sitting in the darkness with nothing to do but wait, I went over it one more time, even though it was too late to do anything about it.

The porters on the dock used thick gunnysacks as cushions for their backs when carrying heavy loads. I had brought some onto the ship to make a bed, and to protect myself from the coarse material I put sheets of cardboard on top of them. I took my shoes off and tried my bed for the first time – it wasn't too bad, I thought.

The ship was scheduled to set sail at eleven o'clock that morning. It was a long wait, so I decided to get some rest. Unfortunately I was too anxious to sleep. Wouldn't it be great if I could fall asleep and wake up once the journey was over? I thought to myself. Lying there, I couldn't help but check the time every now and then. I had always been an impatient man – waiting was something I never liked – but this time I had to wait in order to have a life at all.

Darkness plays such tricks on you. You lose all sense of space and time, and fear comes at you from all directions. I got all philosophical and nostalgic as I sat in my hidey-hole waiting to depart. Poor Ardavan, I thought, what would the future hold for him? I owed him so much. I was on my way to Australia thanks to his sharp mind and positive attitude. If it hadn't been for his courage, stamina and persistence I probably wouldn't have come this far. He deserved this escape more than I did; mostly, I wished he were with me. His company and boyish good humour would have made the journey so much easier to bear.

The lump I'd had in my throat for days now did not go away in the depths of the ship. Not only was I leaving my homeland behind, but also my parents and grandmother. Would I ever come back? I wondered. I tried to stop thinking about the past; it only made me sad and moody. I needed to have my wits about me if I was to succeed with my version of *The Great Escape*.

A sudden bang right next to my ear startled me. For a moment I had no idea what was happening. I was scared. Then I realised that one of the engines had been switched on. A few minutes later the noise got louder as more engines kicked in, one after the other. In less than half an hour I wouldn't have heard my own voice even if I'd screamed. As the fuel began pumping through the engines, so did the excitement running through my veins. It started off with a smile and little by little it turned into laughter; before I knew it I was screaming in elation, letting the past weeks' anxieties out. 'Here we go! Here I come, Kasra!' I yelled. 'Here I come, freedom! Here I come, Australia!' I was filled with joy – at last, after eight hours of waiting we were on the move.

I was as excited as if I'd already made it to Australia. The cacophony didn't bother me at all. I lit a candle so I could see enough to connect up a light bulb. In my previous visits to my new home I had taken note of the wiring and worked out how I could have a source of electric light. My first attempt to wire up a makeshift light source was disastrous. I got a shock that jerked my arm back, and the pain in my right arm remained for hours while I looked for the insulated pliers. It wasn't a job to do in the dark.

A few hours had passed since we had set sail from Bandar Abbas when the ship came to a sudden halt. I couldn't understand what was happening. When I'd worked as a coal heaver I learned a lot about the bulk carriers, as well as details of the journey. I knew that once we left Bandar Abbas the only stop – if everything went well – would be our destination, Australia. But the engines had fallen silent and I'd no idea why. At first I welcomed the silence, but as it dragged on and we remained stationary I started to worry. I wanted the noises back and began to hate that silence. Hours passed and nothing happened. Something must be going on, but there was no way I could find out. The vessel could be in some sort of trouble, or on fire, and there was nothing I could do about it. I was at the mercy of fate. Only now did the full implications of my surreptitious journey hit me.

I kept imagining that we were moving, but we weren't. It was all part of the disorientation of being sealed off from the world in solitary confinement. The first day passed, then the second. All sorts of things went through my mind, made worse by the humidity, darkness, an ear infection that I seemed to have contracted since I'd boarded, the pain of a small sore I'd developed on my back from crawling through the low shaft, and the diarrhoea I'd had a few days prior to leaving.

Suddenly I fell into a total panic. I remembered that someone had mentioned the customs search, but I had totally forgotten about it. Would the custom officers come down to this part of the vessel? I didn't know what to do. Time passed so slowly. I thought about going on deck to see what was happening. Several times I went towards the tunnel, but each time the fear of arrest and its consequences kept me right where I was. What was taking so long? I decided to try connecting the light bulb again, but then I worried that fiddling around with the circuits might be picked up somehow and raise suspicions about a stowaway.

By the fourth day I was practically suicidal. I wondered if I'd badly miscalculated the length of the journey. Would I have enough food and water? Did the twenty-three days I'd been told the voyage took include delays like this?

On the fifth day a sudden jolt followed by the familiar sound of the engines starting up was such a joyous moment that I decided to celebrate it. I opened a bottle of Islamic non-alcoholic Mâsha'ier beer that I had brought along with me. It was warm and tasted disgusting but I didn't care. We were setting off again.

Now that the customs search was over, I felt more relaxed and content. I wanted to rest and also to attend to my ear. My right ear was still very painful, and pus mixed with blood kept running out of it. Physical pain or illness was the last thing I needed and it wasn't something I'd planned for.

I made another attempt to get the light bulb to work and on the second attempt I was successful, which brought some light and joy to my den. I tidied my space and tried to make it as comfortable as I could. Had I had a mirror, I'd have seen myself looking like a wild animal, trapped and injured in a dirty, rusty hole.

After I had sorted myself out, I began to feel bored. I wished I had brought a radio with me; of course, it might not have worked down there. I also realised I'd forgotten to pack razors and shaving foam. I was going to look like the Count of Monte Cristo by the time I reached Australia. One by one, things that I should have brought and had forgotten came to my mind – a book, for example, would have comforted me and helped to pass the time.

A couple of days into the voyage proper my watch stopped working. I had no means of keeping track of the dates. I tried to count the days from when we left Bandar Abbas – a Monday – so it would have been Friday when we set sail again after the delay. Suddenly a character from one of my favourite stories came to my mind: Robinson Crusoe. I remembered how Crusoe kept track of dates by cutting a line every day on the bark of a tree, so I decided to do something similar.

To help me keep track of the days, I drew a chart on the inside of a soap wrapper of the next twenty-three days, which I crossed out each night. I had to crawl to the hatch where I came in to see if it was daylight or night-time. At least it gave me some exercise!

I had also worked-out a dietary programme to make sure I'd have enough food to see me through to the end. No meals would be feasts, obviously, but I reckoned I had enough to keep my stomach full. Then my dietary regime received a bad blow. The thirty Lavash – the flatbreads – that I'd brought with me carefully wrapped in plastic, were completely covered in mould. There was nothing I could do to salvage even a tiny piece. This was going to have a devastating impact on my eating plan and heralded tough times ahead. I felt demoralised, and panic set in once again. But there was no point getting upset; there was simply nothing I could do. I still had my tins of tuna, beans and stew – not much to survive on but it was all I had.

My plan was to spread out my two daily meals, one during the day and one at night. Luckily, I didn't have to worry about water. I ate my food slowly and chewed every piece so thoroughly that it went down almost without needing to swallow. But despite slowing the process, my meals hardly lasted five minutes and as soon as my first meal of the day was finished I looked forward to the next. What worried me most was how I could survive on such a meagre diet until the end. What if the ship broke down, or had to stop somewhere for a day or so? Twenty-three days was a long time to live on so little. I scolded myself for not bringing extra. I should have anticipated emergencies.

There were no toilets down there, so I had to use plastic bags; but interestingly enough that was the least of my problems. Eating so little meant I hardly had anything to worry about! Another miscalculation was that while we were in the northern hemisphere, the days had begun getting shorter, so I didn't have as long to wait for sunset, but once we passed the equator the reverse was the case. I tried to readjust by sleeping through the day and waking up at sunset.

I also toyed with the idea of coming out of hiding under the cover of darkness in the hope of stealing some food or leftovers from the kitchen. I found it hard to deal with the hunger; it wasn't something I had trained myself for or was used to. The work as a coal heaver had made me much stronger, but I started losing weight rapidly and worried it would have an impact on my energy levels. I tried to convince myself to stay below; it was too big a risk.

Eventually, ten days after we set off, common sense surrendered to my empty stomach and I decided to go up as soon as it fell dark. A few steps up the ladder and I realised how weak I had become; by the time I got to the top I was totally exhausted. Slowly I opened the hatch a crack and took a peek out, fearing that someone could be standing right next to it. There didn't seem to be anyone around, so I stepped out and took a huge gulp of fresh air. It smelled and tasted of the sea. I was so wrapped up in enjoying clean, salty air that I let the hatch slip from my fingers. It fell closed, making a thunderous bang in the silence of the night.

My heart leapt. Like a burglar surprised by a returning housekeeper, I immediately looked for cover. I cursed myself for being so clumsy. I would never forgive myself if such a foolish mistake was to ruin everything. I crawled along the bulwark towards the kitchen, located at the back end of the ship. I was dressed in black to give me some better cover at night, but the moon was full and the whole deck and surrounding ocean was drenched in its light.

I had not gone more than a few yards when I noticed a pair of legs only a few feet away. I froze. After a few moments I looked up; the sailor near me was puffing on a cigarette while looking out at the ocean. He hadn't seen me! Then I heard a conversation getting closer. They were behind me. I look round. It turned out that while creeping along the deck I had passed two other crewmen without realising it. They weren't far from the hatch; they *must* have heard the noise. I felt exposed and scared. It wasn't safe, but the wind direction had changed and the smell of cooked food coming from the kitchen was making me salivate. I couldn't make up my mind whether to continue or to retreat. Going back was impossible; even if I had been able to get past the two crewmen a second time unnoticed, I definitely wouldn't have been able to go down the shaft. But I couldn't stay where I was either – there was nowhere to hide – so I continued crawling like a toddler, wishing I had eyes on the back of my head to check what was happening behind me.

The excitement of getting closer to the kitchen suppressed any sense of fear. I was like a dog following a smell. I finally made it, but seconds after crawling into the kitchen, someone came in through its other door. I could hear my own heartbeat and was convinced the other man could hear it too. Slowly I backed out of the kitchen and exited through the same door I had come in and waited. I had been extremely lucky – had the crew member walked into the kitchen through the same entrance I had, he would definitely have seen me on the floor. The man remained in the kitchen for a while. My stomach was rumbling louder and louder. Food was only a few feet away but there was no way I could reach it. My head was telling me that it was simply too dangerous to hang around, while my stomach begged me to stay and hope for the best. I waited a bit longer but soon common sense kicked in and once I saw the coast was clear, I got back to the hatch as fast as I could. After that night's experience, I decided it was better to be hungry than to get arrested. I had already coped with a great deal of hardship and I wasn't prepared to lose it all for a piece of bread.

I had never felt time pass so slowly in my life; food was never far from my thoughts. When I fell asleep I dreamt of bread. I could smell it in my dreams, and when I touched it, it felt warm and fresh. But as soon as I was about to eat it, I woke up. Once awake I could still feel the warm, freshly baked bread in the palm of my hand. It was torture!

One night after waking from a food dream, I remembered a notebook I had brought with me. I had intended to keep a diary, thinking it would be a pleasant way to pass the time. I took the notebook and pen out of my rucksack and, after pondering how to start, I set it aside. I didn't know where to begin. Then I thought I could write down my dreams, so I took the notebook out again. But as soon as I put pen to paper, my dreams faded away. In the end I wrote one word – 'Bread'. I was never in the mood to write again.

The water pumps were located at equal distances below deck and sounded like dogs barking. Often they barked in unison, at other times they took turns. At their worst they sounded like wild hungry dogs running loose in the corridor from one end to the other, looking for a way out. The water pumps became my arch-enemies, the allies of hunger, keeping me awake. They were far worse than the noise of the engines. I tried shoving pieces of tissue in my ears, but it was pointless. The noise penetrated my skin and engulfed my entire being in a horrendous symphony. The noise generated by the engines kept me company on the journey, but when the water pumps joined in, it nearly drove me mad. I tried to cope by picking out music in the rhythmic noise. The music I heard changed depending on my mood. Sometimes the pumps played happy songs; other times, the most melancholic melodies. Mostly they played nothing but irregular, nerve-racking clatters. Every now and then I recited some poetry and hummed along with them, but most of the time the constant banging, bashing, slamming and thumping drove me up the wall. Surprisingly, though, I began to get used to it. How adaptable the human mind could be, I thought. I wondered how long we could put up with inhospitable environments before deciding to set ourselves free, irrespective of costs or consequences.

But better days did eventually arrive. I felt the change in temperature as the ship sailed into warmer and calmer waters. Somehow, the noises lessened too. I wasn't sure if it was the effect of warmer waters on the ship's body or if it was me imagining it all.

There wasn't much room to move around in my den, and I was feeling stiff and sore from sitting around most of the time. I needed to get some exercise in order to stay healthy. The early hours of the morning were the only times I could come out.

Having reversed my days and nights – sleeping during the day when the ship was busy and staying awake through the night – made me feel relatively free. Once I realised that after dark there weren't many crew members on deck, I began coming out. I stood on the ship's forecastle, not far from the hatch, doing exercises and stretches. I loved to look out at the ocean. The air finding its way into my lungs made me feel more alive and free with every breath.

Far away in the distance I could see flickering lights. There were also huge mountains rising into the night sky. I didn't have the foggiest idea where in the Indian Ocean we were or which countries we were sailing by – Java or Sumatra perhaps. The ocean was immense and seemed all the more so in the dark. It was truly terrifying. It was so calm that it felt like we weren't moving at all. The only signs of movement were the little white waves pushing away from the side of the vessel. Some nights the dark clouds couldn't bear the lump in their throats any more and burst into tears. I stood there on deck getting soaked in the warm rain. It made me feel alive.

Meanwhile, I kept my eyes on the sky like a lover searching for a familiar face in the crowd, hoping every night to see the Southern Cross wink at me.

As time went on I got used to my diet, but I felt weak every time I climbed those forty steps. I barely had the strength to hold on and pull myself up. Days were crossed out on the chart that still bore the scent of the soap, until finally one day a strange silence jolted me out of a deep sleep. I stared into the dim light of the chamber for a few minutes, still sleepy, confused.

'The engines!' I suddenly said out loud.

It was the engines and the water pumps. They had stopped. Everything was dead silent. I hadn't experienced total silence for such a long time. I suddenly knew what was going on. How long had we been motionless? I picked up my chart. I'd had to go way beyond the twenty-three days I originally mapped out.

'Australia!' I yelled, no longer caring if anyone heard me.

I had reached the end of my journey, a journey from death to life, from limbo to rebirth, from fall to spring.

I felt energised and euphoric. It was time to come out and get off the ship. Halfway up the ladder I heard noises on deck, but couldn't wait; I had waited for too long.

I climbed out cautiously and quietly and took cover in a dark corner. It was dark, but the floodlights lit up the deck and the surrounding areas. Like a cat in a trap I scurried from one nook to the next. When I realised that I couldn't get off as easily as I'd hoped, I had a momentary fit of panic. Then suddenly a member of the crew was walking towards me. He was a sailor whom I had met back in Bandar Abbas. There was absolutely nothing I could do. He was bound to see me. Crouching down was not a solution.

I turned my back to him and looked out towards the sea. I could hear his steps getting closer behind me. Trying to keep my voice calm I asked him quietly to show me a way out. I quickly told him what I had been through and begged him not to say a word to anyone. He stood there staring at me, puzzled and speechless. He couldn't believe his eyes. I was at his mercy, my entire future was in his hands. I took a gamble that he was among the diminishing number of Iranians who still had respect for their fellow countrymen.

He showed me a ladder, about fifteen feet up, against the wall of the quarterdeck and told me that every two hours it was put across for the crew to get onto the jetty. But, he warned me, it would be impossible to get to it without being noticed by the officers who were usually nearby when the ladder was out. He promised to keep his mouth shut and left.

It was only now that I was able to take in the scene around me. The jetty was nothing like the ones I had worked on back in Bandar Abbas. I had never seen anything like it before. This jetty was at least three miles long, stretching far out into the sea to where we were anchored. It was supported on massive iron piles and was just wide enough for a car. There were no workers, no coal heavers or anyone else as far as I could see. Even if I managed to get onto the jetty, I'd be easily spotted for I'd be the only one walking along it. I could never have anticipated this scenario. No one had ever spoken about how different the Australian port facilities were to ours.

A mere few miles stood between me and freedom. I could see the lights on the coast of liberty. I had come thousands of miles, but the last few were proving to be the hardest.

My initial thought was to jump in the water and swim ashore, but I would have been noticed. A few crew members were coming my way again. I hid behind piles of ropes and winches. They stopped to chat, but I'd have to pass them in order to get to the jetty. I thought I could walk past them, ignoring them completely, even if they saw me. If things got out of hand, I could jump in the water. I just didn't want to waste any more time. I jumped from the ship's forecastle onto the deck and walked slowly, pretending something on the jetty had attracted my attention. I headed towards the ship's cabins. I was tense, my palms sweating. I had almost reached them when the sailor I met earlier appeared in front of me.

'Just follow me,' he said in a low voice.

I had no idea what to do. Could I trust him? I didn't even know his name. He could save me or have me killed. But he was my only ally and accomplice; he was the best chance I had of getting ashore. He took me to a cabin and told me to stay there until daybreak. He warned me not to go near the ladder. I didn't say a word. Like a petrified child, I did as I was told. He closed the door and left.

The hardship and pain I had endured throughout the journey, plus the months of preparation, kept flashing before my eyes. I kept telling myself that I had to succeed, that I could make it; I wasn't to think otherwise. My heart beat faster and faster. At any moment I expected the door to open and that would be the end of that.

The thought of jumping into the water scared me stiff: I had read about Australia's shark-infested waters when I was in Tehran; also, there was no way I could jump nearly one hundred feet into the water without being noticed.

I waited for a few hours behind a desk in the cabin, clutching my knees to my chest. I had asked the sailor to get me some biscuits or anything he could find but he never returned. I didn't know what to do. Waiting for him seemed pointless, and the longer I waited the more restless I got. The waiting reminded me of the days when we first set sail and the time had gone by so slowly, like a turtle going up a hill.

From the cabin window I could see the dark sky getting paler by the minute. Soon the sun would be up. Suddenly the engines started and I panicked. I knew I couldn't wait any longer. In a few minutes the sun would be up. I put Mâdar's picture, the penicillin bottle containing the soil of Iran, the silver box containing Mâdar's hair, my expired and unused passport, the emblem of the Lion and Sun with the Pahlavi crown above it still shining brightly, and the US dollars from the sales of my apartments into a small freezer bag I'd brought with me. I sealed the bag tightly and pushed it down my shirt, securing it under my belt. I was ready to go, but I still had no idea how I was going to get off the ship. I had had a rope with me, but it had fallen from my shoulder next to the hatch when the sailor came towards me. I had to go back and get it before the rising sun blew my cover.

I hurried to the hatch; luckily the rope was still there. I picked it up, rushed to the quarterdeck at the back of the ship, secured one end of the rope to a hook and dropped the other end over the side. Holding onto the rope as tightly as I could, I stepped over onto the shell plating and quietly climbed down the rope. But it was short by about thirty feet, so I had no choice but to let go and drop into the water. I had to avoid making a big splash. I clamped my arms tightly to my side, pointed my toes and let go of the rope.

The water was icy-cold and I accidentally swallowed some of it. But soon I regained control and focused on getting away from the ship quickly. I began swimming towards one of the piles supporting the gigantic jetty above. I felt extremely cold, a sensation I hadn't had during my four-week voyage. When I reached the jetty there seemed to be nothing to climb up on and no place to rest for a few minutes. I put my arms around one of the piles and tried to find a step under water with my feet. I was too close to the ship and it made me nervous. Looking at the bulk carrier from below terrified me. It was a monster from the Islamic Republic that even here in free Australian waters was watching me like a hungry hawk.

I felt a sudden burning sensation on my legs. I couldn't see anything but the stinging was getting worse. I let go and began swimming again, telling myself to remain calm and not to tire myself needlessly as I might end up swimming the whole distance to the shore.

It was getting lighter and I was totally exposed, but there was still a long way to go to the coast. I was exhausted. Then I spotted what looked like a rusty old ladder. I swam towards it and discovered it was what I'd hoped it was. It was truly a godsend. I got all excited, but when I reached it, it proved to be harder to climb up than I'd anticipated. There was little strength left in me; I couldn't believe how difficult I found it to pull myself up those few steps. It took me a while but I finally succeeded. At the top of the ladder was a room made entirely out of thick, hard rubber.

By the time I stepped into the rubber room, the sun was out and I could feel the temperature rising. I got out of my wet clothes and lay them out to dry. When I sat down, I noticed minor cuts and bruises on my legs and feet. Here are my shark bites, I thought, and it made me laugh. It was the first time I'd laughed in a long time.

The port was in full swing. I could hear noises from the ships and a few cars that passed overhead. A conveyor belt was transporting coal to the *Motahari* so it could make its return journey. I lay on the hard rubberised floor. It was dry and I was grateful to be safe, although I was starving. I knew I had to wait until the ship left before I could come out. But that wouldn't take long – the technology they were using meant that the ship would be filled with coal in no time.

After that I don't remember a thing. I must have fallen asleep in exhaustion. When I woke up I felt as if I had been pulled out of a dark tunnel. I sat there looking around me wondering what had happened and where I was. Having slept for days next to noisy engines and water pumps it was the strange silence that had woken me up. I peeked out of the rubber alcove. The sun was dazzling. It was my first encounter with the sun for over three weeks. My eyes hurt at first but I enjoyed its warmth on my face. It made me feel alive. I thought of it as a good omen. I was excited and, above all, a free man, despite the fact that I had not officially yet entered Australia.

My clothes had dried out completely and I put them on again. Then I climbed a spiral staircase up to the surface of the jetty and had a good look around. My ship had sailed away; the empty space where it had been anchored was a joyous sight. I started to walk towards the shore, enjoying the new smells and sounds around me. I wasn't in a rush any more. I couldn't have rushed even if I'd wanted to – I had no energy left. I was extremely hungry, thirsty too, but excitement cancelled out all other bodily needs. I heard cars approaching from behind. I turned and tried to flag them down; the last one stopped for me. The driver was a middle-aged man in a white shirt and khaki shorts.

'Police station, please!' I said in my best English. 'Take me to a police station. Please!'

By the end of 1983 Amnesty International had recorded 5,447 executions in Iran since the revolution of February 1979, of which some 400 took place in 1983; the total number of executions was certainly much higher, with hundreds of executions reportedly taking place unannounced.

Amnesty International Report,
November 1983

Chapter Twenty-two

IT WAS 21ST NOVEMBER 1983, the driver told me. He eyed me
suspiciously. I couldn't blame him – I was dirty, must have smelled,
my beard had grown long and untidy, and I was asking odd questions.
I tried to behave as if there was nothing wrong with me.

'You work here, mate?' he asked.

I wasn't sure what to say. Where could I begin? Would he believe
that I had just arrived in Queensland from Iran?

After what must have seemed like a long pause to answer a simple
question, I replied, 'No, I don't work here. That's why I need to
report myself to a police station.'

'Have you been fired? Had a row or something with your chief?'
he asked.

'Oh, no, nothing of that sort.'

'Have you done anything wrong?'

'Yes,' I replied, but immediately wished I hadn't. 'Well, you could
put it that way. It all depends how you look at it.'

He looked confused. He kept his eyes on the road then, after a
brief silence, said, 'Good on you, mate. That's very noble of you to
turn yourself in.'

We left the coal terminal and headed north. The countryside looked fresh and lush. I heard myself sighing; for a moment it reminded me of the Caspian coast. All along the coastal belt I saw wet, dense rainforests.

'Can I ask you a question?' I asked.

'Sure, fire away.' He glanced at me.

I looked out at the scenery. 'Where are we going?'

He paused for a moment. 'Well, we're on our way to the police station. Isn't that where you wanted to go?' He was frowning.

'I meant which city or town. What is the name of the place we are heading to?' I asked politely.

'We are in Shire of Sarina,' he said.

I could see him out of the corner of my eye checking me out from top to toe again. The Shire of Sarina? The word 'shire' made me think of Robin Hood. Why would there be a shire in Australia.

'Sorry, I didn't catch that,' I said. 'Can you repeat it, please?'

'We're heading to Mackay. That's where the police station is. I live there, too, so I can drop you on my way.'

I thanked him and said no more, but he chatted on. 'It's getting hotter every day now.' He pointed to the sun. I didn't feel hot at all; the vehicle's thermometer only showed 22°C. 'I'd just finished my last inspections at the terminal when you stopped me,' he added.

'Terminal?' I asked, feeling a little confused.

'Yeah!' He frowned again. 'Where I picked you up, mate. The coal terminal. I work there,' he informed me while looking at me thinking I must be nuts. 'Dalrymple Bay Coal Terminal is one of the largest in the world.'

'I see,' was all I said.

He hadn't raised his voice or anything but he looked a bit agitated. I wondered if it was the 22°C that was bothering him or my bizarre circumstances. After that, he didn't talk much – just told me that we'd be in Mackay in about thirty minutes.

I was fascinated by the lush green countryside and happily looked out the window, drinking it all in until we eventually reached Mackay. I had no idea what to expect. It didn't seem very big. Minutes later he pulled up outside a building.

'Here you are, mate. Good luck. It was nice meeting you.'

We shook hands and I got out. Before he drove off I leaned in the open window and thanked him.

'Don't mention it,' he said and sped away.

I felt a little nervous. Since I'd got in the car I hadn't thought of Kasra at all, but now as I walked across the road towards the police station, I wished he were with me. Inside the station an officer was sitting behind a desk.

'Can I help you?' he asked, looking up when the door slammed behind me.

I kept looking at him without saying a word. A voice in my head was telling me I was crazy for asking to be brought there.

The officer looked me up and down. 'Sir, can I help you?'

I must have looked like a tramp. The word 'sir' echoed in my head. It was funny to be called 'sir' when I looked such a mess. An idea sparked in my mind, just in the nick of time.

'Can you tell me how I can get to the centre, please? I am looking for a hotel,' I said politely.

Once he gave me the directions I thanked him and left. I walked away as fast as I could; I didn't want him to change his mind and bring me in for questioning. *What were you thinking?* I scolded myself.

I followed the directions he'd given me. At the junction of Sydney Street I turned into Gordon Street, and, if I'd remembered his instructions correctly, I would soon reach Nebo Road. Apparently there were several hotels there, but I was far from sure that they would give me a room. I stopped outside a hotel called Boomerang and looked around, mentally preparing myself to approach the receptionist. *Should I smile or look serious?* I wondered. I decided to just walk in and be as natural as I could.

'Good evening, sir.' A young blond male receptionist welcomed me with a fake smile.

So far so good.

'Hi,' I said with a sigh, intended to indicate that I was tired from a long day of hard work. 'I'd like to have a room, please – just for tonight, maybe tomorrow as well.'

'No problem,' he said, pulling a form out from a drawer and placing it on the reception counter with a pen. 'If you'd fill in this form, please, I'll arrange a room for you.'

I thanked him.

'I'll also need ID.'

'What? Sorry?' I asked.

'I-D,' he said, spelling it out carefully.

I had never heard the word *Aydee*, so I asked him what it was.

Thinking I was pulling his leg, he laughed. 'An identity card – driving licence, passport, that sort of thing?'

'Oh, that! An ID, okay.' I had my old passport with me, more as a souvenir than an official document, but I was sure the words 'Imperial Government of Iran' wouldn't cut it in Australia.

'I'll have to go and get my bag from my car,' I said to the receptionist as I crossed out my name on the form.

'Thank you, sir,' he replied, taking the form and the pen away.

I walked out, sure that the young man would get me into trouble. I had hoped to get a room, clean up a bit and make that phone call to Kasra, which I had rehearsed over and over in the ship.

Fifteen minutes later, I was back at the police station. The officer I'd spoken to before got up from behind his desk and asked if I'd got lost.

'No, officer,' I said. 'I found a hotel, but I changed my mind and came back.'

'What for?' he asked.

'I need to tell you that I am an illegal immigrant.' I looked him straight in his eyes.

'You're a what?' He was almost laughing.

'This may sound crazy to you, but I have escaped from Iran by hiding in a bulk carrier for almost a month. I just landed on Australian soil an hour ago or so.'

The expression on the officer's face changed as soon as he realised I wasn't kidding. I told him everything.

'I'm also very hungry. I've hardly eaten anything in the past few weeks.'

After the officer had made a few phone calls he told me it was too late that day to do anything. He directed me to a cell and asked me to wait until he came back. I lay on the bed there; it felt so comfortable. A little while later he reappeared and gave me a brown bag inside which was a toothbrush, toothpaste, a few razors, shaving foam, soap and shampoo. They had become luxury items to me. I couldn't remember ever having appreciated any present as much as this before.

'How much do I owe you?' I asked.

'You have money?'

'Some,' I replied sheepishly.

'Don't worry,' he said. 'Just get cleaned up. The showers are at the end of the corridor.'

'Can I have something to eat? I'm thirsty too,' I said as he walked back to his office.

Minutes later he returned with a cold glass of water, which I drank in one go.

'Can I have another one?' I asked, feeling a bit embarrassed, but he didn't seem to mind.

He returned while I was reading the labels on the soap and shampoo bottle.

'My name is Murphy, Lieutenant Murphy,' he said, this time presenting me with a larger glass of ice-cold water. 'Finish cleaning up. Then we'll go and get you something to eat.'

Having witnessed the brutality of the Revolutionary Guards – the Pasdars – back home, this policeman's compassion and empathy really touched me. I almost kissed his hand. But I made do with thanking him profusely.

I went off to take a shower and to shave. I was in there for well over an hour. It wasn't just the obvious dirt that went down the plughole; I also washed away the feeling of being confined in that ship and the smell of fear. Once I looked human again I knocked on the officer's door. His eyes nearly popped out of their sockets when he saw me.

'My God, I didn't recognise you!'

I smiled. I hadn't felt so good for a long time.

'I'm hungry too,' he said. 'Let's go and see what we can find.'

It sounded like music to my ears. He sorted a few papers and files on his desk, called another officer and told him where we were going and we left.

'What do you fancy eating?' he asked.

'Hamburgers!' I answered, almost before he'd finished his question. 'I'd love to eat a hamburger.'

He laughed.

We drove in a police car to a takeaway restaurant less than a mile down the road. Everything was so new to me. The Australians drive on the same side of the road as the British – the wrong side of the road, as far as I was concerned – and I was fascinated by sitting in a car on what would normally be the driver's side without having a steering wheel in front of me. Every time another car approached I thought we were going to have an accident. I had no recollection of having paid any attention to driving on a different side of the road when we were on our way to Mackay. I guess I'd been in shock then.

'I can't wait to have a hot meal,' I told him. 'Can I have two burgers? Please?' I must have sounded pathetic.

We stopped outside a restaurant. Its neon light came on as we stepped out of the car. It must have been his regular hang-out. The girl behind the counter seemed to know him. She was in her twenties and I couldn't help staring at her. I suddenly realised that it was the first time I'd seen a woman's hair in public in over three years. She looked happy and free.

While waiting for my burgers, chips and Coke, I couldn't take my eyes off the burgers that were sizzling on the other side of the counter. I was drooling like a dog. I felt embarrassed, but after not having had a hot meal for almost a month, the smell of cooking food was driving me mad.

A man in his late sixties walked in. He seemed to know the girl too.

'G'day, luv, me mouth's as dry as a dead dingo's donga. Gissa coldie.'

I just looked at him, totally lost. I didn't know they had different languages in Australia.

'What on earth did that guy just say?' I asked Murphy. 'Was that an Australian dialect?'

He burst into laughter. 'Well, I suppose you'd get used to our slang if you lived here. But no, mate, that was no dialect, that was English.'

Murphy found my shock amusing, but if they all talked like that old guy I'd be in deep trouble.

I devoured the burgers and I thanked Murphy several times. I'm sure he felt sorry for me. How many times in his life would he have had someone from the other side of the planet just appear at his police station. He asked me to tell him about myself, and when I had finished he said that he'd only seen such things in the movies or on the news.

After we'd eaten, he took me back to my cell and informed me that he had contacted Canberra. The officials there would be taking over my case. I told him that my best friend was a doctor practising in Sydney, and that I would like to contact him first thing the following day. With a good meal in my stomach I felt I had enough strength to speak to Kasra and deal with his shock at my news.

That night, at the police station in Sydney Street, I got the best night's sleep I'd had since leaving Tehran four months previously. Early the next morning I was woken by other inmates shouting; a few of them sounded as if they had been involved in a fight. When I got out of bed I was suddenly hit by a wave of homesickness. I hadn't felt lonely since my first night in Tabriz back in 1974. Even though I was bored at times on the bulk carrier, I had never felt alone. But this was different; the feeling was intense and powerful.

I had already washed my face and brushed my teeth when an officer opened the cell door and told me that I could take a shower and get some fresh air in the courtyard. There were about ten other prisoners, arrested mostly on minor charges – petty theft or drinking and driving, that kind of thing. They all seemed decent to me. One of the young chaps approached me while I did some stretches.

'G'day, howzit goin?' I'm Carl.' He stretched his hand out.

I shook it and introduced myself.

'Whatya here for?' he asked.

He had a funny accent, a bit like the man in the burger bar. I explained that I had escaped from my country, Iran, and was waiting for the authorities to look into my case. 'What are you here for?' I asked, hoping to stop him from asking too many questions about my situation.

'Drank too much last night at a paaty, didn't I, then tried to drive home,' he said. 'They brought me in to sleep it off. Dunno how much they're going to fine me.'

Soon, other inmates gathered around and we chatted. They all seemed very nice, and my first impression of Australians was very positive.

Just after nine in the morning, an officer stepped into the courtyard and looked around until he saw me. He pointed at me and summoned me with his finger. I told him about my case and asked if I could make a phone call.

'Follow me, Mr Azad,' he ordered. 'My name is Harker. Two gentlemen have just arrived from Canberra to deal with your case.'

He walked into a large room and I followed him.

'Here is our illegal immigrant,' he announced.

The two men, both wearing dark navy suits, got up and shook my hand. Mr Robinson was a tall man in his late fifties; a younger guy introduced himself as Richard Watts. After checking that I understood English, they told me they were from the Department of Immigration and Multicultural and Indigenous Affairs. I only understood part of that name, but I didn't care. I just wanted to be reunited with Kasra, or at least to call him.

There was over an hour of questioning. I filled out form after form, signed papers, and had my picture and fingerprints taken. None of the formalities worried me. Once that was done, Mr Robinson went through the forms and put them in order. Then he looked me straight in the eye.

'I'm very sorry, Mr Azad, but we will have to send you back to Iran. As a matter of fact, the ship you came in on is waiting right now to take you home.'

I panicked. All I heard was his voice repeating itself in my head: 'back to Iran, back to Iran'. I began to tremble and burst into tears. I fell to my knees in front of him, begging him not to send me back. I told him that I was a homosexual and that sending me back to Iran would result in my execution.

Time stood still in that moment. I had said out loud that I was gay! I stopped crying, but it felt as if I had confessed to a murder. I was petrified. I had spoken the unspeakable. It was all out now. Here I was, coming out in an Australian police station of all places. It would have cost me my life in the Islamic Republic; in Australia it would allow me to have a new life.

The idea that I might be deported had never crossed my mind. I was prepared to do anything – to wait in that cell for as long as it took, years if need be – anything to avoid being sent back.

'Please, sir!' I begged. 'I have nothing there. No family. Everyone is dead. My only family and life is here, in Australia. That's why I came.'

I could see that Mr Robinson hadn't expected such a reaction from me.

'Mr Azad, please sit down and calm yourself,' he said.

He and his colleague quietly exchanged a few words. Then he turned to me.

'We've covered all the formalities. That was just a little test of my own invention – the final test, you might call it. You said you have a boyfriend' – I sat back in my chair – 'who is now an Australian citizen and a doctor. If he confirms your statement, you are free to go until your asylum application has been fully addressed and dealt with.'

Relief instantly washed through me.

'However, you would need to report to the nearest police station on a weekly basis until your visa is granted.'

I said nothing. I thought that was the easiest request anyone could have asked of me, after what I'd been through.

'We'll arrange for you to fly to Sydney today,' he continued, 'accompanied by my colleague Mr Watts. By the way, have you contacted your partner since you arrived in Australia?'

'No, sir.'

'Okay then. We thought that maybe you'd want to inform him yourself of your arrival.'

He pushed the phone towards me.

My hands were shaking as I picked up the handset. I began dialling his number, the number I knew off by heart.

'You don't need to dial the 0061 any more,' Watts said, smiling.

I could hear the phone ringing at the other end and suddenly felt as if I couldn't breathe. I held the phone out to Mr Robinson, who, looking bemused, took it from me.

'I'd like to speak to Dr Arjomand, please,' he said into the receiver.

My heart was pounding.

'Dr Arjomand? Dr Kasra Arjomand?' he asked. 'Good morning, I'm going to pass the phone to someone here who would like to speak to you. My name is Kevin Robinson and I'd like to take a few minutes of your time afterwards.' He gave me the phone.

'Kasra!'

'Pedram?' He sounded bewildered.

'Hi, Kasra!' I said in Persian. 'Yes, it's me. I made it!'

He kept repeating, 'Oh, my God. Oh, my God,' in English, which I thought was funny. He even sounded Australian too! Then he switched to Persian.

'Pedram, where are you? Who was that man? I don't believe it!'

I had never felt so happy in my life. 'I am at a police station in Mackay,' I said in English so the men in the room could understand, and burst into tears.

'Mackay! In Queensland?' he squealed. 'Oh, my God! How? When?'

'I arrived yesterday,' I told him. 'Mr Robinson is an immigration officer. They want to confirm my statement with you – I told them that my boyfriend lives here, and we will then fly down to Sydney. Will you meet me at the airport?'

By this time he was crying too. 'Of course,' he said quietly.

'No more tears, please,' I said to him in Persian and then switched back to English. 'There have been enough tears. I have to pass the phone to Mr Robinson who wants to speak to you. I'll see you soon.'

I had rehearsed the moment when I would tell Kasra I had arrived so many times, yet when the time actually came it was all so different. I had been lost for words. But at least I had been given the chance to break the news to him myself. It was very considerate of the officials to let me do that.

Mr Robinson told me to get ready to leave. I wasn't at my best. I had lost a lot of weight and looked a bit gaunt. But I didn't care. A few hours later, Mr Watts and I were on a Qantas flight to Brisbane, where we had to change for Sydney, a distance of nearly two thousand kilometres of absolute beauty. I sat at a window seat, transfixed by the breathtaking scenery all the way along the coast.

It felt as if I was in a dream: I was in a Western country, I had regained my freedom, I had finally come out and I was going to meet my boyfriend – life couldn't have got any better, I thought to myself. Hours later, on the very last leg of my long journey from Bandar Abbas, I was reading a copy of *The Daily Mercury* I had picked up at the police station in Mackay when Mr Watts tapped me on the shoulder and pointed out of the window.

'Oh, my God!' I exclaimed.

I couldn't believe my eyes. We were over Sydney, the sun was shining, and this jewel of the South Pacific was truly a marvel. I burst into tears.

'Mr Azad, are you okay?' asked Mr Watts.

I looked at him and, as if a heavy weight that I had carried on my shoulders for so long had been lifted, I said, 'Never better.'

He gave a reassuring smile. 'You'll be fine.'

'Never better,' I said as I looked out the window.

The political intrigue and medical mistakes that killed the shah of Iran

The shah was a victim of changing politics and his own missteps — a man beyond help, a scion of a dynasty cast on a long and troubled wandering. Kalhor noted that most of the doctors he talked to said 'if the shah was an average Joe walking into any major hospital in any major city in any country, he probably would have been cured.'

LA Times, November 2017

Epilogue

It's six o'clock in the morning. I quietly got out of bed half an hour ago, took a shower and made myself a large cup of coffee. I've been drinking from my Lion and Sun flag mug for almost thirty-four years; its bright colours have faded. Kasra is sound sleep. I normally wake up very early in the mornings, but today is a special day and I wanted to be up earlier than usual so I could get some work done before the day's activities begin.

The air at this time of the year is fresh and, at this time in the morning, a bit nippy, which I love. I had opened the windows in the study before sitting down at my desk. The breeze through the open windows brings in the scents of flowers from the garden. I find the spring weather very agreeable. It fills my old lungs with life, lifts my spirits and keeps me optimistic for a better future. As I sip my coffee I'm looking out over the sea at the Sydney skyline. Now that I've reached the final chapter of my journey, I seem to have gone totally blank. How should I finish it?

It was thirty-four years ago today, 21st November 1983, that I set foot on Australian soil. A few days later – at Sydney's Kingsford Smith Airport – I was reunited with the man who turned out to be

347

the love of my life. When I held Kasra in my arms that day, I felt as if my mission in life had been achieved. I didn't want to let him go.

I remember us both crying, despite the immigration officer beside us and the crowds of onlookers at the airport. I remember that moment as if it were yesterday. I wanted to look at his beautiful face, but I was too scared to let him go in case I lost him again. It was surreal. Nothing else mattered in that moment. Even now, picturing that day in my mind's eye, I still can't find the words to describe how I felt. The closest I've ever managed to get was at a book club a few years ago when we were discussing love: 'It felt as if I could touch for the first time and see for the first time,' I told the group, 'but I couldn't say a word. Words just weren't enough.'

It took a few years for me to adjust, settle, feel at home and truly embrace my homosexuality and be proud of what I had achieved in life. Despite having my beloved partner and many loyal and loving friends, I was never able to let the past go completely. Eventually I went back to the classroom to teach English again, and I began to connect with my students once again, keeping with me always the memory of my Three Musketeers. My students were immigrants from all over the world, people who had come to this beautiful land for all sorts of reasons. I'm sure every one of them, too, has a story to tell.

I never lost contact with Iran. To this day it remains an integral part of my everyday life. I follow its news and read every book that comes out about it. I've never lost hope that one day light will triumph over darkness in my homeland.

Little by little, step by step, we all put our lives back together and managed to give them new shapes. Parastou got married and still lives in Tehran; she has two kids. Ardavan enrolled in the Iranian army and served his time as a conscript but, luckily, was never sent to the front. Later, he married and left for New York where he now lives with his family. Armineh has been living in London with her English husband and continued to practise as a partner in a law firm. We have kept in touch throughout the years; she and her husband even paid us a visit a few years ago. And our dear friends Gilda and Vartan finally got married. They too left Iran with their children and made a new life in Toronto. Having access to the internet allows me to talk often to Richard, my wonderful penpal of those golden years. He lives with his wife and children in London, and they see Armineh from time to time.

The memories that have been pouring like a waterfall into the river of my thoughts while I have been writing this account have taken me on a journey that has been both happy and cheerful and hard and painful. But I needed to go back through them in order to leave behind something of far greater value than any material possession. I hope that one day, people will read this memoir and learn a little about the story of Iran – who we were, how we lived and get a flavour of the paradise our ancient homeland used to be.

I haven't been back to Iran in all these years. I yearn to see my country again. I'd like to visit my parents' and Mâdar's graves. The greatest gift I could be given today would be to walk down Tehran's Pahlavi Avenue when its old birch trees are covered with snow, to stroll on the foothills of the Alborz in spring or swim in the warm waters of the Caspian in a hot summer. On every wall in almost every room at home in Sydney is a reminder of our land of roses and nightingales.

Since the unfortunate events of 1978 my beloved country has hardly been out of the news headlines. The country that used to set an example for developing nations, has represented nothing but death and destruction for nearly four decades. 'The men of God had promised paradise but instead opened the gates to hell,' said our ageing Empress Farah so eloquently in a recent interview. My only plea to the younger generations, who make up the majority of Iran's population today and who will be responsible for the Iran of tomorrow, is to think and to choose wisely. We have all paid a heavy price for the mistakes made almost four decades ago.

So what I began a year ago, when I decided to put my new-found free time to good use, has now come to an end. As I write the final chapter, the youth of Iran have risen again, this time wiser and bolder than ever before, demanding the restoration of the Pahlavi monarchy.

About the Author

Ingrid Leksand was born in Stockholm, Sweden, in 1960 and moved to the UK with her family when she was five years old. Ingrid's life is divided between her two favourite cities, London and Stockholm, although she has lived most of her life in England.

From Fall to Spring is her first novel.

.

Printed in Great Britain
by Amazon